"I HAVE SHARED THIS TALE WITH OTHER FRIENDS," SAID CASEY, "ONLY TO WATCH THEM AGE AND WITHER AWAY."

There was a great sorrow in his voice, and a touch of frustration. "I have tried many lives, and been many things. In the beginning I was most assuredly a man, with all a man's infirmities. I grew old as a man—then suddenly I was young again, and have remained so ever since, though I can take the appearance of age or any other feature of man when it suits me.

"I was a shaman of the People: a medicine man. I had gone to the mountaintop to fast, in hopes that the spirits would speak to me. Then I took the cup: the spirit of the sacred mushroom steeped in water. It is hallucinogenic—which compounds the mystery of my transformation, since I could not tell what was fact and what was fantasy. I have a memory of an awesome flame and terrible burning pain, then of a satisfying inner peace such as no other I have ever known. I believed at the time that I had been with God.

"I have since learned otherwise."

In the Face of My Enemy

JOSEPH H. DELANEY

BAEN
SCIENCE FICTION
BOOKS

IN THE FACE OF MY ENEMY

Copyright © 1985 by Joseph H. Delaney

A Baen Book

Baen Enterprises
260 Fifth Avenue
New York, N.Y. 10001

First printing, November 1985

ISBN: 0-671-55993-1

Cover art by Kevin Johnson

Printed in the United States of America

Distributed by
SIMON & SCHUSTER
MASS MERCHANDISE SALES COMPANY
1230 Avenue of the Americas
New York, N.Y. 10020

In the Face of My Enemy

1. Kah-Sih-Omah's journey begins here, in the Sacramento Valley of California. To the east is the Sacred Mountain; to the east of that the Valley of Winter. Immediately to the south is the Valley of the Strangers, from which the People were taken south.

2. The journey ended at the modern site of Mexico City, then on an island in a lake.

3. After his encounter with the Sun God, and a generation of the peace he brought to the region, Kah-Sih-Omah disappears and begins his wandering. He follows the Caribbean Coast south, then crosses the Isthmus, where he marries and lives for a generation as a fisherman. When at last he sails away, attempting to cross the Western Ocean, he is shipwrecked off the Chilean coast.

4. Attempting to cross the desert, he reaches a mountain glacier in which he is entombed for 12,000 years. When he revives, he finds the ice age is over and that a hundred miles to the northwest aliens have organized humans into a workforce in an effort to repair and refuel a grounded spaceship. After their defeat and a battle with his one-time ally, Ketzal, Kah-Sih-Omah is entombed a second time, this time for 4,000 years.

5. After roaming South America for centuries, Kah-Sih-Omah visits the lands of the Mayans. While he is there, a man in a skin boat washes ashore. Kah-Sih-Omah knows he came from across the Eastern Sea, and decides to follow the coast north and see where it goes.

6. At the time of Kah-Sih-Omah's transformation—about 18,000 B.C.—glaciers penetrated far south into North America. Kah-Sih-Omah had thus avoided the northern sections of the continent. Now he begins to hear stories of great, hairy strangers with metal weapons, who cross the Eastern Sea with ease in great canoes. In his cautious search for them he encounters, then impersonates, Amundsen.

7. Kah-Sih-Omah lingers in Iceland for a generation, until the great plague arrives and kills his family. Then, with no further ties, and much intrigued by the sagas, he abandons the old Amundsen-persona and becomes Omahhsen.

8. Rearming at Cherbourg, he sails south, entering Gibralter at night. The straits

are defended by Saracen galleys, which assail them from both shores. In the ensuing battle. Omahhsen is sunk, and while adrift, meets Marcello, a monk, who observes his differences and concludes the northerner is a saint. He becomes Omahhsen's companion in a journey across North Africa.

9. First at Alexandria and later in Jerusalem, Kah-Sih-Omah gains access to ancient writings which convince him he is a sibling of Christ, and of other immortals who still wander the Earth. He commences a journey to the east, which will cover all of Asia and return him to Europe in the earth 16th century. At this point, he learns that Europeans have rediscovered the western continent.

10. As an immortal, taking the long view, Kah-Sih-Omah realizes that wealth is power, and that power begets knowledge if properly used. He therefore acquires wealth and invests wisely. The last decades of the 20th century find him entrenched in Arabia as the fabulously old and wealthy Omar C. Kazim. As his own fictitious son, he locates and belatedly recovers the computer once belonging to the alien engineer, Ketzal of Coatyl, from which he extracts and disseminates the secrets of interstellar travel.

Prologue

The broken creature hung suspended on fields of force, amid devices half matter and half energy, flung into patterns and functions unfathomable to but a few minds in all creation.

"It is loathesome," said one voice to the other. "Does it live?"

"Its life force is near extinction, but now static. It is primitive, yet I believe it truly thinks."

"It intrigues you?"

"Indeed. As it is now, so we once must have been. I will, therefore, know this being, and ourselves of yesterday."

It probed the body of the beast, and knew it, and was saddened. "Tragic," it remarked. "I have descended into its cells. What ghastly inefficiencies. They battle: they eat each other. They are predator and prey within the organism. Equilibrium may be briefly achieved; never harmony."

"The damage appears complete. What will you do?"

"I shall make repair; observe it in life and function."

The being touched the broken form. With disciplined force he built anew according to its pattern.

"Fascinating. It lives. For a time there is balance. It struggles to retain this, but the struggle cannot endure long against the inner conflict. It spends its energy to forestall destruction, yet it spares enough for thought."

9

"That is conjecture."

"No, it is fact. It is conscious of its existence. It conceives the flow of time. It questions its reason to be. It calls itself . . . Kah-Sih-Omah. This is sentience."

"Perhaps, in time. It does not presently appear probable. If it snatches only fleetingly at this sensory flood, how can it learn?"

"Perhaps it learns only small things. We may yet determine this, for I grow curious. Perhaps we shall never again pass this way, yet if by chance . . ."

"What will you do?"

"I shall change it: bring discipline, provide order. You will perceive its present lack."

"Indeed. Observe: the cells replicate, and as they replicate they drift. The process is unfaithful and unhealthy for the creature, yet the organism permits it. It is as you said; they eat each other."

"I shall adjust."

"How? The drift is cumulative. Each replication deviates a little further. Chance alone determines how far. It is the pattern that is faulty. The fidelity of replication cannot endure under purely chemical control. More is needed."

"Restraint? Yes. Brilliant."

"You set yourself an exceedingly difficult task."

"True. It will be challenging. Observe: these large cells function differently. They are the keys. They interconnect throughout the organism. They are the vehicle of its consciousness. They are subject to the being's command."

"If such it has."

"There is room within them for innovation. I shall form echelons of them, and install cross-controls. Command will ascend to the being's core of consciousness."

"The endeavor seems worthwhile. I shall observe your efforts. I may, perhaps, comment."

"I would be pleased if you would do so."

Again, the boundary obscured. Matter melded with its higher state. Suble changes followed.

"Interesting. Satisfaction must surely be yours."

"Indeed. Observe: even as we watch, its wounds heal, its form regenerates and returns to it. Control descends from its center of consciousness into the cells."

"It is still loathesome."

"It now need not be. Its will controls. Perhaps the creature hears you. Properly contrite, it may experiment and find a form more pleasing to you."

"It lacks the intellect."

"No, not the intellect; the experience. It has lived but the instant nature gave it. I have given it eons more."

Time passed. The dalliance ended. The need which had brought visitors to this young world was satisfied. Their vehicle, having probed the bowels of the mountain and found, extracted, and refined the fissionables it sought, now rose from the blackened slag pit where it had rested so long, and resumed its journey between suns.

Their toy, transformed—and this time safely out of harm's way—watched, mystified. It did not comprehend the works of gods—nor now, even itself.

Book One

Ancient Lights

There was—nothing. There was not even that ghostly grayness that hovers immediately below the threshhold of awareness, nor the fuzzy numbness that signifies flesh immobilized too long.

There was nothing.

But the mind was clear; alert and inquisitive. The mind was never still, never unoccupied even, in true sleep, either troubled or enchanted by fantasies from wakefulness—but never, Kah-Sih-Omah's consciousness insisted, by another dream.

Yet he was so tormented.

He waited.

Tingling! The first sign. A red blur, the second. With feedback came control, and pain—burning pain, burning reminiscent pain exquisite in degree, stifling in its overwhelming presence. Unbelievably, it rose higher, washing like mighty waves of fire, driving the limbs into spasm.

They shook. They shook the body. It writhed; it suffered, but not endlessly. An ebbing followed. Circulation was restored, the pain subsided, and the will took hold.

The will seemed strong, stronger than it had ever been—and always it had been mighty. The body depended upon the will for preservation, and the wisdom of the will and its determination. The will was first, the body second. As the will went, so went the body.

He opened his eyes. And in this instant Kah-Sih-Omah knew that change had come. He was not the same.

These were not his hands that stretched out, palm up before eyes that saw clearly, up close, as they had not for so many winters. Smooth and strong and steady, flexing muscles vital with power and tendons taut across bones that did not ache, he made fists of them and stared in awe. Where was he?

Surely, this was death. Death alone could mend old bodies, raising them new in spirit out of their corruption.

A shaman knew death. Death was a spirit—part of the Great Spirit, who was the earth and all that lay upon it, who gave all things birth and for a time nurtured them and made them grow strong—as Kah-Sih-Omah had once been strong, and now was again.

What the spirit created it also destroyed, when the time had come and its purpose had been served. Just as in the spring the grasses sprang from the womb of the pregnant earth to flourish in the summer when the spirit in them was strong, so did winter come and the spirit destroy what it had made.

He, Kah-Sih-Omah, He-Who-Waits, had waited out his years and withered and fallen under the scythe of winter, where he waited more. There was no other explanation for where he was, and what had happened. He was new.

How, then, had he died?

He rose, shaking at first, rocking back and forth, unsteadily testing the tall straight body which was now his, unbent by pain and stiffness.

His clothes were gone. He was indeed reborn. He was naked before the searing light of the noonday sun. Yet there were shadows on the land: stark, dark giants of shadows, over which the heated air shimmered and the wind blew hot—hotter even than the sun could have made it in many days of ceaseless shining. He looked again, this time more carefully. His new eyes had been playing tricks on him. Now he saw that the very Earth was burnt, her flesh blackened. He had not imagined the fire that raged while he passed.

He was alone. Stretching far out across the blackened shadow, clouds hovered across peaks of jagged mountains. Nowhere did the man see life. Was this to be a lonely time, all the world his alone? Was the Great Spirit that cruel, to give him youth and vigor yet deny him the pleasures these could bring? Was there no game to hunt, no fish to catch, no men for company?

His people! His people were not here. How was he to endure without his people? He must have them.

The man searched memories for the faces of all he had known who passed before him—some of them long ago, some friend, some foe, some as men and women, some as children, some his own children or of his own blood. They were not here. They must be here. He must find them.

He burned: not from the fury of the sun, but from the quest. He turned to look, to search the land in its fullness, to see what had been changed and what was still the same.

Much was. The shadows alone seemed different. The shadows consumed much, but they were minuscule compared to the vastness of his Earth. His mountain endured, there to the west.

It lay where the sun would journey as it settled to make way for the night. There he would go, and dwell, and recollect, and contemplate the interval of winter which he had so lately shaken off.

He rose and walked; the long strides of youth consumed the way between the man and the mountain, oblivious of sharp stones and sticks.

In this waterless waste of stifling heat and hovering dust the insects of the world of death flourished as prolific as in the world of life. A serpent threw his coils across the man's path, observed the man briefly, then fled into a cache of rocks.

The man passed, noticing, thrilled, as joyful as the serpent in its life, for here was at last the sign he sought, and he was heartened.

He climbed; climbed along a route familiar; a route traversed a thousand times in the world of life, a route unblemished by the footsteps of other men, because it was the spirit's land on which he trod, with the spirit's leave.

Here, again, was change. Here was more shadow—which was not shadow, but the ghost of a great fire. It was the enduring blackness of searing, not the transitory blackness of night. Here winter had come early for the grasses and the misshapen bushes that clung in clefts wherever soils collected.

Strange! The man found this strange. Here the shadow cut a swath that ended at the edge of the sand. He glanced out at the sand, following the track of the shadow across it into the greater shadow farther away. The sand had joined. He could see its juncture where the wind had blown loose grains away, and left it hanging there, as a log hangs over a stream, and on the other side, where lighter grains had been wafted up, the budding growth of a new dune. He wondered at the workings of the spirit.

He climbed, but not as he had climbed the mountain last, with pain in every step, and throbbing head and tortured chest. Now he possessed not merely the vigor of youth but youth's impatience, and youth's exuberance of life renewed.

He had learned. He was wise. In the old life he had wasted much. Now he wasted nothing: not a sight, not a smell, not a sensation. He savored all, each step an ecstatic adventure, whether it brought pain or pleasure. Both he cherished, for both were the same sensation in different degree. A man deprived of one lost the other, and a wise man knew it.

The summit intruded, faster than the man realized. He vaulted over, tumbling off a rock and seizing creepers for support. Here the air was thin, and he labored against it.

Resting briefly, he searched for tracks; his tracks, from the other life. He was determined to discover whether or not this was the place he had died, determined to find and see the remains of what he had been.

He found none, but he found where his body had been. Old and battered, his medicine bundle lay on the ground, half covered with windblown sand. Nearby, enduring beyond life, his talismans were strewn, as if waiting.

He squinted into the retiring sun at them, then reached with hands trembling not with age but with anticipation. He gingerly lifted the necklace; still it broke, scattering pierced teeth upon the ground as the string crumbled.

He-Who-Waits paused; pondered. His head began to throb. He strained for the memories that he was certain the spirit, if it were a kind spirit, must have left him as his bridge from the living world.

They would not come. He could not make them come. He could no more conjure up the memory of his rebirth than than that of his original birth, so many winters ago that he could not count. It seemed to him that the spirit was malignant, that it taunted him, tortured him, played with him. And then he saw the bowl, and knew that his passing had occurred in trance. Life had departed upon the wings of a dream.

Kah-Sih-Omah, bewildered, sprawled amidst the scattered serpents' teeth. Without the bridge he had nothing. He needed it as badly as the newborn baby needs the warmth of its mother's body and her soothing voice to still the terrors of birth. He had nothing.

He lay there for a while, resting until the sun descended. His mind would not be still. He had some memories, and therefore some answers. He knew his name. He knew what he had been. He knew his wife—and his children, both those now living and those who had passed. He knew the names of all the People. He could give each name a face. He could give name to all the plants his people used and all the animals they hunted.

And the memories did not stop there. With the freshness of yesterday he could now recall the names and faces of all his boyhood friends. He could remember with astonishing clarity all those precious boyhood adventures to which the grown man looks back with such wistful fondness.

Night fell. The sun fled behind the door of his lodge, flirting awhile with Earth in brilliant blood-red light and long shadow. In his place the first stars appeared.

In their faint, cold light the breezes tempered, hinting frost before the sun returned.

Kah-Sih-Omah sat, motionless, crosslegged, striving for inner calm—the only state in which there was any hope the spirit might receive him—and allowed his mind to open wherever it would. Unclothed, he would impose a harsh burden on his body, but it seemed a small price to pay were he made whole by it.

She came. She was thin, crisp, new and virginal, the points of her crescent sharp, her features gleaming. Behind her, faint but looming, lurked the shadow of what she had been and would become again—like the man, the new and the old together, inseparable.

He waited. She rose, higher and higher. He stared into her face—loved her—begged her help. She was mother to all; mother to me, he thought—*He-Who-Waits*, alone and afraid.

A glimmer—a twinkle! Was it real or was it in the mind? He felt the mind recoil to give it room, to let its feeble presence grow in strength. He yielded will, sank into softness almost fleshlike, yet strangely cold. Wisdom was his. He was young only in appearance. His inner self was old. He knew the trance approached; he could feel the beat of its wings as it hovered near. He braced his being against the bite of the talons. When they struck, he was gone from the embrace of the earth.

He hovered above it, looking down. He had found himself. He now watched himself in the last moments of his old life. Soon, he knew, he would watch his body die. He knew that even in this dreadful hour, he would not—perhaps could not—look away. He-Who-Waits would watch until the end.

There! Beneath him! His image, as he had been—Kah-Sih-Omah, He-Who-Waits, sibling of the serpent, the eagle and the bear, Shaman of the People of the Eastern Mountain—sat motionless, oblivious to the chill wind coursing up the mountainside. Legs crossed, hands folded, he gazed at the shimmering form of Our Mother Moon, lean in the sky.

A moment only, was his to observe—to perceive the

frailties of the body—to admire, in detachment, the strength of his own will.

With speed beyond perception, a change. Something mighty hurled him from the pinnacle. He felt the fire of doom, the shock of gnawing pain. At once the image dimmed, now viewed again through eyes rheumy with age. Time itself contorted when he blinked. Suddenly, the moon waxed broad and fat.

For an instant he was two spirits—two minds, joined but separate. Two hearts, one weak and halting but unafraid, the other strong but full of terror, beat within the vision.

And then he saw the open bundle, contents heaped in disarray beside the remnants of a tiny fire, saw the curled and broken fragments of a wafer of sacred mushroom.

He saw the ancient hands, gnarled and quivering, that gripped the cup of the broth and blood from the wafer. NO! He shouted, but it emerged a whisper: unheard, unheeded, uesless. It could not stay the shaking hands that rose to wrinkled, toothless jaws, nor close the lips that opened then and drank the demon down.

The demon plunged into the depths of the man, the spirit of the man into the depths of the vision. The spirit, trapped, would see not fact, but only such illusion as the devious mushroom spirit might allow.

Thus he watched the spark appear—a cosmic birth, it seemed—arising from the edges of Our Mother Moon. It grew rapidly, glowing fiercely, fleeing her, suddenly filling half the sky, dwarfing she who gave it birth. In that instant she vanished like the cold mountain wind, in her place the bloated spirit of the spark, howling furiously in a voice deep and thrumming, filling the ears with pain. The spirit at once entered the man.

Commonly, spirits used a natural opening. The spirit of the mushroom entered through the mouth, and that of the fire through the nostrils. This spirit's fingers entered through the skin, causing the hairs on the body to rise as did the spirit of thunder, which killed those it entered.

This spirit did not kill as it entered, so it was not the spirit of the thunder—and it had not consumed his belongings, so it was not the spirit of the fire. That fire, licking out in enormous tongues from the spark's edges, was many times farther away than a man could hurl a javelin when the spirit called it back.

Though the roar had abated a hot wind remained, blowing fiercely against him as he rose, tottering, to face the mighty mass of the spark. It rested now against the earth, which glowed beneath it even as its own glow waned.

The struggle began, the hulking ash of the spark against the man. The prize was the spirit of the man, which the spark wanted, and for which it must have come here to the sacred mountain.

The spark was the stronger. Having entered it now departed, erupting through the skin, which grew taut and itched, and glowed eerily. Kah-Sih-Omah's spirit was dragged from him—and with it his blood, which oozed from lips that pleaded with the spark to leave him be. The spark heard, but persisted, and filled him first with pain and then with blackness. With the blackness the pain ebbed.

The blackness too endured for a time. Somehow, this time was strangely peaceful. Something pleasant touched him: a wave of awareness washing through a great sea of mist, trailing haunting voices asking questions. His spirit echoed through the past, recalling answers . . .

Recalling.

How? Was his spirit safe?

Kah-Sih-Omah's eyes opened; saw only the grimness of the mountaintop in the natural darkness of the night. The vision had ended.

With a heavy heart, Kah-Sih-Omah realized the mushroom had stolen any truth he might otherwise have found. All was suspect, no better than conjecture.

Reason insisted that something had interceded to rescue him from the spark he now perceived as the spirit of evil. What else, if not good spirits? His remains were not on the mountain where he had died. His medicine bundle was, so something had taken his body away. Who, if not they, had done this?

But there was one thing more, whether it was a trick

of the mushroom or one played by his own mind,—the dim recollection of voices.

He suspected the mushroom, because he knew spirits spoke not in words through lips, as men did, but with thoughts subtly injected into the mind. Still, might not a man, accustomed to hearing through the ears, be mistaken if curious spirits asked his name?

He paused on the thought, struggling at recollection. More came, and it did not matter anymore to him whether it was real, because he did not understand. In the manner of spirits when they spoke to one another, he could not understand them. They did as they wished with him and did not tell him what or why. As it was with all spirits, so it was with these, who left him as ignorant as they had found him. This was the nature of spirits.

The vision had faded, but into the void it left in Kah-Sih-Omah's consciousness the cold wind and thin air rushed, each with its own silent fury. He shivered. He knew that he could not stay here on the mountaintop even with a fire. It would soon become far too cold to permit him to cling even to this new life arisen out of the death of the old.

The sky told him that. The sky was not the sky of the time he died. The spirits who moved across it were different spirits. They were not the spirits of revival and rebirth, precursors of the sweet spring grass and newborn animals, but those of the coming death of winter.

With a shudder, not just from the growing coldness but from the stark realization that death and rebirth was a far lengthier process than he had ever dreamed, Kah-Sih-Omah rose to his feet. He must leave here, travel down the mountain and find shelter in the warmer valleys below.

He stooped down, scooped the sand off the deerskin, and gathered up such of his birthright as he could—all that he had been allowed to bring from the world of the living into the world of the dead.

It was little enough: a gourd, a bowl, some wisps of singed fur, and a handful of pierced serpents' teeth.

These he gathered up and rolled into the skin, then started off through the darkness to the foot of the mountain, in the direction of the setting sun.

Kah-Sih-Omah trudged across valley sands hot enough to burn bare feet. His no longer were bare, but covered with green skins, taken from the animals he encountered and which, even here in the land of the dead, he slew as easily as in the land of the living.

And why, he asked himself, should it be otherwise? Was not man, dead, and in the land of the dead, the equal of man live, in the land of the living?

There had been a time when Kah-Sih-Omah had feared death, though it was unmanly to do so, and of course because of this he had shared these thoughts with no one. Now, reborn, he could see how foolish that had been. As a dead person he still had all the things he had enjoyed when he was alive; better still, his body was new here and could do much more.

He did not know where death would end, if death had an end, as life had. He did not see how the cycle could end, except to give way to the next part of his existence, as did the earth itself. Perhaps, he thought, the spirits create men and place them in the cycle, and watch them go around it. This seemed reasonable, until he began to ask himself why the spirits would want to.

He could find no answer to that question. He could only tell himself what he, as a shaman, had always told the People—that spirits do as they will, whether men understand or not.

As he walked toward the wintering ground of the People he found he cared less about the motives of the spirits than about reunion with all his old friends and acquaintances, who had also died and come here. Every step he took brought his anticipation to a new pitch.

He knew the People would stay in their traditional hunting grounds even when they died. Where else would they go but to the valleys they had hunted and the streams they had fished in life? There was no reason to leave these places; therefore, this is where Kah-Sih-Omah would find them.

He looked down at those parts of his body he could

see and wondered if they would know him in his new form. Probably they would not know him, until he told them his name. Perhaps they would laugh at him when they saw the rudeness of his clothing and caught its ripe scent. Perhaps they would gather around and poke fun at the crudely flaked point on his spear, and chide him for his ineptitude as a hunter.

He would become abashed. And to explain, he would throw open his robe to reveal the necklace of serpents' teeth which he had recently and so painstakingly restrung. He would show them his medicine bundle, with its exquisitely detailed symbols newly cleaned and partially repainted. Then they would know him, and understand that if his skills as a hunter were not as sharp as those of others, his skills as a shaman had remained undiminished.

Now he began to find signs. He came across the remains of a great-tooth, which the people had killed by driving it into a gully whose walls it could not climb again.

They had done with this what they always did. Because they could not carry the beast away except in pieces, the People had come here in a body and hacked it into small parts, which they had roasted and eaten until the flesh turned.

They had abandoned the carcass to the birds and other scavengers, who in days reduced the bones to greasy, shiny brightness, of interest only to ants, and gone back to their camp on permanent water.

Kah-Sih-Omah followed the tracks easily, though in the interim rain came and washed part of them away. By then, however, he no longer needed to follow tracks. He could use his eyes instead and see the wisps of smoke rising from cookfires out of the winter valley.

Once he caught sight of these his pace quickened and he was grateful to the spirits of death for the gift of this strong, new body. His enthusiasm drove him to use it ruthlessly, almost to the point of abuse, as what started out to be an exuberent sprint became a dogged race of endurance to gain the mouth of the valley ahead.

He came upon a regular pathway, one on which the grasses had been trampled by many feet, a game trail used by the People regularly on their forays up the slope of a hill, on which the climbing horned beasts dwelt. He gazed up at it and saw people.

His heart became gladdened at the sight of other men, like him, here in the land of the dead. He stopped to catch his breath, waited, and watched them as they approached. They were not yet within a distance where voices could be heard, but soon—

The eyes he had now were new eyes, and he saw much better than he had with the old ones, so what would once have been a blur for many, many more steps was now a clear, sharp image from which he could pick features and details. The man nearest trotted ahead of another who was burdened by the weight of a carcass across his shoulders. In the first man's hand was an axe with a twisted haft, which had become his namesake.

Kah-Sih-Omah felt his pulse quicken, not only because he was at last to be united with his people after what must have been a long separation, but because of a distinct feeling that something was wrong.

It was the body that Bad Axe wore which was wrong. That Bad Axe had died did not surprise him. The man was nearly as old as he, and had long suffered from some of the same infirmities that Kah-Sih-Omah had. And he had brought them along with him into the land of the dead.

Bad Axe approached still closer, but his pace had slowed and the axe in his hand was rising, as it would rise against a stranger until his intentions had become known. Behind him the other man had closed the gap and had shifted his burden to the other shoulder, so that Kah-Sih-Omah could see his face. The face was that of Bad Axe's youngest son, but it was not the face that Kah-Sih-Omah remembered. It was older; at least a winter, perhaps two winters than it had been when last Kah-Sih-Omah had seen it. Something was very wrong about this.

Kah-Sih-Omah did not move. His rude spearpoint trailed on the ground. His arm hung limp at his side. His mind seethed, with wonder and consternation. How long had death taken?

They stopped a good ten paces away from him and stood, studying his features. The boy again shifted his burden, slinging the dead animal onto his left shoulder, reluctant yet to put it down on the ground, but wary enough to want his right arm free to wield a weapon.

Bad Axe had had enough of ignorance. "Who are you, stranger? What do you want of us?"

The words fell on Kah-Sih-Omah's ears with a warmth totally unsupported by their gruff tone. These were the words of one of his people. He paused an instant to savor the sound before he answered. "I see you do not know me, Bad Axe, because I have changed. I am He-Who-Waits. I have returned."

A look of suspicion washed across the other man's face, and his axe arm rose a little higher. His eyes began to squint a little, and he cast a nervous glance to his side where his son, too, now held an axe.

Again Kah-Sih-Omah had to struggle to conceal his astonishment. It was glaringly apparent that Bad Axe's vision had deteriorated badly in the time he had been gone. It was apparent that the old man was all but blind. Probably he hunted the near hills with his son because no one else would go with him, and because he dare not go very far away from camp.

"Kah-Sih-Omah . . . I hear your words; I know your voice. But your voice is strange now. Where have you been?"

"On the sacred mountain, I believe. It was from there that I have lately journeyed. It was on the sacred mountain that I passed. I did not know that you and your son had also passed."

"Passed? Your words are strange. I do not know your meaning."

Behind Bad Axe, his son was drawing near, whispering something to him that Kah-Sih-Omah could not hear.

The older man listened for a moment, then shook his axe arm and whispered something back. The axe arm suddenly descended, and he stepped closer. "My son says you are not the shaman, but I believe you are, for I have known you all my winters, Kah-Sih-Omah, and your voice rings true. Will you come with us to the village?"

"I will come."

Bad Axe turned, and stepped away toward the half-dozen or so columns of smoke that rose above the hill separating them from the stream, alongside which stood the lodges of the People.

Kah-Sih-Omah followed, checking the length of his own stride to match that of his companion.

But the boy fell behind them, and Kah-Sih-Omah had an uneasy feeling about this, because the boy's suspicion remained with him, and the muscles on his axe arm remained taut.

"You smell bad, Kah-Sih-Omah. You have the stink of death about you. You wear green skins."

"The spirits left me nothing but my medicine bundle. I passed far from where the people were. There was no one to prepare me."

Bad Axe did not reply, but shambled on toward the village.

Kah-Sih-Omah began to feel uneasy at the man's silence. Bad Axe behaved as if he did not understand what Kah-Sih-Omah had told him, and Kah-Sih-Omah was beginning to wonder if there might not be some difference in the way each had passed. Perhaps his own situation, because of the direct intervention of the spirits, was somehow unique. Perhaps he had been given this new, young body because in some way his old one was unfit. No, that did not seem reasonable—Bad Axe had most assuredly as great a need. After a few minutes of such mental struggle Kah-Sih-Omah gave it up, and concentrated on the panorama which was developing ahead of him.

Their approach had been noted by the people in the village, who watched them come. In the forefront, dogs snarled, and sniffed the air for the scent of this stranger.

"Stranger"?

The thought struck Kah-Sih-Omah like a bitter winter wind. He knew at once that there was far more amiss than he could have imagined. He recognized not only the faces of all the people in the gathering crowd, but also the features of the dogs—he knew the dogs. The dogs had passed along with the people!

Even more appalling was the fact that *all* the faces were there. To Kah-Sih-Omah, this could only mean that something terrible had happened to the People— some disaster, which had taken all of them, wiped them out. He wondered, with mounting horror, if any of the People survived in the world of the living. It did not appear to him that any had. All of them, from the old men and women, to the youngest children, seemed to be here in the crowd which now surrounded him.

He stopped, shocked at this realization, and turned to Bad Axe, who had dropped a little behind him.

Bad Axe was no longer the shambling, almost placid person he had been during the march into the village. Now he stood poised in an attack position, weapon raised high, eyes glaring, face contorted, muscles tense. Beside him, in like posture, stood his son.

Others approached Kah-Sih-Omah, who stood bewildered, still with his spearpoint near the ground.

"Seize him," Bad Axe shouted. "He says he is Kah-Sih-Omah; he has the Shaman's medicine bundle."

From among the crowd, men with weapons appeared— men Kah-Sih-Omah knew, but who did not know him; who scowled at him and moved with menace in their gestures. In a moment they had encircled him.

In a final act of conciliation his hand relaxed its grip on the haft of the spear and it tumbled to the ground.

Instantly someone seized it, and an instant later its crude head had joined the other weapons pointed at him.

"What is the matter with you people?" he shouted. "Why do you treat me as though I am a stranger, when all of you have known me in life? Why do you behave as though I were an enemy?"

The answer was another volley of thrusts.

"I *am* Kah-Sih-Omah," he shouted. "Do not be deceived by the changes the spirits wrought on me. The spirits made me young again, that is all they did. I do not know why they did so—they did not tell me—but within, my spirit lives as always."

There was a great murmur, followed at once by a

shout from behind the crowd. The voice of the shout was well known to Kah-Sih-Omah, and in this he found comfort. It was a voice of great power and great wisdom, of the man who led the People. It was a voice that for many winters past had taken the counsel of Kah-Sih-Omah, and who perhaps would take it now—it was the voice of the Man-Of-Thunder, Ruhu-Doh-Sah, champion of the hunters, leader of the people and friend of Kah-Sih-Omah.

"Let him by," someone mumbled. The circle broke and in the gap appeared a man of stern visage and shoulders broad and brawny, trailing silver locks unbound by braids, as was the custom among the People. On his face was painted his sign. Around his wrists were amulets of the hunt which Kah-Sih-Omah had himself fashioned, containing talismans to which only he and their bearer were privey. This, he told himself, would be the test.

Ruhu-Doh-Sah, weaponless, his mighty arms folded across his chest, looked upon the form and face of the stranger who called himself friend, eyes straining, searching for signs of recognition. Ruhu-Doh-Sah, being younger by far than Kah-Sih-Omah, would not have known the young shaman, but it was not necessary that he should; not for the test.

For a long time he stood there, and then his face took on a troubled look. The eyes rose and met Kah-Sih-Omah's own for a brief instant, then dropped. "The voice," he said, "is that of the Shaman. The form is not. I do not know this man."

The circle started to tighten, as though the words were the trigger to a snare that would now unleash a forest of jagged spearpoints. Kah-Sih-Omah was lost.

"No," he shouted back at Ruhu-Doh-Sah. "This is the work of the spirits who aided me in passing. Let the circle widen, Ruhu-Doh-Sah, so that others may not hear our words, and I will offer proof."

"What proof have you, stranger, other than the bundle, which you might easily have taken from the Shaman? He was old. He was infirm."

"Have you fear of me?" Kah-Sih-Omah knew that Ruhu-Doh-Sah did not fear him. Ruhu-Doh-Sah feared no one and nothing, and he could hardly ignore such a challenge with all of the people watching.

"Do as he says," Ruhu-Doh-Sah's voice boomed out. "I will hear this stranger's words." His arms rose in a gesture.

"Now," he said to Kah-Sih-Omah, when the circle had widened, "tell me; how came you by the Shaman's voice and upon his bundle, and by what right do you claim his spirit?"

Kah-Sih-Omah knew that denial with words would be a futile gesture. He would instead offer the proof he promised. "Within the amulet upon your left wrist there lies the tooth of the cat which stabs, pierced in four places, which represent the wounds the teeth make. Around it is wrapped, with a string made of the entrails of the same beast, tufts of its fur with which have been smeared its saliva, blood, and urine. This is the talisman which gives you strength.

"On your other wrist is the amulet which gives you wisdom. In it is the dried eye of the great bird of prey which lives atop cliffs, together with one of its feet, all bound together in a cluster of feathers with a thong beaten long and thin from a fragment of the sun. There is no other such fragment in all the world."

Ruhu-Doh-Sah's face reflected the amazement he must have felt at hearing this revelation. His jaw dropped and one hand fell to his waist, where a dagger hung in its sheath.

For an instant, Kah-Sih-Omah almost believed the other man was convinced, and his lips parted to speak.

But all at once Ruhu-Doh-Sah gestured furiously, and the circle closed swiftly and tightly once more around Kah-Sih-Omah. Again, spears menaced him from every direction.

"He has stolen the spirit of the Shaman," Ruhu-Doh-Sah's voice roared, though in it there was the curious but unmistakable cracking of fear. "That is how he knows. But he is not the Shaman."

"He claims to be dead," Bad Axe shouted above the growing murmur. "He says that the People are dead."

Ruhu-Doh-Sah's voice boomed out again. Again, fear filled it and he made no effort to conceal that fear. It was not unmanly, but wise, to fear an evil spirit. No one would think less of him because he did. "Bind him! Bring him to the village. Let the woman see him. And someone must find the Shaman."

Nothing else would have so astounded Kah-Sih-Omah as these last words. The Shaman! *He* was the shaman—there was no other; there was no need of another! And the People! The People did not know—they did not believe themselves dead!

And then he realized what Ruhu-Doh-Sah meant: the People had a new Shaman, Kah-Sih-Omah's successor. He would be another old familiar face, his pupil as well as a relative, the son of Kah-Sih-Omah's long-dead brother; Hono-Yoko, He-Of-Many-Visions, so called because he often fell faint upon the ground and shook violently, and bit his tongue.

When Kah-Sih-Omah had gone off to the sacred mountain, Hono-Yoko had wished to come along, but Kah-Sih-Omah had forbidden it. He was, at the time, still unsure that Hono-Yoko possessed the qualities requisite of a shaman. In the young man he had observed flaws, not the least of which was a propensity to use his knowledge to bully others. Kah-Sih-Omah had been entertaining the idea of taking an additional apprentice so that he could be certain a worthy successor was available when he passed. Obviously, when Kah-Sih-Omah had failed to return, the People had passed his mantle to his nephew, who no doubt now would have extreme reluctance to part with it.

Kah-Sih-Omah submitted meekly to the bonds. He had no hope, and no other course than to wait and see what happened. Should he bolt, he would find a dozen spearpoints in his body before he had completed the first step, and yet to stay would probably mean the same, in a slower manner. He did not know what effect such wounds would have on his new body, which he had believed already dead. Could he be killed again, and pass again, to yet another place? Kah-Sih-Omah didn't know. That was the trouble; he knew next to nothing about his new self, except that he loved his people and wanted to stay among them, if they could be persuaded to allow it.

Kah-Sih-Omah lay there, in the otherwise empty lodge, upon a pile of robes: old robes, tattered, torn, and with the fur worn off them; robes no one wanted any longer, and so did not care if they took on the odor that surrounded him.

His wife had come and looked into the door of the lodge, then entered and stayed the afternoon, studying him with rheumy eyes. She had grimaced at him, revealing nearly toothless gums, but had not spoken. Her behavior seemed to him to be the strangest of all. As old as he, as infirm, her spirit had begun to leave her long ago. She was not, as yet, incapable of caring for herself, but that was in her future; her near future, that was plain to see.

For a while, when she had first come, Kah-Sih-Omah thought he saw on her face a faint spark of recognition. It gave him hope, for she was among those few of the people who remained here who had known him well as a young man, and he knew that she remembered better those times long past than those of merely yesterday. She would recognize him if anyone could.

Yet it appeared to him that she did not. He spoke to her, first of natural things, as a man is accustomed to say to his wife, and she did not answer. He told his account of his passing, and she listened with apparent interest, though there was no sign of understanding. Only when he began to talk of those secret, intimate things between them did her eyes brighten for a time. The time was brief. Too late, he learned that what he had interpreted as a sign of her affection for him was really a sign of fear.

She did not believe him either. Instead, she began to curse the demon she thought he was, and spat upon it, reviling it for having stolen her husband's spirit and taken his medicine away; for having come here to steal yet more from his people. Presently, alarmed by the rising tumult within, the braves who guarded the lodge had entered and led her away.

They left behind a Kah-Sih-Omah crushed and broken by this as he could have been by nothing else. Then, without a thought as to how this might sound to others who would hear, he too began to curse the spirits. He cried out from the pain the spirits had brought to him, to make him different from all the rest of the People. *Why*? What was his crime?

Again the opening of the lodge became filled with faces, first the two guards and then others. They came, led by Hono-Yoko, dressed in ceremonial robes, his face painted in the ancient pattern of the dance of death—the dance by which the People mourned the passing of a beloved member, and with their prayers, fortified his spirit against the hostile forces which would attempt to injure him while he was in the helpless transitional state.

At the sight of this, Kah-Sih-Omah became immediately solemn and silent. The truth was beginning to dawn on him; perhaps the people were right, and he was wrong. Perhaps they were not dead at all, as he was. Perhaps this was why he saw them as they had always appeared, and why they had not been transformed as he had been.

Transformed? Suppose he *had* been merely transformed—transformed, not killed! Not dead? Could it be that he had not died at all?

Somehow, that thought was more crushing than any blow which had yet fallen. How cruel the spirits could be, if they had done this.

"Leave us," the new Shaman said to the guards. Hono-Yoko's voice was curiously high-pitched, shrill, yet his order fell on ears eager to obey him. They left hurriedly and without a moment's hesitation.

"So, Uncle; you appear to have fallen on hard times."

"You know me?" Kah-Sih-Omah was astonished.

"Of course I know you. Who else could you be but Kah-Sih-Omah? Who else knows the things you know?"

Kah-Sih-Omah paused to digest this development. He didn't know whether to believe Hono or not, yet he wanted desperately to gain an ally, and until now, no other possibilities had appeared. Finally, he threw caution to the winds and confessed. "I am He-Who-Waits. I am younger, healther, stronger, but that is the work of the spirits. I remain who I always was."

"I believe you, Uncle. Tell me of your experiences

with these spirits; tell me where you have been for two winters."

"Two winters?— But— I thought it was only one."

"No, Uncle. It has been two. The first we waited for you to return, then went to the valley of the great tooth. Returning in the spring, we passed near the sacred mountain, which was newly changed."

"You have been there?"

"Not to the summit, Uncle, but to that of a mountain nearby. I traveled there alone."

"Why?"

"To see your spirits, of course. But the spirits concealed themselves, and I saw only their works, where they dug mightily into the sides of the mountain."

"Even I have not seen them, Hono. I have only heard them in my mind."

"Had the spirits words for you?"

"None which I presently comprehend. I know only that they spoke my name occasionally. I was entranced at the time."

"For two entire winters?"

"I do not know how long. Why do you ask?"

"I am merely curious, Uncle."

"No! No, Hono—you are more than that. What do you really want of me? Why, if you believe I am Kah-Sih-Omah, have you not released me, or told the others who I truly am?"

"There are complications, Uncle. You see, your reappearance, in this strange form, has frightened the people. You have especially frightened Ruhu-Doh-Sah, who believes that you are indeed an evil spirit, that you have eaten the spirit of Kah-Sih-Omah and acquired his medicine, and that you hunger for his. The people wish to be rid of you, but they do not believe you can be killed and they are afraid to attempt it."

"You do not believe I have passed—but, Hono, I have passed. I must have. How else could I have been reborn?"

"I do not know precisely what magic was involved, Uncle, but I have seen very great medicine since you went to the sacred mountain. With my own eyes I have seen the great egg of the spirits—greater even than the

length and breadth of this valley, and higher than the
highest of the hills around it."

"There is no egg, Hono; I saw none."

"True enough. The spirits have gone, have they not?"

"How do you know that?"

"I saw their signs in the sky . . . first, a great blazing
tail of fire when they came, which was at night, shortly
after your departure, and then, more recently—just before you reappeared—I saw a cloud in the direction of
the sacred mountain, and I think perhaps, had it been
dark, this would have been of fire also. The omen was
clearly connected with you."

"Then I did not imagine it all. It was not a part of the
trance. The mushroom had nothing to do with it."

"You took the cup?"

"Yes."

"You fool! That is why you do not know what happened to you. And I thought . . ."

"What, Hono? What did you think?"

"Never mind, Uncle. In any event, I should be pleased
if you would tell me what you do know."

"While I am bound?"

"That is for your safety, Uncle. Were you free, like as
not, some nervous warrior would plunge a spear in
you."

"And, if I tell you . . ."

". . . then I will assist you to escape."

"Escape? Why should I wish to escape? These are my
people; I am their Shaman."

"The people follow me now, Uncle. They do not know
you."

At last, the words had been said. Kah-Sih-Omah was
not surprised. He had been afraid since Hono had first
appeared, enrobed, that the boy's ambition had gained
the upper hand. Having tasted power, he would not
willingly give it up, though he must eventually lead the
people into grief for it.

Hono was clever. He had displayed great initiative,
and though Kah-Sih-Omah could not readily see what
advantage might be gained from the information, he
knew that Hono believed and hoped there was one. He

also knew that once he spoke he would be of no further use to his nephew.

Sadly, Kah-Sih-Omah had seen the boy's strength of intellect before he recognized the weaknesses in his character. His physical disadvantages had long been apparent, and he had apprenticed Hono partly because of them. He had known Hono would never make a warrior or a hunter, and his intention had been to give the boy a chance at life.

But Hono's ego had grown ponderous. Because he was weak he hated those who were strong, and more than once had turned the magic Kah-Sih-Omah had taught him to the satisfaction of his growing craving for power. Kah-Sih-Omah had seen this fault in others. There were tribes where shamen ruled instead of reason, whose people and whose neighbors lived in constant terror of them; insecure men who debased their gifts and led their people into wars of conquest, and took from the earth more than was their due or need. He could see now that his nephew was one of these.

Kah-Sih-Omah's course was therefore clear—defiance. "Then work your medicine, Nephew," he replied. "Discover for yourself, if you can, what it is you wish to know. I will tell you nothing."

"As you wish, Uncle. But as I have said, the people follow me. Should I suggest to the People that roasting the spirit over a slow fire might end its intransigence, the People would doubtless obey." He rose to his feet. "I must leave to officiate at the dance of death in honor of Kah-Sih-Omah's spirit. When I return we will talk more of this, and perhaps in the interval you will recant." He smiled, turned, and left the lodge without another word.

Presently, drums sounded, beating out a slow dirge. Then the chant began, led by Hono, extolling the virtues of Kah-Sih-Omah, late the Shaman of the People, now passed.

Such quackery! Yet the contradiction appeared to escape the notice of the people. How, Kah-Sih-Omah asked himself, could Hono tell the people Kah-Sih-Omah had passed and still claim his spirit was imprisoned? It was not honest and it made no sense, but there appeared to be nothing Kah-Sih-Omah could do about it as long as Hono enjoyed the people's confidence. Was there no way to expose his nephew's trickery?

He could think of nothing, especially while a prisoner. Even free he might do no better, but he would have more options. He resolved to become free. Thus far, escape had not seemed necessary, because he had believed the People would eventually recognize the truth. He had not attempted to free himself.

Now, with that alternative unquestionably gone so long as Hono's sway prevailed, Kah-Sih-Omah began to test his bonds, flexing muscles and straining against them until the tough fibers of the rope bit into his flesh. He found the bonds were strong and would not yield.

He must, therefore, try another way. He began to relax his limbs instead, and seek to utilize what slack he could find in the loops. To his surprise there was some—more than he had hoped for, and he began to wonder why he had not noticed it before.

He worked at it for a long time before he managed to work his fingers around the first loop. There fingers were young, and supple, not like the old, stiff ones he had once had—which, had they been bound, even more lightly, could not have moved, much less been freed.

The first loop was the key to all. After that he had slack to spare. Manipulating and straining, this was transferred to the other loops until there was enough to release one hand. After that, only moments elapsed before Kah-Sih-Omah was standing next to the door of the lodge, rubbing his hands together to restore circulation. He glanced down at them. They felt somehow different—looked somewhat different; slimmer, longer, he could not decide what it was about them. But it did not seem to matter much now that his bonds were off. What mattered was that the hands were strong.

He could perhaps then have thrown open the door and bolted past the guards, who from their post had riveted their attention on the ceremony across the clearing. But this would have meant immediate pursuit, and Kah-Sih-Omah did not want that. He wanted a silent and unhurried departure, so he went to the far wall of the lodge and began to dig under it.

At first he made good progress, but when he got beneath the soil he encountered clay, which required tools. He found these in the form of sticks from the wattle, and with a stout, sharp one he chiseled the earth away and pushed it behind him.

He had almost finished his tunnel when the drums stopped. This told him that the ceremony was over, and he dug even faster. If his assessment of Hono was correct, the next encounter with his nephew would occur with very little delay.

He threw the sticks aside, brushed out the remaining dirt, and crawled into the hole, sliding on his back, head first. He had his torso through when the lodge door opened, and one leg out before the shout rang out. Then, someone grasped him by his other foot, which was still in the hole, and tried to pull him back in. His makeshift moccasin slipped off and whoever it was lost his grip, whereupon Kah-Sih-Omah jerked his leg out and sprang to his feet.

Other shouts rang out; at least two men, probably his guards, were in the lodge, but Kah-Sih-Omah knew that they would immediately rush out and pursue him; that probably the whole village would then join in.

He had to move fast—get out through the valley's comparatively narrow opening before it could be blocked, and gain the open plain where he had some chance of outrunning them.

He raced for it, leaping over firepits and tentpoles, and dodging startled people not yet aware he was the object of the alarm. He raced by Hono, still adorned in the feather- and quill-decorated robe he had worn in the dance.

Hono glared at him, and shouted orders at the warriors nearby. Some of these were also in ceremonial dress, but nevertheless snatched up weapons and gave immediate chase.

Kah-Sih-Omah plunged onward, making for the opening, grateful for the surprise which had enabled him to get this far unchallenged. He did not want to fight. A wound, however slight, might prevent his escape, and certainly he wished to harm none of the People.

He cleared the two low hills that marked the entrance

to the valley. Sentinels posted high on each looked down and brandished spears, but did not join in the chase. They were there to give alarm of dangers approaching the valley. They would not leave this post, and in any case were too far away to be any threat to his escape.

The panic which had gripped Kah-Sih-Omah up until this moment suddenly left him, as he saw the way ahead was clear. He broke out into the grasslands and raced toward the eastern mountains. There was still pursuit, and he knew when he looked back and saw Yengoos-Waha, swiftest of the People's runners, that though this new and splendidly fit body gave him a chance, it was no more than that. He would need all its power and all its endurance if he were to get away.

He stopped for an instant to tear off the other crude moccasin, which was slowing him down, then stretched out into long easy strides, breathing deeply and regularly in tempo with the movements of his legs. What a joy it was to run again, whatever the circumstances, and feel the wind in his face. How differently he felt now that he was young again. He felt as though he could race on forever.

This was curious—his activity had been both furious and strenuous, yet he had not tired. He was still not tired though he had already run half the length of the valley. His breath still came easily and unlabored, with none of the tortured aching he remembered from his youth as the price of such strong effort. The muscles in his legs were still supple, not tense and knotted as they should be, considering the killing pace he maintained. He could not help but wonder at this, which would have seemed so natural to him were he still convinced that he was dead, but was so decidedly unnatural for a man alive.

Confident now, he glanced back, to see that his pursuers had dwindled down to two. He knew that one of these was Yengoos, who was dogged, and who would not end it until he dropped. He could tell from their strides that they enjoyed no such advantage as he; that they were tiring, and that soon pursuit would digress into a lengthy ordeal, slow-paced but steady, its continuation dependent as much on tracking as running.

This was what disturbed Kah-Sih-Omah: the possibility that when he had evaded close pursuit they would one day reappear, having followed his spoor, and he would then perhaps be taken by surprise.

Thus, he could not do what he really wished to do—hover near the People, watching over them, trying to devise some way to make them understand who he was so that he could free them from the growing and evil influence of Hono.

He must instead go on to the high ground where rocky soil and scanty vegetation would not retain his tracks, and then cautiously circle back to where the People were.

Without a break in the running except to drink at a brook, Kah-Sih-Omah traversed the distance to the foothills in what remained of the day. His pursuers had long since disappeared behind him, hidden by the horizon and the tall grasses. Fortunately, since he was unarmed, nothing menacing crossed his path on the way.

It was not yet the season of the thunderbeasts, who later, closer to winter, would roam these plains, eating and wallowing in the grass. Even in the late autumn it was too hot and dry for the great-tooth, whose thick hairy hide required shade or moisture lest he cook inside it from the heat of the sun.

The other, smaller animals feared man, and avoided him. These fled at Kah-Sih-Omah's approach, even faster than they would that of a great cat. They knew that of the two predators, man was the more deadly.

Kah-Sih-Omah reached a low escarpment just beyond the edge of the bush. The sun was then growing low in the sky, so that the goats who pranced on the rim cast long, inviting shadows and were easy to see. This was the time of day when men customarily hunted them, and they were wary, but not so wary that had he a weapon he might have eaten meat that night instead of dry nuts and gritty roots.

He could not risk a fire, either for warmth or to keep the animals away, because he knew that it would be seen; that Yengoos, and any still with him, would run the night through, if need be, to take him in the morning. He was, considering what he had learned of himself in recent days, by no means sure they could, still, he did not relish the thought of mortal combat. He was not yet used to life.

There was a cave of sorts, carved by wind and water into the base of the escarpment. It was into this he crept for safety in the night, while he fitfully slept away the hours of darkness.

In the morning, feeling fit and fresh, he mounted the rocks and gazed out onto the prairie, eyes searching for those motes of darkness which, cast against the light expanse of grass, might betray the presence of pursuit. He saw such motes, but from the pattern and the numbers he judged them to be grazing animals, and therefore did not worry.

He passed from the top of the escarpment into the next valley which, though less well watered than the one in which the People were camped, was just as large. Here he saw many of the small grazers, collected in little herds scattered across the valley floor.

Some ate peacefully and undisturbed. Others were not so fortunate, being visited periodically by turmoil and confusion, during which times they bolted and scattered erratically. Kah-Sih-Omah did not like this. He knew that it meant the presence of large predators among them, most likely the great stabbing cats who, because they were slow and clumsy, haunted the edges of the grassland. There they frequently waited in ambush, unmoving and unseen, to pounce upon any unsuspecting animal who wandered into range. Even armed, a man was normally no match for one of them. Worse, they generally hunted in pairs, so only a large party of men could cross their range and expect to live.

Kah-Sih-Omah must cross it. He had no choice. If he didn't, he faced not only purposeful discovery by Yengoos, but inadvertant discovery by hunting parties from the village, who would be driven to forage here when game grew scarce close by it. Once past it, he could also circle to the north and hide in the foothills near where the People were camped. He could be close to them and yet unseen.

He acquired a hand axe, no real weapon but better than nothing. When he reached the far wall of the valley and entered rocky ground once more, he intended to fashion a new spear. At the moment, he had neither flint for the head nor wood for the handle.

He was fortunate to a degree. He came very close to making his goal. He was crossing a place of mixed grasses and low bush when first he saw the cats.

If they saw him as well, they gave no sign. Their attention was not on the man but on the several half-grown deer who grazed close to where they lay concealed.

Kah-Sih-Omah squatted down, nevertheless, and took note of the wind. It was against him, and against the deer, who thus had not caught the scent and fled.

Kah-Sih-Omah lay quietly, hoping there were no other members of the group of cats nearby. He didn't see any, but that did not necessarily mean there weren't any. He kept hidden, and he kept quiet, just in case. If the cats succeeded in catching one of the deer, as seemed likely, he knew the answer to the question would be rapidly revealed, as every cat nearby would rush to share the meat. He hoped he could use those moments of distraction to bolt out across the remaining flatland and gain the rocks on the other side.

Perhaps a more experienced hunter, more familiar with the habits of animals than Kah-Sih-Omah, would have anticipated the danger and avoided it. Kah-Sih-Omah was not a great hunter; he was a shaman, whose interests lay not with behavior in the hunt, but with the more general behavior of the animals' spirits and the way these affected men.

Thus, when the cats, which hunted by sight, pounced upon the deer, whose noses had not warned them but whose ears did, the deer bolted—bolted in the precise direction of Kah-Sih-Omah's hiding place. Again, had he been an experienced hunter, he would have remained motionless and let the cats charge on past him, because he would have known that it is the movement of game which triggers the cat's interest.

He did not know that he was safe in hiding. He thought he was the object of the charge because he lay in its path. Alarmed, and in panic, he followed a natural instinct. He jumped to his feet and ran from them. After that, he had no chance.

There were two of them, a female and a big male. The male was ahead when Kah-Sih-Omah bolted. He continued on to chase the deer, who now, in full flight, had turned and raced inward toward the comparative safety of the herd.

The female, however, was not as confident as he that one could be caught. She stopped short at the sight of Kah-Sih-Omah, decided that here was something a little slower and more certain, and pounced on him instead.

The first blow of her massive front paws knocked him to the ground. She was on top of him instantly, poised to stab with gleaming upper fangs as long almost as Kah-Sih-Omah's forearm. He could feel her fetid breath beating down upon him.

The fangs descended, one on each side of his neck, so that both missed a vital area. Instantly the beast withdrew and tried again. This time she cupped her front paws, with claws extended, around Kah-Sih-Omah's back. Without some additional and miraculous intervention by the spirits, Kah-Sih-Omah's new life seemed about to end.

The intervention came not from the spirits but from the male cat, who having lost the chase to the deer was now intent on sharing whatever the female had caught.

She did not want him near, and growled savagely at his approach, turning her head to bare teeth even as she continued to hold Kah-Sih-Omah firmly.

The male chose that moment to strike. He did not want all her kill, just some of it. A few mouthfuls would do. He got them.

The jaws of the cat were massive, and muscled well. When they closed around Kah-Sih-Omah's left leg his flesh parted more swiftly than the bone, which merely cracked. But with a savage twist of the male's head the bone parted too, piercing and ripping whatever muscle remained intact when he rushed away with it.

Kah-Sih-Omah's agony was excruciating, his scream blood-curdling—frightening even to the cat, who leapt lightly away for an instant. Her mouth opened for a long moment after that, to issue forth a long and threatening growl at the male before he trotted off and her attention returned to her kill.

Meanwhile, Kah-Sih-Omah's autonomic system had taken over bodily functions in their entirety. Triggered by the gross shock of the trauma, his consciousness mercifully fled, and he fell limp.

To the cat, lack of movement equalled death. Her thinking was not complex. She did not, therefore, renew her effort to stab Kah-Sih-Omah, but instead grasped him by the loose skins with which his torso was covered and raised him off the ground. Pausing a brief moment to determine the whereabouts of the thieving male, she found him devouring his stolen morsel near the base of a small tree. She went the other way, somewhat round-about, to get to the lair where her two half-grown cubs lay. A mother, she thought first of them. Their weaning was in progress and her milk supply was drying up, but they would learn to eat this meat, even though to her it stank.

Kah-Sih-Omah, unconscious, deep in shock, was spared the further terror of the precarious climb the mother cat made in wild and daring leaps from rock to rock, up the face of the precipace.

She took her time, and was careful to hold her prize tightly in her mouth as she rested, though at times it hung out over the sheer edge, dripping blood to spatter on the rocks below. Presently, panting fiercely from the exertion, she made her way along the narrow ledge that led to the shallow depression.

It was her cave, now, but evidence abounded that in the past it had been inhabited by all manner of other creatures, including some of the great scavenger birds, whose ruined nests had collapsed between two long, pointed boulders which stood before the cave entrance.

Inside it, in the wide mouth, the cubs waited impatiently, mewing wildly. The cubs wanted milk. They made that clear as soon as she was inside. They sniffed only briefly at the meat she bore in her jaws before diving underneath her in search of tastier fare.

She was a loving if somewhat savage mother. She would, insofar as she was able, indulge them. She threw Kah-Sih-Omah's body down upon the floor and lay down in the cave mouth, where she could watch the approach in case the male decided to come up to rob her again.

Probably, he would not. Males had a healthy respect for the ability of the mother cat to defend her young, and the ferocious determination with which they did it. Still, a mother never knew.

She did not allow the possibility to trouble her greatly. Instead she rolled over and let the cubs nurse. Never did she give another thought to her prey. Never did it occur to her that it yet lived. Never—never, for the rest of her life.

Pain! Pain unbearable, but pain with a shadow—a shadow of greater pain, now gone.

Light! Fiercely glaring, painful in and of itself—the full face of the afternoon sun, burning its way even through closed eyelids; penetrating deeply into the brain.

Fuzzy numbness—detachment—vertigo, violent but receding.

Fetid stenches—rotting feces, rotting flesh, rancid fat, decomposing blood.

Buzzing sounds—no! The sound of labored breathing, mewing, scratching sounds—tiny growls.

The recovering sensorium enveloped it all, while the mind responsible for interpretation yet languished in shock. It must not continue to do so.

Kah-Sih-Omah's will proved less able than his pre-brain. Though its status was the lowlier, it had resisted the strain to which the loftier lobe succumbed. It had salvaged and preserved what was left of the body which sustained both, much to its credit; but being what it was, had no awareness of that fact.

Awareness came to Kah-Sih-Omah in another great wave of shock. He knew what had happened and he knew that he could not really be alive. With his own eyes he had seen the great cat tear off his leg and run away with it, while his life's blood spurted from the stump.

That was bad enough. Amazed as he was to find himself alive, in relatively little pain, and conscious, still he was horrified when he discovered the reason—the mother cat was feeding the cubs before she fed herself. His turn would come next.

In his panic, thoughts, not always rational, came fast

and furious. His impulse was to flee, yet reason ruled this out. She would catch him instantly, scrambling along on one leg. Probably she would catch him almost as easily, even if he had two.

Also, he was cornered. The cave entrance lay beyond two immense rocks, and she and the cubs were between them. There was no way out. He must fight!

How? He searched for weapons and saw none; not even a sizable stone lay within reach. All he could do was throw himself upon her and attempt to strangle her. That avenue did not seem promising.

He had hardly dared to breathe since the instant he opened his eyes, lest he attract the attention of the cat. How, then, could he move fast enough even to reach her before she bounded on top of him and stabbed him to death?

He couldn't. He could do nothing. He must simply wait for the end.

The end? Was it really the end? Was this the purpose for which the spirits had prepared him, for which they had given him renewed youth? Was this magnificent body fit only to feed this mindless beast? Was it rational, was it fitting that this be his end?

He could not believe it was, yet it seemed inevitable. And it was a question that, if he did not solve it in this life, might continue to plague him in the next. If there was one thing that Kah-Sih-Omah believed in, it was his assessment of life as a cyclical mechanism. His present dilemma seemed to support that idea. If it didn't, then the spirits were indeed wasteful.

What, then, did they require of him? Belief in them? They had that. Reverence? That too he gave them. They had no need to torment him to have their proof. Again, why was he—*what* was he to them? Why did they behave so mysteriously when all they really had to do was tell him what they wanted and he would do it?

Something was wrong with that idea. He searched his memory for the key. He found it—found it in a fuzzy thought that he had never before recalled, but now did because it was significant—a spirit had said it—thought it—whatever, however, it was there—*"It is primitive, yet I believe it truly thinks."*

To think! Is that their test for me?

Kah-Sih-Omah bent his will to it. He strove to do as he believed the spirits had bidden. He believed that somehow, even in the darkest moment he had ever known, they meant him to survive.

How?

Somehow, within the boundaries of his circumstances, the spirits expected him to find the way—which meant there *was* a way.

Very good—reason belongs to man, as does brute strength to the animal. This is the difference in their spirits. Man thinks, man plans; animals do not. Animals are wary—man is wary also, but man thinks, so man takes caution a step further—man plans, animals do not—man plans, animals do not. Why does this make a difference?

Why! Why! Why! What is a plan? What are the elements of a plan? What is the purpose of a plan? Purpose? Purpose? What is my purpose?

Answer—Purpose, immediate: to avoid being eaten. Purpose, general: to survive. Purpose, ultimate . . . unknown.

Question—What circumstances, if any, favor the first purpose?

Answer—Life continues during this interval, while the cat is distracted.

Again—there are no other favorable circumstances.

THINK!

The cat is foolish.

What?

Foolish—should the rock tumble she will be crushed.

What rock?

That rock.

The cat does not care; why?

The cat cannot anticipate; the cat can only react. The cat cannot plan.

THINK!

I am a man—my purpose is to survive, to ponder the ultimate question in the light of attendant circumstances until I have derived its answer.

THINK!

Push!

Kah-Sih-Omah pushed. One strong leg taut, back braced against the cavern wall, he pushed against the awkwardly balanced rock. Beneath its outer edges an incrustation of the cave's detritus crumbled, and a gap formed, as it teetered.

A man could have avoided what to the cat was certain doom. A cat's four-footed stance permits no options for its leap. It can leap forward a long way and backward a little, but it cannot leap to the sides, as bipedal creatures can.

The mother cat leapt forward, trusting to speed and agility to save her, but she did not have enough of either, any more than she had had the intelligence to avoid the position of peril.

Now she lay, back broken, chest crushed, and fast expiring, while her cubs looked on without apparent interest.

Behind her, farther inside the cave, her assailant—maimed, weaker, far more feebly armed—triumphed with intellect, mightiest of all the known forces of nature.

Kah-Sih-Omah could not move the stone from her, nor could he hasten her release. She suffered and, at length, died while her cubs watched.

Kah-Sih-Omah's own situation was grave, but to his surprise he had no pain. He had had fierce pain in the beginning, and copious bleeding, to judge from the evidence he could still see. He knew that he should be dead, either from shock or from loss of blood, but he suffered neither at the present time. Unlikely as it might seem, it was even probable that he would live.

But was it desirable? How could he possibly survive without any help, far away from his people, where life depended on catching food and avoiding being caught for food? He could not run; he could not walk; would never again do either. Kah-Sih-Omah had known individuals whose limbs had been lost. An arm caused little difficulty, and most people who lost one could live relatively normal lives. A leg was another matter—though again, he had known a few who made do with sticks. Were he still a shaman, still among the people, he could function, but never as a lone hunter.

But wait! Could he say that? Was it true? Perhaps it was another test. Somehow, deep in his mind, the spirit had lurked, and by means of his prompting Kah-Sih-Omah had been induced to reason his way out of certain death. Was this so different?

What had he done to solve that problem? —He had merely taken note of the circumstances and used them. He could do that again.

By straining to the utmost, Kah-Sih-Omah could just barely see the end of his stump. The stump was ugly but the amputation was relatively clean. The end of the hip bone was not visible, having broken above the bite and then been drawn out. Here and there a stretched tendon protruded or a severed vessel still oozed drops of blood. But over the face of the wound a filmlike covering was forming that Kah-Sih-Omah supposed in time would become a scab, and thus protect the wound. He did not wish to interfere with this by covering it up. He decided to leave it bare, though when he moved he took care to keep it out of the dirt.

He found this to be easier than he had supposed. By adopting a three-legged stance he could get around the cave quite well, even climb over the toppled stone to get at the remains of the birds' nests.

This was important. The material in them insured that he would have fire with which to drive off other predators, and to cook those with whom he had already done battle. That night he dined on the roast haunch of the mother cat, and fed tasty tidbits of her meat to her kittens, who ate it eagerly.

"Your turn will come," he told them. "Eat; grow fat; be tender; for the ultimate question remains to be answered, and this man intends to survive."

Astonishment—pure, stark, and utter astonishment: evidence in the face of fact which totally and unequivocally defied all established reason. In its way it was altogether as horrible as the loss of his leg had been— and it was real. Its reality was unquestionable.

Three days Kah-Sih-Omah had reposed in the cavern, with only the cubs and insects for company. Three days all of them had fed off the carcass of the dead mother cat, now stinking and bloated around the edges of the stone which had crushed her. Flies, attracted to the stench, buzzed endlessly over it, while ants creeping up from their hill somewhere below carried off a steady stream of tiny fragments.

Kah-Sih-Omah could do little to relieve the situation here. The stone had been just within his capability to upset; it was far too heavy to move. He would have to abandon the cave and hope the cubs would stay with him. He needed their bodies for food.

He had been making preparations to depart, fashioning a protective cup out of his clothing with which to cover his stump, when he noticed that something curious was happening to it.

He felt around it, probing for the bone, which if it was sharp might irritate the flesh which had grown over the end of the wound. Now, amazingly, the stump was sloughing off the scab, revealing a healthy-looking pink flesh beneath.

The stump was longer than it had been—and the bone had grown to match!

That had been startling enough, but there was more. This time, Kah-Sih-Omah was certain that his imagination was not to blame, because his mind was totally clear, and up until that point had been at ease. But: his stump was growing warts—five of them—and they looked for all the world like tiny toes, arranged in the proper pattern, at the edge of another pink and puffy patch of tissue that looked something like the sole of a human foot.

At this moment he sat, holding up the stump in both hands, staring at it. He was sweating profusely, and the sweat was trickling down through dust-encrusted brows, burning his eyes. His breathing was rapid but regular, though the pace was nothing compared to the pace of his thoughts.

Was it possible—the spirits remained in him, even now, and were making him a new leg?

He knew it was. The spirits had proven their potency by doing what they had done before by doing something far more difficult—replacing his entire body. How could he say that what he was seeing was impossible in the face of such evidence?

But it is not natural, his inner self kept saying.

Man cannot say what is unnatural to spirits, was his most comforting answer.

Kah-Sih-Omah moved out of the cave. The cubs stayed, for a time, but joined him later on the rim, at the fire, to which they were now accustomed and did not fear. They had come to associate the fire with feeding, and they sat around it, waiting patiently.

Kah-Sih-Omah had nothing to feed them. He was himself ravenously hungry. Of late, hunger had driven him frantic, though he had supposed thirst would be his primary problem. He had reasoned that out too. The spirits provided. Somehow, what he ate satisfied also his need to drink, and part of it was being used to build the leg which was now forming.

Because he believed that, he did not hesitate, but quietly strangled, skinned, and cooked the smaller cub, and shared him with his brother. "Time enough," he told the cat, "for your existence to end, but it appears mine never will until the ultimate answer.

"I am a prophet—that is what I am." Kah-Sih-Omah faced this morning with optimism. And why not? He was moving—on two good legs. Not fast, not gracefully, for one was still shorter than the other. But it held him, and without pain. And it carried him and his pack, stuffed to the brim with dried roast goatmeat, gained with persistent patience aided by a sharp shard of flint, which he had bound to a convenient stick with the guts of the great cat's child. Kah-Sih-Omah was exuberant.

There was not, he believed at this moment, any peril which he could not overcome, any situation he could not master so long as he enjoyed the aid of the spirits. True, they had tested him sorely and he had suffered much, but they had also rewarded him with a new life which promised to be infinitely more interesting than the old one.

Why he was chosen instead of someone else, Kah-Sih-Omah did not know. But there again, though the spirits had not reposed their confidence in him, he felt they would in time . . . and time, it seemed, was to be his in abundance.

While he walked, he pondered the implications of that. What, exactly, would it mean to live not one lifetime, but two? Two? Only two? No, that was also wrong. He had been given more than that—he had been given a succession of lifetimes; he had been given all the time there was.

Then, the answer came to him easily; it meant wisdom—it meant experience. It meant an opportunity to learn all there was to learn about the world around him, time to study whatever he came upon which might prove to be of interest, and time to ferret out and understand that which mystified the minds of curious men.

He was such a man. He had always been so. Curiosity had driven him into his calling, because he was not content to leave things be, as others were. To him, it was not enough to observe that the face of the heavens and the form of the earth changed periodically, seemingly at the whim of something greater than man. He must also measure the change, however crudely, and ask himself its purpose.

He knew, from the frustrations this curiosity had already generated, that explanations came only very slowly, and only after the expenditure of much deep thought—and that sometimes, even that which seemed simple was not at all.

Guardian

The People had no convenient way of reckoning time. They had no need of one. Some, more curious than others, threw various numbers of fingers and toes before them and claimed that each of these stood for a full moon or a winter. But these were the pretentious ones, and Kah-Sih-Omah had never included himself among them. Because he was the shaman he concerned himself not with what men did to account to themselves, but what nature did to account to the spirits with whom his duties dealt.

Nature knew its year—one summer, one winter—and was content with that. Each summer the snow melted and the grass turned green and new life grew to take the place of that which autumn had weakened and winter had killed. That was the way things were.

In the heavens, as a sign, were the sun and certain stars to herald the coming of each. These every man could see and therefore know that one or the other change approached.

If still he were unsatisfied he had only to watch the animals to whom the system and cycle pertained, and they would tell him the same.

But Kah-Sih-Omah found of late that neither method applied to his present purpose, which was to go and find the People, and seek the society of men again.

He had not seen them for many months. Where were the People now? Where would he find them, if they still existed? The People wandered, as did other bands of men, seeking water, following game, making war on one another and taking new lands. Finding them might be no small undertaking. Kah-Sih-Omah's personal need to do so was considerable; hence his anxiety, which grew with the passage of each day and even with the passage of each footfall.

This expedition was no hasty thing, as his flight from the village had been. Kah-Sih-Omah was armed in ways no other creature could match. His senses mimicked the best that nature had to offer.

No other man would have recognized him as a man. He was something more than man, and something less than god. He did not plod, but loped along on graceful stiltlike legs fleeter even than the antelope's, which ended in great splayed feet like those of the hump-beast.

A head, adorned with great flaring ears, caught every sound that crossed the prairie. A nose, somewhat snoutlike but reminiscent of the nose of man and laced with thousands of tiny, intricate nerves, did the same with faint scents wafted on hot winds.

His weapons, however—should they ever be needed— were the weapons of a man: a massive club studded with sharp spines of flint, a long-hafted spear tipped with polished stone, a bola of rawhide. With these, with his speed of flight and with man's finest tool, a powerful and imaginative mind, he was invincible. That which he could not outfight he could outrun.

These were the gifts of the long winter spent in his sheltered valley, striving to know himself before attempting to understand the People. He had learned a great truth. Though the method which enabled such miraculous works remained in the realm of the spirit, his own will controlled what happened to his body. He thought perhaps there was no indwelling spirit other than his own, though its awareness had been enhanced by his creators and its powers magnified beyond those of ordinary men. This seemed to mesh with observation, and to be far simpler than his earlier theory.

It led to even grander observations. Having eaten his

neighbors in the valley of winter, he saw, except for size and shape, no difference between their bones and his. Could it be, he asked himself, that only the spirits are different—that all creatures of the earth share much the same needs and the same senses? Suppose his spirit, when his leg was gone, had wished to grow not the leg of a man but that of a deer, or a cat, or a frog—or not a leg at all, but a fin or a wing? And if his body could grow a leg, why not fur, and fangs, and horns, and claws?

He tried, and found he could—and so he did. With easy, confident power, he indulged himself in experiments so foreign to human thought they astonished even he. He changed at will, so often and so rapidly that the most perceptive and careful mind could not follow all the metamorphoses he underwent. While he dwelt in the valley of winter he tasted the lives of all who dwelt around him, becoming for a time each of those that the limits of size and bulk permitted.

Thus when spring came he was ready. He could take the long strides which now consumed the grassy trails the great woolly horned beasts had made across the parched vastness of the high plain, where now almost nothing of worrisome size remained. In the summer's heat all had departed, migrating to cooler lands with softer, sweeter graze and permanent water; all save the humpers, who needed little of this, and whose awkward heads rose from time to time above the sea of grass in curious gaze at this interloper more improbable in appearance than themselves.

The plains ended in foothills which lay below the mountains limiting the broad, dry valley. Here snows, caught in passage during winter, melted and steadily fed trickles of sweet water to the lowlands. Here the grass again was green, and here, where prey was abundant and fat and wary, lurked the denizens absent from the withered plain.

Kah-Sih-Omah abandoned his stilts but kept his senses sharp and weapons handy. He added strong talons to his feet, and a coarse fur to protect his skin from thorns. Where once he had loped, now he crept with catlike stealth, eating well and often. By night he added fire to his arsenal, a foresight that proved entirely worthwhile. As often as not in its light he found the reflections of great limpid eyes, waiting silently to wet the fangs which lurked below them.

Kah-Sih-Omah did not fear them. He sometimes watched them pace for hours on end, frustrated by the inadequacies of their simple minds, which while they would not admit defeat, continued to persecute the animal with hope. And he was glad that he was a man, with a man's mind and a man's foresight.

He did not cease to marvel at himself. He knew that he was yet ignorant of his full capabilities. But he regretted that he had not known these abilities when last he enjoyed the company of the People. Had he only known then it would have been so simple. He could have returned to them not as a stranger, but as one they knew: his former self.

Kah-Sih-Omah planned now to do just that; to be what he had been, at least on the outside, so that the People would have no fear of him when he found them again.

Again he was troubled by the concept of time. How were the People now? How many would be left who would remember Kah-Sih-Omah as he had been? How many more now hobbled, crippled by age, blind, deaf, and infirm of sense and memory, who had been young and vital at his last appearance?

Never mind; he would not be strange to them. When he reappeared he would wear the face and the form of their true shaman. If . . .

. . . if Kah-Sih-Omah could reproduce that face. It suddenly struck him with absolutely crushing force—with reality, stifled by assumption so long ignored—that there was one face in all of his acquaintance that he would not recognize, because he had never seen it. His own.

How little we know ourselves, he thought. And it was true. Man could never see himself as he saw others. Even his reflection, a pitiful shadow sometimes observed in dark, murky waters, was false, and did not show the real man, but something reversed from the true face. He tried to recall that reflection—found he could not. Either dimness of the memory of youth, or the more recent memory of maturity, one or the other, remoteness of time or failing vision conspired to deprive him even of that. He could never appear before the People except with the face of a stranger.

He trekked to the lands near the sacred mountain, searching out the trails the People customarily used in their migrations while they followed the movements of game. Here there would always be water; here there would always be danger. He went to the site of their village, the one from which he had fled, hoping here there might yet be a straggler or two, some infirm or wounded warrior who could not travel with them to the summer grounds, who waited with his family for the Peoples' return in autumn.

But there was no one. His hope had not been high that there would be. Generally a straggler's lot was a perilous one, without the strength of the People for protection. Kah-Sih-Omah found not even the bleaching bones or rotting scavenged flesh of any who had stayed and died alone.

There came the season of return, and so he waited with futile patience, each day searching the horizon for signs of scouts and hunting parties. The animals came; the People did not, and Kah-Sih-Omah was greatly saddened.

What had happened to them? Had it been war, or sickness? Were the People lost? Or had they simply chosen paths different from those Kah-Sih-Omah had always known?

He thought this last unlikely. The habits of the People changed but slowly, and never without compelling reason. Change was perilous; and a good shaman, who loved the People, discouraged radical departure from established policy.

But the People did not have a good shaman. The People had Hono, and Hono was an incompetent charlatan!

Kah-Sih-Omah began grieving for the People. He set off toward the lands from whence came summer, ever wary for signs of the People.

He passed well beyond the sunlit side of the sacred mountain before he came upon the spoor of man, but it was not the spoor of the People. It was that of strangers who had no business here.

There was a valley, not far ahead, somewhat resembling Kah-Sih-Omah's valley of winter, where he had waited and played while the People became lost to him. While it would be strange indeed to find them there, in this season, he resolved to go there. He knew that if they still adhered to the old ways this is where they would spend the winter; they always did, as did the great-tooth, on whom they then would prey.

He found—trouble; trouble in the form of squat, dark, heavily muscled strangers who wore not skins, but something lighter; soft, and gaudily decorated, as though they did not care if game could see them coming. He believed them to be hostile as well, although he took care to avoid encounters which might have supplied proof.

Instead he watched them from concealment, sometimes close enough to determine that they spoke in words he did not understand. Sometimes he saw their weapons in use; strange weapons these, at first appearing puny but, upon demonstration, proving deadly instead.

Kah-Sih-Omah was accustomed to missile weapons. His people used both the bola and the javelin, the latter thrown great distances with the aid of a device which lengthened the arm. These men threw smaller missiles, tipped with black stone points and winged with feathers, by means of a thong stretched between the ends of a springy branch. With it they easily killed the largest game, and from a distance far greater than a javelin could be hurled.

Groups of them roamed the woods outside the mouth of the valley. Others, stationed day and night on heights overlooking the entrance, scrutinized all who entered and departed.

From his own vantage point on an adjacent hill even Kah-Sih-Omah's augmented eyesight could discern little beyond the fact that great forests of stumps were all that remained of the lofty trees which once had grown on the inner walls of the valley. There was no doubt at all in Kah-Sih-Omah's mind where these had gone. All along the rim of the valley stood curious huts from which, day and night, there erupted smoke.

That was not the full extent of the metamorphosis the People's valley had undergone. There was much more that did not fit his recollection. Most curious of all were the plants that grew now on the valley floor, not scattered as those of Kah-Sih-Omah's acquaintance, but in neat rows and patterns he had never seen before. Somehow, he knew, the strangers in the valley had caused this also.

But where were the People? When would the People come? When they came, where would they winter? Their winter valley was already occupied.

A horrible possibility occurred to Kah-Sih-Omah. Suppose the strangers had come long ago—suppose the People had been driven off—suppose they would never return? He knew that could have happened. Worse, perhaps there had been war, and the People had lost. What then? He knew the answer—then Kah-Sih-Omah would always be alone.

He knew that his reasoning could be close to the truth. It explained much of what he had seen—or rather, what he had not seen: signs of the recent passage of his People.

Still, it was always possible he was wrong. If he was, the People would eventually appear, but if they did they would be ignorant of their plight until they had confronted the strangers and learned of them. But they would not be arriving in a body; they would arrive in small bands straggled far apart—hunting parties, not war parties. They would be weary from their long journey, without adequate supplies of food or bases in which to fashion weapons. Moreover, the women and children—the true treasure of the People, whose loss the People could not survive—would be in jeopardy.

Kah-Sih-Omah studied the situation carefully and at length. He knew what he had to do; he had to warn the People.

But what would he tell them when he found them? That an unknown number of strangers had come, who had strange but powerful weapons, and taken their wintering grounds?

This knowledge would help but little, and he knew no more—yet. If ever there was a time to use the special talents the spirits had given Kah-Sih-Omah, this was surely it.

This thought, he suddenly realized, was profound. Of course! It was obvious! How could he have been so blind as not to see it? Kah-Sih-Omah berated himself for his abysmal stupidity—that denseness of mind, that slovenliness of thought that now abashed him so.

This was his purpose, his ultimate purpose—this was his charge!

He had groped for it, speculated about it, fretted over it, carried his imagination to its extreme limits of wild and idle fantasy—yet missed it all the same, as man would, despite the best efforts to the contrary of all his gods.

He, Kah-Sih-Omah, was guardian of the people. Such was the commission the spirits gave to him; such was his sacred duty. His imagination could now rest. Secure in his destiny, He-Who-Waits would now become He-Who-Watches-And-Protects.

That day Kah-Sih-Omah fashioned weapons such as he had seen the strangers use: potent weapons of great utility, of silence and light weight. That night he tested them in the hunt, and triumphed easily over a great horned woolly, much of which he roasted and ate.

The next morning, though engorged and stuffed with energy, he wore the normal form of a man—the man the spirits lately made of him. And then Kah-Sih-Omah climbed—climbed the steep, sheer wall of the sunlit side of the valley, to the heights which overlooked it.

Here he found no sentinels on guard, and had known there would be none. There was no need of a sentinel to watch for eagles, and in the mind of mortal man none but an eagle could mount these cliffs.

Kah-Sih-Omah did so easily. With arms and legs supple and outstretched, like a great spider he crept upward across the glazed face of the cliff, clinging with all the tenacity enhanced muscles could produce. Fingers and toes, elongated and provided with rich supplies of blood, first found, then expanded and filled tiny crevices between the layers and fracture lines of rock, pulling his body ever upward.

By noon he was halfway up the cliff. By dusk he peered from the summit out across the valley floor. He crept carefully along the top of the ridge until he overlooked its center, where the stream irregularly bisected it.

Even the stream was different. Like the beaver, the strangers had dammed it up. Unlike the beaver, they created not one pool but many, and from each they had dug many ditches. Kah-Sih-Omah conceived at once the purpose of these. It was obvious, for along each ditch, profusely and copiously watered, the plants sown in neat, evenly spaced rows grew tall and prospered.

Even then people walked between the rows, working at something; what, Kah-Sih-Omah could not tell from this vast distance and in the fading dusk.

He looked across the valley at the winter side, where all the trees had gone into huts, these also spaced evenly and neatly in rows. People abounded—more people than Kah-Sih-Omah recalled ever having seen in one place in all his life—several times more than the number of his own People. So many! His task would be awesome. Should the People, upon arrival, be forced to make war, even Kah-Sih-Omah's presence among them might not make any difference.

He threw off the agonizing mantle of dispair at once. He was favorite of the spirits; the People were favorite to him. The spirits would not permit the People to be lost.

Still, the spirits would expect effort from Kah-Sih-Omah. They would not fight for him; they would demand he do his duty. Thoughts once again turned to his purpose in climbing the cliff, and Kah-Sih-Omah made ready the execution of the rest of his plan.

When he had first discovered the marvelous manner in which he could control his form, he had experimented with many others. Eventually, he had mastered all of them that were within his capability of size and bulk. Yet there remained one to which he had long aspired: that of the great raptor, the eagle, whose travel with free and easy speed and power through the medium which seemed made for him alone had caused envy to well in Kah-Sih-Omah's heart.

He had tried, over and over again, to emulate the eagle, but he found that whatever configuration he espoused he was simply too heavy, unable to summon the energy to work the great wings he needed to gain the air.

He had then abandoned the eagles' manner and sought a substitute, which, though less satisfying, did permit him to imitate some of the powers of birds. Taking his example from other heavy creatures who had done the same, he had contrived to stretch a membrane of skin between his extended limbs and glide. Thus, at great peril, and often with much pain, after his own fashion Kah-Sih-Omah learned to fly.

He was so prepared now, but somewhat hesitant. Never before had he launched himself from such a height. Never before had he jumped into the night, and always before his prospective point of alighting had been a safe one. Here he did not know what he would encounter on the way down, or after he was down.

He was still adding touches even as he waited. Daytime eyes were useless now. Night eyes, though they would not give him color, were better. From the patterns of the owl and of the great cats he fashioned these, grateful that he had taken care to store the energy to do so.

Kah-Sih-Omah had learned, through experiment, that there were two orders of reorganization: one a simple spreading, expansion, and relocation of existing organs and tissue, the other the creation of tissue and special organs which did not already exist. The first required less effort, but both were expensive in terms of energy consumed.

The flight mode was expensive. It required him to shed bulk, whereas metamorphosis into a terrestrial type was cheaper; he could simply increase density. In this instance, the biggest problem Kah-Sih-Omah would have when he reached the bottom of the valley was finding and consuming enough energy to revert to a more plausible form.

He was away, the cliff face now far behind him, and soaring now after an enormous drop occasioned by the need of his supporting membranes to accumulate lift.

For a while Kah-Sih-Omah was unsure that he had sufficient altitude to carry him across the valley and still remain aloft long enough to study its features and inhabitants.

He was, however, spared this problem, because about halfway down he began to encounter warm, rising air, the product of the daylight heating of the air and the trapping of pools of it within the steep walls of the valley. He had to be careful always to turn into the wind that now rushed out through the valley's mouth, but forewarned of it, he did this easily.

Below, details were beginning to become visible. The plants the strangers grew had fruit of a fashion. It grew in elongated pods, several to each man-high plant. He could easily see that he had been right about the ditches. Their purpose was to water. And he now believed that what the people did among the rows was to destroy other plants that tried to encroach on those they grew. All over the ground he could see where the dirt had been loosened and raked up around the roots of the plants.

Kah-Sih-Omah used the rushing wind at the center of the valley to slow both his speed and descent, maintaining his height with careful twists of the ends of his leathern wings. He needed time to select the route of his next pass, because his instincts told him there would be time only for one. He had not shed quite enough substance and he carried too much equipment.

He chose a pass over the clumps of huts on the winter side of the valley—a careful peek down at the people who milled around the cookfires and the children who frolicked in the clearings.

What he saw shocked him. Flying swiftly over on silent wings about twice as high as he could shoot one of his new missiles, he saw and heard familiar things—familiar words, familiar styles of clothing. For a moment his heart galloped in joy, and it was with great effort that he resisted the temptation to wheel into the wind and land.

That would have been foolish, even without the implication of his next observation. The People would have been frightened. And they would, no doubt, have attacked him, not realizing he was a man and a friend.

The other thing that stopped him was the fact that he saw only women and children on the ground. There were no men, and this was a bad sign.

It was a sign that perhaps he had arrived too late to intervene and prevent them from being conquered—that they had already been conquered. He had seen this sort of behavior before. It was a common practice, followed by many tribes: kill the able-bodied men, who enable the tribe to resist; keep the women for their pleasure and the children for their work.

He turned his wings to the right, spilling air in his turn but speeding into the valley's center. There he caught the stream of air again, but utilized it differently. This time his objective was not altitude but the cushioning effect of its speed beneath his wings. He settled swiftly into the center of the great field, demolishing many of the plants in the process before awkwardly folding his wings to begin another change.

Kah-Sih-Omah was grateful for the solitude the empty field allowed him. These changes required time, and distraction was always very devastating to the process, since it interrupted the necessary concentration and sometimes diverted the effort into grotesque formats which later had to be corrected.

Kah-Sih-Omah took his time. He had long ago discovered that careful planning was worth the extra investment. This time his plan was changed, both by reason of his diminished body mass and by what he had seen on the ground. He sampled the fruits the strangers were growing, found them both tasty and nourishing, and could have used them to raise his energy level. He did not choose, however, to resume his own format, but stopped the process when it had reached an intermediary and undifferentiated human level.

Then, observing that the effort had eaten away the interval of early evening and carried him into true night, he crept to the edge of the plantation to examine the settlement from the ground.

The children were all gone, no doubt sleeping away the exhaustion of the day's activities. Most adults were gone too, and there remained toiling in the light of the fires only a few old women whose duties must have been to clean up after the evening meal.

Kah-Sih-Omah studied them, noting both features and behavior. They all moved slowly, as he once had, restrained by their infirmities. His emotions coursed between pity for their station and envy of their relative immunity from molestation. It was the latter that convinced him this was the ideal form to assume.

His reasoning seemed sound. Were he to appear as a man he would be in constant danger of discovery, and discovery would lead to fighting. He could not appear in the guise of one of the strangers because he knew neither customs nor language. Sensibly, he should assume the female form, for which he had now about the right bulk—but were he to allow himself the pride of a comely appearance he might invite trouble of a different kind.

But an old woman . . . that was safe. In that form he would be undesired, unnoticed, unremembered, and secure. An old woman shambling determinedly along, particularly if she carried something useful in her hand, should be able to go almost anywhere unmolested.

Kah-Sih-Omah made the transformation, molding the form to that of the woman he had known best in all his life: his wife, surely now long dead, though he had no way of knowing for certain.

To this new guise he added subtle changes to insure that when he walked in her form there would be no startled gasps or cries of ghostly recognition from those who had known her in life.

He was then ready for the next phase of his plan, one necessary before he could walk again among the People, or let the People see him: he needed a robe. Nudity was not an embarrassment among the People, and had its occasions among them, but it was considered crass when not appropriate. Such would be the case in the coolness of this night. So, Kah-Sih-Omah must skulk around in shadows until by chance he happened on something to wear. He did not expect this would take very long, considering the quantity of laundry hung outside to air and dry after washing. The Peoples' habits had not changed.

Soon, suitably accoutered in his stolen clothing, Kah-Sih-Omah could walk among them and speak to them, and they to him—if he dared.

Did he? Kah-Sih-Omah did not yet know. It would be hard, considering the time that had elapsed since he had last held conversational speech. In the solitude since rebirth he had often spoken to himself, sometimes in voices other than his own natural voice, because it amused him to do so. But these were utterances totally under his control, containing only what he had himself injected into them.

In this place, Kah-Sih-Omah expected the words he heard to bear a real burden of woe, and he was therefore loathe to hear them.

He nevertheless strolled confidently and casually until he came upon an old woman kneeling next to a fire, working with a stone, grinding something and muttering to herself. She was the nearest to the shadow where Kah-Sih-Omah lurked; here was opportunity. With much apprehension he sallied forth to visit with her.

His approach brought no reaction except a blank stare when finally she noticed him. Then she raised her head slightly, turning at the sound of his bare footsteps. The light of the fire shone on her face, half covering its features with craggy shadows. Amid these shadows burned two brilliant sparks, but these were the wild sparks of nature and nature's rules, not the sparks of intellect.

It was apparent, from Kah-Sih-Omah's first glance at her, that intellect had long ago departed. Were further evidence necessary, it was to be found in the muttered, mumbling dirge that hummed in chaotic disarray across toothless jaws. She sang the dirge chant from the Dance of Death.

Try as he might, he could not persuade the woman to speak. She continued endlessly with the chanting and the grinding, from time to time reaching down to dump from the lower stone that which the upper one had crushed: a meal made from the hardened form of the fruit the strangers grew.

He could not do otherwise but to listen to her, though her words were jumbled and slurred. He knew the dirge, of course, but only certain parts were common to the ceremony. The bulk of it consisted of a litany of the virtues of the person who had passed. Kah-Sih-Omah wanted to know who this was, if he could understand her. He hoped it might have been someone he had known.

He listened on with but half an ear, struggling at the same time to remain alert to the other sounds in the night. Without warning and almost without recognition the name came—softly pronounced, distorted, as words sometimes were by the afflictions of the aged brain—*Kah-Sih-Omah!*

His mind reeled at the thought that someone still remembered him; still sang of him and mourned him. Who *was* this woman?

He studied her face again, this time far more closely. She met his eyes with the same blank stare as before, but all the while crooning on, rubbing the stones together with slow motions of her thin arms and gnarled hands.

Failing at recognition, he touched her. The touch was thrilling; his first tactile contact with another human being since Hono had ordered him bound.

The woman did not resist the trespass, but she stopped moving; stopped singing, and merely stared.

"Who are you?" he whispered loudly and frantically into her ear. "Tell me your name."

"Loh-Waha-Lona." She had answered without hesitation, but with an idiot's smile. She turned her face downward then, as if in shyness, and groped again for the stones.

Kah-Sih-Omah was stunned—speechless. Loh-Waha-Lona, Hono's mother.

His heart pounded so hard he could not help but fear that others could hear it far away. Who were these spirits to think that mortal man could stand such devilish torture? Whence came their right to heap such massive abuse as this upon his head? To taunt one whom they have made ageless with the battered, withered husks of friends driven mad by the burden of their years? It was too much to give the spirits, even for the sake of the People.

Kah-Sih-Omah, despite his strength, was helpless. He could do nothing but hug her close and weep, even as the small distraction he had provided lost its hold on her dim mind. Witlessly, her old mind reverted to the only thing on which it could still focus. The stone resumed its grinding motion, and the mumbling dirge began anew.

Kah-Sih-Omah stayed with her until he had heard it all, then left her alone with her mindless toil. He could stand no more that crackling voice; a voice that once had been so soft and sweet and strong and full of joy. Better *he* had died, as she thought, than live to see her the way she was. Better *she* had died than reach this point.

Kah-Sih-Omah wandered no more among the people that night. He would wait for the morning. For the remaining hours of darkness he lay huddled alone on the hillside, taking shelter from the wind in a shallow ditch, thinking about the People and how they had changed.

They had allowed Loh-Waha-Lona to become what she was. This was not the old way of the People. The old ways of the People took care that such things could not happen. Had they continued to follow these ways, Loh-Waha-Lona would long ago have passed, while she still retained the wit to want to. She would even now enjoy peace and happiness with her kindred spirits, spared the indignity of losing her soul, with useless life drawn out perhaps for many long miserable winters. She would, instead, have passed high on some lonely hilltop or in the middle of some broad plain, swiftly, relatively painlessly, the fangs of some great cat or wolf the merciful instruments of her relief.

Kah-Sih-Omah had previously given little thought to the disadvantages of his ageless state. Now he had to, because above and beyond all the other differences between himself and other men, this was the greatest and the cruelest. He had not previously regarded the spirits as cruel; he had believed that cruelty was foreign to their nature. Now he knew it wasn't, and he wondered, *What torments lie ahead for me?*

He rested not at all that night, but embarked, bitter and vengeful, as soon as dawn had broken and people began to stir, to make a survey of the camp.

During the night, his body had subtly changed. He could not bear to hold the form he had; it was too hideously truthful. He altered it, not yet with youth and youth's attendant dangers, but with that which was as close as he could come to she who once wore it in her middle years, her best years: when she was no longer young, but not yet old—his favorite recollection of her.

Lah-Waha-Lona was not about when he descended. Kah-Sih-Omah was thankful for that. Her presence disturbed him, for reasons he understood far too well. He had shirked a duty he was well aware he had—one he knew was his far more than it was, or had been, that of the People, but one loathesome to contemplate. He was, as far as he knew, her only living relative, and it was therefore his obligation to take her out on the plain and help her to pass.

With an almighty effort, he drove this from his mind. He had another mission to consider, another purpose to achieve. To help the People who remained, he must find out how they came to be here. To do that, he must talk to them. He must search out faces, make mental changes in them, account for the ravages of years when he had not known them, in order to determine if he had known them before.

This effort failed largely because here there were only women, and it was with the men that he had had the most contact and therefore knew the best. Occasionally he thought he recognized a name when he heard one mentioned. Once or twice he was asked his own name by women who looked at him curiously and with suspicion because they did not know him.

Kah-Sih-Omah was ill at ease whenever he answered, using a name he had drawn from his imagination and telling she who inquired he was in fact a stranger, having lately come here from far away; that he was from another group of the People who spoke the same language and who were perhaps related.

But this deception, too, was less than satisfactory. Simple conversation was difficult. Meaningful conversation was impossible, until he encountered a talkative child.

The boy was of eight, perhaps ten winters of life. He was a bright one, and he was not shy. He came to Kah-Sih-Omah first because Kah-Sih-Omah had a full plate of food, and the child was still hungry. He stood by and watched Kah-Sih-Omah eat, until at length Kah-Sih-Omah understood, and gave the plate to him.

The boy ate ravenously, scooping up great gobs of the ground fruit with his fingers and shoving them into his mouth. When the plate was empty he licked it, and then his fingers as well. Never once during this time did he speak, but when he was finished his eyes told Kah-Sih-Omah that he was grateful.

"Who are you, boy?"

The boy hesitated an instant, nevertheless he answered. "I am called Toh-Pan-Gah, Child-Of-The-Dark-One."

"Who was your father?"

"He was called Hono. He is dead."

Kah-Sih-Omah was immediately seized with a chill. This momentary distraction of his attention brought a new realization: others watched—and mumbled.

The boy took note of this and began to tremble. "I must leave," he said, and would have bolted away had not Kah-Sih-Omah grasped his arm and restrained him.

The other women who watched now drew closer, muttering louder. Their lips were curled, and whispered curses filled the morning air.

The boy wiggled free, and ran through a narrowing gap in the circle of women. Those nearest hit at him as he ran. Soon he had disappeared between two of the buildings and was seen no more.

"You have only recently come to us," explained one of the women to whom Kah-Sih-Omah had earlier spoken, "and you do not know of him, or of his father, therefore you are forgiven this. But he is as a dead child; he is not of the People. His spirit does not belong among the People."

Kah-Sih-Omah nodded. There was nothing else he could have done, unless he was prepared to reveal himself. A dead child—a dead person—received no help from the People—no food, no shelter, no comfort, no weapons. A dead person was supposed to leave the camp of the People and go where they could not see him—where he could die in truth, and usually quickly did, at the fangs and claws whatever uncaring beast happened across him first.

"The strangers do not follow our ways. They allow the child to wander where he will within this camp, and being women we can do little to stop him. But he is the child of the evil one and we will not help him."

Kah-Sih-Omah recognized this as an opportunity to bring himself up to date. If he could get this woman to tell him what had happened, perhaps he could devise a means of setting the people free. "I am, as you said, a stranger, and am thus very ignorant. But I would like to know of this Dark One, and how his people came to be here."

"The Dark One was a fool, whatever else he was, and some say that was many heinous things—that he trafficked with the spirits of darkness and evil, hence his name, and that it was he who stole the soul and the medicine of Kah-Sih-Omah."

"Kah-Sih-Omah?" Kah-Sih-Omah was intrigued to learn his own place in things.

"Our great shaman; a good leader, whose medicine kept the people safe and prosperous for many years. When I was a small girl he was taken away by the spirits on the sacred mountain, or so the Dark One told us. Some say that Kah-Sih-Omah later returned, transformed, and worked many wonders, but that the Dark One denied him, and drove him away because he wished to take his place. Ruhu-Doh-Sah, my father, told me this."

"How came your people into this valley?"

"That too was the work of the Dark One. The Dark One said that all of the lands that lay within the shadows of the sacred mountain belonged to the People; that the spirit of Kah-Sih-Omah had given them to us and would protect us. He said that upon the mountain dwelt the spirit of summer who could drive away the spirit of death; that if the people remained, and if they believed, summer would be ours always.

"So we stayed. Many did believe. And when these strangers came they told us they had traveled from lands where it was summer always, and more believed the Dark One.

"The strangers said that the People must leave the lands of the sacred mountain, and that they must come here. Then the Dark One refused. He told the warriors that they could not be killed, so long as they remained there. But in the battle which followed they were killed and did not rise again as the Dark One had promised.

"We women and the young children the strangers brought here. The young women they took for their warriors; the rest work to make the plants grow."

Kah-Sih-Omah did not inquire further of her, but let her ramble on in a litany of woe, listening with but half an ear. He wandered away just as she summoned the presence of mind to ask what misfortune of his own had brought him here.

But in any case the conversation could not have endured much longer, because the strangers came among them and one by one each woman and child fell into the growing column of laborers who trudged toward the field in the center of the valley.

He did likewise, not wishing to draw particular attention to himself by balking. He knew that he had much to learn before he could understand what the strangers were doing here and do anything to help the People.

He had already made an assessment of the possibilities for the Peoples' escape, and did not like them. He could see that there were enough of the superbly armed strangers to stop any such attempt even if the people were able to get out of the sheer-walled valley, which appeared impossible.

The crowd reached the edge of the field. There, each received an implement with which to loosen the soil around the bases of the growing plants and clear away other plants around them. Then, having been assigned a row for which he would be responsible, Kah-Sih-Omah began work.

He studied these plants as he passed by them. He

could not recall having seen anything like them before, and concluded that they had been brought here by the strangers just as the People had.

From time to time Kah-Sih-Omah stopped work to examine the plants in detail. At first he could not conceive of a people who did not hunt in order to live. It had not occurred to him that such a thing was possible.

Yet apparently it was, since the strangers did it. Evidently the plants produced enough food so that they did not have to hunt. *They did not have to move, either!* That to Kah-Sih-Omah was a startling revelation—a people who did not have to follow the whims of the animals upon which they lived—who, moreover, could store food for later use.

The People could do this with some things, but as a rule meat did not keep well, even when dried, and it was then relatively unpalatable. Fruits known to the People fared better, but not as well as these apparently did. He had seen these in their hardened state, as they were being ground, and concluded that this food was durable indeed. He could then see how it was possible for the strangers to live.

Kah-Sih-Omah finished one row and started another. The labor was not onerous to him, since he could adjust his body for comfort. But around him the signs of the People's suffering were everywhere. Some who labored in this hot sun were far too old and feeble to be here, yet they toiled along with the rest, even as the sun grew higher and the day hotter.

His eyes searched the towering tops of the plants, alert for the sight of some old face that he could puzzle out to be that of an old acquaintance. But it was useless. He found none.

When the sun reached its zenith the work stopped, and the People went to the edge of the field to rest. Here, warriors collected their implements and herded them back to the settlement, where they received food and water. Again Kah-Sih-Omah saw no one he recognized, but found the other women friendly enough and soon, in the guise of a newcomer, he had gleaned a great deal of the popular knowledge and myth of the strangers.

It was then that he learned of a great chief among the strangers who held the People captive, whom all the strangers obeyed. He lived, it was said, in a great lodge beyond the farthest field, surrounded by a number of lesser chiefs and by many warriors.

It was to this lodge that the young women had been taken, as companions for the chief and his lords, since they had brought with them no women of their own kind.

Kah-Sih-Omah was much disturbed by this news. He knew that it meant eventual extinction for the People as he had known them. It was not uncommon for conquering warriors to kill all males capable of bearing arms and to assimilate the women and children into the conquering society. The People had never practiced this, but the People had seldom made war. War was too expensive a thing for hunters to wage.

He knew then that he must find some way to free the People who remained and take them out of this valley, far away from the strangers—that he must do this before the strangers' culture had taken hold on them, and before the children of the People had begun to regard this as natural. And he did not know how this could be done.

Briefly he considered another change of form: that of one of the conquering warriors, or perhaps a younger, more attractive version of his present self, either of which might enable him to get inside the great lodge and study the enemy's strengths and weaknesses.

Neither of these seemed promising. He could not speak the strangers' language, and as a warrior would quickly be detected as an imposter. And not only would his appearance as a young woman be difficult to explain, but he found the implications of the guise unbearable.

Torn by indecision, Kah-Sih-Omah waited many days, each filled with grinding, monotonous labor in the hot, dusty fields. Yet each day he gleaned a little more knowledge of his situation.

He realized now, for instance, how few of the People were left—and how difficult it would be, with only one man among them, for even those few to survive if they had to depend on the old ways of the People.

Regardless of the fact that the practice had been forced upon the People by conquest, Kah-Sih-Omah knew that by the cultivation of plants the People could feed themselves—while he, as the only hunter among them, could not. The People were trapped between two alternatives, each of which led to their extinction as a separate cultural group. And even he, with all the powers the spirits had given him, appeared impotent to change those facts.

He knew that this could not be true. The spirits had made him the guardian of the People. There was simply no other reason for his continued existence. Kah-Sih-Omah was troubled by a new thought. The ways of spirits were devious. Still, if the spirits wished to preserve the People, why did they not do so in a more direct manner? Why should they torment the People as they had? What was the meaning of it all? Why should they test Kah-Sih-Omah so severely, place him in a situation so patently insoluble by any of the means apparently at hand? Had they not tested him sufficiently already?

For the first time Kah-Sih-Omah contemplated the possibility that he might fail the spirits, and thus fail the People as well. It was not, after all, ordained that he should prevail, but only that he might strive to prevail. For all Kah-Sih-Omah knew, the Peoples' survival might not matter to the spirits. The spirits might be interested in them only as a part of their test of him. The effect of such speculation was to drive Kah-Sih-Omah frantic.

The plants grew taller, and their leaves turned golden. Inside their swollen husks their fruits did likewise. It was no longer necessary to dig among their roots, for their winter had come to them on the hot breath of the nights. They needed no more water, and so the laborious opening and closing of dikes ceased.

No more did the People file out along the single rows to work the earth. Now crowds of them, carrying baskets, moved along the rows in masses, hacking the golden husks away and bearing them to the edge of the field where great heaps of them began to grow and where the still hot sun dried them even more, until they were as hard as flint itself.

Then it was that the Great Lord came himself to see, one early morning, dressed in splendid robes and carried on a seat mounted on poles. Each of his bearers seemed almost as richly attired as he, and behind him there followed a retinue of his wives and retainers, who deferred to him and did his bidding.

Kah-Sih-Omah stood in the crowd which watched as the procession approached, studying those strangers who came closest. He had not seen any before but warriors, and these only rarely and from long distances, as they held themselves aloof from the People.

Others told him that this was the will of the Great Lord, who now owned all of them, as a man might own a spear or a pair of moccasins, and just as he owned those of his own people who accompanied him here to the Peoples' lands.

Kah-Sih-Omah found the concept repugnant, as well as unfathomable. He did not see how a man might be owned, except by himself; or why anyone would want to own another, even if he could. Nor could he understand why, among these conquering strangers, there were none who rebelled against this Great Lord. It seemed to him that this would be a natural thing to do.

When the lord drew closer Kah-Sih-Omah studied him as well. Aside from his clothing, Kah-Sih-Omah could see nothing in the man that was different from others of his own kind. He was no bigger than any of his warriors, who were generally shorter though more bulky than Kah-Sih-Omah's People. Observation did not, of course, reveal whether the lord was wiser than the others, and Kah-Sih-Omah thought perhaps this might be the principal difference. He looked around for signs that this was so.

The procession stopped in front of the mountain of drying produce, and the lord's chair was lowered. He rose, gathering his robes around him, and stepped off to examine the harvest.

Kah-Sih-Omah was fascinated at the intricacy of decoration on the lord's robes. Not only did the costume include a brilliant cape of feathers and some very elaborate quill and beadwork, but some of this was bordered in threads beaten from pieces of the sun, such as he had himself once woven into Ruho-Doh-Sah's amulet.

But such quantities of it! Kah-Sih-Omah had had no idea there was so much of the sun's substance to be found. He marveled at it.

Even more he marveled at the animal who was companion to the lord, and which joined him in the inspection of the harvest. It was a great gray wolf, a huge one whose great fang-studded jaws hung open and whose tongue, trembling as it panted from the heat, dripped saliva on the ground.

Yet, with a word from him, the wolf obeyed the lord, and did as he bid it, instantly. It was not even tethered, and bore no mark of subjugation to man other than a collar that Kah-Sih-Omah could see was also decorated with pieces of the sun.

Kah-Sih-Omah knew of dogs. His People sometimes kept them, though like as not when the hunting was bad the dogs wound up roasting over their cookfires. And he knew that dogs sometimes mated with wolves; these too his People occasionally kept in camp. But he had not ever before seen such a magnificent and powerful beast so close to man, and who obeyed man and was comfortable with him. Kah-Sih-Omah felt fascination in this beast's forbearance, expecting, at any time, for jaws to turn, and grasp, and rip as nature had always willed they should.

His eyes tore themselves away from the image of the animal, and turned back to the men. The wolf had told him all it could; the men would tell him more—if he could but understand them.

Their language was a mystery to the People. None of the People spoke the language of the strangers; at least, none of those who labored in the field did. Their instructions came from those of the strangers who had learned some of the tongue of the People, but these did not associate closely with the People and for the most part kept to themselves.

That would not be the case inside the great lodge, where certainly those women the strangers had taken would be taught the strangers' language. If he could

talk to some of these women—learn what they had
learned about the strangers—then perhaps he could find
some way out of his dilemma.

Again Kah-Sih-Omah considered a change of form, so
that he might enter the lord's household. This time,
however, he would enter not as a woman of endangered
virtue, or as a warrior in peril of discovery, but as the
one creature to whom all except the lord deferred—as
the wolf!

In execution, Kah-Sih-Omah needed two changes of
form—the first into that of one of the lord's servants,
whose features he studied as the lord inspected the
harvest. He had observed that the servant had a defect—
he could not speak. And so, in his role, Kah-Sih-Omah
would have no need to speak.

He could have stopped there, but he didn't, knowing
that although the man could not speak he would still
have habits and peculiarities an imposter could not
hope to imitate except after very long, detailed observation. The persona of the wolf was already a familiar one.

Thus Kah-Sih-Omah made his plan and chose his
time to leave. It was the evening of the day on which
Loh-Waha-Lona finally passed. Kah-Sih-Omah left the
other women with a heart considerably lighter, knowing
that she, at least, was finally free.

He was able, dressed in both the clothing and the
form of the servant, to penetrate the great lodge without being challenged. For a while he explored the
inside, and discovered to his amazement that it did not
seem intended to be permanent. Much of it consisted of
the same strange substance of which the strangers
made their clothing—a light, fluffy, close-textured material made of woven strands of plant fiber. Great ex-
panses of this hung across a framework of long poles
and formed the roof of the structure, while other, somewhat heavier pieces divided the interior into sections.

Though it was flimsily made, it was by far the largest
such structure Kah-Sih-Omah had ever seen. For a long
time he followed the maze of corridors formed by the
hanging fabric, glancing into the shadows cast by the
torches set at intervals at the tops of poles. Deep in the
center of the maze there was a warrior standing guard,

who would allow him to go no further, and who gestured furiously when Kah-Sih-Omah's face expressed consternation.

He knew this must be where the Great Lord reposed. He judged the lord was making merry, because of the maidenly squeals that emanated from within. He tried to listen and see if he could understand any of the words, but the warrior tired of his presence and drove him off with a flourish of his club.

Kah-Sih-Omah retreated down the corridor. Having learned as much as he could as a man, it was now time to search out the wolf. He did this as a wolf would have done it—by enhancing his senses as much as was consistent with his human appearance and using them to locate his quarry.

He found the wolf, unguarded but tethered, at the rear entrance of the great lodge, where it rested upon a heap of the dried stalks of the recently harvested crop. Beside it, its surface caked with dust, lay the remains of the wolf's most recent meal, a haunch of deermeat. This wolf, thought Kah-Sih-Omah, lives well indeed, with men to hunt for it.

Sated, drowsy, and accustomed in any case to the proximity of men, the wolf was not wary as his wild brothers would have been. It allowed Kah-Sih-Omah to approach without restriction, not even bothering to rise to its feet, preferring to submit to the hand that reached down to scratch its neck. In its indolence and naiveté it did not realize that the hand sought not its friendship but its extinction. The hand retreated briefly, paused long enough to draw a long sharp shard of flint from beneath Kah-Sih-Omah's garment, then savagely chopped back down on its neck.

The wolf died without an outcry, its spinal cord severed, its throat pierced. It lay in a growing pool of its blood next to the remains of the deer. While he still had fingers of sufficient suppleness to do it, Kah-Sih-Omah unfastened the wolf's collar and fitted it around his own neck.

As a man in transition, Kah-Sih-Omah dug briskly into the ground, with claws that with every passing instant became less the nails of a man's hand and more the talons of the wolf. In a very short time he had a hole large enough to hold the body, and by then an observer would have been hard pressed to see any difference between he who dug and he who lay dead on the ground.

Kah-Sih-Omah carefully scooped the dirt back into the hole, packing it down as solidly as his now smaller feet could manage. What would not fit he scattered, and then he concealed the grave further by scattering out the leaves.

Finished, with little of the night left to rest, Kah-Sih-Omah stretched out and closed his eyes to dream the dream of the wolf.

The Time of the Wolf

If the lord noticed any difference in his companion, he gave no sign of it. Kah-Sih-Omah had been very apprehensive when the servant appeared and untied the tether. He knew that in the dim light and under the stress of the situation there had been subtle details which had escaped his notice, and which might at first appear odd to someone familiar with the creature he had replaced. He was grateful that the wolf had been a large animal, certainly too big for one man to lift, because it had been necessary to increase the density of his flesh in order to match it to the volume of the body.

But these were physical things. More important was his inability to comprehend the commands men gave him in their own language, and this was the part he feared the most.

He need not have been fearful. Beneath it all he was a man, with a man's experience and a man's intelligence. He found embedded in every vocal command a silent one which he could read—a subliminal tone; a faint unconscious gesture. These were enough. Together with his greater power of memory he easily matched, within the space of a morning, what it had probably taken the wolf a moon or more to learn.

His role as the companion of the great lord was not unpleasant. He had duties, to be sure, chief among which was to sit beside the seat of his master and appear fierce to others and docile to the lord. He managed this quite well at first, when the situation was new to him and he more easily remained alert. But there were also long stretches when the lord entertained others of his People in dull conversation which Kah-Sih-Omah could not, as yet, understand, and when he became bored.

Fortunately, no one questioned the wolf's right to nap if he chose, and Kah-Sih-Omah survived this ordeal as he had so many others. As time went on the persona, at first difficult to hold, particularly while he slept, became habitual, and soon there was no danger of any lapse of form.

The wisdom of Kah-Sih-Omah's choice of formats became more and more apparent as time went on, particularly as the lord did not spend all his time in conversation on tribal matters.

Frequently he dallied, and when he dallied, of necessity it was with his young consorts from among the People.

Because he was a wolf there was no thought of excluding him, so Kah-Sih-Omah saw all. Moreover, he heard all, including words spoken in the tongue of his own People and transitional conversations in a mixture of that tongue and that of the strangers.

Thus he made a beginning of learning the strangers' language. More important, he was at last able to find out what had really happened to his People. It was a revelation, strange in its own way yet far simpler than that fragmented account he had heard in his first days in the valley.

It had all been quite serendipitous. The strangers had come, not at the will of and by direction of the spirits, but from simple curiosity. This great lord, who was but a lesser lord in the lands of his people, had come here simply to see what was here to see. His people lived in the land of the summer sun, in a great valley midway between two seas where snow never came, even to the tops of their highest mountains except when it was very cold in the lands of the People.

Kah-Sih-Omah at first had difficulty with the concept of two seas. He knew of one, of course, but he had not ever seen it, since it lay several moons' journey toward the setting sun. Two seas were indeed a curiosity, and as he learned more about these strangers his admiration for them mounted.

If what he was learning was true, they were quite remarkable, and quite different from the People. He discovered that the strangers regarded the People as backward, because they lived by hunting, and moved around, and had not many possessions.

In contrast, the strangers neither hunted nor migrated, but claimed vast lands as their own and planted the crops they had harvested here as well as many others. They did not live in lodges made from skins or bark as the People did, but in lodges made of stone, or of the earth itself.

This last Kah-Sih-Omah had some difficulty in believing, since he could conceive no way to keep such huts from tumbling down. But the strangers appeared to be a resourceful people capable of many other great wonders, and eventually he was able to take this on faith.

By that time many other things he had learned disturbed him far more, particularly after he discovered that these strangers intended shortly to return to their own land and take what remained of the People with them.

The strangers were men mighty in arms. They had many marvelous weapons besides the bows, with which they could shoot their obsidian-tipped arrows many times farther than the strongest man could hurl a spear. They used long knives, fashioned of razor-sharp slabs of stone set in wooden holders and capable of severing a man's head from his body in one stroke. They wore padding of various materials, which ordinary weapons, such as those the People had used against them, could not penetrate.

All these things had contributed to the defeat of the People, but among them there was no one reason so important as the strangers' concept of war.

War, as Kah-Sih-Omah had known it, was a series of skirmishes between small parties of warriors whose object was to inflict humiliation on the enemy or carry off his goods.

With the strangers it was different. Kah-Sih-Omah learned that some of their wars involved many times the number of warriors than there had ever been of his People; that the objective was to kill as many as possible and occupy land; that sometimes great numbers of the enemy were captured and held, and made to labor for the victor, or were simply killed if their labor was not needed. In a hunting society, such as his own, this made no sense at all, since the wealth of the land was in the animals on it, and one piece of land was generally as good as another. To people who lived by growing things it was different, since all land did not grow things equally well. Gradually, Kah-Sih-Omah began to see how this apparently simple difference in diet had generated two distinctly different ways of life.

The spirit of winter began to linger near the valley. He signalled his presence with rains which grew increasingly frequent until they became more or less continual. In the highlands the rain fell white, and the tops of the mountains were covered with snow. The horned climbers descended, to join the great herds of thunderbeasts who darkened the plains with their numbers and fattened on the sweet grasses the rains had awakened.

As it grew even colder small herds of the great-tooth joined them who, protected from the cold as they were by their great bulk and thick fur, attempted to enter the valley and frolic in the ponds that in warmer times had watered the strangers' plantation.

But they were driven out. Even the great-tooth, it seemed, could not match in strength these dusky men of the south. Many fell to them before the animals learned who their masters were, charging into clouds of stinging arrows which penetrated even their tough hides.

The People feasted as never before. Throughout the lengthening nights great fires burned and the smell of roasting meat permeated the valley like a cloak.

Predators entered as well, and fared no better. The great long-toothed stabbing cats wilted as the arrows pierced their bodies, their skins and fangs destined to become yet another part of the Lord's regalia, their spirits added to his totem.

It was a good time for both these vastly different peoples. As the People feasted, so too did the strangers, but they did so in a far more subtle way.

At first Kah-Sih-Omah did not understand what was happening. He could not tell what the men were doing with the great baskets of pulp which they carried into the Lord's camp from the slopes of the surrounding hills. He could see no use in it, and it stunk badly; more so as it aged. He knew the plant, of course. It was the plant of leaves like spears, which grew prolifically in the less well watered areas and which very infrequently extended an enormous stalk from its center. When the stalk flowered, the plant sickened and died, after which pods on the stalk broke open and the seeds fell out.

The strangers had chosen only the stalked specimens as the source of their pulp. They placed it in huge earthen vessels and crushed it, periodically adding water and meal from the grain they had so recently harvested.

After a time they dipped out the foul-smelling juice, strained it, and drank huge quantities.

It was at this time that Kah-Sih-Omah's ability to control the sensitivity of his nose proved very beneficial. He could otherwise never have stood the odor. He could not imagine how men could bring themselves to drink this—until he observed that it had a strange effect on them, and then he guessed the truth.

As a shaman, Kah-Sih-Omah had known of hallucinogens, and employed them in his calling. He did not know this particular one, and he had not yet conceived them as having any recreational value; nevertheless, since that seemed to be the way the strangers employed this drink, he resolved to test it himself. It was a revelation.

He was at the lord's side when the opportunity arose. The lord was entertaining some of his consorts, and vice versa, and it appeared that the drink had seized them all to some extent. Kah-Sih-Omah watched, and waited his time to sample. This came when the others were occupied in a pursuit which under other circumstances would have disgusted him, but which was now fortuitous.

Without any hesitation he rose to a two-footed stance and plunged his muzzle into the open-topped crock.

Without the smell the drink proved quite palatable, though it stung his tongue as it washed past. Being a wolf, he must, of course, lap, but as he swallowed the liquid he was fascinated by the warming sensation it created throughout his body. This was nothing like the sacred mushroom, whose spirit suddenly sprang outward and seized the mind. This spirit was less subtle—and—the effect was pleasant.

He could feel this effect immediately. There was no area of his body it did not seem to penetrate. In his careful analytical way Kah-Sih-Omah studied its behavior. He was not long in deciding why the strangers drank it. Like he, they doubtless enjoyed the glow it gave them. Kah-Sih-Omah decided that the drink was good, and drank some more of it.

Presently, however, he stopped. He found he was the center of attention. The lord had interrupted his dalliance to watch him, as did the women who were there.

He learned the name of the drink—*pulque*—about the time that he discovered its principal effect. He took his feet off the rim of the vessel, to drop to four-footed stance—and promptly fell over.

Kah-Sih-Omah was terrified. He had lost control of his body. His limbs would not obey his mind, but went their own way. Struggling to rise again, he feared the loss of control would extend to the format he was holding—that he might not be able to prevent an involuntary reversion to his real physique. If that happened—

It must not happen. He abandoned all efforts to stand, and lay down on the floor. He knew that he could not fall off the floor. With all the will that he could muster he concentrated his attention on holding his shape, and closed his eyes and covered his muzzle with his paws.

His companions, having imbibed as much or more than he, were highly amused at this—and vocal, exhorting him to take another drink. When he did not the lord seized him and pulled him into the pile of bodies strewn across the cushions to join in their merriment.

Kah-Sih-Omah was assaulted with caresses. Hands reached out to stroke his fur, to roll his body within a circle of them. He was terrified even more at this because while outwardly a wolf he retained all the emotions and passions of a man. These rose in him, despite all efforts to resist, each time one of the women touched him.

He felt his resolve slipping away, dimmed by the drink, which seemed not only to possess its own will but be determined to overcome his. He could not allow this to happen. If he did, his form would begin to change, and that would bring disaster.

So, with a mighty effort and a yelp, he leapt from the circle, attempting to run but succeeding only in staggering. He fell several times before he reached the entrance to the chamber and crept out through the curtains. Behind him, peals of raucous laughter rang out.

He was now relatively safe. Moreover, he could concentrate a little better. He had taken a foolish risk and now regretted it. But—he had learned. He now knew the power of the spirit in this drink, and that was knowledge useful to a shaman. He resolved to learn more.

Bearing down, concentrating as hard as he could, his consciousness reached into the farthest corners of his body, where the spirit worked its will on him, and sought the spirit out. He found it—though it was a feeling rather than a thought, that showed itself as little lumps of chaos in otherwise orderly tissue.

Without knowing how he did it, he willed his body to collect these lumps and convey them away from his head, where he knew the will reposed. This done, the sensation of chaos left him, and his limbs lost the ethereal lightness that the drink had brought to them. Inside, in the great organ that lay in the center of his body, he concentrated the material and isolated it, testing various combinations of body constituents to see if he could recreate it.

This was an exercise that he had done many times in the past, ever since he had known that his body could mimic other forms. To copy the spirit of the pulque was no more difficult than recreating any other substance his body used or needed, once he knew its structure.

Finished, with a clear head again, Kah-Sih-Omah took

special care to preserve a sample of the spirit, which he stored in the great organ against the day when it might be useful. Then he sought out a place of safety near the lord's chamber and went to sleep.

When the snow was thickest on the tops of the mountains, the lord announced that their journey to the south would begin at the end of the next hand of days. Servants began to strike the great lodge and to bundle up the lord's possessions into packs.

In the part of the settlement occupied by the People the news met with trepidation and grumbling, though the work of the strangers occupied the hands that might otherwise have devoted themselves to mischief. For many days the People labored long and hard, rubbing the grain from its inner core, weaving baskets of reeds in which it could be stored and carried.

Armed strangers stood nearby to watch, to discourage any of the People who might be tempted from secreting supplies of it so that they could stay. Many tried this, because they did not wish to go with the strangers. They did not know how they would be treated in the land of summer.

"You will be welcomed," the lord said. "You will be as we are, and live as we do, and enjoy what we have. We will be as one people."

Kah-Sih-Omah heard these words also. It was clear that the lord, as a person, liked the People, and in their way the people seemed to like him. Kah-Sih-Omah himself had grown fond of his master. But sophisticated as he had now become, he still had difficulty with the strangers' concept of order. All his long life he had known only the tribe—had assumed that all societies were thus organized, and that to all peoples the tribe was all.

In the tribe there were understandable and sensible rules. What was not ordained by tribal custom was forbidden; and it was forbidden that strangers, who did not share the blood of the tribe and its customs, could ever be a part of it. Rarely were there partial exceptions. Even marriage outside the tribe was not the same as marriage in it, and the offspring of such marriages as did occur were often as not regarded as outsiders even though they practiced its customs from the moment of birth.

These strangers knew no such restraints. They regarded membership in their society as a matter of simple preference, on the part of both the individual and the society. They were prepared to accept the children of the People as their own if, as they matured, the children accepted the role.

After lengthy study and much thought on the matter, Kah-Sih-Omah could at last concede that, given the culture they had, there was some logic in the strangers' system. At the same time he was loathe to allow the People to be assimilated, though there appeared to be no suitable alternative if they were to survive. Even were he to find a way to break them free, they could not hope to survive until the passage of years has brought the tribe's boys into manhood. Kah-Sih-Omah resolved not to interfere, but instead to attempt to preserve the People's identity within the alien society, until this occurred. He could see no other way.

It was then, burdened with this responsibility for the future of his people that Kah-Sih-Omah began to appreciate the true implications of his immortality.

The trek began on the skirts of cool winds blowing down the slopes of the mountains to the north, across the massive snowfield the spirit of winter had laid upon the land.

Animals, driven to the floor of the valley in their search for food, dotted the plains. Great herds of woolly horned beasts, their faces and forequarters thick with matted fur, turned heads into the wind and kept watch for the fanged cats and the packs of hungry wolves.

Kah-Sih-Omah was closely watched now and always tethered, because his master feared that the call of the wild ones might reach out to him, and that he would answer. He did not, of course, have any such aspirations, and though he could have escaped at will he found his present circumstances quite suitable. He trotted now, beside the lord's litter, within sight and hearing of all of importance that passed between the lord and his retinue.

There was a river which flowed southward. They came upon it on the second day, when the sun was high. It traveled on the low ground between two ridges of mountains, turning as they did, and thus shutting out the wind.

There was rain, sometimes in torrents, which raised the level of the waters and sometimes delayed the procession while they waited for it to recede. Kah-Sih-Omah recalled many cold days of wet fur even though by judicious use of body oils he was able to keep his skin dry.

For the People there was hardship. The People were not accustomed to travel in winter. Always they had sought out a sheltered valley, built stout lodges, and enjoyed warm fires. Here, as they moved, they could have none of these.

Exposure therefore weakened many of the older ones, who became ill. Many died, to be buried along the trail, the wolf who was not a wolf a silent witness to it all, watching his culture slowly melt away. These old wise ones, the reservoirs of the Peoples' past, the guardians of its culture, would be sorely missed. Kah-Sih-Omah contemplated the arrival of the day when only he might remain of them, and was saddened.

The weather improved as they traveled south. The walls of the valley opened and the river became broad. The rains ceased, and mounds of coarse gravel began to replace the grasses that fed the herds of thunderbeasts.

The thunderbeasts gave way to small herds of deer, and of the great, awkward, splay-footed desert dwellers—who alone, save for man, could traverse the barren dunes of sand which lay ahead, because they needed little water.

Man could do so because he had foresight enough to carry water with him. And he carried much; all that he could. Still, the desert was broad, and here exposure took its toll of still more of the old ones. The People, already few in number, became fewer still, and Kah-Sih-Omah was remorseful. He believed that he had erred; regretted his choice of inaction, which had allowed this tragedy to come about.

In hindsight he could judge himself harshly, and the

spirits harsher still. The spirits he blamed more even than he blamed himself, for they had known of this. He was certain they did. The spirits knew all of man's travails; they were the authors of many of them.

Again Kah-Sih-Omah felt deep despair, and frustration that his physical powers were of no assistance under these circumstances. Once he had believed himself armed and armored against any threat. Now he knew that this was not true. He did not possess that one faculty which would have made it true: the knowledge of what was to be.

The spirits had found him ignorant and left him no better. They had sent him forth to grope his way across the face of the Earth until the end of time. He suddenly found himself wondering if he could endure it—or if he must.

But for the People, for whom he still harbored some small hope for salvation, Kah-Sih-Omah might have yielded to that grand experiment which was the end of all grand experiments—to set himself upon a course of personal extinguishment and see if the spirits interfered. More and more of late he wondered if they would—and what his lot might be it they didn't. Somehow he could not imagine the spirits would allow such drastic disobedience to go unpunished; that they would rob him of the peace of passage he had always taught, and believed, was the right of every human spirit.

And so he persevered. Faithfully and steadfastly he plodded along beside those other human spirits to whom the fates now attached him. More of the People died before the sands began to give way to lands better watered and more hospitable.

Here there were other men, known somehow to the travelers though hostile to them, who neither hunted nor grew food, but herded small horned animals instead. Occasionally they skirmished with the travelers, mostly because the lord had ordered his warriors to forage upon the herds. Always the herdsmen lost; at first, Kah-Sih-Omah thought, because their numbers were fewer and their weapons inferior.

But that was not so. He knew it when a great battle ensued, when hordes of herdsmen congregated at the neck of a narrow canyon through which the travelers were passing. They were defeated here as well.

Kah-Sih-Omah was astounded at what happened. He had seen battles before. He had witnessed brave acts. But never had he seen warriors form themselves into positions where they could both protect one another and attack their adversaries in strength—this was new to his experience. It appeared foolish at first, but it worked. Beneath the hail of arrows the small force of archers, protected by a wall of spearmen, melted away the disorganized wave of attackers, who fell in great numbers before they could get close enough to fight. Kah-Sih-Omah gasped at the slaughter.

In this demonstration he found a lesson, one of the greatest he had ever learned: the power of a man derives not from what he is, but from what he knows. Kah-Sih-Omah would never again forget that.

The travelers continued on, closely watched but not molested by little knots of wary herdsmen. The lord continued to forage as long as they were in the lands of the herders, but soon this rolling, relatively treeless grassland gave way again to higher hills. These grew into mountains once more as they continued toward the land of summer, and but for these the heat of the day would surely have been unbearable.

As it was Kah-Sih-Omah was steadily shedding fur, melting away his outward illusion of bulk, becoming lean and hungry-looking. He had been in the form of a wolf for almost an entire summer and winter now. He had learned enough of the strangers' language so that he could have passed for one of them, and occasionally had been tempted to try.

He resisted this temptation, unwilling to create a mystery, as the disappearance of the lord's wolf would surely be regarded. Besides, the form had proven extraordinarily convenient, and promised to keep him always on the leading edge of the news.

News had begun arriving as soon as the procession threaded its way through the high mountain pass that opened the way to another great valley. This valley was vast. On its summer-side slopes dwelt people who were not hostile to the travelers, but seemed to know them;

and though they spoke another language, could be understood by certain members of the lord's entourage.

They were, Kah-Sih-Omah learned, not friends, but allies; people conquered by the lord's people long ago, who had become as their conquerors, who had adapted their culture and were under the great lord's protection. They behaved with deference toward Kah-Sih-Omah's master and escorted him into their greatest city.

It was the first city that Kah-Sih-Omah had ever seen, and although he considered it grand at the time it was a small and relatively poor one. Here he saw for the first time a building constructed of piled stones, and at length understood why they did not fall down; they were bound together by some manmade stone that had been placed between them.

Here for a time the travelers remained, resting, repairing equipment, and gathering new stocks of food. What they had carried was now almost exhausted, and but for the meat the foragers had taken or the hunters caught had been their staple, and had grown quite monotonous.

Foods new to Kah-Sih-Omah appeared, although being a wolf, he was not encouraged to eat them. Besides grain the city people supplied various types of melons and fruits, many of which were quite sweet. But there were some varieties which, though juicy, were highly acid, and made his mouth pucker when he tasted them.

There were great nuts which grew in clusters at the tops of tall, coarse-leaved trees, and long, mushy fruits of bland taste which grew in even greater clusters on broadleafed bushes. It was clear that the natives had planted many of these things where they now grew and depended upon them for sustenance, and Kah-Sih-Omah's admiration for the native culture grew. He now could see why the lord's people had regarded his own people as backward—they *were* backward, though previously ignorant of the fact.

It was clear also, in the faces of the People, that they liked the new things they were finding here in the land of summer. Many children seemed to know nothing else but life on the trail. Many had learned to speak the language of the lord's people. Some spoke it, even to one another, in preference to the tongue of their birth. Kah-Sih-Omah listened, and he was sad.

They moved on, descending again to the floor of the valley, whose walls gradually parted and soon became many days' walk from one another. Here there were forests, until they reached the center and it became evident that the inhabitants had cut and burned the trees to make room for grain fields.

Though watered as well as it had been in the valley on the side of winter, the grain was sickly by comparison.

Here their travels took them through villages of thatched pole huts, past silent, sullen-faced watchers who, though they yielded ground to the lord's minions as they passed, seemed to do so grudgingly.

Being where he was, Kah-Sih-Omah could hear the comments of the lord's confidents, and he knew that these people were not the willing allies of the lord, but a resentful, conquered people who wanted to be free of the strangers' rule. While they passed through these villages the archers marched with arrows notched, and warriors kept weapons ready.

By this time Kah-Sih-Omah was beginning to gain some insight into the culture he and the People had entered. He had not believed this could be so vast as it proved to be. He could see now that the People had been not only culturally backward but insignificant in terms of numbers. Many of the *small* villages along the trail held as many people or more than had his tribe.

This, together with the demonstrations of the fighting capabilities of the lord's warriors, convinced him that his decision not to lead the People in resistance to transportation had been wise. That realization tempered somewhat the criticism he had been heaping of late upon himself.

Now a new theory was forming, destined to replace the older one, which was outdated. These followed one another rapidly these days, as Kah-Sih-Omah struggled to reconcile his own passivity with the mission he still believed had been imposed upon him by the spirits. Why not, he thought, a greater destiny for the People, here in the outer world of wonders he could now see existed there? It was not, he began to think, entirely irrational, in view of the strangers' custom of adopting outsiders into their culture.

It could well be, he reasoned, that the People—with himself to lead them—might eventually survive to dominate this culture, as the lord's people did now.

He knew that they had not always done so. He was in the thick of most of the political discussions the lord had, seated at his feet whenever he held court. He was aware that the dominating thread within this vast sea of men was force, and the threat of force. Without force, of which the lord's faction happened at the moment to wield the most, the political integrity of the area would vanish, and there would again be many smaller groups of people in contention with one another.

It now seemed more logical to Kah-Sih-Omah to believe that the spirits' purpose was far more complex than he had once believed, though his role in it was more obscure than ever. How much of this originated with his own feelings of inadequacy he was not prepared to guess, or even to acknowledge these feelings to himself. But he had waited, as his name implied; and waiting, at least, appeared to have done no lasting harm.

The time came when the valley could no longer be called a valley, when its mountainous boundaries lost themselves in the dimness of distance against the looming horizon. It evolved into a flat plain. Relatively well watered, it supported vast forests and bush so thick that but for trails hacked through it by nearby inhabitants it would have been all but impassible.

Even as it was, the progress of the travelers was slow except where the trail touched a city. Here, the need of the natives to travel to and from their fields generated a great deal of local traffic, hence the way was easier.

Kah-Sih-Omah observed that the character of the cities was changing, too. All that they had passed through of late were larger than those in the hinterland. All contained more buildings, and more and more of these were stone. Increasingly, they were littered with statuary and decorated with symbols. Some boasted streets paved with slabs of stone, and well-developed water supply and drainage systems.

Instead of setting up a camp at the edge of the next

town on his itinerary as he had formerly done, the lord imposed on the hospitality of his local counterpart and was entertained by him. As a part of the lord's immediate party Kah-Sih-Omah could observe much.

Of late, all of the inhabitants through whose lands they passed were racially and linguistically identical to the lord, and Kah-Sih-Omah might have supposed that relations would be cordial. They were in fact not cordial at all, but filled with intrigue and suspicion and envy.

As an animal, Kah-Sih-Omah was mostly ignored, but on occasion he was also abused by his host and the servants of his hosts, who, fearing his master, yet not daring to show their enmity toward him, used his pet to vent their anger.

Kah-Sih-Omah became wary of them, and listened ever closer to their words. He became adept at flight, whenever it appeared he might become the target of a kick or a missile. He was quick to arch his fur and bare his fangs whenever intimidation seemed the wise course. Thus, in his own way, Kah-Sih-Omah adapted to the hostility shown him, and interposed such defenses as befit his station.

The time came when this was not enough, when passivity no longer sufficed; then Kah-Sih-Omah became aware that the lord and all his entourage, including all the surviving People, faced a far more serious danger.

"Always," a drunken host, just out of earshot, had muttered to the lord's wolf, "they come to steal, while they smile at me. Today—like you, wolf—I wear his collar, but one day ..." The gesture which followed was obvious, even to a wolf: a finger cautiously drawn across the throat, to signify the gaping smile of bleeding death. That night Kah-Sih-Omah lay sleepless at the young lord's feet, fangs ready, senses keenly alert, while his master dreamed.

By this time Kah-Sih-Omah knew a great deal about the political structure of the culture which now controlled the People's destiny. He knew that every city along their route was under the charge of a great lord like his master; that often as not these lords were his brothers: the children, by his many wives and concubines, of the greatest of all the lords, who ruled all from a central city somewhere farther to the south.

So long as their sire lived and ruled, order was maintained, and the rivalries did not break out into open warfare. But each sibling contemplated and awaited the death of the great lord, or the coming of some misfortune which might enable that son to unseat and succeed him.

Meanwhile, these princes toyed with one another, superficially correct, on occasion even cordial allies ... but never friends. Kah-Sih-Omah counted himself and the People fortunate in one respect. His master, their ruling lord, was favorite of the great lord—his heir apparent, though how much loyalty that would inspire and how much good it would do when the moment of succession arrived was a point on which he could only conjecture. It had taken, as he later learned, almost an entire generation for the present great lord to eliminate all the rivals to his own claim to supremacy.

Suddenly this society which he had come to admire, which had accomplished so much and which held such promise, revealed its one great flaw to him. It turned each man against his brother. Its leaders were not its wisest men, but its most ruthless. What appeared to be an advantage for his master was not. It was a sentence of death unless he followed his father's way.

And for what? A few short years of self-deception that he was somehow better than other men? Had it not been so tragic, Kah-Sih-Omah would have been amused. To him this empty lust for power was a foolish quest. Were they each to succeed, no lord he had met could begin to rival Kah-Sih-Omah's power or match what he knew must had already been an inordinately long and healthy lifetime. And yet, for the sake of such a petty thing, here in this city, within the very walls of the building in which Kah-Sih-Omah reposed, a rival sibling contemplated taking life—not one, but many, and risking his own, in order that he might face one less opponent when the moment of succession came.

The trek ended, in the steaming heat of late afternoon. Almost magically the jungle vanished, and there lay before the travelers an enormous lake fed by a dozen or more streams whose termini had been dammed at intervals and from which slim, straight canals extended through fields of the intensely green grainstalks.

In the center of the lake was an island connected by causeways to the shores, and on the island stood by far the grandest city that Kah-Sih-Omah had yet seen: dozens of buildings of stone, hundreds more of wood and wattle, and people in such great numbers that Kah-Sih-Omah compared it with an anthill. It was the capital city. It was his master's home, and the home of the People until Kah-Sih-Omah could find one more suitable for them.

As he trotted along the causeway behind the lord's litter, Kah-Sih-Omah felt the cool breath of the water, before which the oppressive heat of the jungle fled, and looked out upon its face. Occasionally he could see fish swimming below the surface, some pursued by diving birds, whole families of which hunted them together. Curiously, flowers grew in the water, and Kah-Sih-Omah at first thought they were rooted on the bottom. Later he noticed that they moved, floating on their broad leaves wherever the wind took them, trailing their roots behind them.

The city proper was entered through a gate in a low wall which extended for some distance on either side of the causeway, and which appeared to be a part of the city's defenses. Near the gate squads of archers gathered in a cluster and made obeisance to his master, who ignored them from the curtains of his litter.

Kah-Sih-Omah was not tethered. Nevertheless he could not leave his master's side, though when he stepped off the causeway he wanted very much to do so—he wanted to see what would happen to the People.

The People were fewer still than they had been when this journey started. Moreover, they were scattered around, the older women and the children in one group and the younger women who had borne children of the strangers in another. Glancing back, Kah-Sih-Omah could see some of them far to the rear, gaping around at the wonders as shamelessly as he. He knew that the end of the journey also meant loss of easy contact with them, and he was greatly disturbed by the fact. He made up his mind to abandon his guise as a wolf as soon as it was practical, and to rejoin and care for the People.

In the end, he did not see where they went. The entourage began to filter down a broad street lined with magnificent stone-walled buildings, which blocked his view at the first corner they turned.

By this time, something else had seized his attention— something never seen before in any of the other towns they had passed through. It was a walled enclave, reached by crossing a surrounding ditch over a wooden bridge, then passing through a gate beside which archers stood. Once through it, Kah-Sih-Omah could see that near the top of the wall was a catwalk, reached from the ground by ladders upon which archers could stand and shoot.

The greatest lord was cautious. Living here in this fortress he was no doubt safer from attack, both by his own people and by outsiders, but Kah-Sih-Omah asked himself what joy a man could find in life if he could not live in the world as the spirits had made it. It seemed to him that there was no difference between being a leader and being a prisoner.

Inside the walled enclave the streets were narrower and each turned often, sometimes for no logical reason, except perhaps to make them easier to defend. Kah-Sih-Omah trotted onward, waiting to see, and at length passed with his master through another gate.

Inside this one was a large courtyard surrounding another building of stone. This building had several levels connected by stone steps. Its walls, except the lowest, were pierced by many tall, narrow windows. The first level apparently was solid, and the entourage mounted its stairway to the second level.

Now Kah-Sih-Omah could see an immense structure, so large that at first he did not believe men could have made it. But there it was, like an artificial hill, rising higher than anything else in the city. Each of its four sides consisted entirely of steps which narrowed as they rose and terminated at a huge flat top so large that it could easily have held all of his people. At each of the platform's four corners stood a brazier in which fire burned, and in the center a curiously shaped table of stone.

Kah-Sih-Omah wondered briefly what this might be, but then became more interested in something else he saw—gargoyles.

These were hideous caricatures, some in the form of animals but grossly distorted, as though the carver wanted all of them to conform to the same design. Others, while just as hideous, were more easily recognized as effigies of human skulls. Moving closer to the walls, he could see that all were inscribed—each stone bore something, though commonly the carvings were not very deep.

Where there was room for display, the carvings seemed intended to tell stories. Panels of them, sometimes of motifs repeated in different poses, ran in series. None of them made very much sense to Kah-Sih-Omah, but all impressed him with their ghastly morbidity.

Inside, carvings gave way to frescoes, and occasionally to tapestries. Small pieces of statuary stood along the corridors, whose floors consisted of the first polished stone slabs that Kah-Sih-Omah had ever seen. While he marveled at the city, and in particular this building, he could not help thinking how long and hard these people must have labored in order to build it all.

He admired the strangers for their industry and their skills, but he found he was most envious of them for the vast store of knowledge that they possessed. He knew the People could never have built such a place—not as they were when he lived among them, or as they were now, but someday, perhaps. But then he asked himself whether the People would be happier if they had this, and he found he did not know the answer, any more than he knew his own role in all of this.

Once past the inner wall, Kah-Sih-Omah was taken from his master and placed in a small room without furnishings. A servant brought him water and meat, then left him alone to speculate upon his situation. For a while he did, beginning with the continued suitability of his disguise. He realized he no longer needed the form of the wolf. He could now easily go out into the city in human form, speak to people, look around, and do whatever else he chose, perhaps even locate and visit with the People.

Something stopped him. He did not know precisely what it was, and at first he was inclined to regard it merely as personal reluctance to leave a role in which he had grown very comfortable, to trade the known for the unknown. But the feeling endured, and grew.

It had come to him first as a feeling of uneasiness—a portent of impending doom, without face, without form, without apparent reason. Now, it gnawed at him. It was as though his enhanced senses had detected some evil at the ultimate limit of their range, but could not bring it close enough for him to see clearly.

So Kah-Sih-Omah hesitated—and he watched.

It was several days before he saw the lord again. In the interim servants came and fed him, and groomed him, and took him out into the courtyard for exercise. Here each treated him with the utmost kindness.

The occasion of his next meeting with his master was a celebration of the party's return from their travels—a great feast, held in a pavilion in the open courtyard on the other side of the great house, where Kah-Sih-Omah had never been.

It occurred in the early evening, by the light of many torches. It included a pageant—a dance of those warriors who had gone with the lord, who acted out the experiences they had had along the way. Donning masks of the animals they had seen, these fell, one by one, from ritual wounds delivered by the dancers, and one by one their tanned skins were brought to the throne of the great lord and unrolled at his feet.

He accepted these gifts graciously and examined each one in some detail, before turning to smile at his heir, who sat on his right hand. "You have done well," he said to his son. "You have shown strength to your enemies, and that is good. Let them see this, and fear it."

There too sat Kah-Sih-Omah the manwolf, head high, glancing around at what was taking place. To others his curiosity seemed natural enough for a wolf, and after the first casual inspection, he was ignored as always.

But Kah-Sih-Omah scanned the crowd with a shrewdness of purpose no animal had ever matched, searching out faces, making mental notes of things that interested him. He saw in the crowd some of the consorts the lords had taken from among the women of the People. These looked upon the pageant wide-eyed, their faces reflecting the awe each must have felt to be here, to see this, dressed in such finery as they had not known to exist a mere winter or two ago—and pleased, it seemed, to have it.

Kah-Sih-Omah was disturbed by the sight. No less extinction than death of the body was death of the culture. Should this go on, the People would pass as a people, painlessly but just as permanently, within a generation.

True, many of the ways of the strangers were good. Much of what they had was useful. But in acquiring it they had obviously sacrificed a great deal of what he had always regarded as the birthright of every man— his individual freedom of choice.

As he watched, he wondered how it had all come about. The strangers seemed so single-minded, so cohesive in their submission to the authority of the lords, this even though any fool could see that against their massive numbers their leaders could not prevail, should the commoners decide to exert their united will.

There had to be more to it—and there was, though at the time Kah-Sih-Omah did not know that the reason was before his eyes, seated inconspiciously in the upper tiers of the structure on the other side of the plaza. These were men curiously aloof from the rest of the crowd, somehow different, even beyond their peculiar dress, white robes with broad red stripes. They whispered to one another, their lips carefully shaded by their hands.

The pageant came to an end, and the feasting began. Much pulque was drunk and camaraderie prevailed throughout the plaza. In place of the dancers there was entertainment of a different kind—acrobats, tumblers, jugglers, wrestlers, and more dancers, this time female as well as male. Kah-Sih-Omah had never seen anything like this before. He was both astonished and disgusted. The decadence of this society was revealed to him with increasing clarity as the celebration wore on.

He could not allow the People to become a part of this society without making some effort to change it. As that appeared to be an impossibility, he would have to find some way to lead the People away. Again the apparent disinterest of the spirits disturbed and angered him. It seemed to him that they had failed him in their silence; presented him with a choice that really was no choice.

The next day, Kah-Sih-Omah saw how true that was. That day his master attended his father at court, taking with him the wolf, his totem and symbol of power.

And Kah-Sih-Omah looked for the first time on this culture's true rulers—who ruled all, without right, but by guile and cunning and lies. They were the shamen of the strangers' city.

Were he himself a common man, ignorant of the ways of such as these, Kah-Sih-Omah might have been deceived as was apparently the court. He watched and saw, not enlightened men of wisdom, but superstitious, gullible men, eager to believe every lie that they were told, no matter how preposterous. And these shamen, it seemed, exploited the preposterous on a large scale, pretending skills and powers that they could not have had.

Every shaman on occasion casts futures, using such devices as seem appropriate to individual tastes. Kah-Sih-Omah had done it, though never with any great confidence that the signs he read had any bearing on reality. When he did it at all it was to reinforce his own reason, to bolster with magic some sound decision to which logic had led him—never to win on a point supported only by conjecture.

These shamen did, over and over again, rolling knuckle bones across a polished tray, then reading signs they said they saw. True, they did so upon instruction of the great lord, in response to his questions about certain of his vassals—but as a skilled shaman himself Kah-Sih-Omah could read, as easily as they, the signs which appeared not on the bones, but on the face of the great lord himself.

They knew, from these signs, what the great lord already thought, sensed suspicions perhaps already raised by reports of spies, and cleverly reiterated his own half-formed opinions.

"The Sun is your brother," one unctuously said to him, "and loves you. He watches over you. You will, therefore, enjoy long life, Lord, and victory in all your wars, which will be many and glorious. Your brother, the Sun, asks only the hearts of your enemies for his own." And he cast out the bones again, and smiled.

Court continued for much of the day. Kah-Sih-Omah grew weary of it to the extent that some of his napping was not feigned. In his waking moments he witnessed the most momentous of decisions, including many of life and death, pass on the strength of guesses or worse.

Kah-Sih-Omah conceded willingly the cleverness of his dishonest brethren. They were clever—clever enough to have convinced their leader that there were confined, within the other building in the plaza, spirits who at once possessed great power and were so gullible as to allow mere men to imprison and control them.

Kah-Sih-Omah knew this was not so. He knew spirits. Spirits were largely disinterested in the affairs of men, and interfered only at infrequent intervals and for the gravest of their own reasons. Even the least of them could not be confined for very long, and none he knew of followed any will but its own. He, himself, was living proof of that. The words of these shamen were pure lies.

This was bad enough, but it was made far worse by their apparent lack of motive. There must be one, Kah-Sih-Omah knew; there had to be benefits derived from this great deception. It made no sense otherwise.

The session ended with Kah-Sih-Omah of the opinion that the land of the strangers contained many mysteries. He would therefore have to learn a great deal more about this society before he could make a judgment; perhaps chance occasional forays outside this guarded compound. He knew this would not be easy, and a convenient method eluded him for many days.

An answer did ultimately present itself. As he attended more and more sessions of the great lord's court and learned its ways, he discovered that many people passed in and out of the enclosure with ease. Some were lesser nobles of the city; others were merchants, both local and from afar, with whom the leader traded. And the great house held another class of inmate, one whose status exceeded that of all except the great lord's—the foreign emissaries.

Learning as he did, by listening and watching with careful attention to obscure detail, it was some time before Kah-Sih-Omah had sufficient facts to comprehend the political situation within this society. It was far more complex than he had previously supposed. He had at first been of the opinion that the land of the great lords existed in relative isolation, composed only of cities and peoples under his domination.

This was not so. The great lord was only one of many, and to Kah-Sih-Omah's amazement he was not even the greatest. Farther to the south there were other civilizations larger than this one, with people who spoke different languages and had different customs.

All of these neighbor civilizations interacted—sometimes peacefully, through trade, and sometimes violently, in war. At present there was relative peace, the greatest of these having surrounded themselves with allies and buffers against one another, and the system having achieved a sort of equilibrium.

One function of the emissaries, some of whom were not true emissaries at all but hostages, was to preserve that equilibrium for as long as it appeared in the best interest of his homeland to do it. Another function was to gather information of interest to his own homeland. As a result, palace intrigues and rumors were important things.

Many of these originated with women or were controlled by them, something Kah-Sih-Omah at first found odd. Later, having considered the advantages some women had, he realized it as an excellent way to place spies in the bedchamber of a rival. It was no wonder that the great lords exchanged their daughters in marriage as a means of sealing alliances. The system seemed to work poorly, yet it endured, probably out of inertia and apathy—and because, as Kah-Sih-Omah began to be more and more convinced, the great lords enjoyed intrigue.

To Kah-Sih-Omah, the most amazing thing about the

study he made was that it revealed to him the true extent of the differences among men.

In the old lands of the People most tribes were much alike, speaking substantially the same language, and adhering to the same or similar customs. They traveled, but always on traditional routes, and so did not often encounter strangers. Those they did meet they generally shunned and ignored if this was possible, or fought in genocidal war if it was not.

Here, in the lands of summer, it was not that way. Many completely unrelated languages were to be heard; many physical types could be seen, many diverse cultures rubbed elbows with one another. Among them, the People were as a mere handful—an insignificant drop in a great ocean of men. Were it not for the wondrous transformation the spirits had worked on Kah-Sih-Omah for the purpose of preserving them as a people, his resolve to do so might then have been lost.

But it was not lost. It continued to drive him, as it had since he learned of their peril—until it drove him abroad in the nighttime. "I must go to the people," he told himself resolutely. "I must incite them to recall their past."

Though he had held the form of the wolf for what seemed forever, Kah-Sih-Omah had not abandoned his studies of the technique of metamorphosis. He had, instead, perfected it, honing his skills to a new edge. By careful observation and intense concentration he compiled a repertoire of characters, burning the physical features and behavioral characteristics of each firmly into his memory. He hoped that by having thus laid in the matrix he could achieve rapid movement from one persona to another. Still, he was careful to choose those which did not vary a great deal in size.

Because a wolf's opportunity to steal was a good deal less than his opportunity to eavesdrop and he looks decidedly unnatural carrying clothing around, Kah-Sih-Omah's excursions grew in stages, beginning with the servant who cared for him, who slept in quarters nearby.

The servant commonly drank pulque in the evenings, when he had nothing to do. Kah-Sih-Omah had only to open simple latches on his own door and that of the servant's in order to enter, after his augmented senses determined that the servant was asleep.

Even then Kah-Sih-Omah took no chances that he would awaken, but fortified the pulque's deadening force with an injection of the base substance given through a hollowed and finely pointed claw.

Thus on that first night, when Kah-Sih-Omah stole into the servant's room limping on three legs, he established a firm pattern and made the most radical, most difficult change in the safest of all possible places and under ideal conditions.

To leave the great house, when Kah-Sih-Omah did so, normally required two more. In his early forays he selected the forms of local nobles whom all the guards recognized by sight. Soon, however, he found that he could save much effort by the simple acquisition of one robe—the long, flowing, crimson-on-white of the temple shaman.

These men walked about city and palace at will, without challenge, whenever they wished. It was almost ridiculously easy; Kah-Sih-Omah could get by with one change. For this he was grateful, though he found the awesome influence of these individuals to be chilling. Their power in this society was immense.

For many, many nights, whenever he safely could, Kah-Sih-Omah roamed the city. Outside the palace, except near a few establishments where entertainment was provided for the citizens, the streets were generally empty. He could leave the palace and go anywhere without encountering anyone, if he chose. Only the shoreline of the lake had sentries, alert for anything crossing its broad, deep waters.

He found many of the People quartered together in the same neighborhood, though it took a long while for him to discover this. One night when he was certain that he was in the right location he altered himself, covered his priestly robe with a cloak, and rapped at one of the doors at random.

Fortune smiled. His rap was answered by Seh-Kho-Tan, daughter to Ruhu-Doh-Sah, whom he knew from their days together in the fields. But she had known

Kah-Sih-Omah as a woman, and was alarmed to find a strange man standing in the doorway.

Fearing she would cry out, he spoke at once in the language of the People. "I am He-Who-Waits," he said to her.

Had he struck her, she could not have been more devastated. She knew that all the men of the People were long since dead, and that none of the city's strangers would have bothered to learn her language, much less speak it as flawlessly as this man. The shock, combined with the informities of age, was too much for her. She fell faint and began to sink toward the dirt floor of her hut.

Kah-Sih-Omah was quick to prevent this, seizing one scrawny arm and holding tightly while he grasped her around the waist.

She weighed but little, not that it would have mattered. Kah-Sih-Omah's present body was that with which he had awakened after his transformation, with ample strength to support such a small burden.

The hut was not otherwise empty, but had other inhabitants: another old woman and several children. The children remained asleep, but the other woman stirred, peering at him in the dim moonlight, and cringed into a corner. She too had heard the short conversation at the door, but whether she failed to recognize his name or whether she was simply too frightened, Kah-Sih-Omah could not tell.

He resolved to break her fear, and did. "Make light, that we might see each other," he told the woman. "And clear a place for her to lie."

The woman obeyed, seizing an earthen vessel in shaking hands and holding it in front of her face. In this was a coal, glowing on a slow-burning cake of rotted wood banked with its own ashes, and intended to be used in the morning to kindle cooking fires. It would, instead, kindle a light for them.

The old woman found tinder, and soon a flame erupted from it, from which she lit a brand. It was in this light that she saw Kah-Sih-Omah's face.

"You are a young man. You cannot be Kah-Sih-Omah, yet you are of the People. I know this."

"I am of the People; that I swear to you. I am Kah-Sih-Omah—that I also swear."

Seh-Kho-Tan was reviving, uttering small, weak moans, which grew into hysterical cries.

"Stop!" Kah-Sih-Omah said to her sternly, his voice full of command. "Hear me. What I say is true. I am Kah-Sih-Omah, and of this I will provide proof, first to you, then to the rest of the People." He was holding her down on her cot now with a hand on each shoulder.

She continued in her hysteria, and he shook her. "Look at me! Look into my face, and tell me what you see."

She now had something other than her own fright on which to focus her attention, and stopped both her struggling and her squeals to do as he ordered.

Suddenly the squealing started again—as she realized what was happening to Kah-Sih-Omah's face. It was changing into a face she knew—that of her companion in the fields.

Kah-Sih-Omah could see more reassurance was needed. "I have been with you and with the People all this time, just as I am here now. I am your shaman." His features began to revert. "Tell me; did you know your father's totems?"

"Yes," she struggled to answer, though her voice was weak.

"Who else would know them?"

"No one who now lives."

Kah-Sih-Omah then began to describe them in detail, as well he could, having made them himself. "Who then, am I, Seh-Kho-Tan, if I am not the shaman?"

"You are the shaman," she gasped.

But her eyes had been on the priestly robe, visible beneath the cloak. Kah-Sih-Omah could not be certain she really believed him. Perhaps her faith would take a long time to rise. He did not know. He knew only that before the night was over and the rising of the sun compelled him to return to the great house that he would announce his presence to the People through these women.

Kah-Sih-Omah knew that in choosing this manner, in preying on their fear and overawing them with powers that to him were natural and explainable, he too strayed from the true domain of his calling, claiming more than was really his to claim. But he convinced himself that the circumstances were compelling enough to justify this slight deception.

"It was the summer of the great thirst," he began, "when the rains refused to come and the grass on which the thunderbeasts feed was thin and sickly. You will remember this."

She did not reply.

"The People were hungry and fearful, and grumbled, because the hunting was hard. Your father came to me and asked for signs, but I had none to give him then. I sought these on the sacred mountain, and journeyed there alone, though I carried a burden of many winters on my back.

"There I waited, fasting for many days, beginning as Our Mother Moon appeared. As she fattened in her sky I grew weak on the mountain below her; still she gave no sign to me.

"I despaired. She knew this, and took pity, though I thought at the time she was angry, for from her own body she gave birth to spirits of fire, who came to me, and burned me, and caused my senses to leave me.

"When the spirits of the fire departed I was as you see me now. I did not understand. I thought that I had passed. I returned to the lands of the People, but your father did not know me and all but Hono were afraid of me. You will remember this."

Seh-Kho-Tan nodded, but said nothing.

"Hono alone believed me when I told him who I was. He had been to the sacred mountain and had seen the signs. He wanted the power of the spirits for himself.

"In those days I had not yet full use of the powers the spirits had given me, nor great understanding of them. These I developed through meditation while I was gone from the lands of the People, and I learned to take the form of many things, as you have just seen me do.

"Having thus prepared myself I sought the People, but I found them too late. It was not until after Hono had led them down the path of ruin, and all of the warriors had been killed. Then I could only wait, and watch over the People, while I studied the ways of the strangers and sought a means of deliverance. Thus you knew me well as the woman who labored beside you in the fields in the strangers' valley."

"But she is gone. I thought she died."

"She did not die, Seh-Kho-Tan. She never was. But I am. So long as the People need me I will be nearby."

Seh-Kho-Tan was one whose wisdom had grown with her years. This was the reason Kah-Sih-Omah was so overjoyed that he had found her. He saw in her all those qualities which in a man of the People would have made him a leader. Stifled no longer by the accident of birth, she could rise to this new leadership.

But wise are they who search for flaws in great truths. Seh-Kho-Tan would not blindly follow even such a man as he. "Where are the People, Shaman? I see but handsful of old women who remember the ways of their fathers. The young women have no men of the People. They have gone with the strangers, and their children are the children of the strangers. Why have you permitted this to happen? Why did you wait so long?"

Kah-Sih-Omah had long ago asked himself the same question. He did not try to explain to her. Instead he resolved to have her aid in making a new beginning. He would risk much, in carrying out this plan; part hope, part faith, and part deception; but it seemed worth it. "We will begin anew. The People," he said, "will rise to a new greatness. We will recreate them, as the spirits recreated me."

"How, Shaman?"

"We will restore their identity. We will keep them separate even here in the land of the strangers, until they are many again, and strong enough to go their own way."

"I do not understand."

"The spirits intend that I transcend time; that I shall be their bond to the past, and their link to the forefathers they have never known. You, Seh-Kho-Tan, must tell the People that I am here among them, and that I watch and wait with them."

Seh-Kho-Tan looked up at him and blinked, but gave no other sign.

It was clear to him she understood now: she was to be

midwife, and attend the birth of his legend. But, he asked himself, can she ever know how dear will be the cost to He-Who-Waits?

Thus Kah-Sih-Omah carefully tutored her; this is how she must tell his story, or as much of it as he dared, with such embellishments as to him seemed needful though they were less than the truth. It was the version of his travail which was to ripen into legend and trail the People as long as they were the People, throughout many generations until both finally died.

Kah-Sih-Omah made much of his transformation, supplying missing parts from his own conjecture so that it had continuity and sounded rational. He did this with an aim: to preserve in them the myth of the spirit's purpose in transforming him—to protect them while he led them into greatness.

Kah-Sih-Omah left them early that morning, spellbound, enjoined to silence before the strangers of what they had seen and heard, but admonished to tell the People he was near, and that he watched even as he waited. He returned to the wolf's form, touched somewhat by the vanity of his plan. He was, at that moment, no different than he had ever been, though he felt different. He was, in fact, exactly what he supposed he was—a shaman of the People, casting spells.

Protector

The great lord was dead! The news was stark, disturbing even to the wolf, who was supposed neither to notice nor to care. But he had been walking with his master in the courtyard at the instant when the young lord received the news. Like his master, he was stunned.

Their respective reasons for being shocked were far different. The young lord both welcomed and dreaded the news; dreaded it because even in this normally callous society there was some affection between himself and his father, and because it probably meant a long, hard, bloody struggle to keep his father's legacy.

Kah-Sih-Omah's reasons were more personal. He feared the approaching chaos might be very bad for the People, most of whom had only lately heard the news of his own mythical existence, and a few of whom truly believed it yet. Now fully half the people—the young women, now consorts of strangers—dare not be told, lest Kah-Sih-Omah be mistaken for a rival prince contending in this struggle for power, and the People thereby suffer. It could not have happened at a worse time.

The young lord, now king, acted swiftly. He had had a plan ready for this situation. He ordered his warriors to seal off the city, allowing no one to pass through the portal onto the causeways except for his own royal messengers and priests. All outsiders attempting to en-

111

ter might do so, but inside the city they would stay until he let them go. Especially, he did not wish the foreign emissaries to leave bearing news of the succession. Were these to escape he might find foreign armies crossing his borders, their leaders courting the favor of his siblings and entering into alliances with them.

The young lord's plan called for a deception, one cleverly employed by the great lord during his own ordeal for power. Runners went forth to all the subject cities, commanding the presence of their ruling lords at court in the name of the dead king, to give him council on a plan for war in the south, against a neighbor who was both rich and vulnerable.

The new king then waited, with his army, for his adversaries to walk into the trap. Not a few did, but not enough. Somewhere among the new king's subjects was a traitor, or more than one traitor; one was all which was needed.

Civil war followed. Kah-Sih-Omah had never learned the concept, but he soon discovered its meaning.

"We must prepare the People, Seh-Kho-Tan," he told her after the first battle. "Chaos reigns in this land of the strangers. Crisis is coming, and they must be ready to meet it."

Little news had reached the city. That which had had filtered through so many lips it was not possible to distinguish fact from rumor. But Kah-Sih-Omah had come from the battlefield with first-hand knowledge, so she listened carefully as he described his last day as a man-wolf.

"I was at the prince's side, as his totem—perhaps as his friend." The memory of it was painful for him to relate. It was still quite vivid—the prince, falling in death, his skull broken by the blow from a heavy club, his royal blood and brains splashing on Kah-Sih-Omah's fur, even as the man-wolf's slashing jaws tore at the throat of the axeman. He had been true wolf to the end. He could do no more for his master.

"I bolted off the battlefield, bounding over the corpses of the dead of both sides, dodging arrows and javelins until I reached the bush, where I hid until nightfall. Later I stripped the armor and weapons off a dead warrior of the other side and spent the night at the new high lord's encampment. I gathered such information as I could, and in the morning marched into the city with his army.

"You must go out among the People, Seh-Kho-Tan. Tell them we must have no side in this war. They must remain calm, and wait. Tell them they must make a place for as many of the women as I might send to them from those in the great house, who are in danger."

He lied to Seh-Kho-Tan, and through her to all the People; but he did so once again for a purpose. The women of the great house were in no danger. The new lord would not harm them, because he considered them his property now that he had taken the city. What Kah-Sih-Omah really feared was continuation of the war. He wished to gather up the People and leave with them before that happened, if he could find a way to do so.

And he did have a plan of sorts; not a good plan, but a plan nevertheless, one that called for the assistance of as many of the lesser lords whose wives were of the People as might be persuaded to join him. Again and again, Kah-Sih-Omah donned the corporeal mantle of a slack-jawed temple shaman, and he roved the great house. But he found the women in little fear, most of them having guessed their value as a part of the spoils of war.

Some of these did listen to the admonitions and fled the great house, taking refuge among the People in their quarter of the city. Others, more stubborn, doubted the legend and demanded proof, which Kah-Sih-Omah gave them. Any who had seen a transformation never again doubted, though in the end this action placed the People in even greater peril. Kah-Sih-Omah did not know that then. He had not been a god long enough to know divinity's disadvantages.

And ultimately, his plan failed. There was no hope for it because there was no time. There was no time because the war was no longer civil, but foreign—his master's worst fear had materialized. Now, approaching from the south, a foreign army marched into the strangers' lands, grinding away the fragmented resistance with ease.

The city's new prince fled to the north, to the city from which he had come, and there made an effort to gather allies and march back with them. This plan also failed. His enemy pursued him far too closely. He was forced to fight where he stood. Ultimately, he died where he had fought, and all the land fell under the sway of the invader—and the central city remained sealed.

Kah-Sih-Omah wandered through its narrow streets in various guises, taking care always to avoid doing or saying anything that might bring attention. The people he encountered, mostly of the strangers, were apprehensive but resigned, as though they knew what was to come. Strangely, none would speak of it.

He resolved to return to the great house—and found that entry into it was easier than ever before, because the invaders did not yet know who everybody was.

There were, however, those whom they did know well, and those whom even the conquering prince treated with deference. Observing this, Kah-Sih-Omah at once realized how the entire tragedy had come about. His own master had been betrayed. His lord's father had been murdered; he had been fed a poison that caused a natural-seeming death. The shamen had done it.

Now they talked of it among themselves, these same shamen who welcomed their counterparts from the south with open arms, and now moved freely with them about the temple of the gods they shared.

They were now the power, not the southern prince who reigned as conqueror of the northern empire. Yet they too were afraid. They were afraid for their gods, for whom they had done all this. They feared the influence of a powerful new god of whom they had heard rumors, who walked among the people they had conquered: a god for whom they searched, but without success. Kah-Sih-Omah knew then why the commoners had been so secretive.

But Kah-Sih-Omah misconstrued the basis of the priests' fears. He was a simple man who favored simple explanations. He did not understand that these men feared not the idea of gods as gods, but the idea of gods in the minds of men.

Not until he donned the persona of a minor shaman of his acquaintance, whose absence from a certain feast he took steps to assure, did Kah-Sih-Omah discover the truth. These men did not believe in the existence of their own or any other god!

"We must root this rumor out," the high priest raved, "stop the propagation of this nonsense at our own gates, lest all our creatures fall, and our power with them. We are too few to rule by other means."

"Lord," a voice answered, "the belief of some seems very strong. We put these to the test of fire, yet they believed even as they died that this creature would save them—burst forth as a great wolf and tear away our throats."

"Yes," the high priest countered. "I have heard such stories too, and others even more preposterous, and some of them I liked because they serve our cause."

He went on, waving aside all interruptions. "You know of the wolf, but do you know whence the story rose? No. Then I will tell you.

"The young prince kept this very wolf, said to be the god of these barbarians in a clever disguise. He is gone, it seems, last seen on the battlefield with its dead master, whom he was powerless to protect. Somehow the ghost of him remains, and so these people believe what it pleases them to believe, the same as all men do.

"Our way is clear—challenge. It is one thing to talk, another to act. I say we must act. We must compel this new god to act—to defeat the Sun, or die. And of course we will allow no such thing to happen, will we?"

Kah-Sih-Omah heard their laughter and felt its chill. He did not know then what they intended, and could not ask. He slipped away to think.

When the shamen did act, it was fiercely and savagely, with the violence of blindness grown from desperation and terror. It was too late for Kah-Sih-Omah to lead the People away. It was too late for anyone to leave. The city was sealed off. It was destined to become a city of death. And Kah-Sih-Omah blamed himself, as though it was his doing to have planted fear in the priests as he planted hope within his People.

Day and night the conqueror's warriors stood two hands deep at the causeways. Nothing moved on the lake, unless they first carefully searched it. They gathered up the People—all of them, the old women, the children, the young women and their husbands and children—then those of the strangers who had gone with the young lord into the lands of the People. They penned these up in one corner of the city.

So the People did not suffer alone. The city had become one vast prison. Fully half of it was under guard by invading warriors. All who served Kah-Sih-Omah's former master or he who had defeated him were there, and from the marches outside conquering warriors brought still more captives.

Kah-Sih-Omah continued to move about at will, to seek a way to get the People out, though it seemed impossible in the face of the awesomely tight grip in which the conquerors held them. He despaired that he could only wait, and watch for opportunity.

It did not come, but rumors did: rumors confirmed by the sight of sweating captive warriors, driven with whips, who hauled great statues of stone through the streets of the city, and up to the pinnacle of the many-stepped structure that stood behind the great house.

At first Kah-Sih-Omah did not believe the stories he heard. But then came the great stone, lumbering through the streets on rollers, dragged by many, many hands of struggling slaves, crushing the paving stones beneath its weight.

This too they took to the pinnacle, where masons labored for days to set it firmly with mortar, as they had the four gruesome statues of the conqueror's gods, and dress its surfaces for use.

Time became Kah-Sih-Omah's enemy, racing madly along toward madness greater still, and still he could see no way to stop what was about to happen. He had no plan that promised anything but failure. He floundered in indecision; he knew deep anguish. The time of his greatest test, perhaps the time of his fulfillment, might be near at hand—and he was unworthy and unready to meet it.

The city began to swell. From other cities nearby the warriors of the conqueror herded people into it. Some were shamen, allied to those who served the gods of the conqueror. Some were headmen from villages which raised food for the city. Some were newly in the pay of the conqueror and anxious to gain his favor. Others were commoners, tradesmen and artisans, sent here to watch and return with tales of what they had seen.

At last, Kah-Sih-Omah realized who the real rulers were to be. Not the chieftain of the southern warriors, fearsome though he was. It was to be the bloodthirsty gods who waited atop the pyramid of stacked stones. Theirs would be a rule of terror—a tyranny not merely over the bodies of men but of their thoughts, an incursion into the very spirit. He could think of no worthier object for the wrath of the true spirits who had created him and sent him forth.

And at last, though it was a time when great tragedy loomed for many others, Kah-Sih-Omah knew a sort of inner peace. He realized now what the spirits wanted of him. They had seen far ahead in time, and in their wisdom they had given him the powers to triumph over this evil.

He knew now also that his responsibility was far broader than he had once supposed. He was not simply to be the guardian of the People, but the guardian and protector of all men, bound to nourish what was good and vanquish what was evil. His destiny was at last revealed to him.

He was resigned; he was resolved. He knew now what must be done. He must take that final step which he had always avoided and acknowledge to himself his own nature—that he was, in fact, a superbeing. He must indulge in an ostentatious display of power, a display so rawly awesome that it would never be forgotten. There was no other way; only greater magic could overcome magic.

Champion

Time grew short. There were many whom Kah-Sih-Omah could not hope to save, because he could not prepare within the time remaining to them. Though he was what he was, still he was as dependent on propitious circumstances as any other shaman.

Kah-Sih-Omah salved his conscience with the thought that perhaps this, too, was the will of his benevolent spirits: that the people could not conceive evil until they saw it, and that only by the perception of evil could good be appreciated. The people *must* perceive it, because only the people, acting in unison, could prevent other evil men from repeating this history.

The people who watched, standing in the hot sun as a silent, sullen throng, saw much evil. They were not allowed to look away from it. Any who did were seized and bound and thrown among the captives who waited their turn to climb the stairs of death.

All day long the victims marched in queue, guarded on each side by solid lines of the conqueror's warriors. Armed with clubs and jagged-edged swords the warriors prodded them along, careful to inflict no mortal wounds, though many victims tried desperately to provoke them into doing so.

The priests worked diligently, seizing and dispatching victims as fast as they could, until the gutters carved in the stone overflowed with the blood and the corpses piled up faster than the warriors with their litters could carry them away.

The smell of death pervaded the plaza. It would hover even after the sun, in whose name and for whose glory these atrocities were being committed, dropped into the pit of night. Nor would it end even then; the captives were too many even for the fervent servants of the sun god to sacrifice in one day. Tomorrow it would go on, and the day after, and the day after that, until all the captives were dead or the new god appeared to do battle.

This was only the first day.

And it was a day of great sadness for Kah-Sih-Omah, who stood, a nondescript man in this large and essentially faceless crowd, waiting as he always had, for greatness to come to him. He too looked that day upon the face of evil, appalled that men could believe such cruelty pleased any spirit, or that there existed any spirit so capricious as to tolerate it. He knew then that, loathesome as he was, the high priest had spoken true. It was one thing to talk, and another to act. If the sun were not challenged—and defeated—the grip of these evil men would never be broken. It would grow until it had engulfed the world.

The windows of the great house were high and narrow even on the upper floors, where their presence was not a hazard to the strength of its walls. Its builders knew this, but they clung to stubborn uniformity in their design. Thus the openings were too small to pass the body of a man even were he able to reach them. It was no impediment to Kah-Sih-Omah, who simply dislocated joints and wiggled through. Harder would have been the ascent of the wall, above the busy and closely guarded plaza, but Kah-Sih-Omah had not taken that way. In the same manner as he now entered he had crept out a more sheltered opening and then on long, sinewy arms had swung hand over hand around the edge of the roof.

Fully half his body was through the opening by the time he could look down and search for handholds to aid his descent. He found little that would help except for a stone socket halfway to the floor.

It extended out from the wall, meant to hold a torch in place. There was no torch in it now, so Kah-Sih-Omah slipped limber fingers through and tested the strength of the socket. It did not yield. In a moment he was down.

There was little light in the room, so Kah-Sih-Omah adjusted his eyes for night vision. He gathered his body into its normal mass configuration and approached the sleeping woman.

She was young, hardly more than a child, with womanhood only a few winters upon her. She was the youngest daughter of the deposed lord. But she was not a small person as women went, and for this Kah-Sih-Omah was grateful. He would have trouble enough as it was, retaining the impersonation.

She did not sleep a normal sleep. She had succumbed to the will of the spirits of sleep. There were many kinds of these, and Kah-Sih-Omah could not determine by looking which the sungod's priests had given her. It did not matter greatly, so long as its spirit remained in her.

Kah-Sih-Omah had much work to do. He would labor long into the night. The deception must be as perfect as he could make it. Detection would be fatal—if not to himself, then to many disciples of the new god.

He looked around for a place to hide while he began the gross transformation. The room offered few choices. It was a large room with little in it except for the pile of cushions on which the woman lay and an alcove in one wall, the front of which was covered by a curtain.

He went to it and looked in, delighted to find that it was empty, and slipped quickly inside to begin the metamorphosis.

In this instance internal changes were far more important than external ones. Kah-Sih-Omah packed his body mass to a density half again normal simply to conform to requirements of size. To do this it was necessary to reduce the usual internal cavities to almost nothing, and he would therefore weigh a great deal more than his outside appearance would suggest. This was the greatest danger and his greatest fear, though he was hoping whoever carried him would be too excited and distracted to notice.

The body Kah-Sih-Omah built this night was the most complex he had ever worn, and the most survivable. He added special valves to the great vessels leading to his heart and lungs, then budded two more hearts, one of which he grew to size. He armored it in cartilege rings and concealed in his abdomen, equipping it with valves with which to shunt into the great abdominal blood vessels. The other remained a bud, but he attached it adjacent to the normal site so that it could rapidly be brought up to size and function if needed.

Kah-Sih-Omah had fortified himself with nutrients before he began his climb. He had spent much of the preceding day concentrating the biological fractions he knew his body needed and used. He had discovered the functions of many of these by experimentation, by simple trial and error, and though he did not always understand how they did what they did, he was reluctant to omit any of them. Most of these had been stored easily within the less dense male body he had started with. Now there seemed to be no room for them, or for the buds of other spare organs: a liver, a pair of kidneys, an extra lung; or for the packets of hormones, enzymes, blood fractions, and specialized cells that made up his rapid regeneration system.

He decided to cheat, enlarging the body slightly wherever he could—wherever it was not likely to be noticed. He made it slightly taller and bulkier, endowing the girl with fuller hips and breasts. The latter became storehouses for all the spare organs whose normal situs was within the thorax.

Before the night was half over Kah-Sih-Omah had completed his skeletal and internal changes, including the armoring of the most vital nerve trunks, without which even his body was helpless. Then he set to work on the cosmetic features, which took much longer to finish.

He was ready by the predawn. When the priests arrived to bathe and groom the victim and to dress her in the ceremonial white robe, it was the imposter they found in her place. The real woman was safely concealed in the alcove beneath a pile of cushions. The waxen, drugged features they saw in the light of their torch were convincing.

More priests entered the chamber and took charge of him. Kah-Sih-Omah was lifted to his feet, eyes still closed. They expected him to walk; therefore he concluded the drug they had employed permitted this, and he walked, stiffly but steadily, between two of them. Thankfully, the pace was slow, and he did not stumble. He hoped they would not notice that he peeked at them occasionally through half-closed eyelids.

They did not notice. After descending to the lowest level, they entered the living corridor of warriors which extended across the courtyard and up the wide steps.

A chant began as Kah-Sih-Omah appeared. Drums and cymbals accompanied it. This was to be a far different ceremony than had occurred the day before. The former had been an act of vengeance on the part of the conqueror. This was to be his obeisance to the sun; the sacrifice of this choice prize to gain the favor of the sun. A rival god could hardly ignore this challenge to take the prize away.

Ascent was synchronized as precisely as the priests could time it to the coming of sunlight. That was a part of the objective: to greet the sun with this feast the moment his face appeared. Already there was enough light to make the torchbearers superfluous. The faces of the crowd below could be distinguished one from another, and one kind from another.

The composition of the crowd was different, too, for this sacrifice. Fewer of the city's natives were present, more of the conqueror's people. It was clear that there would be less sympathy among these spectators but, stealing a look one last time before strong arms lifted him and placed him on the altar, Kah-Sih-Omah hoped there would be more fear.

Kah-Sih-Omah lay there face up, body resting in the hollow carved in the stone, unbound because of the drug. He had glimpsed the altar briefly as he approached it, noted that it had been washed and that the grooves in its sides were no longer filled with stinking, clotting blood. Still, the smell of death lingered like a pall in the quiet of dawn, when the chanting and the drums abruptly stopped.

Kah-Sih-Omah felt the chill of the stone slab. Since he did not believe it could make any difference now, he opened his eyes to see what the priests were doing, though he was careful not to move.

On each side of him stood a senior priest. The one on his left held an immense ceremonial knife fashioned of polished obsidian, honed to absolute perfection of sharpness, and embellished with a hilt of carved jade. The priest on his right held an axe of the same material, whose function would be to split the breastbone, should this be necessary to extricate the heart. Behind him, barely visible, were two junior priests whose task, Kah-Sih-Omah knew from the previous day, was to hold down struggling victims, then carry the bodies away.

He waited calmly, not from drugs as they thought, but due to his resolve, and with the absolute assurance that the spirit within him was greater by far than the mythical power of their god.

From somewhere above and behind a single voice rose in chant, in the language of the conqueror, and floated eerily down on the breath of the morning breeze. It reached the crowd below, where it echoed in the voices of those who watched and waited. The light began to grow, and between his feet Kah-Sih-Omah could see a glow on the rim of the far-off mountain. It was not yet day, but day was about to be born.

The chant rose. Kah-Sih-Omah, though he could not understand the words, could guess their meaning, an entreaty to the sun about to rise: foolish, flattering phrases, flowery words, appeasements no one could expect to deceive a true and wise god—words meant only to deceive worshippers who heard them. Kah-Sih-Omah's concept of the divine was entirely different. He conceived god as a spirit far man's superior in intellect, on whom man was totally dependent, not as a collection of capricious spirits that wily priests could manipulate, as they so easily manipulated men.

Then came the spark of sunlight. With it came the moment of absolute truth, when Kah-Sih-Omah's faith would be tested by the spirits within him. At that instant the will moved the body. The valves of Kah-Sih-Omah's heart slammed shut, though the heart continued to beat. All around it biological switches closed off the great nerves. All functions were shunted off to the new auxiliary system that Kah-Sih-Omah's body had built, one unsuspected and therefore safe from harm.

His eyes were open wide now, staring upward into the face of the figure that had swept from behind and entered his sphere of vision. This was a figure tall and sinister, face masked in the skin of the sun—bright, polished, flashing the light off points fashioned to resemble rays. Below it a robe glowed with threads of the same material, which bound the shafts of decorative feathers to the cloth. The image in Kah-Sih-Omah's eyes at the time the knife flashed down was that of an immense and evil bird of prey.

He felt the thrust of the knife as pressure, not as pain. The point penetrated deep into his chest, then slashed toward his head, ripping the cartilege of his breastbone as it went. Kah-Sih-Omah, though secure in the knowledge that he was essentially unharmed, vicariously shared the terror he knew must have overtaken the minds of all the other victims as they died. Through his mind rushed furious anger that men would do such things to other men, and resolve that his ordeal this day would end it.

An arm, its sleeve thrown back, thrust out. A hand—strong, with fingers flexed and probing—entered Kah-Sih-Omah's chest, seized his heart, and ripped it through the slash. With a practiced, flicking movement, the hand that held the knife severed its vessels. Blood spurted out in a fine mist. Caught by puffs of wind, it settled across the altar as the priest in the feathered robe held it high for the crowd to see and chanted to his god.

On the altar, Kah-Sih-Omah allowed his body to grow limp. Though his eyes remained open, they did not move, and he feigned death.

Arms grasped him, raising his limp form erect. From the gaping wound in his chest the pooling blood flowed out, staining the white robe.

They conveyed his body to a litter farther down the pyramid. His heart remained in the hands of the high priest, who continued to chant as he paraded around the altar four times before depositing his grisley prize on a tray, which he then carried down the pyramid and through a door in its side.

The task of the high priest was finished—or so the high priest thought. The remaining sacrifices would be the labor of others.

Warriors brought these now, ten at a time, not drugged but bound with strands of hemp rope, against which they struggled so violently that their arms bled. None could escape through these efforts. More than one of them would die, here on the altar of the sun, before Kah-Sih-Omah was finished with the work he had to do.

He could go no faster. The process took time, and perfection was the only acceptable result. He had begun the restoration even as his regular heart was severed, allowing only such bleeding to occur as was required for the plausibility of the drama. While his body was being raised off the altar, the heart bud was already migrating into regular position within his chest and the inner layers of tissue separated by the wound were beginning to close around it.

Simultaneously, the substances his body needed to regenerate the wounded area poured into his bloodstream. The armored heart in his abdomen vigorously pumped them toward the regeneration area. The chief delay was reconstruction of the tiny nerves and blood vessels in proximity to the incision. But already the new heart was functional and beating, in unison with the other heart below.

At this point Kah-Sih-Omah could switch the spare one off, though it remained an important part of his preparation for the next phase of his plan; and he kept it on standby status.

Ideally, regeneration should take place under calm, quiet circumstances, since concentration was an important part of the process. Kah-Sih-Omah held his concentration desperately, fully aware that the screams of one dying victim presaged, only by moments, the death of the next. He knew he could not save them all even if he acted prematurely, but he could not avoid unconsciously counting the victims who died while he was preparing himself. By the time the inner layers of the wound had bound themselves together he had counted one hand of fingers. By the time the outer skin had closed and he was removing surface scar tissue, the fingers of his other hand had been exhausted.

Kah-Sih-Omah knew that his resurrection must be dramatic, and that he must have the instantaneous attention of all the people in the crowd below as well as the priests at the altar above. He must take immediate and total command, and keep it until his task was finished. He braced himself erect against the stone step that bit into his back. And then, every muscle taut, he gave a mighty shout in the language of the People. He allowed but an instant for the startled watchers to focus on its source, then jerked his blood-stained body to its feet.

For an instant he stood motionless, gazing at the transfixed mass of bodies, all unmoving as if frozen in a single frame of time, faces contorted and awe-stricken. And he knew at once that he had not only succeeded, but succeeded beyond his wildest expectations.

There was utter silence as he stood there, blood-soaked white robe fluttering about him in the morning breeze—then a murmur as he turned, raising one arm upward, to point toward the altar, where a victim lay pinioned beneath the arrested knife-arm of a senior priest.

Again Kah-Sih-Omah shouted, this time in the language of the conqueror—"No!"

And then he moved to halt this arm of death. As he took his first step upward, the knife dropped from the hand of the priest and fell on his victim's chest. With this gesture, a murmur began to rise from the crowd.

Kah-Sih-Omah began to climb in earnest, moving steadily up the wide steps. Those in the crowd below had seen him carried down, chest a ruined mass—and seen him rise without a single blemish. Now those above would also see.

The victim bolted off the stone altar, scrambling to his feet despite his bonds, and wriggled past stupefied attendants who made no move to stop him. He stumbled down the steps between retreating warriors and toward Kah-Sih-Omah, who stopped and embraced him. The intentions of this miraculous personage were thus made known to the crowd. Behind him the low murmur of astonishment from the warriors and the priests grew into a roar of panic.

So riveting was the event that all around Kah-Sih-Omah seemed paralyzed. He could certainly understand why. What they were seeing was no unnatural that the mind revolted in shock. He had not only anticipated that this would occur, he had counted upon it, to enable him to gain control of this crowd.

The warriors who herded prisoners or whose mission had been to preserve order were not excepted from the effect. They stood motionless and indecisive, the same as all the rest, sword arms slack, weapons drooping toward the ground. Who, Kah-Sih-Omah reasoned, seeks to kill one they know is already dead? They have seen the woman die; seen her heart torn out, still beating, from her chest; seen it exhibited in the hands of the high priest and her bleeding body lying lifeless before their eyes.

Now they see her rise and walk, and cry out and point accusing fingers, and comfort a captive—and she is whole again, without so much as a blemish.

Kah-Sih-Omah moved toward the warrior nearest him and seized from his belt a stone dagger, and with it hacked away the ropes that bound his first disciple. And then he gestured to the others, and they came to him. One by one he embraced them and severed their bonds.

Then he turned again, still holding the knife in his hand, to look upward where the high priest now stood, having heard the tumult and climbed to the altar from the other side of the pyramid.

This was to be a confrontation—the only confrontation. Kah-Sih-Omah knew this. So did the high priest—and the crowd. As Kah-Sih-Omah had come to life, so now did the watchers. Some were still motionless, their attention directed to the pyramid, but others had begun to shuffle their way out of the throng.

Kah-Sih-Omah ignored all except the high priest, whom he now approached step by careful step, watching the contortions on the face of his murderer—a face he had not previously seen because it had been covered by a mask. He wanted to look deeply into the eyes and spirit of a man who could do what this one had done— wanted to understand what drove such men. That was all Kah-Sih-Omah really wanted then.

The high priest did not know this, but he knew that what he now saw was impossible; that there was, in fact, no such power to be derived from the rising sun; that it was an illusion, his creation and that of others like him. He would not yield control of his illusion, would not allow himself to be deceived by some clever substitution. He would concede nothing as Kah-Sih-Omah approached— except that he would surely be attacked.

Kah-Sih-Omah intended nothing of the sort. He had not known the high priest would be there; he had expected all the priests to flee. He wanted only to gain the summit, where he could begin the second change of form; one to be made more rapidly, more easily, because it was his own true form, which he could assume in only moments.

That was his intention.

The high priest stood his ground, a fact somewhat troubling to Kah-Sih-Omah, who did not mean to share the attention of the crowd with him, but did not know what to do to stop him.

Serendipity intervened—violently. The high priest waited until Kih-Sih-Omah was only a step or two away and then acted, bending down to the step, there to snatch up a javelin dropped by a retreating warrior. In the instant it took Kah-Sih-Omah to shunt in his abdominal heart the high priest thrust the javelin's head completely through Kah-Sih-Omah's chest.

A roar from the crowd peaked with the high priest's thrust. When Kah-Sih-Omah did not fall, there came a hush so stark that heartbeats might be heard.

With the silence a wave washed over the high priest's face. He stared at Kah-Sih-Omah with bugging eyes. He had fallen deeply into the illusion—he was transfixed, his muscles frozen as fast as his face had been.

On the pinnacle, only Kah-Sih-Omah now moved. He seized the shaft of the javelin in both hands, bracing its butt against the bloody altarstone. Effortlessly, he eased forward, pushing it through his body, then reached back, gripped it tightly, and drew it out.

Kah-Sih-Omah held the javelin high. His eyes searched the small crowd still on the pyramid until he found a warrior who had not fled. To him Kah-Sih-Omah tossed the bloody javelin—then pointed at the high priest. He had had enough of this evil man.

The warrior was a test of Kah-Sih-Omah's power—a critique of this miracle. His next act would constitute the only real proof. "Kill him!" Kah-Sih-Omah shouted, in his own masculine voice and the tongue of his murdered lord. He pointed at the devil in the feathered robe. An instant later, the robe was stained with the evil blood, and the priest sank sprawling across the stone altar.

Now Kah-Sih-Omah was ready to finish his transformation and resume the form he had so long abandoned, so that the People would know him and feel comfortable with him; so that they would follow him when he left this place; and so that all who might try to stop them would know that he was their shaman, whom the spirits had touched and favored.

He gestured to the warrior who had killed the high priest—now waiting behind him, the javelin still firmly clenched in his hand—and said in the language of the city, "Go to the great house, to the room from which the priests took me. Find she who looks like me, and bring her here."

Then, ignoring the startled expression that spread across the warrior's face, he rushed the man off with another gesture, and sprang up to the top of the altar. He tore off the bloody robe, and gestured to all to gather near to watch the transformation.

The people approached him cautiously; reverently. They feared him, yet they also feared to disobey. Only those among them who had been captive huddled close. Kah-Sih-Omah looked down at these and searched their faces. He wanted to know their thoughts not through words uttered at a later time, but from their expressions, recorded on his memory as the People experienced them. He wanted, as every shaman does, a gauge of the potency of his magic.

There was a face in the crowd he recognized, though

it had grown and changed, and the body which carried it was taller, fuller, and more muscular in the coming of manhood than it had been when Toh-Pan-Gah was a child.

This face Kah-Sih-Omah watched especially closely as he began, because in its impressionable youth he saw the hope not only of his People, but of all people. It did no harm that, though the relationship was distant, he was of Kah-Sih-Omah's own blood, perhaps the last of that blood.

The form of the woman left him, subtly at first. Kah-Sih-Omah's bones grew, forming a frame on which the condensed tissue could expand to its true density. Where the softness of woman had been, muscle now rose in powerful bands across his chest and shoulders, trailing into arms still outthrust toward the people. He stood, a man in the making from the remains of a woman twice-slain, a symbol of the power that grew from adversity and prevailed over it.

All the while Kah-Sih-Omah watched, and his watching was rewarded. Awe, fear, hope—all of these were there—he was their focus—he must always be their focus, and that focus must always be as powerful as it was at this instant.

But would it be? Kah-Sih-Omah was unsure. For the People, perhaps the answer was yes. He intended to remain with the People, always. But what of these others, whom he would leave? They especially must remember him, because they had already once fallen below the level of man's true spirit.

He therefore considered. Few had known him as he had been; most knew only of him, through exaggerated fables circulated since they had been in the city. Those who had really known him largely had passed, their words of him grown dim in the minds of those they had begotten because the appearance of the shaman had been ordinary. That was easily changed.

Kah-Sih-Omah began. Black hair detached from his scalp and tumbled around his feet. In its place a pale fringe began to erupt.

At transformation's end, a memorable man stood atop the pyramid of death, alive and vital, gazing down at the people.

He was pale; as pale as the light of the predawn sun.
His hair and beard were as spun sunlight, and wreathed
his head as the sun's rays wreathed the face of the sun.
The beard was a nice touch, he thought. He had made it
thicker than common, even among these hairy men of
the land of summer. The People were less hairy, and
customarily plucked the whiskers out as soon as they
appeared; thus his facial hair would impress them even
more. Kah-Sih-Omah was pleased.

He looked down at the crowd, hoping to see signs that
they were also pleased. Though he had seen some rushing away when his transformation was beginning, there
appeared to be even more people watching now. He
took careful notice of who they were.

There were, he could see, many former captives, now
unbound, but mostly cluttered together. Oddly, few warriors had left; most had stayed, and so had some of the
minor priests, who before had mingled with the crowd.
The largest segment of the increase was made up of the
People, who now pressed at the forefront of the crowd.
He could see why. Seh-Kho-Tan, the daughter of Ruhu-
Doh-Sah, was there—she who was perhaps his last surviving friend and confident had brought them. And
Seh-Kho-Tan knew who this was atop the pinnacle. She
had seen transformations occur before and knew the
purpose of them and the man beneath them.

Comforted by the sight of this solid face from his
past, Kah-Sih-Omah raised his arms again, signaling
for silence among the People, who had taken up a low
chanting of his name. His people stopped, but others
took up the words. They thought the People were making obeisance to Kah-Sih-Omah as they did to the sun
god. They did for Kah-Sih-Omah what they would do
for the sun.

With growing horror Kah-Sih-Omah realized he might
have taken the transformation farther than he should
have—that perhaps he had created an erroneous impression, one that he must quickly eradicate. He shouted
angrily.

He knew not all in the crowd could hear him or understand his words, though he spoke in a voice filled with
power. "I am not the god of the sun, or any god at all. I

am Kah-Sih-Omah, He-Who-Waits, shaman of the People, messenger of the spirits who made me and gave me the powers you have seen.

"I come with the words the spirits have for men. They are angered by what you have done—there is no god who demands this, or wants this, and you must not do it. I come to show you the way the spirits wish men to live."

Even as Kah-Sih-Omah spoke the last of his words a new murmur rose from the crowd. He did not wish to appear startled, but he was curious enough to look around. When he saw the girl stumbling up to the pinnacle on unsteady feet, he breathed a sigh of relief. He had forgotten that he had sent for her.

Though she did not understand what was happening, still recovering from the drug, Kah-Sih-Omah added the event to his program. He could see now how wise he had been to summon her.

He gestured to the warrior to walk with her down the remaining steps and out into the crowd. There, curious women opened her robe, examining her body for wounds or the signs of wounds—and finding none, renewed their chant of Kah-Sih-Omah's name.

Kah-Sih-Omah had a few moments of respite to concentrate on his next actions. He knew that he had perhaps at last begun to fulfill the spirits' will. He wondered if now he must really die, as he would have naturally long ago had they not intervened. And he wondered what would happen to the People, still captive here in this strange land far from the home of their ancestors and still with few capable hunters among their tiny group.

He found reassurance within his own thoughts. He knew with certainty that, unlike the deities conjured up by men, the real gods were not cruel. Never, Kah-Sih-Omah reflected, had the spirits been truly unkind to him, though he had often thought so because he did not understand.

Nor, he began to believe and hope, would they be so unkind now. Instinctively, Kah-Sih-Omah knew that his task was not finished. It had only just begun.

He-Who-Waits waited, and changed. Gone was the form of the man, the lithely muscled body he had worn for the space of a generation, while he roamed and taught others what the spirits had taught him. But, while he was the beloved shaman of many, his ageless body threatened him with that which he abhorred the most—false godhood.

He approached his present course with much reservation, wishing fervently that there were some other way. He knew there wasn't, though he might at any time have simply melted into the crowds of the city in another form and with another face.

He couldn't. Simple disappearance would not accomplish what he must accomplish. Were he to vanish, sooner or later the People would make him into images as they had done before with gods—though he had always forbidden them to do so, taught them otherwise and banished from their graven art the images of the old gods of the sun and moon, those bloodthirsty gods he had fought so long and hard.

He-Who-Waits sat, perched on the sunward precipice of his sacred mountain. It was the place where those who waited below would last have seen him, where he wanted them to think that Kah-Sih-Omah had died.

There is nothing so final as death. To a whole people there is no memory so vivid as the passing of a god. This was Kah-Sih-Omah's purpose here, his body contorted into freakishly long thin, hollow bones and leathery flaps of tough, dark skin.

He had come here when the day was new, accompanied by many hands of his disciples, all skilled shaman of a new class schooled in his teachings. Among them were several bright young men of the People, including the sons of Toh-Pan-Gah, who had grown old in Kah-Sih-Omah's service and passed this last season. These few he especially cherished, for they were of his blood.

He did not allow this inner favoritism to show. It was a flaw in him that others must never see. He permitted it in himself only because it could be concealed. Such was not the doctrine he taught as the spirit seemed to be teaching him—that there is no essential difference between men, despite what men think. They are all the same.

He-Who-Waits looked out to the horizon, so dark since the sun had set in the west. It was not so dark now.

Light began to appear—cool light from she who had shown Kah-Sih-Omah the way to the spirits.

Kah-Sih-Omah wondered if at this moment she was also rising at the sacred mountain where his new life had begun. He resolved, if the spirits permitted, to some-day go and see. Perhaps the descendants of the People would be there. They could go, if they wished, whenever they wished. The People were free.

But for Kah-Sih-Omah there was no hurry. He had time enough—more than enough, to judge from his continued vitality. More than any man had ever had before, with no sign that it might ever end. As far as he could tell, he had aged not a day. He was as sound of wind and limb as the day the spirits created him.

Our Mother Moon burst out between two mountain tops, full and fat and bright, and beckoned to Kah-Sih-Omah.

He-Who-Waits waited but an instant more. There was time for one more thought before he passed, a pleasant thought and one immensely satisfying—that at last he had found and understood the spirits' purpose and fulfilled it. It was to bring order, to bring peace. He, Kah-Sih-Omah, had done this—by his words, by his example, without a single moment of pain to any man, without a single death—because he *was*, and because other men could see he *was*, through the power of the spirits.

But would it last, after he was gone? Kah-Sih-Omah did not know. Only the spirits knew. As they had tested him, so did Kah-Sih-Omah test man and challenge him to ferret out the purpose of his existence, as he believed at last he understood his own.

He-Who-Waits rose on spindly feet, extending fragile leathery wings to gather up the wind. Then he leapt into empty space, plunging downward until the air was stong enough to lift him.

He turned, face into the wind, eyes fixed upon Our Mother Moon, and sped silently across the breadth of the valley, sinking slowly but steadily, trading altitude for lift and speed.

She twinkled at him as he watched, rippled much as she had when he had last taken the cup. But it was not the spirit of the mushroom playing tricks, but his own emotions showing through his reason, that brought him to tears.

He looked down to the base of the mountain, where around their fires his followers huddled against the coolness of the night, faithful to their promise to keep his vigil and watch for his sign until it came to them.

Even as the lights of the fires dwindled into pinpoints it was time for Kah-Sih-Omah to turn.

He heeled into the wind and spread his wings to their fullest, maintaining trim with subtle movements of the muscles at their tips. Carefully judging his speed, he slowed himself so that his image would drift lazily across the brightness of the moon. This was their sign—*he* was their sign: the giant bird of night unknown in nature.

On this night a new legend would be born—the legend of Kah-Sih-Omah's passing. Storytellers of the future would recite it, perhaps with much embellishment, probably without complete accuracy. There was no harm in that so long as this symbol helped preserve the words of his promise—to come again, as man's champion, in time of peril and need.

Those on the ground below did see the final flourish of the sign, and would remember, for a time.

Kah-Sih-Omah would remember always, as he wandered unrecognized, across the length and breadth of the universe, the loneliest creature in it, waiting for its end. That too was his destiny.

He made his landfall quietly, settling on the grassy plain with silent majesty, all wasted on the dull-eyed beasts who watched for a brief time and then went on, as beasts will, about the business of life.

There emerged from this savannah, with the dawn, a nondescript man who trudged his way toward the hinterland, who never once looked back.

Glimpses of the Dawning

Kah-Sih-Omah stepped lightly from rock to rock, placing his feet carefully on each slippery surface, testing its ability to bear his weight before committing to the next step.

The stream was wide at this point, though shallow enough that the punishment for a misstep was merely a soppy moccasin. Still, the season was well into autumn, and the water would be cold. He preferred dry feet.

Halfway across the stream he stopped and looked around. On both banks, the turning leaves of the beech trees rustled lightly in the wind. Beneath him the brook barely murmured. He listened for other forest sounds; heard none. He was disturbed. Silence in these woods meant danger.

Kah-Sih-Omah paused long enough only to search the trees on the far bank, to insure that within them lurked no immediately dangerous foe: no bear, moose or cougar. Then he continued, moving in the same careful way until he stepped from the last stone onto the mud and gravel bank.

He saw it—the footprint of a man, already half filled with seeping water; only one, all others having fallen on firmer ground where the signs would be more subtle.

Doubly cautious now he bent to examine it closely, touching its edges, rubbing the mud between thumb and forefinger to see how far drying had progressed. The track was very new—its maker had passed this way only heartbeats ago.

Other signs he read revealed this was a big man, heavy, feet shod but not in moccasins. He examined the toe of the track, which was not in water; found the marks of the tiny nails the strangers used to hold the thick soles to their sandals.

So, they were about: one of them, at least. He had never seen the strangers, though he had met other men who had. They were very big and very hairy, and were fierce, with good weapons, and therefore very dangerous to stalk, as he stalked this one now.

Kah-Sih-Omah had no evil purpose in this. He wished simply to meet them, and learn of them, and learn from them. He had come upon their tracks before, but always they were very old ones. He had followed the rumor of their presence for many moons, journeying from his accustomed haunts in the south to these cold lands of the far north, for that sole purpose.

Kah-Sih-Omah finished his examination and moved onward, searching for other signs. He found one: some drops of blood, fallen on a drying leaf, splattered in a pattern which indicated the distance dropped had been almost the height of a man. There was not much of it, and Kah-Sih-Omah did not think it was the blood of the stranger. More likely, it had come from game the stranger had killed.

He went on. A little farther up the trail he found more signs, which confirmed this: two more distinct tracks and a gout of fur, stuck in the crevice of a low branch. He immediately revised his estimate of the man's weight, assuming it to be less, now that he knew his quarry was burdened with the carcass of a deer.

Armed with this knowledge he could hurry. He knew now that there was little danger of discovery, and that he followed only one man. He knew that the strangers generally lacked the skills he had at woodmanship and that this one would be unlikely to notice him if he were reasonably careful.

The trail followed the creekbed, which showed evidence that it was sometimes much larger than now;

that in the spring, when the snow on the low mountains melted, it became a torrent, sweeping rocks and debris along to scour its banks clean of vegetation. Kah-Sih-Omah saw nothing growing which had not sprung up in the current summer, and no beaver dams. The beavers were a practical sort, and avoided such violent streams.

The spoor grew ever fresher. Sooner or later he would see the man, and then he would have to make a choice of where to confront him. He knew from talking to others that it would be, in every respect, a confrontation. The strangers spoke no known language, and were reputedly very quick-tempered. Moreover, a single individual would likely be more belligerent than a group, which could find comfort in its numbers.

There was a curve in the stream, which took it off to the right, and on that side the bank was not only higher than the other but heavily overgrown with trees and brush. The curving of the stream around this had caused brush to accumulate during floods, and because of this the stranger had been forced to walk in the water in order to get around it. Kah-Sih-Omah would have to do the same, else cross over the pile; something that would make more noise than he wanted.

He gathered his resolution behind him, prepared to step into the water and endure the misery of wet feet, when he heard the scream. The scream was bloodcurdling, though it sounded more of rage than of terror. Kah-Sih-Omah ducked nearer to the brushpile. And he saw something moving beneath one of the logs.

Immediately he pieced the scenario together, that which he could see and that which he could deduce—and he knew what trouble the stranger faced, even before he heard the growls of the mother bear whose cubs lay hidden in the brushpile.

And it was then that Kah-Sih-Omah's bow rose in his left hand and his right reached over his shoulder to draw an arrow from the quiver. In an instant this was notched, and he trotted through the water and around the bend of the stream.

There he saw a sight unusual in the extreme—not one bear, but two, both intent on taking the same prey.

The stranger was fighting both of them at once with a

great two-handed sword, too close to them to use his own bow. At his feet lay the carcass of a doe, the object of the male bear's avarice. Before the stranger was the female. He had already cut a deep gash in her flank and was preparing to address his next thrust at the male, who was behind him.

Kah-Sih-Omah could see where help was needed, and he shot his arrow through the male's throat. Before the first arrow had struck he had the second notched, ready to impale the female.

She struck too fast for him, and when the stranger turned he stumbled over the carcass of the deer. The female was on him almost before he struck the ground.

Kah-Sih-Omah's second arrow buried itself in her back, but she seemed hardly to notice. His third penetrated deeper, apparently striking her heart. She gave a mighty growl and collapsed across the body of the stranger.

Kah-Sih-Omah notched and shot another arrow into the male, who still moved feebly—then rushed forward to see what he might do for the man.

It was apparent at once the man was doomed, his throat crushed by a blow from the bear's paw. He could only gurgle and spit blood. He was beyond help.

Kah-Sih-Omah rolled the body of the bear off the man and spread him out as comfortably as he could for those last moments. There were not many of them. Mercifully, he died quickly, leaving Kah-Sih-Omah all alone to contemplate death's massive visitation upon this otherwise beautiful glade.

Kah-Sih-Omah stooped and studied the stranger, noting the vast difference between him and all the other men he knew. The stranger was taller and rangier, though about as heavy as he. His skin was pale, slightly mottled with many small dots of color on the face and neck, the first freckles Kah-Sih-Omah had ever seen. A thong bound a patch of leather across the man's left eye. Beneath it the socket was drawn and sunken, the eyelid heavily scarred.

Most striking was the stranger's hairiness. He had, in addition to a full reddish beard, a great deal of hair on his limbs and chest. To Kah-Sih-Omah this was remarkable, though less so than the stark absence of hair on the crown of the man's head, revealed when his head gear tumbled off. Among all men that Kah-Sih-Omah had met, baldness was artificial, not natural.

But he had seen another head like this, long ago, near the southern end of the continent, where the two great seas he knew approached each other closely. That man had been smaller and older, but he also had come from the east, washed ashore in a skin-covered boat, racked with fever and hovering near death.

It had been Kah-Sih-Omah's great tragedy that neither of these pale men had lived more than moments after he chanced upon them. The first had died raving in delirium, waving a small shining fetish in Kah-Sih-Omah's face. Kah-Sih-Omah still had it tucked in his medicine bundle, a lump of the sun's sweat beaten into four lobes. Curious, he opened his fallen companion's tunic and looked. Perhaps these two had been countrymen.

But the dead man's chest contained nothing but hair-covered scars of many old, healed wounds.

Kah-Sih-Omah retrieved his arrows from the bodies of the dead bears and took a careful look around. He found no other spoor. No other strangers had lately passed nearby. A great sadness filled him. No one but he would ever know what happened to this man, or how it was he died here, unless Kah-Sih-Omah now searched out the man's companions. He knew there must be a camp somewhere nearby, otherwise the man would have cached the deer and gone for help to take it back. Big as he was, even he could not have carried it very far.

Contact had been Kah-Sih-Omah's objective. But the effort could become very complicated, and he would now have to be doubly wary. He had counted on making friends with the dead man and establishing the rudiments of communication before approaching any others. Now he had no idea how his overtures would be received, or how he might tell anyone what had happened.

He pondered long and hard before it occurred to him there might yet be a way. It was a method he had never before dared try, because it promised to be both risky and distasteful—a mental congress with the corpse.

On occasion in the past he had done this with the living, sparingly to be sure, as it was dangerous to the hosts. There had been accidents. Still, where was the danger to a man already dead? He was confident he could protect himself, and what he knew of the nature of the nervous system suggested that for a time after death the cells in it could still function, if given the proper stimulus, and provided the wait was not too long.

He made up his mind to attempt it. Here was an opportunity, possibly unique, to satisfy his curiosity and answer the questions about this new type of man. Resolved, he made ready, swiftly dragging the body to a place of concealment and safety. It would not do to be surprised by some other predator while in this relatively helpless state.

A hollow beneath the bole of a fallen tree, exposed only on one side and the entrance blocked by the body, satisfied this requirement. Then, with a tendril of his own substance, he penetrated the corpse's neck, entering through the opening at the bottom of the skull and tapping into the brain stem.

A violent twitching of the body followed, as his own life forces activated the body's reflexes. Quickly he insulated his probe, to keep the drain as low as possible while passing through the prebrain. He did not want the distraction that the reception of his host's sensations might provoke—not now. He would take these, of course, and examine them later, at his leisure. For now, he simply mapped the route and sent his probe following its course to the great trunks farther up.

At last he reached the seat of memory in the stranger's temples, and carefully activated a small part of it. He did so sparingly, since his own system now powered the cells and the energy costs were enormous. With live subjects this did not happen; with them he merely directed, and did not drive.

A short period of experimentation revealed that the cells lost vigor after discharging a couple of times, then began to die. Kah-Sih-Omah realized that his time would be extremely limited. He must find out all he could in the next effort.

He peeled the corpse's memories, most recent first, from layer after layer of the cortex. The first of these were of the trauma of death, and nearly overwhelmed him. Essentially immortal himself, he was much intrigued by the phenomenon of death. For an instant he was torn between temptations—one to retreat, the other to explore. Through sheer strength of will he chose the former, though he carefully implanted those memories for future study. He could not spare time to contemplate them now—he needed the dead man's language.

The language was deep, having been learned, as most are, when his host was a child. Getting at it was an extremely onorous effort. Kah-Sih-Omah was deluged with sensations which he did not understand, but in which his host's vocabulary lay buried. He finished with the kernel of the dead man's persona, but that was all he got. The rest of the sensorium was imperfect. He did not then understand why this should be, since the recent visual memories were so stark and so complete. He did not discover the true reason until he was withdrawing. Then, when his probe passed through the great trunks of the cerebellum and entered the auditory area, he realized what was wrong. This man—Amundsen—had had a congenital hearing defect.

Suddenly it was over. Though extremely fatigued, and disoriented by the division of his own sensorium between two separate, distinct sets of memories, sensory and motor systems, and emotions, he now partially understood the hairy men.

Kah-Sih-Omah then rested, gathering his strength, and tried to decide what to do next. His choices were not easy. The question now was not how to tell the man's family and companions what had happened to him, but whether to tell them at all.

On one side of the argument rested the fulfillment of Kah-Sih-Omah's own quest, a fulfillment already millenmia overdue. On the other was the right of one who had passed to have his passing mourned. In the end, he yielded to his own self-interest. His quest had been such a long one.

He had known for many thousand years that the world was immensely large, that beyond the seas were other continental masses where men of different cultures lived.

But though he had yearned to visit these places, they had been beyond reach. His one attempt, long ago, had been an abysmal failure, convincing him that the distances were simply too vast for men to traverse. He had believed the passage of the man in the skin boat had been a rare accident, the fault of one of the great storms that sometimes raged at sea.

Then had come stories that changed this. These hairy strangers—he groped for the word in the new language—these *Norse*, did what he had for so long regarded as impossible: crossed and recrossed the seas at will.

To reassure himself on this point, Kah-Sih-Omah took the time to search through the memories he had just acquired, and visualized the knorr.

And he then knew what it was he must do. He must pursue a third alternative. He regarded it as somewhat more than incidental that in that course lay ease for an aching conscience.

The wind changed. It had all day blown from the sea, which was warm. Now it blew off the land, from the north and west, and was cold. Helga, wife of Lars Amundsen, saw in this an omen of worse to come, as the sun retreated farther to the south and deep snows followed. This land was harsh enough already, and would be harsher yet when winter came.

As it rose, the wind began to whistle and find its way through chinks in the upper walls, where the unmortared joints between the stones were not flanked by earth. At times it raised the thatch, thick though this was and weighted by rough-hewn planks and stones as heavy as Lars could lift. Helga could only hope that when the snow fell its drifts would seal that. Meanwhile, she would continue to stuff the chinks with mud and dried moss, and huddle around the little hearth built into the back wall.

She paced the one small room, treading softly on the dirt floor, lest she waken her sleeping twins, only a summer old, born the day the wild men burned the knorr and killed Thorwald the Fat, who owned it.

She found a chink, and carefully tore off a portion of her dwindling supply of moss. She would have to find more soon, but it was much in demand and growing scarce near the camp. Mud this evil place possessed in great abundance. It caked everything that touched it. Half their meager harvest of grain had been devoured by it while yet in the fields.

Helga turned, holding her hand high and running it along the wall to feel for more breaches. She found too many to stuff with what material she had left. Reluctantly, she abandoned the task for the moment and turned her attention to the hearth, where a pot of porridge still bubbled weakly, though it was out of the flames. It had been ready to eat long ago, but Lars had not yet returned.

Helga cleaned her hands as best she could and sat down to rest on the rough bed. Hans, the boy twin, stirred briefly but did not open his eyes. His sister, Heidi, continued to slumber peacefully. Helga breathed a sigh of relief. She was in no mood for nursing.

A sound outside caught her attention, and she rose carefully to go to the door. It was not a proper door, and worked with difficulty. Having no iron to spare for hinges Lars had built it in a rude track, so that it must be slid open. It made a great deal of noise in the process, and Lars had no appreciation of what that did to the children. He could not hear it, or them.

She opened it herself and looked out. He was there. He had a deer. Her hopes rose a little at the sight. At least this land occasionally provided meat, and the hunter was entitled to keep half of what he killed.

Lars had not noticed her—would not until he turned and saw her. Now his back was to the door, and he had the deer hung, ready to skin.

She stepped out, careful to avoid the muddiest spots, and walked around to look at the deer. She had not expected Lars to do more than scowl at her. This was his customary greeting.

Lars spoke her name! Spoke it clearly and recognizeably, then gazed stupidly at her as though this were an everyday occurance.

It wasn't. He had never before managed more than a garbled croak, communicating mostly through gestures. She stood there with her mouth hanging open in amazement.

His next reaction was a smile—something else he did but rarely, usually only when full of ale, but Helga knew there was not a drop of strong drink left in the entire camp.

Lars turned his attention back to the deer. With deft strokes of his knife he prepared it for flaying, then expertly jerked the pelt off and spread it across a nearby pole.

Next, he labored a moment and detached a haunch, which he held out to her. Bloody though it was, she took it and retreated into the hut, still dumbfounded, still mute.

He joined her inside a little while later, to erect the spit for smoking the meat, and that was when she spoke to him, for the first time ever with any expectation he might be able to hear her. She uttered his name while his back was toward her. She was shocked wide-eyed when he acknowledged.

"You heard me?"

"I heard you."

The voice fell strangely on Helga's ears. She felt suddenly lightheaded.

"But how—you have never been able to hear any but the loudest sounds. . . ."

Kah-Sih-Omah watched hands, because the movements of hands often said more than the tongue did. He watched Helga's hands creep down her bodice and grasp the thong that hung between her breasts. These rose, bearing the mate of the small fetish he had in his medicine bag. And he knew she thought she understood.

She said nothing more about it, but took a rag and used it to lift the pot from the fire. She carried this to the low shelf on the other side of the room.

He finished skewering the meat and walked up behind her, to stand and watch her with the ladle, dipping out porridge into two wooden bowls. A long battle with his conscience began—whether to speak the truth, perhaps to break a heart already heavily burdened with misery, or by silence let an unspoken lie live. He never got the chance to decide. She took that from him.

Later, searching carefully through the purloined memories, he was stricken by her courage in doing what she did then. She had turned to throw her arms around his neck and hug him.

Helga had not been happy as wife to Lars, though she had reconciled to it. She had not been a willing bride. She had been taken, and the consummation of the marriage had been an act of rape, though in the custom of the Northmen it was lawful. Helga was his by wager with her father, and which her father lost to Lars. Yet, strange as these circumstances were, Kah-Sih-Omah realized something had eventually grown of it—something that made these already awesome people more awesome still. He met the embrace with silence and shared it with Lars, to whom he would become indebted ever more deeply as time passed.

When at last she let him go, wiping away a tear with one hand while she handed him a bowl with the other, he knew he could never tell her. It would have been too cruel.

The rest of the settlement took the news with no less astonishment, though none believed as Helga did: that it was the work of the meek god whose fetish she now wore in full sight of all.

They preferred the old familiar lore and ancient myth, the deeds of their humanistic gods. To them it was Odin's reward, his admiration for Lars' conquest of the bear. Never wasteful of such resources, and less so under circumstance so severe as these, the Norse retrieved the bears, roasted and ate them. And though there was no mead, or ale, or even beer to wash down the greasy fare, and no great hall in which to feast, the spirit of the Viking rose and rejoiced with Lars.

Lars was new. It was as though his unhappy and quarrelsome spirit left him along with his affliction.

Kah-Sih-Omah, now Lars in fact and thinking as well as form, now found himself in a position that the old

Lars could never have achieved. He had somehow emerged the leader of this handful of hands of determined Viking souls.

Somehow, no one knew how, he made peace with the wild men. He talked to them, and now they traded with the Vikings: food for the Northmen's iron. But there was now little left of what the Northmen had brought, and though the smith had searched for ore none had been found. One day there would be no iron left except in the blood of the Vikings, and trade would all but cease.

Kah-Sih-Omah knew they could not survive without it—not unless they followed his counsel and lived as the Indians did: abandoning agriculture, for which the land was unfit, and becoming hunters and fishermen.

The Vikings would not do this. They were stubborn. They believed that someday others would come, bringing ships to take them home again—that they must stay where they could be found, instead of going inland where the game was more plentiful.

Though Lars had not been a particularly intellectual person, he had kept himself informed about things. Through his memories Kah-Sih-Omah knew that the Vikings had all but abandoned any plans for further settlement of Vinland, as they called this land. A century of failure was enough for most of them. The distance was simply too great to sustain colonies, and transport too uncertain and too hard. He was also aware that Thorwald's knorr had been blown far off course, that he hadn't landed where people at home thought he would.

Therefore, he reasoned, no one would come—or if they came, would look in the wrong place for survivors of Thorwald's colony. He discouraged as much as he could the ideas advanced by some to trek up the coast on foot and search for other colonies. He did not believe there were any.

There came a time, however, when he could tell his arguments were losing their force—that people wanted so badly to go home that they were seeing salvation in shadow. He had to offer something.

"We will build a knorr," he told the people, who had assembled in council.

"How? There are no shipwrights among us. We have no iron left for fittings."

The voice was that of the smith. Kah-Sih-Omah could understand and sympathize with him. The need for his skills was vanishing with the iron.

But Kah-Sih-Omah could claim experience none of the others had. He knew that ships might be built without iron, or any metal whatsoever. He himself had done this.

So he told the smith, "Make us the tools. We will build the knorr."

They did not build a knorr, or anything like a knorr. They built instead a large-sized copy of the fishing boats used by the fishermen who lived along the isthmus far to the south. Kah-Sih-Omah himself could not have conceived their result before it emerged. The idea of a planked vessel had simply not occurred to him until he was able to draw on Lars's memories.

The resulting effort was clumsy, but proved fairly seaworthy. It had a keel and could make way against wind and current. It was not a knorr but it was the best they could do.

They built it in autumn, and during that part of winter which was warm enough for men to work. In the spring they loaded up and sailed north up the coast, to the place where great fogs covered the sea.

Signs of the Northmen were found along the way, the remnants of small villages where people like them had once lived. But according to the Indians, ships had come long ago and taken the people away.

There was a choice to be made then, with the short summer in flight. Either they must sail south again or move an untried ship out into open sea. By his own lights, Kah-Sih-Omah would have chosen to coast south, because he knew of no way to travel through the fog. But the smith had an iron fish, which he hung on a thong above the helmsman's stool, whose tail pointed always to the south. With this direction known, Lars's memories told him, they could find first Greenland, then Iceland.

Many tense days followed. At first the water was cold and covered by a perpetual dense fog. Then, suddenly, though the fog got even denser, the water was warm, and they could discard the heavy furs they had been wearing. At length breaches appeared in the fog, so that the sun could aid in navigation as well as warm the people, and at night as occasional star showed through.

The Northmen had great skill in the use of the stars. Before the iron fishes appeared they nevertheless sailed wherever they would. They had done so for centuries, and penetrated throughout all the lands of the earth—or so they thought. Only Kah-Sih-Omah knew differently for certain. Nevertheless, he was very much impressed with what they had done. They were a remarkably audacious people, and despite the fact that many of their customs seemed crude and cruel to him, he truly admired them.

Fishing vessels began to appear. Some of these stayed at sea continuously for many, many days, and their crews knew with seemingly absolute accuracy where they were at any given time. Those aboard the makeshift knorr were ridiculed at first, before their circumstances became known, though afterwards, people spoke of their adventure with admiration in their voices. It had been no mean feat of navigation.

Escorts took them to a town called Reykjavik, where many of them, including Helga, had kinsmen. Though Kah-Sih-Omah, used to warmer, sunnier climates, at first found it bleak and rainy he decided he could endure it because he liked the people and found their culture fascinating. He had been in larger cities many times before, but never in one with such versatility of crafts. The Northmen's use of iron implements he found particularly interesting. This seemed to make all the difference in the world to a culture, turning men's passions outward against the earth itself, instead of one another.

Arriving as they had, on the wings of misfortune, the survivors of Thorwald's ill-fated colony at first had little but what the townsmen gave them. But there was the vessel they came in, and there were fish in the sea, and they used these things to turn misfortune into substantial success. They could stay out far longer and they could carry more; so, in time, the venture prospered.

Lars/Kah-Sih-Omah did not own it all himself, but as the leader he had the leader's share. He used his newfound wealth to make Helga and the children as comfortable as he could, though Helga seemed to want little more than a liveable house and his own company.

Kah-Sih-Omah soon realized he could not simply bolt away from this, though he longed to continue onward, across this northern sea, and explore Europe, of which he heard much of interest.

Friends also counseled him to seek adventure. Europe, they said, was in foment. Throughout its rich countryside booty abounded, there for the taking—and the taking was easy, particularly along the coasts. Together, they told him, they had gold enough to get a ship, and the strength of their arms to get more gold still. Warriors would flock to them on the promise of a share.

Kah-Sih-Omah never managed to understand this lust for the yellow metal. He valued the iron more. Gold had its uses, but too often spoiled the men who touched it.

He did not discourage the others who wanted to go. He himself would wait; live out this life for Lars, watch his children grow and Helga's beauty fade. When she was gone there would be time enough, and he would still be here.

Years passed. Kah-Sih-Omah did not repeat his error of former lives, but tinged his sparse hair and luxurient beard with white, wrinkled his skin, and limped along like other old men whose youthful wounds, once badges of pride, now visited pain upon their bearers.

In the great halls along the waterfront a new saga was heard, sung of Hans, Lars's son, who sailed away one day intent on taking England from the young Danish king—and who very nearly had. Kah-Sih-Omah/Lars had grandchildren now, and roots, and a rusty sword that long had hung unused on the pegs above his hearth. For a time this room was all the world there was.

A ship touched the port, bringing new sagas of deeds of daring and valor from sunny lands of sand and black men, called Africa, and gold and strange fabrics and scrolls of curious writing.

Kah-Sih-Omah/Lars listened to these tales as often as he could, hobbling over cobblestone streets to the great hall as many nights as Helga would allow. And there in the light of the logs that blazed in a hearth as long as many ships, while rivers of ale flowed on every side, he drank the singer's wondrous words instead.

Thus, without traversing the gulf that lay between, he learned of many great nations and many kinds of men, and of their contentions with one another. Beneath all these lay greed and gold, which seemed the force that drove them. Ahead, like harbingers, like shields, rode banners justifying all, signifying ideals shouted from the throats of men while they butchered other men. Man seemed by nature always eager to die for ideas, provided only these were not quite clear to him.

Kah-Sih-Omah found in that thought a seed of his own future. He had not previously been well acquainted with Helga's religious beliefs. She was not very vocal about them, and at the time few others in the community shared them. But that was changing. There were more Christians now, and they had built a small temple where they went to worship one of the same gods of which the new saga sung. From time to time Helga went there and returned, strangely composed, to sit silently for hours with her knitting.

Hans arrived home, scarred, limping, but in command of the ship in which he had first sailed, bringing with him booty from a place called Byzantium, on the shores of a great inland sea. Much gold had he, and many scrolls in curious script, and a wife by capture, called Illona—a dark beauty whose belly was big with child, who spoke with a strange accent but who could read the scrolls.

Kah-Sih-Omah made her welcome in his house, and by so doing welcomed death through its doors as well, though he did not at the time know this. Within days its presence was horribly apparent.

Heidi's children were the first to feel it: chills, high fever, profuse vomiting and finally convulsions. They died, never having developed the signs that Kah-Sih-

Omah later saw again and again, in faces all over Europe, Africa and Asia: deep pocks, the badges of survival. Helga did. Her fevers broke into an eruption—fierce red lesions covered her head and spread down her body, where they first hardened, then broke.

She died, and so did Hans and Heidi, and Heidi's husband and many of Kah-Sih-Omah's neighbors. In the harbor Han's knorr lay at anchor, her crew dead or dying of the plague that now ravaged all of Reykjavik.

Kah-Sih-Omah was immune, of course. So apparently was Illona, soon to bear Lar's last grandchild. Together she and Kah-Sih-Omah gathered up their dead, loading them aboard the old ship which had come from Vinland. A knorr towed it out of the harbor, into the open sea, and with his own hand Kah-Sih-Omah touched her pitch-smeared decks with fire. He stood with Illona in the knorr, weeping with her as the past first burned, then sank.

They returned to his house, empty now of all they both had known, silent and dark, where at last Illona seemed to find comfort in the reading of a scroll. Kah-Sih-Omah felt a loss no less acute than hers, and sat there mourning perhaps more than she, because he knew less of death than she did. She could contemplate death because she knew that it would someday claim her. He could not, because death could not.

It was then that Kah-Sih-Omah weakened, and reached back. In a fit of agony he touched forbidden memories, the last moments of the life of Lars.

He felt it! He saw it. He heard it faintly and even smelled it. There was the glade, tucked in between the lofty trees, their leaves fluttering in the breeze, their branches bare of life, abandoned by birds alarmed at the prospect of imminent battle. At once those blurs of black fur filled a panorama of vision. Wherever he looked, there they were. He was at once aware of the odors that rose from them, musky and ripe, powerful enough to drive from his nostrils even the stink of his own terror.

The deer fell to the ground, to lie across the instep of the left foot and catch it, and in the end to doom the man. A sinewy arm rose, high above an unseen head, whose eye perceived not itself but watched the advancing foe with steady and determined gaze.

The sword sang as it flew from its scabbard on the man's back, its song too faint for him to hear, its heft both crushing and comforting.

Muscles tensed, coordinating with the eye, seeking weakness, seeking advantage. The she-bear's flank appeared, unprotected. Thrust or cut, that was the question. He chose to cut, perhaps an error in judgment, perhaps a trick of fate, an awesome wound but one not immediately fatal.

Turning—astonishment at the flight of a stranger's arrow, violent, uncontrollable rage, centered on the presence of red men, here—now—when distraction was least affordable.

Turning—greater astonishment—more distraction—another arrow, swift, piercing, but again off the mark, as though the red man toyed with these hapless combatants, so he could stalk the winner.

Pain! Fierce, stifling, choking pain! A warm gushing, a numbness—stark awareness that through that gaping red slash which followed the claws of the bear his life flowed outward in a torrent nothing could stop.

Faintness! Tightness across the chest, numbness in the arms, weakness in the fingers that grasped the bloody sword, the knees buckling, the langorous descent, and finally the snap of limp neck muscles that threw his face toward the sky.

One last image bloomed, then blurred. One last muscle trembled, and then the world ended.

Nothing of it remained, not even the last image. For that fleeting instant alone Kah-Sih-Omah had seen his own face.

He awoke. He was lying on the rough stone floor, head propped against the bulge of Illona's unborn child, eyes open and staring upward around her breasts, at her mouth. The mouth was moving, contorting in cadence to rapid heaving breaths that suddenly racked her chest. Kah-Sih-Omah's ears, until then deaf, now seized his full attention—drawing out, as though across the vast gulf of the lifetime he had already lived, the piercing sounds of Illona's scream.

Abruptly, consciousness returned. Time normalized. Perspective changed. Kah-Sih-Omah's head was dropping toward the flagstones; Illona's heaving torso was in frank retreat, rising as she straightened from her crouch, her mouth still a twisted red blur.

Kah-Sih-Omah marshalled all his strength, both that of his body and that of his will. His body was strangely weak. He felt tired to the bone. Glancing down, he saw why—knew why Illona had screamed.

He was not Kah-Sih-Omah/Lars anymore. He was not a Viking. The pale wrinkled skin, the bristling body hair, the withered sagging muscles—these were gone. He was again the man he had been when the creators departed the earth—renewed through the medium of Lars's final trauma.

Despite fatigue and giddiness he leapt to his feet, again encapsulated in a seemingly personal cell of time. Illona was falling now. Her throat no longer rippled with the force of her scream. Her eyes were closing. Her limbs appeared to be going limp. She would fall into the fire unless he were quick enough to stop her.

He lunged, reaching forward to grasp her, felt her flesh in still trembling fingers. In that instant he had her. She was safe from the fall. He eased her slowly to the floor, intending to try to revive her.

It was not to be that simple. Illona's time, it seemed, had come, perhaps because of what she had just seen. Having once begun, nature could not be stopped by any means that Kah-Sih-Omah knew. Nature went only forward. The best that Kah-Sih-Omah could do was gather such padding as he could from around the room and find her something in which to wrap the child when it arrived. He did this, then waited.

There was no mystery in the rest of it. A grandson arrived, ignorant though his mother was of the event. Illona slumbered through the birth.

Kah-Sih-Omah cut the cord and tied it, then wrapped the child in a shawl of warm wool, and placed it in Illona's arms.

She wakened at that moment, saw first the child, then him.

Kah-Sih-Omah feared she might bolt upright. He reached forward to take the baby should that happen.

Illona drew it back, though this time Kah-Sih-Omah was convinced her fear had left her. Her face was not the same.

She spoke, her voice weak, pleading for reassurance. "You are still here," she said, in halting, heavily accented Norse. "You are real."

"As real as your child," he answered.

"Please! Let them rise."

"Rise? Who?"

"The dead."

"But I cannot do that." Kah-Sih-Omah realized at once that the shock had massive impact.

"You have the power."

"Illona, who do you think I am?"

"You are the Christ."

He could not dissuade these thoughts. He knew, through Helga, who Christ was, but not that this particular power was claimed for him. He did not like the idea, within this city of death, of personal identification with a god who could reverse it. He had been confused with gods before, always unpleasantly. He therefore slowly reassumed the Lars persona.

As she watched, Illona remained in a state of near entrancement, glassy-eyed, incoherent. She spoke rapidly in her native language, as though he should understand her.

At first Kah-Sih-Omah feared the baby might not be safe with her, but eventually Illona reached a state of relative calm and displayed enough interest in her child to attempt feeding.

By then, though he was Lars again, she gazed at him through a knowing smile that said he wasn't fooling her at all—that she knew who and what he really was.

For days thereafter he continued to watch her carefully, avoiding conversation with her as much as he could, hoping now that he looked like Lars again she might question the authenticity of the experience and eventually deny it to herself. He knew that this sometimes happened. He could recall other instances where this had occurred.

It became clear eventually that nothing of the sort

would happen to Illona without his help. That was the morning he discovered her out on the street, preaching his divinity to neighbors, who thought her addled.

What he did next he did with much regret and with the greatest of reservations. He had never attempted anything like it before and did so now only in the hope of saving Illona's sanity. He invaded her mind and took the memory of the transformation away. She was a willing subject, because what he proposed coincided with her belief. When he was finished, he was no more to her than the grandfather to her child.

She was, however, much more to him. To expunge her memories he had first to find them. To find them he had to explore. In exploring he necessarily intruded on many other memories to which this one related. Once he did this, they remained as his own.

He emerged with competence in a new language, Greek, the language of most of the scrolls Hans had brought from the Byzantine. It was this fact that crowned a growing mass of fortuitous circumstances, and augured the belated passing of Lars. He waited but the time it took suitors from the many widowed warriors of the city to find Illona, and then though the funeral was, as much of the Great Grunter's existance had been, an illusion—he committed Lars to the flames.

They did not know who he was, this man they were to follow for a time. He called himself Omahssen, and strangely, he seemed to know all of them and all their fearsome strengths and all their petty weaknesses.

He had appeared out of nowhere, on the waterfront, announcing he would buy the ship of Lars's son, Hans, and hire a crew to sail it. Many thought it but the jest of one so young and so unscarred, until they saw the gold he had. A lesser man would never dare display this. This giant did. All Reykjavik's thieves together could not have taken it away.

With this gold he gained the knorr and all the men to man her, setting sail not at dawn, as by the custom, but at dusk, with forty sweating Viking warriors bending sweeps against the tide.

The night, he said, he chose for the sake of its stars,

and ringing truth from his words, he lounged in the ship's bows, reclined on the head of the dragon who broke the waves for her, staring ahead, unmoving, clad only in light cloak and iron helm against the growing chill that darkness brought.

Presently, with the south capes cleared, others shipped their oars and slept, trusting the west wind to blow the night through and fill their great square sail. When the sun returned its rays fell first on Omahssen's face. When it had risen high he crept beneath the folds of the spare sail, stowed amidships at the base of the mast, sometimes to sleep, sometimes to pore fitfully over the strange script of one of the many scrolls he carried in a brass box.

Throughout the days that followed he did the same, keeping his own counsel, aloof from them, joining neither in their merriment nor their quarrels.

Some were disturbed, finding their new leader so morose, and wondered if his spirit matched his hulking form. Rumors rose about him, though these were softly spoken, passing lips only when he was in the farthest reaches of the ship. Some said his sword was rusty, though none had ever seen it drawn; that he had come from fabled Vinland, and that he sailed in search of his brother. Rumor, though, was all there was to be. Omahssen spoke little enough, and never of himself at all.

They sailed on, the iron fish pointing abeam, as far as the Faeroes, though they did not touch there as many thought they would. Instead Omahssen turned the ship southeast, toward Ireland, and they thought he might raid there; though the land was poor, with little worth the stealing except in towns that other Vikings like themselves had built.

But he landed them openly at Limerick, sailing in on the high tide, finding anchorage before it receded and left them settled in a sea of mud.

Omahsen did not raid. Instead he haunted Limerick's great hall, chasing rumors, asking foolish questions, listening gullibly and with childish awe to the most transparent lies its drunken denizens could muster.

And then, still without a word to the crew of his purpose, he squandered yet more gold for cheese and sausage and rock-hard unleavened bread. Sadly, he bought little ale, and no mead, though Ireland's mead was excellent.

The crew grumbled mightily. Their disappointment in Omahssen mounted. Discontent was rife, still he would not divulge their destination. Some warriors deserted Omahssen to follow new leaders inland, trailing rumor that a great army was rising there and battle against the Celts was in the offing.

Rumor grew into truth. Other knorrs arrived, bearing heavy burdens of warriors, some of these Jarls in the service of Knut, young king of Denmark and of England, which lay across a narrow channel to the east, and these took horse and rode away.

Twenty of Omahssen's warriors rode with them, but Omahssen's sword remained in its scabbard. He went alone each day to the ship to await their return, though he thought it unlikely that they would, as most now thought their leader a coward.

Many long days passed. Then, across the eastern horizon, horsemen appeared, heralds, bearing news not of mere defeat but of disaster. Behind them others straggled in, some on horseback, most on foot, heads bowed, weapons trailing, many badly wounded; behind them refugees, driven from the lands they once had wrested from the Celts; behind them Brian's minions, determined to kill all who had escaped Clontarf.

The city swelled. Northmen, Omahssen at last among them, waited atop battlements. In the harbor ships hastily provisioned were moved to deeper water, against the day when the last refuge of these harried Vikings might lie at sea.

But battle did not come. In time the siege lifted, this new high king too unsure of his own, against whom he must now guard his own back, to risk a further confrontation. He could deny them the interior, nothing more; and in time, the Vikings thought, the Celts would again quarrel among themselves as they always had, their petty chieftains easy prey for men who fought together.

Omahssen then gathered a new crew about him, and again set sail, now bound for the Norman Duchy of the Frankreich, to join other ships in a voyage south through dangerous waters. This was but a journey of days, though the sea was angry and they raced just ahead of the fangs of a great storm that raged from the troubled north.

In the yards of Cherbourg he added a ram to the knorr's bows and braced it against the dragon. Archers joined his crew. Great baskets of arrows and bundles of spare oars cluttered the deck. Leather buckets hung from pegs beneath the gunwales.

Again the deep of night was chosen to sail this armada between the great promontories that guarded the entrance of the inland sea: a wise choice, since at first light strange galleys sortied from the southern shore and chased them.

The Northmen had the wind at first, and at first easily kept the distance. But then the galleys from the south were joined by others coming from the north, and from the decks of his knorr Omahssen could see dark columns of smoke from signal fires burning along the shore. He knew that more and more of these strange-looking ships would soon sally forth to meet them.

At midday the wind failed. Without its aid the heavier knorrs were slower to make way than the lighter craft of their pursuers. Despite the efforts of the warriors straining at their sweeps the distance closed, until at last it became obvious that what strength remained to them was best saved for the confrontation that inevitably would come.

From the lead ships warriors turned burnished copper to the sun, flashing signals to the others at the rear. As one ship, the armada prepared to turn about and meet the foe which harried them: a foe who now possessed nearly twice the ships the Northmen had.

Omahssen found his ship now on the van, bearing down on rakish hulls full of the darkest men that he had ever seen. He stood behind the figurehead, over the ram, and waited.

A sleet of arrows rose to meet the knorr. He raised his shield against them and drew the long sword, now bright, now shiny and sharp. From the rear the Viking archers answered, impaling many aboard the first approaching galley.

It turned, avoiding the ram which would have shattered it, preferring instead to slip between ships and harry them with missiles. Some of these were burning and set small fires on the knorr's deck which warriors hastened to smother.

A collision occurred in the next instant, shattering an enemy galley and heaving many of its oarsmen overboard. Ropes, trailing grappels, sailed overhead, their claws biting into the enemy's hull, holding it fast on the ram, while arrows continued to whistle past in both directions.

The clang of steel rose to a din. Warriors boiled over the rail and leapt to the enemy's deck, where great two-handed swords and battleaxes had some room to swing.

The enemy met these with determination and valor, though his weapons were lighter. The dark warriors were commonly protected by armor, which evened the odds of battle for them but quickly doomed any who fell overboard. This was an observation most Viking warriors quickly made. They pushed as often as they slashed or thrust.

Omahssen's warriors rapidly overwhelmed those of the enemy, who were fewer in number owing to their smaller ship, and the fact that their oarsmen did not fight.

Omahssen was about to order the hulk fired as soon as they could disengage from it, but wondered why the surviving rowers had not jumped overboard and swum away. Then he saw the chains, and realized with horror that they could not leave. They were slaves. He ordered the torches extinguished, and his own rowers to carefully back away. This hulk and its captives was no peril to the Vikings. With luck they might yet remain afloat.

By this time his ship was under attack by several enemy vessels at once, and out of position to use her ram. Shields held high on their outboard arms to ward off arrows, warriors manned oars to push at the enemy hulls and keep them at bay. Archers dueled each other, filling the sky with arrows.

Many fell, impaled. Others broke shafts from heads

buried deep in their bodies and fought on as long as
they could. Omahssen himself, struck twice, did this.
Still leaning on the dragon, protected somewhat by the
rail on either side of him, he hung over the nearest
enemy vessel and lopped such heads as came within the
reach of his blade, a bloody wound in one thigh, another at the base of his neck.

Other knorrs were now rushing to aid them. One
rammed a ship on the port side and drove it against
Omahssen's, where it was crushed between them, captive oarsmen and all.

All over the surface of the sea, strangely calm now
that the wind had died, little knots of combatants tore
and slashed at one another. Ruined hulks, some with
oarsmen clinging to fragments of timber, some afire
and blazing, littered the waves. The odds were changing, but clear victory would for a time be still in doubt.

Omahssen, alone among the wounded, was in no peril
of death. When respite from the battle came he used the
time to repair torn tissue around the missiles, then
flexed new muscle in careful sequence to expel them,
driving them in the direction of their barbs, until they
popped through the other side. But he did not dare to
close the wounds entirely and staunch the flow of all
the blood. Some had already seen him stricken, and he
wanted no new rumors flying with the rest.

Presently, his knorr was for the moment free, though
missing many warriors formerly manning her sweeps.
Not enough of her own remained to gain the speed to
ram and so instead he pulled her into position to board
such ships as other knorrs now engaged with grappels.

Much slaughter ensued. Much blood flowed. Many on
both sides perished. But it had become apparent long
ago that the knorr was the favored vessel and the
Northman the fiercer warrior. Given no additional im-
ponderables, there would have been no doubt of the
ultimate outcome.

But one came. It was at first only a curious speck on
the horizon, though it was a large one. Far from the
scene of battle, the Northmen had not allowed its approach to concern them. But when it hove near enough

for them to see it clearly they watched it ever closer, and wondered what it was.

When the smaller ships abruptly broke off the fighting and rowed to join it the knorrs gave chase, and there was much rejoicing on their decks. Though exhausted and breathless at their oars, the Vikings roared out challenge. Mighty oaths were sworn to sweep this enemy from this sea, then take his homeland, his women and his gold. While the distance closed stewarts broke out ale, holding horns of it to the lips of thirsty warriors as they rowed.

And then, disaster. Flying fast, building speed to ram the screen of galleys that huddled ahead of this strange lumbering craft, the knorrs were hard to turn and impossible to stop. Many continued onward even when struck and hulled by the cloud of huge stones that rose from the big ship's deck.

Lighter and faster, the enemy galleys dodged the knorrs, only enough remaining in the screen to protect the larger ship from boarders. Too big and too heavy for any ram the knorrs carried, this strange craft also carried a massive array of armored pikemen, and her archers shot from protective parapets mounted high above the decks on masts.

Omahssen recognized the danger of this at once, and ordered his warriors to back their oars. He knew they could not approach this ship yet; not until the remainder of the light galleys had been destroyed and they could maneuver freely.

These small ships now pulled desperately to encircle the knorrs, to prevent them from breaking away. The reason was apparent with the next salvo of missiles.

These were not mere rocks, dependent on the force of their fall for the damage they inflicted. These missiles burned fiercely as the flew. When they struck a ship, water could not smother them. They must be lifted on the blades of many swords and thrown overboard, else they set afire everything they touched.

The situation aboard Omahssen's ship became desperate. Attrition had taken its toll. Too few warriors remained to both row and fight. He must choose one or the other.

He chose to fight, it being apparent that this could not be avoided in any case because the local concentration of enemy galleys was too great. This left his knorr dead in the water, no great disadvantage under the usual circumstances, but these were not usual. It made her an easy target for the catapult crews.

In all, three missiles struck Omahssen's knorr. Two which burned struck amidships, one piercing the planking near her keel, then dropping otherwise harmlessly into the sea. The other fired the tiny deck on which the helmsman stood to steer. The third, a great stone ball, splintered the dragon figurehead and hurled Omahssen, unconscious, into the water.

For Omahssen this battle was over. Soon it was over for everybody, as those knorrs still afloat and manned changed their tactics to fight a running battle with the enemy galleys beyond the range of the catapults.

Consciousness returned but slowly. As soon as it did the body revived as well, and those automatic defenses the creators had built into it gave way to Kah-Sih-Omah's will.

Floating face-down, he had not breathed at all during the interval in which his senses had abandoned him. His body was starved for oxygen, having leached from his tissues nearly all it dared to take. Though his muscles were consequently weak, he managed to flail his arms vigorously enough to bring his face above water, where he snatched great breaths of salt air as rapidly as he could.

When he had restored his depleted reserves, he fashioned flotation organs to spare himself the effort of treading water. Then for a while he searched the sea around him for signs of the combatant navies.

But the ships had gone. No remnant of them remained except an occasional plank, or an arrow shaft floating point downward or a soggy leathern fire bucket. He looked up to search out the sun but could not find it with exactness, since clouds had begun building to the west. Neither could he see any land, though he thought it might be near and only his lowly vantage point prevented him from seeing it. Seeing land was paramount.

Until he knew in which direction it lay it would be pointless to start swimming.

So, he simply waited. Presently the light failed and stars appeared. Much later, the moon rose. In the interim, Kah-Sih-Omah collected a half dozen of the arrows which had floated by, and tucked them under a thong around his waist. He had not yet seen any of those large voracious fish which commonly infested most seas of his acquaintance, but he wanted to be prepared if any came.

All through the night he floated free and unmolested, staring ahead at the lapping waves and upward at the stars. He could not tell in which direction he was moving, or if he was moving at all. Currents in this sea seemed more sluggish than in others he had known.

Long before the sun rose the horizon grew pale. Just as it started into pink it cast a silhouette at him, unmistakably a silhouette of heads. They bobbed on waves perhaps half a hundred paces away, otherwise unmoving.

For long moments Kah-Sih-Omah continued uncertain these were men. Then, once he had decided they were, he was uncertain what kind of men he saw. As none had moved, and under these circumstances were not likely to be belligerent, he paddled silently closer.

From the new position it appeared to him that they clung to a plank for flotation and that there were three of them. Closer still, he could see they were not Northmen, but oarsmen from a sunken enemy galley, and chained to the plank on which they floated. Finally, with the sun rising, and the light better, it occurred to him that they might all be dead.

One obviously was. The broken shaft of an arrow protruded from his temple. Another, when a wave turned him, displayed a surely fatal gash across the throat. The third, floating face upward, arms outstretched, and bound tightly by the loop of one of his chains around the end of the plank, had no obvious wounds. In him, Kah-Sih-Omah thought he perceived just the barest hint of respiration.

He paddled closer and confirmed this, gazing at this dark young man for long moments before he could detect the shallow rising and falling of his chest. He was slight of build, though he looked wiry. His head contained a fringe of black hair through which his crown shone in the dawn, and on his face there was a thin growth of beard.

Kah-Sih-Omah grasped the plank and clung to it. Under his added weight it settled enough to immerse his companion's face, and he stirred, though Kan-Sih-Omah quickly let go the plank.

The man's eyes opened. He had simply been asleep.

Then terror filled those eyes, as they realized the visitor was a huge and ferocious-looking Viking, one of those who sunk the ship on which he rowed.

Kah-Sih-Omah spoke to him in Norse, intending to calm and reassure him. But Norse is a rough tongue, filled with harsh gutturals and glottal stops, and it quite apparently alarmed him. Kah-Sih-Omah, for want of any alternative, tried the only other European language he knew: his untried Greek.

That produced first astonishment, then confusion. The other man retreated from him as far as his bonds would allow, but did not reply.

Kah-Sih-Omah examined the corpses, noted they were similarly chained to the plank, and decided that unless he could be freed of them the live man would soon sink. In a day, two at most, the plank would become waterlogged and would no longer support them. He drew the dagger from his belt and set himself to the grisly work of severing wrists.

The alarm in his companion's eyes receded as the bodies floated free and the plank rose. Kah-Sih-Omah returned the blade to its sheath and threw one arm over the plank. He watched the other man intently, from time to time uttering some joviality at him. In time, the small reactions for which he watched so closely convinced him that the man knew Greek—perhaps imperfectly, but knew it none the less, else how would he know that Kah-Sih-Omah was hungry and would greatly relish feasting on his ears?

Having obtained the responses he wanted, Kah-Sih-Omah set about to repair whatever damage his remark had done. "I jest, of course," he said. "Fish, even raw, are more to my taste than gristle. To catch one, I shall require bait."

He drew not the dagger, as the young man feared, but one of the arrows. He held it in one hand, and with the other, shaded his eyes and stared downward into the depths. "I see that our dinner fancies your toes even now. Take care not to wiggle them." He ducked his head under, and remained submerged and motionless for an inordinately long time.

Suddenly there was a flash of movement. Kah-Sih-Omah's arm rose, a fish impaled on the arrow. Beneath the surface the man could not see that the bait had been, not his toes, but a lure with the appearance of a worm, which grew on a stalk from his companion's own foot.

Kah-Sih-Omah jabbed the head of the arrow into the plank and took another from his belt. He went down again, and soon had another fish. Then he drew the dagger and gutted them, and sliced off fillets, which he laid out in a row along the plank. He ate half of them, but left the other half for the dark man.

It was a long time before hunger tempted his companion, and when he ate it was with obvious distaste. Raw fish did not suit his palate very well. He was, nevertheless, grateful, and though his words were heavily accented his Greek was good enough to express his thanks.

"Who are you?" Kah-Sih-Omah asked his somewhat more relaxed companion.

"A slave."

"That I knew. I meant, what are you called? Where is your home? You need not be afraid to answer me, you know. I am your captor's enemy."

The man seemed to relax after that reassurance. "My name is Marcello," he replied. "Once, I am from Sicily."

"I do not know where that is," Kah-Sih-Omah replied. "Is that where you were captured?"

"No. I left there when still a child. My father took me to Rome . . ."

"Rome!" Kah-Sih-Omah had heard much of Rome. "Tell me about Rome."

"I saw little of it. It is a large city, once a rich and powerful one. Perhaps by some standards it still is."

"You do not know?"

"I entered a monastery, which was cloistered, and grew to manhood there within its walls. We seldom ventured out. It was forbidden. Then I went with a group of other monks to Spain, and there the Saracens took us all. Those two you cut adrift were monks like me."

Monks too, were newly familiar words to Kah-Sih-Omah. They were curious men who did peculiar things, but many were reputed to be very learned, and a few were wizards of note. Some of the scrolls he read occasionally mentioned this.

He could not believe his luck! Such men knew of Him, perhaps some even knew where He might be found. Kah-Sih-Omah, though he had studied these writings very diligently, had not been able to decide what all the words really meant. The accounts seemed to have been deliberately couched in obscurities, with little that was exact. On the one hand, there were many vivid accounts of the Other's passing. On the other, it was said that he remained nearby always.

The shaman side of Kah-Sih-Omah's persona discounted much of what he read as obvious embellishment. But underneath it all he knew there lay substantial truth. No legend endured for very long without such a basis—and this one displayed enormous vigor. It seemed to Kah-Sih-Omah that much of the world hereabouts followed the Other. The wonder of it was that He should prove so difficult to locate.

But then, Kah-Sih-Omah understood. He knew the travails that could attend the existence of one such as he. He had himself endured them often enough. How could he blame the man for seeking such peace as he could find, and such solitude as his followers—these Christians—would allow him?

Of the Saracens he knew much less. They too followed a leader who, like Christ, had passed; perhaps he too another such as Kah-Sih-Omah. They too, it seemed, were fierce in manner and fanatic in thought, just as the Christians were.

Kah-Sih-Omah, in fleeting instants of conjecture, found himself wondering how many immortals the creators might have made; wondered if perhaps the scenario into which he seemed about to intrude might not in reality be a struggle between two of them, in which each employed mortals as his tools. If it was a possibility, he might be very wise to conceal his true nature from all until he knew the truth.

Another day the two castaways bobbed upon the plank. The sun beat down so fiercely that Kah-Sih-Omah's pale skin began at once to redden. No disadvantage in the cool and cloudy north, here, light skin was impractical to the point of uselessness and pain.

Before Kah-Sih-Omah realized what was happening or could do anything to stop it, his body began to slough off the burnt skin, much to the alarm of his companion. He watched with great trepidation as Kah-Sih-Omah's face dropped away like the skin of a serpent.

Marcello fell strangely silent at the sight, and gawked at Kah-Sih-Omah, as though he studied his features in search of recollection. When he saw the new pink skin emerge from underneath the old and immediately begin to tan, he must have understood that all was not as it seemed. His body began to shake and shiver, though the sea was quite warm, and began to chant in a tongue that Kah-Sih-Omah did not know.

Kah-Sih-Omah listened for a while, then spoke. "What is the matter with you? Are you ill?"

The monk paused, but only briefly, then continued. Finally he began a series of gestures, awkward in his bonds, during which he momentarily let go of the plank. When he did he sank like a stone, under the weight of the chain.

Kah-Sih-Omah realized then that the monk could not swim. He immediately dived and dragged him to the surface again.

He was in time. Though Marcello had swallowed much water he was still alive. Kah-Sih-Omah used the chain to bind him fast and safe to the plank, then waited for an explanation.

The words, when they came, were accusatory. "Which are you, Omahssen—saint or devil?"

"I do not understand."

"I did not know you when first you came upon me, but I know you now. You were in the ship that sank my own, in the bow, beneath the figure of the dragon. You had grevious wounds then. Now you have none. There is not a mark on you."

"You are mistaken. The fury of battle clouded your mind."

But the man was not finished. He had clearly thought the situation through. "No! You pretend you are a barbarian, ignorant of civilized ways, yet you speak to me in Greek which is without blemish, and with such perfection as I have not achieved in many years of study and struggle."

Kah-Sih-Omah could think of nothing to say. "The sun and sea play tricks on your mind, monk, nothing more. There was a captive; a woman, from whom I learned."

"As a grown man? Impossible. I know, I am a linguist. Only children learn strange languages and speak them without trace of the old. Your Greek has none of your Norse in it. You are more than you admit. I ask you again if you are the devil, come to torment me?"

"And if I am?"

"I will begin the rites of exorcism. I will destroy you."

"Then begin. Believe as you will," Kah-Sih-Omah replied. He retrieved the arrows which still stuck in the plank and dived below to fish.

He was exorcised. Since the process did not destroy him, as it surely should have, Marcello emerged from it with an even more unctuous manner. He was now convinced, beyond all possible argument, that Kah-Sih-Omah was a saint, whatever that might be. He behaved with a disgustingly servility.

So it was a lonely afternoon, but one of good fortune. A current rose and carried them toward the south, and just as the sun was about to disappear below the western horizon the last of its rays fell upon a sail. Kah-Sih-Omah adjusted one of his eyes for distance and tried to determine the direction of its travel.

Its course would take it ahead and abeam of them, though slowly enough so that with a little work he might catch it, if he were alone. The vessel was very small and did not look like a merchantman, and Kah-Sih-Omah had observed that the Saracen galleys flew no sails. He decided it must be fishermen.

Briefly, he toyed with the idea of making a rapid adjustment and taking a run at it, and trust to luck that he would be able to find the monk again and rescue him. He had already begun to web his toes in preparation when without warning the sail disappeared.

His own experience as a fisherman supplied the answer, and the sight of two more sails after that confirmed it as correct. They were undoubtedly within a short distance of land and the boats, having located a school of fish, had stopped to drop nets. He knew he did not have to hurry now.

The monk did not yet know. He continued to stare wide-eyed at Kah-Sih-Omah, though he had stopped chanting. The situation had become very awkward.

Yet if they were to get ashore, Marcello must be told, so that he could help. Kah-Sih-Omah saw no sense in wasting time, particularly as the current had picked up a little and was rapidly carrying them toward the spot where he had seen the sail go down. "There are fishing boats ahead of us," he said.

The monk's head jerked around, and his eyes searched the horizon. In a moment he turned back. "Where? I saw nothing."

"They have lowered their sails and are now setting nets. Soon they will light torches with which to lure the fish, and it will be very dark by the time the current carries us near."

"These will be Saracens."

"I know." The man's faith in his divinity, if that was what he had been attempting to display, had vanished in the face of this prospective danger.

"They will know that I am a slave when they see the chains, and certainly they will not mistake you for one of their own."

"That too concerns me gravely," Kah-Sih-Omah replied. He did not add that his companion was the reason. "Tell me, do you understand their speech?"

"Enough to respond to commands before the whip stung me, but I am hardly fluent."

"Then we cannot approach them openly. We will have to seize a boat by force." Kah-Sih-Omah began some additional alterations to his body as soon as he made this decision. On the first fingers of his hands the second joints began to swell, and beneath the nails of each a channel formed.

The current slowly took them nearer the lights, which were lit when darkness fell as Kah-Sih-Omah predicted. Three boats in all they saw, each with half a dozen fishermen aboard, sweating over nets. Some were young boys, a fact which should make seizing a boat a great deal easier. He modified one of his biological syringes to dispense a smaller dose.

Kah-Sih-Omah abandoned the plank while still some distance away from the nearest boat, much to the monk's dismay. He disappeared under the water with his dagger clenched between his jaws and never came back up.

For a long time Marcello watched with ever-growing consternation. The current carried him nearer and nearer, and that soon he would be close enough that those on board would see him.

Then, abruptly and to his immense relief, the waters in front of the plank parted, and Kah-Sih-Omah's head appeared. "Come," he said, "you must abandon the plank and follow me. There are nets ahead with which we will shortly run afoul. We will swim around them to the far side of the farthest boat."

"How? You know I cannot swim."

"Leave that to me. Gather up your chain and come."

Intimidated by the warning of the nets and the awesome size of the man who gave the order, the monk obeyed. His faith, he found, had not yet regained its initial vigor.

Something wrapped around his middle, like a very thick rope, and expanded somewhat more as it tightened. Swiftly and silently the two of them began to move in a wide arc around the circles of light.

Marcello expected to be released before the boat was reached, so that he would be free to aid his companion in the struggle with its crew. He was not released, and no crewmen were to be seen. Kah-Sih-Omah grasped for a handhold to gain purchase and with the other arm he hurled the monk aboard.

Marcello tumbled into the bilges and struggled to rise to his feet again, aware that there had been something odd about the arm which had raised him: that it indeed appeared ropelike. Before he could confirm this he stumbled over a body lying next to him. "You killed them," he gasped.

"Be quiet, and stay down. They sleep. They are not dead. Now, listen carefully—place the torch in that tub near the rail and set it afloat. We do not want the others to notice when we leave."

"Suppose they give chase?"

"I have cut their nets and used the ropes to foul the tillers of the other boats. We can be away before they free them, but in the meantime I must tow our boat far enough away so that her sail will not be seen to rise."

The monk did as he was told. An instant later Kah-Sih-Omah had hauled up the stone anchor and dropped it in the bow, and after that he used its rope to tow the boat toward the east, taking advantage of the flow of the current.

When the torches of the other boats were but pinpoints he pulled himself into the boat. In the light of the rising moon the monk thought the bare feet strangely shaped, but said nothing, waiting for Kah-Sih-Omah's next instruction. He had already made up his mind this was no ordinary mortal. He knew of no other saints of the church who possessed such powers but his faith was now rock steady.

Kah-Sih-Omah's next action was to haul up the triangular sail, which he set with ropes to catch the wind slightly abeam. As he stood back to grasp the tiller his feet appeared entirely normal. "We cannot sail against the wind in this," he said, "but this craft hauls closer than most. I will steer south-southeast and gain the coast as far away from here as possible. Tell me, what is Africa like?"

Marcello had taken a seat on a pile of nets and baskets and was staring down at two sleeping people, one a man slightly older than he, the other a boy of perhaps twelve years of age. He contemplated his reply for long moments and then spoke, wondering why a saint would need to ask. But he obeyed. "Africa is very large. The coastal lands are arid, but tillable. The interior is harsh desert, inhabited only by nomads. The Saracens hold all of Africa north of this, from the Pillars of Hercules through the Holy Land, and up almost to the very gates of Byzantium."

"The 'Holy Land'? Why is this land holy?"

"You test me?"

"If that is how you wish to perceive it."

"It is the land of Christ's birth, where he taught, and where he died."

"Died? When?"

"Almost a thousand years ago. Nine hundred and eighty-one years ago, to be exact."

Kah-Sih-Omah fell silent. He began to shake involuntarily. He hastily ordered his nervous system to stop this, and strained to regain control. *A millennium ago, yet they speak of it as yesterday!* The Norse had no use for large numbers; did not understand them and did not use them. Few cultures did, and few men of Kah-Sih-Omah's acquaintance were any different. But the Mayans—they had contemplated them and could express them, and so, therefore, could Kah-Sih-Omah. This news was crushing—a trail a thousand years old, that he must follow if he were to find his brother.

"Then," he said solemnly, "we will go there. We will find Him again. While we travel you must tell me all you know about Him."

Marcello was startled, but resigned. He did not understand the reason why, but he knew that God was testing him through this saint; that his senses were no longer trustworthy, but prey to vision; that he must never again weaken, as he had that afternoon, and question God's motives. It was his mission to obey.

While they sailed, Kah-Sih-Omah removed his companion's chains, using the anchor stone for an anvil and battering the links apart with a dull chisel fishermen used to drive caulking into leaking seams. When they landed in the morning, the sleeves of the boy's robe, which Marcello had exchanged for his own, covered the wrist irons which remained. If he had had any doubt the night before as to the character and nature of his companion it was gone now. The light found Kah-Sih-Omah was no longer a blond, pale giant, but as dark as he, with the curly black hair and beard of an Egyptian.

The saint was a willing and astute pupil, who listened carefully to his every word and asked so many questions that at times the monk despaired of the test. He had not anticipated the depth of it, though he remained convinced of its importance.

The saint seemed an adept linguist as well, and part of each day was devoted to teaching him such Arabic as Marcello knew. The saint never forgot a word, and from time to time when they encountered other travelers he would practice conversation with them, pretending to be a foreigner who wished to improve his knowledge of their language. At times Marcello wondered why it was that God had not provided his saint with that knowledge. At times he thought that perhaps God had, and that the ignorance was only a sham designed to try his obedience.

Kah-Sih-Omah was content, after that first night, to allow the error to perpetuate. It served his purpose well enough. It gave him guide and teacher as well as company of a sort, though he disliked the thinly masked adulation the monk displayed. At times the temptation rose within him to tell his tale as it truly was, from start to finish, and free it of the religious trappings with which others insisted on endowing it. A couple of times he almost did, beginning with a cautious phrase, intending to lead slowly into the narrative.

Marcello was intelligent enough to have understood it, if only he would use his mind, but each time Kah-Sih-Omah tried his gaze was met by a knowing look that said, "Whatever miracles you relate to me I will accept on faith alone." He was beaten.

Their trek was one of months' duration, their manner that of beggars. As they wandered through field and town, bazaar and casbah, Kah-Sih-Omah found these lands no stranger than many others he had traveled, and the lives of the common people much the same as anywhere. He was mildly surprised to note that the hump beasts, called camels here, had survived on this side of the world, and that the elephant, which his ancestors had called the 'great tooth,' also endured, though in a smaller and much less hairy form.

They reached Egypt and in the course of time entered Alexandria, where there were many Greeks and great libraries full of scrolls written in Greek. Marcello became afraid when Kah-Sih-Omah told him he wished to enter and read. Beggars could not do this, he said. Besides, the Greeks were heretics, and hostile to Romans such as they.

Kah-Sih-Omah had not heard this word before, and asked what it meant.

Marcello told him that the Greeks conceived Christ's nature imperfectly and that they had refused to be enlightened by those who knew the truth, and that sometimes they and the Romans fought wars over it. Besides the Greeks, there were other heretical groups within Christendom, but these did not amount to much anymore, having been soundly punished for their errors and repressed.

Kah-Sih-Omah's eyebrows barely rose at that last remark. His theological zoo was growing large, filled as it had become with several sects each of Christians, Muslims, and Jews. Farther to the east, Marcello told him, were many other varieties of heathens, every one as bad or worse than even the Saracens or the Greeks.

They tarried in the Nile delta for many months, during which Kah-Sih-Omah devised ways to enter the libraries and read. He also supported the two of them in quite high fashion, by begging outside the central mosque, his face and body contorted in disfigurement, so that he excited great sympathy in the faithful, whom Allah had commanded to be generous. Marcello swallowed each bite of food he ate with a smirk on his face.

At length Kah-Sih-Omah exhausted the Greek scrolls, but found no satisfactory answers in them. He set about to learn Latin and Hebrew, so that he could read in those languages as well as Greek and Arabic. All the while his somewhat confused but still adulous companion believed in him even more strongly.

They found Jerusalem was as large as Alexandria, and very much older. Kah-Sih-Omah thought the Jews even more interesting than the Egyptians. They enjoyed a literary tradition almost as long as Egypt's, but unlike the Egyptian glyphs, which were complete mysteries even to Egyptians, Jewish scholars read these ancient writings easily. Moreover, these scholars and their repositories proliferated.

Kah-Sih-Omah was surprised that the Arabs, who held political control, permitted this. It was contrary to what Marcello had led him to expect, with all his tales of Muslim savagery. But as he penetrated farther and farther into their domains he began to conclude that they were not, as he had been told, barbarians beating at the outer marches of the civilized world—that perhaps they *were* the civilized world. True, he had yet to visit Byzantium, or the fabled Rome, but somehow he was certain that even these lands could not exceed the wonders he was finding here.

He knew a little bit about those cities from Marcello, but he thought a certain amount of license might have crept into the descriptions. For one thing, he found the Roman number system childishly clumsy. The Arabs had a better one, which included the concept of zero as the Mayans' system had; and like the Mayans, these Arabs excelled at mathematics, which was a true test of intellect.

They learned much from other peoples, but then who hadn't? Both Christianity and Islam had borrowed heavily from the Hebrews, and the Hebrews certainly had borrowed from those who preceded them.

Kah-Sih-Omah felt that at last he had reached a place where he could make progress toward completion of his quest. Again he found ways to penetrate centers of learning and to read. One of his first and most exciting finds was the discovery that much more of the Bible existed than Marcello had ever admitted. There were many other books of it, including one which, when he began to read it, caused the blood to pound away in his temples to the point where he thought the vessels would burst—it was called Ezekiel.

Here at last was the proof! Now, at last, he knew for

certain that his creators had been here too. He was not alone; somewhere on this earth he had siblings.

He had to share this good news with someone. It was bursting out of him. He had no other confidant, so he told his companion, the monk. "My brother is here," he said proudly. "Soon I may find him."

The monk did not understand what he meant. His response was a stutter: "But surely we all know where he is." He pointed skyward.

"That is not what I meant," Kah-Sih-Omah explained. "Forget what you have been told. That is wrong. He is here. He is like me. They who made me also made him."

"They? The Trinity?"

"I mean they—they who came, so long ago, to our earth—who made Christ, and me, and who knows how many others."

"B-but there *were* no others. There was only Him, and how He came to be has been revealed to us. Surely you know that."

"No. I do not know that. I know only that what you believe—what you all believe—is wrong. It did not happen that way, any more than the world, was created in six days, as you understand the term 'day.' "

"But it was."

"No. That is an error of translation. The length of the period is indeterminite in the original Hebrew, and the word you take to mean *day* is properly translated as 'a period of time.' It is the same with the star which your teaching tells us was present at his changing. It was present at mine as well, but it was not a star; it was a deadly fire. The scholars have been too literal. They have inadvertantly distorted meanings. Without this distortion it is all very clear."

And it *was* clear, to Kah-Sih-Omah. Having spent many, many days reading, searching for such errors, and, he thought, finding many, he now had a theory he thought explained why this part of the world had given birth to so many powerful religious movements.

He did not know, at the time, what great injury he was about to visit on his faithful follower and sometime friend. He did not know how brittle the man's mind really was, or how unshakable his faith had been. He did not know, as he set about relating the narrative of his own origins, that the tale would destroy the foundations of Marcello's own existence.

When he finished what he had envisioned as a beautifully clear and carefully rational account of history as it really happened, his companion was glassy-eyed and mute. And when he closed his eyes that night to sleep, he believed he had brought Marcello enlightenment.

In the morning, the shouts of passers-by woke Kah-Sih-Omah early. He peered out the doorway of his lodging to find them pointing at the corpse, swinging from the limb of a tree, face purple in the dawn, limbs already cold and stiff.

Kah-Sih-Omah took a dagger and cut the cord from which Marcello hung, while others grasped the body so it would not fall.

Kah-Sih-Omah carried him inside their room and laid him out on the floor, and closed the door against the ghoulish stares of the curious. He wished to be alone in his grief.

No—that was not the reason. Grief there was, in copious measure, but his remorse was greater still. He was ashamed of his crime. He had thoughtlessly destroyed not just a man, but a mind. He had done it by killing that which had enabled that mind to reconcile itself to its own existence; he had extinguished an idea, the reason for that existence. No other creature had these, or needed them; only to man were they vital.

With them, man dominated his earth. Without them, he had only death. Kah-Sih-Omah had not even that; not yet. His was a greater existence; his an even greater need.

Yet he was presently undeserving, because he remained flawed. He had had eons in which to achieve perfection, yet still he had not conquered his own propensity toward error. He was a man, or at least had sprung from man; yet he failed to understand man.

None who knew the circumstances of the monk's death would consent to his burial within the city. His failing had been despair, and despair was forbidden the followers of Kah-Sih-Omah's brethren.

So Kah-Sih-Omah carried him out into the wasteland, and dug a grave with his hands. He knew the
ritual and so he might have spoken the words, but he
did not. He buried Marcello with silence and what
dignity he could, taking care to be as gentle as he could
in filling in the grave.

When it was done he lingered for a time, gazing out
over the low, barren hills where centuries ago another
such as he had walked, perhaps seeking that same final
peace which Kah-Sih-Omah now sought, doomed to
trek this wasteland until he found it.

Kah-Sih-Omah firmly believed that he had. He no
longer believed that Christ still hovered near, or that he
could be found simply by tramping endlessly across these
barren hills. He could not be nearby; that Kah-Sih-
Omah knew with absolute certainty. If he were, he would
long ago have put a stop to all this bickering about his
nature and his teachings, and ended these bloody wars
waged in his name and for his sake.

But as to the rest ... The quest would continue. It
had been no mistake to come here. The time had not
been wasted, considering the clues which he had found.
Only the loss of his companion generated any doubt in
Kah-Sih-Omah's mind of the wisdom of his actions, but
that which had been done was done and no retreat from
it was possible.

While he pondered that which was, and that which
might have been, Kah-Sih-Omah also struggled to decide his course from here. He had the rest of this world
to search for his siblings, and this world was large.
Behind him lay only his own homeland and Europe, a
land far too heavily settled and too much immersed
in familiar dogma to be a favorable hunting ground.

But to the east—to the east lay yet more deserts, and
at least one other sea. Beyond that, who knew? Vast
lands, perhaps larger yet than any he had yet traveled
through. He could not know until he had been there and
explored them, and the creatures in them, and learned
their habits and their thoughts ... as he already knew
those of many, many others.

It would take a long time perhaps, but Kah-Sih-Omah

had all of time there was, to cross these deserts and this next sea, until he reached the end of time.

Kah-Sih-Omah's outlook had changed much throughout this journey. His perspective had broadened. So had his mind. In all the time there was he now was certain that every scrap of the earth could be trodden over many times, even by one man.

He marveled at that thought—at the sophistication of his own mind. What else but man could stand, barefoot and in rags, in the middle of a desert of trackless sands and plan such things? Ambitious? Yes. Audacious? Yes. Impossible? No, never. He filled his lungs with air and shouted out at the wind, at whoever or whatever might be near enough to hear. "I am coming after you. I will find you, someday, though I must wander forever, to the very ends of the earth and beyond—across that farthest sea of stars. I *am* coming!"

He turned, and stooped, and patted the dust of the grave, and took a rock and marked it, and thought: *And you, Marcello, my friend, I thank, for you have helped to show the way.*

Book Two

In the Face of My Enemy

I am not a coward by nature, though surely there is a little cowardice in all of us. Mine surfaced as soon as I could make out the features of the man disembarking from the shuttle. It was Ivan Carmody himself, my boss.

There are men. Also, there are MEN. The difference is one of kind, not degree; and the mind perceives it instantly, unerringly, and inexplicably.

One approached whom I feared, but to whom duty demanded I explain the other. And I wondered if I could.

My months on Campbell had been filled with many strange experiences—some of which, I felt, were better left out of my report. But Carmody would demand to hear them all. And I knew I would tell.

I was too minor to have met him face to face before. As Secretary of Extraterrestrial Affairs he was the U.N.'s most powerful figure, and its most colorful. As he approached I understood why, for he was imposing. He was tall, with the look of an eagle about him, from the straight white hair he wore combed back to the huge curved beak of his nose. Thick glasses perched on its bridge magnified piercing green eyes that did not blink.

"Kimberly Ryan," the voice boomed. "Are you in charge of this mess?"

I glanced around at the muddy street, the burned-out buildings and crushed equipment. Most of the men who had watched the shuttle's approach had skulked away. "Yes, sir. I have assumed command under Emergency Regulation Number 309," I said, hoping I had cited the right one. I felt his stare on my body, at the rough leather clothing that Casey had made for me. "This is all I have left, Mr. Secretary. Everything burned."

"I'll want to hear your report immediately, Miss Ryan, preferably not out here in the street."

"Yes, sir. We can go to Solar Minerals H.Q., to Mr. Meyers's office. What's left of it, that is. I'll show you the way."

I turned and started off down the street, trying to stick to the dryer spots. He followed along a pace or two behind.

"Where is Meyers?"

"Dead," I told him. "He shot himself just before the settlement, uh, fell, when he thought the aliens were going to fire the building. I can send for Mr. Bigelow, though. He's in charge of Solar's operations now, I guess."

"No, I want your report first. We may be filing charges against the management, including Mr. Bigelow."

I reached the stairs and started up, wondering if the flight would hold both of us in its damaged condition. It had taken a glancing hit from a catapult which had partially destroyed the landing, but Carmody did not hesitate. He trailed me up the twenty or so steps closely enough for me to hear him panting.

We entered Meyers's office and Carmody took it upon himself to sit at Meyers's desk, despite the fact that the chair back was still spattered with dried blood and brains. He propped his chin on his hands, leaning over the desk, and looking right at me. "Find a chair, Miss Ryan. I don't like looking up at people."

I pulled one of the rough-hewn chairs closer to the desk and sat down carefully, mindful that it contained splinters, and when I was as comfortable as I could be in the presence of such awesome power, I asked him where he wanted me to start.

"At the beginning, Miss Ryan: from the time you first set foot on Campbell. And you will omit nothing. Is that clear?"

"Very. But actually, it started before I ever got here. I found that out later. Mr. Bigelow told me."

Carmody slapped the fingers of one hand against his chin. "Whatever," he said.

"Well, evidently he—that is, Captain Corsetti—he was the master of the *Wilmington*—had orders to buy a little time for Meyers before I got here. He called Meyers on the radio as soon as we were in orbit and warned them I was coming. That's an indication to me that Solar management back on Earth knew about the cairn, and meant to conceal it from . . ."

"Forget that part. I'll take care of them. I want to hear about this Indian; what's his name?"

"Kah-Sih-Omah. But we called him Casey. How did you hear about him?"

"Never mind. Get on with it."

"Yes, sir. Well, here again, some of this is second-hand from Bigelow and it was much later when I found out about it, but to begin with I certainly didn't hit it off with Mr. Meyers. He knew why I was here, or thought he did, and he saw his job about to be snatched out from under him. He'd be through if I learned of the cairn."

"Without comments, please, Miss Ryan. Stick to what's revelant."

"I'm only trying to show his attitude, Mr. Carmody."

Carmody seemed to give up at this point. He didn't respond, and I felt safe in going ahead, repeating as much as I could remember, verbatim.

It had started out innocently enough; I'd merely thanked Meyers for meeting me at the dock. His reply had been harsh.

"I didn't come down here for that, lady. I came to check cargo. As far as I'm concerned, you can go back on the next barge. What do you want here, anyway?"

"You know why I'm here, Mr. Meyers. I'm here to make the ecological survey. That's the law. No planet can be opened to colonization or exploitation until the U.N. Ecological Committee has approved it and imposed the necessary restrictions. That's my job, okay? I'm not looking for a fight."

"Nor am I. But I've got enough work to do now without looking after you and wasting time leading you around."

"I don't need looking after. I don't need leading. I can find my own way around. You won't even know I'm here."

I started to leave, and that was when he grabbed me by the arm. It hurt, and I suspected this was his intention. I couldn't shake loose. "Get your hands off me," I demanded. "I'm an officer of the United Nations. You could go to jail for this."

He let go.

"Have it your own way, lady, but keep this in mind: there are 450 healthy construction men on this planet, and no women. Some of them have been here two years without a woman. Maybe I won't know you're here, but every one of them will before you're off this dock." He'd have been all right if he'd stopped there, but he didn't. "Course, maybe that's the way you like it. A girl like you could get rich in the four months you'll be here."

I knew it was a mistake when I did it. I lunged and threw a punch.

He stopped me easily with one ham-like hand. "There'll be none of that, lady. On Campbell I'm the law; judge, jury and all the rest of it. Assaulting me ought to be worth ninety days in the brig, at least. Bigelow," he called.

A big, sleepy-eyed man came over. Meyers thereafter called him Scotty. I didn't know it then, but he wasn't quite as harmless as he looked. Bigelow was the project architect. He was responsible for erecting the landing web, but later it turned out he had a sideline too. He was a part-time assassin.

I went with him to the administration building, where Meyers had told him to take me immediately. Meyers hadn't been subtle about that, although he did try to mask his real purpose. I heard him tell Bigelow to find somebody big, ugly and stupid to be my bodyguard.

Bigelow had seemed nice enough at the time, though he too gave me to understand I was in the way, that they had deadlines to meet, that any delay, however slight, cost the company and the consortium to which it belonged great sums of money, all of which had to be made up by investors who would bid on the minerals when the web was finished. He, personally, feared for his bonuses, which field management would not get if they didn't make the deadlines. And he told me all about the expensive family he was supporting on Earth.

I stood there, locked in a back room feeling sorry for him, and even for Meyers, although I still didn't like Meyers. I was a problem to them, and maybe in their place I'd have felt the same way, guarding against 450 potential rapists.

It seemed like hours before he returned. I amused myself by staring out the one window the room contained. It overlooked a muddy street remarkable for its complete lack of traffic. Then Bigelow came into view followed by a hulking, shambling figure dressed in bib overalls and a hard hat. He wore no shirt, and from beneath his hat fell long black braids, which lay on coppery-skinned shoulders. He was as massive as he was brawny. Bigelow had followed orders in one respect: the man was big. At the time I hoped he was not too dumb, though he gawked around like a tourist. He was not ugly; he was simply ordinary.

Bigelow introduced him as K.C. Oma.

"Hello, Mr. Oma," I said.

"I am called Casey," he replied somewhat shyly. "I am pleased to meet you. Are you ready?"

I thanked Bigelow and followed Casey down the stairs and into the street, walking slightly behind him, watching him. He moved like a shadow, without effort or urgency, and I found myself admiring him for the graceful way he managed that massive form. I had known Indians before. He was tall and light-skinned enough to have been a Northern Sioux, but they were rarely this heavy.

We did not speak until we were inside the suite: a foyer, a kitchen and two bedrooms, all of rough-sawn native timber and sparsely furnished with articles of the same material. "Not the Ritz," I said, "but adequate." Then I realized how dumb that sounded.

I looked around. There was my luggage in the larger

bedroom. I peeked into the other one. In it was a beat-up military-style duffle bag.

Before I could ask the question, Casey answered it. "Mine," he said. "I am to guard you every moment." He sounded as if he really meant it.

I felt the words of protest rise in my throat. But there they stopped, unuttered, and I thought, *It does seem reasonable.* Who could menace me with him nearby? And he did seem nice enough. So I said instead, "Fine, I'll try to be no trouble."

With great innocence he remarked, "You do not trouble me at all, Miss Ryan. Tell me, what is it you will do here?"

"I'm a busybody, Casey. Haven't they told you?"

He shook his head gravely.

I realized I was behaving defensively, making this simple man the object of revenge for the hostile reception at the dock. "Forgive me," I said, "I meant to say I'm here on an ecological survey of the planet, to see if the presence of men will harm it: hurt the local life forms, or create hazards for future colonists, that sort of thing. Understand?"

"Yes, Miss Ryan."

"I'll need to go out in the field, perhaps for days at a time, and I assume that means you'll go too."

"Yes, Miss Ryan. I shall go."

"Have you been out there before?"

"Only near the station, never far in."

At first his answer disturbed me, and I was angered that Meyers had not furnished me with an experienced guide. But after thinking it over, I liked this better. This way I could choose where to go, and this simple man seemed so sincere in his assurances that I believed he could and would protect me, even from Meyers.

"Fine. We'll get started in the morning. We'll need a skimmer. I assume you can arrange that, and that you can drive one."

"Yes, Miss Ryan, I can."

My next question was redundant, in light of what I later learned, but at the time it seemed appropriate, and Casey took no offense. "We'll be camping out for several days, Casey. You'll need to collect equipment and food. I assume you know something about camping and cooking."

"I can manage, Miss Ryan. I will obtain what we need and be ready by morning." He got me settled in, then left me behind locked doors to make preparations.

I did not know at the time what a foment I had caused, or what drastic preparations Meyers and Bigelow were making to insure that I did not leave Campbell with word of the cairn. Though it lay far away in dense woods, and the odds I would find it were astronomically high, they were unwilling to risk even that, fearing that if its existence became known their operation would be halted until we determined what it represented. Perhaps they thought we could consider it a mark of some other race's claim to Campbell and order the planet abandoned.

They had already tried to destroy it, with no success whatever. The effect of modern explosives upon it was nil. Man could not have built it, and he could not demolish it either. Later I learned that Meyers had considered burying it under a mound of dirt, but my unexpected arrival left him no time for that. So they decided instead to destroy Casey, the big, dumb, expendable Indian, and me.

We did not know that then, the morning we left the station aboard a skimmer loaded with death.

At first the day was pleasant, though we were cool to start with, both in shorts, but this area of Campbell was tropical and soon it grew hot, even with the blast of the skimmer's fans to cool us. We headed inland, across the coastal plain where the proto-grasses flourished, but these gave way to a cycad-like growth which was evidently a survivor of the planet's earlier plant evolution. Farther in in the uplands they were rare, supplanted by larger organisms closely resembling terrestrial trees.

There was much of interest to see, and we flew low, just high enough to avoid obstacles, while I drank it in. We spoke little beyond what was necessary to call each other's attention to some new curiosity. I was too excited to risk missing something, and he too tactiturn.

Our course was leisurely, and we followed the streams that flowed down from the highlands to the sea. Here life teemed, and we stopped many times to observe and photograph it, hanging on the skimmer's fans and hovering over small herds of little animals which gathered at the streams to drink.

Campbell was made for skimmers. Its sun was bright and poured its energy into the cells that covered our hull, from which it flowed into the plastic batteries built into it and thence to the motors which drove the fans. Riding in one made me feel detached, as though it was the magic carpet of the old Arabian nights.

Nightfall found us in the highlands, where the air was cooler. Casey set up a tent for me, there among the trees, and we ate from supplies brought from the settlement. Whether out of shyness or due to some unspoken preference, Casey refused to occupy the tent and instead rolled up in a blanket outside.

By then he had demonstrated he was no stranger to the woods. He laid out the camp in an expert manner, with the tent rigidly erect on taut ropes and perched for drainage on a little hummock. His fire blazed brightly and cleanly, fed with dry, dead wood and banked carefully to last the night. Whatever doubts, whatever reservations I had had about the man disappeared that night. I slept as soundly in my tent as I ever had on Earth.

The morning brought the smell of fresh coffee into the tent, borne on a gentle breeze. I rose to find Casey bent over the fire, cooking breakfast. Around us there was a heavy fog which swathed the tops of the trees and blotted out the half-risen sun.

I took the steaming mug from him and tasted it, while he divided the contents of the skillet onto stainless steel plates. It too smelled wonderful, and I found myself drawing deep breaths of Campbell's morning air into my lungs. And I said to him, "Casey, this is why I'm here. Smell that air. Nothing like it exists on Earth—anywhere. All that man spoiled long ago. But I mean to see that no one spoils this."

He handed me a plate, which I took gratefully, but he said nothing. Instead he met my gaze, pausing a brief moment before resuming his task. Had that been a tear in his eye? From the smoke, perhaps. Surely not because of what I'd said. But then, of course, I did not know that Casey had seen it all before.

We ate, struck camp, wiped the condensate from the skimmer's cells, and started off again. More and bigger trees appeared, growing in clumps, not yet numerous enough to become a continuous forest. They yielded a kind of nut, on which fed little beasts about the size of cats. We saw the first sizeable group of them that morning. They were quadrupedal, with good manipulative ability with their front paws, and scurried about gathering and crunching nuts despite our approach.

I did not know a great deal about Campbell's life forms. What I did know came from survey reports made by the first scout teams to visit here, and like all survey reports they covered only the obvious.

They had, to their own satisfaction, ruled out the existence of intelligent life. It was a fairly safe bet, since Campbell appeared to be geologically younger than Earth, and its life consequently less highly organized. There were evolutionary confluences, of course, but on this land mass, at least, these did not extend to large grazing forms or to large predators.

Campbellian protein was organized slightly differently from the terrestrial norm, and utilized different amino acid groups in its structure. Most of it was simply useless as food for human beings, who couldn't metabolize it—but some of it was poisonous as well.

We observed and photographed animals for a while, then began to follow a stream which wound its way through the foothills of the still-distant mountains. Here again we saw teeming life, this time in a pool. The creatures which threw their shadows on its sandy bottom were not fish, but occupied the same ecological position as fish and had the same problems: they were hunted.

The predator beast had fangs in his jaws and claws on his feet. He was no larger than the nut grazers, though he managed to look ferocious, even leonine, as he growled at us. We left him to his fishing and continued.

That night we camped in the foothills. Once again Casey pitched the tent. This time I was not content to bury myself in notebooks as I had the night before and retire early from the weariness of the journey. I had become acclimated to the outdoor life and caught up in the spirit of the adventure. I was resolved to leave the recording of trivia to another day, and instead enjoy those things that made this journey personally memorable.

And so I took over the task of cooking while Casey went to the stream for water. I sat by the fire and drank in the aroma of the food and the still, calm pleasure of Campbell's star-studded night.

Casey returned, looking troubled. At first he refused to tell me why. But I pestered him without mercy, and then he explained.

"It may mean nothing," he said, "but I have found the remains of a fire."

He took me to it, and we examined it by torchlight, along the banks of the stream: charred lumps of wood, so tiny I could hardly see them, scattered around and half buried in the sand. They meant something to him. I would never have noticed them, much less equated them with the presence of men, and did not understand his concern.

"So," I said, "other men have been here, made a fire. Why should this disturb you?"

"Because now I must search for their bones." He reached down and took an object from the sand, where it had been shallowly buried. He brushed away the debris. It was the skull of one of the fish creatures, and it looked charred.

"The creatures of this world are different from those of the Earth. Some can be safely eaten, though they provide little nourishment and taste foul. Most are not safe. These are poisonous, though it appears that they have been roasted and the flesh eaten."

"By whom? Surely if you know this others do as well."

"Yes, it is common knowledge—now. So this must have been done by an early exploration party, dead before I came here. I know of no one missing from the station since then, and the signs are old. I will search again in the morning."

He did, but found nothing except more fishbones. That day I saw the grim side of Casey, for he was morose and troubled, as though he took this as a sign. And in truth it was, for us, as the first of the disasters struck us.

Suddenly our dead reckoner became a dead dead reckoner. It refused to show our position on the console display, but meandered from one side of the screen to the other. We could get nothing but a feeble, anemic-looking blip that rolled around the bottom of the screen.

"Can you repair it, Casey?"

His glance answered even before his words. "It is beyond my skill, even if I had the parts and tools. We will have to work: use the satellite beacon and calculate our position from its next pass. I suggest that we do not move until we have done that." He switched on the radio and punched the red button for the navigation channel.

We waited. The time came and went, but the beacon did not register as it overflew. Casey removed the cowling from the receiver, no easy task without proper tools. He looked into the works and sighed. "Fused. The tuner will not move. There has been a surge of some kind: an arc across the plates. They have been welded together. If I force them, the tuner will break. If I do not, we cannot match the satellite's frequency."

"What else do we have?" I felt peculiarly helpless, since my education did not extend to such technical things, and I lacked the knowledge even to fully appreciate our predicament.

"Nothing. Not even a compass. Modern science replaced such things long ago with gadgetry. I'm afraid we'll have to resort to even more primitive methods."

"Can you find our way back to the station?"

"Certainly. To the east is the sea. We could hardly miss that, and once there we can follow the shoreline to the station. We are not in any danger of becoming lost, but I suggest we do not risk further problems by continuing inland. We should return at once."

Reluctantly I agreed. I was disappointed, but there was still plenty of time. We could get another skimmer and go out again, and this time we'd check it out carefully before we left.

Casey changed course, headed east, and carefully watched the skimmer's shadow on the ground below. He took what he hoped was the proper heading to get us near the station, holding a slight angle to the right and trying to compensate mentally for the passage of time. It was tedious work.

I left him alone, partly because I realized he was very busy and partly in reflection of my own disgust with this unhappy turn of events. I sat there, feeling the rush of wind through my hair and listening to the steady hum of the fans.

I began hearing a click, at first barely audible, which grew louder as time went on.

Casey noticed it too, and cocked an ear to listen. There was a look of concern on his face, as though he anticipated more mechanical problems. Then the sound vanished, and Casey's look went with it.

After that we flew on at a steady speed of about forty-five knots for nearly two hours without a hint of what the mysterious noise had been. With their simple construction and controls, there was little that could go wrong with a skimmer, and neither of us then suspected the click represented anything more than a twig lodged in one of the fan grills.

Then the escarpment appeared. It threatened to run for miles perpendicular to our path. To go around meant risking the loss of our orientation, human senses being as fallible as they are. Casey therefore decided to increase our altitude and climb it, and then to camp on the high plains for the night, which was rapidly approaching.

But as he increased power to gain the necessary lift, the click abruptly returned. It grew into a loud knock, and then a squeal joined it. Together they lapsed into a pounding vibration. I clung to the seat, fearful of being thrown out, for the skimmer had begun to list and pitch. Casey fought to control it, but could not stabilize us. In desperation, he cut the power and we dropped like a stone, our lifting surfaces inadequate to support us without the help of the fans.

Trees, in the path of our steep and rapid glide, rushed toward us. I could see Casey straining with the stick, trying to guide us toward a small clearing near the bend of a stream, but I knew we'd never make it. I was still watching in horror when the ground came up and we struck it with a glancing blow that jolted every bone in my body. We were sliding along the ground, striking bushes and rocks, a cloud of dust and debris rising around us. Then I felt myself being flung forward and knew I would hit the windscreen. Desperately, I tried to duck.

Then I saw stars and briefly tasted blood. After that came darkness.

I do not know how long my personal night lasted. I awoke to the real night, staring upward into Campbell's star-strewn sky and feeling wet and cold. There was pain in my face and in my arms and legs. I could still taste blood, and a couple of my front teeth felt loose. But testing, I found my arms and legs seemed to work.

I strained to raise my head, felt a wave of pain, and dropped back into the coarse sand beneath me. I would have to try that a little more slowly. I looked around again, into the darkness, turning my head from side to side. There was little to be seen in the darkness except a glow on my right, toward a distant hilltop. As I watched, I could see it was creeping up the slope, and the realization came, aided by the acrid smell of smoke in the air, that it was a fire. And then it dawned on me I didn't know where Casey was.

Ignoring the pain this time, I struggled to my feet, took an experimental step or two, and stumbled over something. I strained to see in the darkness of Campbell's moonless night. Below was a shapeless mass. Our tent? No, the satchel of supplies: part of it, anyway. It smelled funny, and I realized it had been burnt.

I groped at it, trying to find the opening and get a flashlight. That was when I heard Casey moan. He was underneath the bag, holding it with both arms. It was *he*, not the bag, who had been burnt.

I struggled with the bag, pulling it downward toward his feet, until at last it slipped off him. I opened it and searched frantically through its contents, until at last I found a shape that was right.

Pushing the switch brought forth a stabbing beam of light. In it I could see the burned stumps of trees, and the ground covered with blackened ash. Grasses, still holding their living form but now consisting only of fragile ash, disintegrated into little puffs as eddies of wind hit them.

I turned the light on Casey and gasped in horror. His fingers were charred stumps. Above them his arms were blistered horribly, and while the bag apparently had protected his upper chest and face, his hair hung loosely around his head, the braids singed off. There was a deep gash in his forehead. The blood had run down his neck and puddled darkly beneath his head.

The moan had told me Casey lived, and the sight told me how badly off he really was. There are few things more painful than burns, and fewer still more difficult to treat. In time, when the protective shock wore off, he would be suffering horribly, and I must then be ready to give him what help I could.

There was precious little in our bag of medical supplies. I searched through it and found nothing even remotely adequate. There was a tube of antiseptic jelly with which I coated the worst parts of his burnt arms and hands. But there were no large dressings, no unguents, and only three ampules of morphine sulfate to relieve his pain. They would not help for long. I decided to wait until his need was greatest before using them. I covered him with a blanket and sat down beside him to consider my own situation.

I was not badly hurt. I had only small bumps, cuts and abrasions. From the looks of the front of my blouse, I had bled profusely from the nose, and while this was sore, it did not seem to be broken.

Alone, with the shock wearing off, I tried to piece things together. I knew what must have happened: the crash of the skimmer, into a rock or large tree, must have ruptured cells in its hull, shorting them out and setting fire to the underbrush. This would have melted other portions of the hull and started more fires.

I did not see the remains of the skimmer nearby.

Therefore I had been removed from the site, dunked in the stream, then placed here on the sand. Casey would have been all right then. And the fact that I had not been burned, or even singed, meant I had not come through the fire. That meant Casey had returned to the wreck to get the bag, and by that time the fire must have been fierce. He'd gotten his injuries retrieving the bag. Why did he risk it?

Then I remembered: the native foods would not sustain human life. We needed terrestrial food. Without the skimmer return to the settlement would take weeks: long enough so that we'd have risked starvation on the way. Casey knew that we needed the bag to get back; that we were isolated and lost, with no expectation of rescue. That's why he'd gone back.

I felt brief anger at him then, for sacrificing both of us. His male mind had told him that he must save me by getting the food, but not that without him I had no hope whatsoever of making it. *I* knew it—and strangely it didn't bother me to know; not like it bothered me to have the responsibility for comforting Casey in what I realized would be his last hours.

As I sat there, all alone in the darkness, I realized I had absolutely no way of coping with the situation. I could only huddle here, wrapped in a blanket, and watch Casey's life pass away along with Campbell's night.

The shock wore off, and fatigue marched in and took me away. For a time I slept. Then the rising sun woke me. Opening my eyes, I could see it was already at least an hour past dawn. I must be up, to see to Casey. I strained to rise, and found that slumber had brought me stiffness to go with my pain. Every joint ached, every movement was agony; nevertheless I did gain my feet.

Around me, the blackened landscape loomed starkly. A hundred yards away the skimmer hung, its bow canted against the bole of a still smouldering tree. Its skin had melted off in the fire, exposing the steel skeleton, now buckled and bent in the middle so that the stern rested flat on the ground.

Casey had not moved; he still lay, arms crooked, beneath the blanket. I could not tell if he was alive, and hesitated long moments before raising the blanket to look.

It would have shocked me less to find him dead. His eyes were open. Incredibly, they moved. He was conscious, and remarkably composed, and he seemed to have been waiting for me.

I gasped at the sight, and it was a moment before I found my voice, "Casey, I have the morphine. I'll give you some."

"No." His voice was strong. It was not consistent with the terrible pain I knew he must be experiencing. "Save it," he said. "I am in control." Then he closed his eyes.

He's delirious, I remember telling myself. I broke. I was not in control.

"Casey, your hands," I shouted. "There's nothing left of them. What are we going to do?"

The eyes opened, again calmly, to reassure me. Again he spoke in strange words. "We will wait."

"Casey, we're lost, hundreds of miles from the station. Nobody knows we're here. I can't get us back. I can't get myself back, much less move you."

"We will wait." His voice fairly boomed at me. "Set up the tent around me, then let me sleep. And wash that blood off your face. You look awful."

Again he closed his eyes, and again I was terrified. Was this merely the product of delirium, or was Casey some kind of superman, immune to pain? He looked so bad: yet he sounded so strong, so positive. For long moments I knelt there, bent over him, watching his chest rise and fall with deep, even breaths. Then I covered him again and went to do as he asked.

I washed away the blood, soaking a bandanna in the cool water of the stream, so that I could go back and do the same for him.

I could not tell whether or not the strain was playing tricks with my imagination or whether I really saw what I thought, but at the time he seemed a little more gaunt, a little thinner, than he had the day before. When I went to clean the dried blood from his face, the gash that had gaped at me so malignantly the night before now seemed tiny and insignificant.

I had to get hold of myself, curb my imagination. Nothing helps do that quite so well as work. So I pitched the tent: not as well as Casey would have, but adequately, then gathered wood and built a fire. I cooked and ate a light meal, then took the dishes to the stream to wash them—terrifying, in the process, the fish creatures which swam there, trapped in an oxbow pond.

Casey slumbered on inside the tent, oblivious of the awesome destruction his body had endured. He did not waken again, though I feared he would at any moment: that he would find his control gone and fearsome pain present, and I would need the morphine.

I pondered now his recovery, where short hours ago I had pondered his death. If he survived he would be helpless for weeks. I looked at the bag of supplies, which was by no means full, and wondered how we could stretch them out. We'd planned six days in the skimmer. On foot it would be more like six weeks, if we could make it at all.

Time passed. I waited silently in the shade just inside the tent flap, and adjusted it from time to time to keep the sun off Casey. Campbell rotated in slightly more than nineteen standard hours. With next to no axial tilt there were roughly ten hours of daylight. As light began to ebb, I resolved the night would not be dark, and that this time the fire would be friendly.

Because of the destruction of vegetation in the area I had to go farther than usual to find wood, but I returned just as the light was about to fail, intending to check once more on Casey before it did. I dumped the wood on the ground and brushed off pieces of bark, then entered the tent and raised the blanket.

He did not stir, but appeared to be sleeping peacefully. Sometime during the day his arms had descended, and now rested across his chest beneath the blanket. Is it the light, I asked myself, or does he look yet thinner than he did before?

Over the bones of his face the skin stretched tight, and his cheeks seemed hollow. Then I glanced at his forehead. The gash had dwindled: shrunk, the way a healing cut does, to a fraction of its former size, as if days had passed instead of hours. This, I knew, was real. It was not a product of my mind. And I knew that what was real was in no way natural either, but I found my attitude about Casey's situation changing. It was not a question of *if* he recovered, but *when*.

Troubled by this perplexing fact and many others, I went outside and looked up into the night. Ahead and low on the horizon was the escarpment, which was probably the best reason I had to be pessimistic. We would have to climb it to reach the sea, and though Casey's miraculous slumber might eventually mend what was left of him, he might survive it merely to join me in starvation. The escarpment was our greatest obstacle, and we had met it at the worst time.

It seemed to stretch out endlessly in both directions. It was both steep and high. And what was nothing to a skimmer was insurmountable to us now. No doubt along its course there existed breaches in its face, where a healthy person could climb up, and I could imagine myself struggling up some steep ravine, slipping on fallen rock and tearing at creepers for handholds. But Casey? No. His battered stumps of hands would be useless, and I simply lacked the strength to get him to the top.

I caught myself thinking, *if only there was help: somebody else nearby.* A useless plea that flashed across my mind about the time I saw, or thought I saw, the fire at the top of the escarpment. Fire? Did I see it or did my mind create the image? It was but a flicker, a pinpoint that flashed across my retinas, then was gone.

I grew cold, and wrapped myself in a blanket. And creeping inside the tent, I lay at Casey's feet, staring at the flickering embers of our own fire. It had not occurred to me, as I fell asleep, that it, too, might be seen from far away.

Morning came. I rose with the sun, feeling somewhat less achey than I had the day before, and now resigned to what was to be. Casey slumbered on, looking even more skeletal, eyes now sunken in their sockets beneath dark lids. But the gash! The gash was gone! Not just diminished, but *gone*, without scab, without scar: not even a discoloration was left. I felt my blood run cold.

With shaking hands I grasped the blanket and drew it

down, past his now-bony neck and across his chest. Through the unbuttoned shirt it, too, looked shallow, and where thick muscles had laced across it ribs now pushed prominently through his skin.

And then I looked at his arms, which rested across his abdomen, expecting to see devastation, perhaps gangrene. Burnt skin had sloughed off and lay in flakes beneath them. Blisters had drained. In place of blackened ruin now appeared smooth pink skin, devoid of any scarring.

Reason told me this could not be: that it was in my mind the fantasy lay. But even as I gazed in disbelief my eyes dropped to his hands, no longer charred and cracking, oozing fluid and dripping life away, bare stumps of useless, tortured flesh. A scream rose in my throat, which at the last minute I stifled, while blood thumped a fierce tattoo and went pounding across my temples.

The hands were whole, smooth and pink, lacking only nails—and at the fingertips these, too, were budding. I dropped the blanket and knelt there, over this strange new Casey, reflecting on what I'd seen, convinced it was not real. Then I wondered: did fantasy deceive touch, as it did the eyes? And some insane curiosity impelled me to reach out. I felt—not charred and hardened ruin— but firm warm flesh, and a pulse, faint, but regular. This time the scream came, shrill and piercing, and echoed down the valley.

Casey stirred. He opened his eyes and smiled weakly, totally obliterating the demonic picture of him that had been forming in my mind, becoming once more only a man. I lost my fear and again I knelt beside him, holding his hand, waiting for him to gain the strength to speak. Whatever sort of miracle was taking place, I was now grateful.

Presently his lips began to move. At first no sound came out, but I bent near and strained to hear, and at last he became audible.

"I have control," he said. "I have rebuilt; replaced the damaged tissue. But my body's reserves are gone; used up. They must now be replaced. Help me."

He referred, of course, to his emaciated condition.

Somehow he had moved tissue into the wounded parts, perhaps at great peril to his system as a whole, and it was this he wanted to protect now. But what was it he wanted me to do?

"How, Casey? Tell me how."

"I need protein: lots of it. I must eat meat."

I started to rise. "I'll get it for you, Casey."

But he held tightly to my hand. "No," he said. "Not from the supplies. Those are for you. You need them."

"Where, then?"

"From the stream. There is food in the stream."

"The fish? But you said they were poisonous." I knelt again, still holding his hand.

"To you: not to me. I can metabolize them; make the poisons harmless. You cannot. Listen to me: you have seen that I am different. Now do as I ask."

Weak though his voice was, its tone was commanding, and I went down to the stream, to trap the fish creatures imprisoned in the pond. Some spare clothing and a length of springy root became a net, with which I hurled the helpless creatures up on the shore until I had all of them the pool contained. Then, with my hands, I dug a passage through the soft mud and sand, so more could enter from the stream.

They smelled terrible, cooking on the spit. I did not know how to clean them. Casey seemed not to mind, but ate every bit I fed him. Throughout the day he ate all I could catch, interrupting his disgusting repast with catnaps in between.

By nightfall he had gained strength to the point where he could sit up. "Tomorrow," he said, "I shall hunt."

I had not troubled him with questions during the long day. In truth, I lacked sufficient insight to ask anything meaningful. I knew only that he was a most extraordinary man, if that was in fact his nature; that the experience I was having was unique to human memory. When the sun set I fell asleep, still wondering whether this was real or a dream.

I rose late, with the sun high outside the tent and Casey gone. I found him outside, transformed. Still thin, still gaunt, but looking fit and now whole, he stood there, moccasins of deerskin on his feet, a deerskin loincloth spanning lithe hips. His hair, now too short to braid, was bound with a strip of cloth. These had come, no doubt, from the depths of the battered dufflebag, along with the curious necklace that now hung across his chest.

He saw me look at that.

"Serpent's teeth," he said, "for luck. One of my talismans. We can use some good luck for a change."

"I hope so," I said. "So far, it's all been bad."

Casey was fashioning a javelin of sorts, using a stick and a sharpened tent peg. "Luck," he said, "had nothing to do with our misfortunes. It was sabotage."

I stared at him for long moments, finally finding voice. "But how, and who?"

"As to the instruments, I cannot say for sure. The fire left little trace of them. But I found the fan-bearing housings full of emery, and that is why they failed."

"But who? Who would want us dead?"

"Not us: you. I am nothing to them, whoever they are. You menace someone at the station. Compelled to guess, I would say they fear your mission here will uncover something which will deny them this world."

"What? Certainly I've yet found nothing which would require that, unless . . ." The thought occurred to me. "Casey, how long have you been on Campbell?"

"About three years; since the first crews came."

"And you've traveled about?"

"Some, though never this far from the sea."

"Have you seen, or heard rumors of, any advanced life forms here?"

"No, I never have. Why do you ask?"

"Because," I said, still not sure I had not dreamed it, "the other night I thought I saw a fire, out on the escarpment."

"Perhaps you did. Maybe it was a search party, out looking for us."

"But they don't know we're lost. We're not overdue yet. And why, if they were men, have they not yet come to us? Perhaps they are not men. This is a big world. And unlikely though it seems, considering the low order of life the planet seems to support, it is not impossible that intelligence arose here. Making, even using, fire requires intelligence of a relatively high order. Certainly well beyond anything we've yet encountered. And," I added, "the existence of native intelligent life is an eminently good reason to kill me. The planet would belong to them. Solar Minerals would be out on its neck."

"Show me where you saw the fire, Kim."

I pointed with reasonable certainty toward the escarpment. *Had he used my first name?* "It's there," I said, "where the dark streak is."

"Then we shall go that way. Now eat, while I prepare packs. I am afraid we must abandon the tent and the less useful equipment, to travel light."

All day we trekked across the scrublands which lay between the foothills and the escarpment. Our goal was the escarpment's base, and it was deceptively distant. The going was difficult; our passage was hindered by heavy brush and gulleys strewn with rocks. When at last we stopped, to camp by a small stream, Casey would not allow a fire. We ate cold food. After that Casey went to work, fashioning snares of tent cordage and setting them by the water.

When the sun set we lay in darkness, huddled together under blankets. Though exhausted, I could not sleep, but lay there wondering if, even with his marvelous skill at woodmanship, we'd ever make it back to the sea. More than that, I believed that now I could summon the nerve to ask the question which had nagged me since the crash: a question I had been afraid to ask, because I did not know if I could live with the answer if I got one.

So, following my impulse, and without further reflection I blurted it out. "What are you, Casey?" *There, I'd done it.*

He did not answer at once, but sighed. "I am Kah-Sih-Omah. He-Who-Waits, in the tongue of my fathers."

I rose on my left elbow and faced him. "No," I said. "Not who; *what* are you, Casey? You know what I mean. You owe me a truthful answer."

Again he paused, as if deliberating whether or not to say anything at all. Again came the sigh. "This is true, Kim. I do indeed owe you that. But I fear that what you ask is unanswerable. I have myself asked the same question too often to remember."

I was becoming angry now, finding courage in my impatience. "Don't try riddles with me, Casey. You aren't, and never were, the dumb Indian you pretend to be, though you play the part to perfection. Admit it: you are more than human. Now tell me truthfully: what are you?"

He protested my anger. His answer rang with sadness all the same, and there was a curious cracking in his voice. "In truth, I do not know what I am, or even exactly how I came to be. I can only tell you this: if I am no longer man, I once was, long ago. I have lived a very long time already. I may never be able to die, however much I may wish to."

A horrible thought struck me. "The fish, Casey! Did you eat them to poison yourself, so you could die?" I pictured myself alone, beside his rotting corpse.

"No, Kim. I ate them for strength, knowing they could not harm me. I desperately wanted to live because you needed me."

I felt ashamed at this and spoke no more, but Casey, having started, seemed constrained to continue; as though it meant something special to him to explain, to have someone share.

"I have done this before," he said. "Some believed me and some did not. I have shared this tale of grief with other friends, only to watch them age and wither away: to leave me in death, all alone, separated from all others by the cruelest of all barriers: time. I am trapped in an eternal present."

His voice took on plaintive tones. There was a great sorrow in it, and a touch of frustration he tried very hard to subdue. "I have tried many lives, and been many things in the time I have already lived. In the beginning I was most assuredly a man, with all a man's infirmities. I grew old as a man—then suddenly I was young again, and have remained so ever since, though I can take the appearance of age or any other feature of man whenever it suits me.

"I was a shaman of the People: a medicine man. This I remember, as I remember all that happened before, and all that happened since the vision which changed me. I had gone to the mountaintop to fast, in hopes that the spirits would speak to me. For many days and nights I waited, and they were silent. Then I took the cup: the spirit of the sacred mushroom steeped in water. It is hallucinogenic, which compounds the mystery of my transformation, since I could not tell what was fact and what was fantasy. I have a memory of an awesome flame and terrible burning pain, then of a satisfying inner peace such as no other I have ever known. I believed at the time that I had been with God.

"When the vision began, I was an old man, perhaps sixty. The People had no accurate way of reckoning time, but in my calling age was much revered. When I awoke I was much as you see me now, and the People did not know me, though I told them I was Kah-Sih-Omah. My wife denied me. To them I was a stranger who had come upon cherished family secrets through magic and overcome Kah-Sih-Omah. I had his medicine bundle; therefore I was more powerful than he, potent though he was. And in superstitious fear they drove me away.

"I did not know then of my immortality. I still feared death.

"I wandered the land as an outcast, perhaps for millennia, certainly for many centuries. I found that within certain relatively broad limits I could control both my form and my features, though radical changes were onerous and required enormous concentration to hold. Minor changes required next to no effort; therefore I could adapt to any tribe and live among them, learn their tongue and customs, and be as they were, until they noticed I did not grow old. I rarely remained that long in any one place, and so, in time, I had no identity. And as time changes men, so also does it change cultures. Even the People lost their identity in the time I had lived.

"When I was young, mammoths roamed the Americas. By the time they passed, I was already intimate with both continents, South and North, and with those who lived upon them. I conversed with each in his own tongue and believed at the time this was all there was to the world.

"Then I learned of great, fierce strangers who visited the far north. Great hulking Vikings with pale skin and hair on their faces, who used weapons and implements of iron brought from lands beyond the eastern sea. I went north, becoming as they were, and lived among them. But they found the land too harsh and the distance from home too great. When they sailed away, I went with them.

"It was in Europe where I began to really understand my plight, for the Europeans possessed a true conception of the passage of time. Here too, I made my first acquaintance with the messianic redemptionist religions of the Middle East. It was an era of foment. Islam and Christendom fought each other on the battlefields, each claiming true insight into the destiny of man.

"I had to know my reason to be. For a time I believed the answer lay in the East, and I went there, seeking to find the purpose my existence served, to end the boredom of useless existence. Still, none could, or would, tell me. I began to regard what answers they gave me as purely parochial. They were seers, such as I had been, whose movements had acquired the trappings of cults and mired themselves in mindless dogma. I knew well the ways of the wizards. I understood their motives, and how wily, indolent men sometimes corrupt a noble concept, using knowledge to acquire wealth and power.

"I wanted none of these, so I abandoned them and traveled on, to India. There, despite more mountains of superstitious nonsense, I remained a century or two and sifted through it, finding much that was good. I found not an answer, but an aid: a truly realistic concept of the vastness of time that contemplated both a beginning and an end.

"And then I knew I was not truly immortal, that I would someday end—if not with the death of Earth, then with the death of the universe. I knew also that, while life was finite after all, it would seem infinite to me, and yet in that infinity—somewhere, out of sight and understanding, to be revealed to me someday—I had a purpose.

"While man remained pinned to Earth, I searched that world over, hoping to find clues. By then I had little doubt that the beings who changed me were no more than an unimaginably advanced race, though it still seemed meet to think of them as spirits. It was not a question of what *they* were but of *who else* they might also have changed.

"In that respect, too, I was different from other men, who only hoped humanity would someday reach the stars. I *knew*—knew that other races had, and that man would; and that when he did I would search the cosmos also, for my creators.

"That story you know well enough—of the great, mysterious Kazim, and of his son, Omar; of their vast wealth, and their use of it to find and seize the key, the alien computer buried deep in the Andes. I was both these men. It was my wealth that brought us here, Kim." He sighed, and paused.

"Yes," I replied, and gave a silent sigh myself. And to myself I silently added, *And it is your character*.

But Casey did not notice. He was lost in his past. "I envisioned space as ennobling, then," he continued. "I believed it marked a new era for man, when he would regard himself merely as man and leave his old vices behind him, buried in the Earth from which they both sprang.

"I was wrong. I shipped aboard the first of man's star-traveling vessels—the *Gandhi*, bound for that world which we now call Herschel, though at the time we could not be certain a liveable world lay out there. In the boredom, passions grew. Intrigues ran rampant—prejudices surfaced and became weapons.

"Kazim had conceived the *Gandhi* as a racial effort. Her components were built by many different peoples, each ignorant of what the other was doing. They were assembled under his control, and she lifted under U.N. auspices.

"But the nations of men died hard. Each nation packed its quota with spies, eager to claim for that nation the full secrets of her construction. They would have wrecked her to get them.

"Inevitably, mutiny flared. I was killed, or so they

thought. But the body that went out the airlock was the captain's, not mine; and I took his place, to reign like a potentate over the bedlam the ship had become.

"It was then that I resolved never again, aside from grave emergency, to allow my differences to show. I became the epitome of the common man.

"So I wait, as I have for centuries, for my sign, preparing myself as best I can for what must come. Now I know my destiny approaches. But it is a lonely wait."

Then Casey spoke no more. I huddled near him, to comfort him. Though I was but an infinitesimal fraction of what he was, he took it, and for a while that loneliness we both felt ebbed, and was for a time forgotten.

With daylight we could risk a fire. I was kindling one when Casey returned from checking snares. He carried one of the nut creatures, and the head of his javelin was stained with blood.

He plunged the javelin into the ground, where it would be handy, and set about skinning the animal with one of the mess kit's knives. Though he had talked a great deal the night before, he was strangely silent now. He finished the flaying, spitted the carcass over the fire, and took its entrails down to the stream to wash them. At the time I thought perhaps he regretted baring his soul to me.

He returned, bearing a glazed mass, which he stuffed into a plastic jar and liberally salted. Then he took the spit from me, turning it slowly until the meat turned uniformly brown and began to crackle, dripping melted fat into the fire.

I watched him tear off a small fragment and chew it carefully. Then he swallowed it and said, "You may safely eat this. Your body will make use of little of it, but it will not harm you, and it is filling. We must now use all the land will give us, if we are ever to reach the station."

Strange words, I thought. His voice carried foreboding, but I did not pry. I now knew that Casey revealed himself in his own good time and at his own pace. I ate what he gave me, and it was good.

Then, while I broke camp, Casey scraped and salted

the animal's hide. He rolled it up and tied it with a thong. "Come," he said, picking up his pack and javelin. Then he walked off in the direction of the wrecked skimmer.

"Casey, that's the wrong direction." I was mystified.

"I know, but come with me. I must show you something."

I followed him, sensing his disturbance, all the way to the stream, where we came to an area of packed sand.

He stopped and pointed down. "Look," he said, pointing to tracks in the sand. "Something stalks us."

Fear washed over me. "What—who?"

"I do not know. It is not human, but it is not a beast, either. I had four snares. All caught game, but three were raided. Only that closest to our fire was undisturbed."

"Maybe another animal . . ."

"No. Animals bite or break the cord. They do not untie the knots. They kill with teeth or claws, not clubs. The thief had a stone axe. He put it on the ground while he took our game. He stepped on it, leaving its impression in the sand. There are the thongs binding head to haft. Observe this footprint. This foot was not bare; it was covered. When the creature knelt on one knee, it did not mark the ground with toes."

I tried my best to see what he saw, but even with his explanation this was not easy. But then, he had been here before and had had time to think about an explanation, and if he thought the thief had not been human I wanted to know why.

"There are other tracks, farther along. They are in soft mud and bear impressions well. And the shape and size of the foot is wrong. So is its articulation. There is no arch, and the foot that made the tracks did not bend in the manner of the human foot. The creature's strides are impossibly long, suggesting a giant, yet it is also impossibly light. There are other signs, less visible but equally informative. We are fortunate that there was only one of them."

"So Campbell has sapients. And Solar Minerals knew it. You were right about them wanting me dead."

"It would seem so. But now we face new danger:

more enemies. That is why I must now make weapons and why I may again have to kill, loathe as I am to do so. But come, we must travel. We can learn nothing more here."

Throughout the day we walked steadily. I found myself taking frequent nervous glances behind, searching the undergrowth for signs of the tall creature. Once or twice I thought I saw something, but Casey assured me there was no cause for alarm.

From time to time he stopped and picked rocks from the ground, slipping them into his pack. Once, while I rested, he went off into the bush to cut a stave. Later, as we walked, he whittled on it. The stave took form and symmetry, becoming a bow before my eyes.

We camped that night at the base of the escarpment, taking shelter in a shallow cave, from whose entrance Casey labored long to erase our spoor. Again we ate cold food, afraid to risk a fire. "Tomorrow," Casey said, "we shall be armed, and make preparation for the climb."

I lolled around the next day watching Casey's wizardry with the rocks he had collected. Pressing shards against a bit of bone, he fractured and shaped them with consummate skill into dozens of exquisitely formed arrowheads. Then, with enough of these, he ventured out to cut quills. Peeled, split, notched, and winged with bits of plastic, these became the shafts of his arrows. Their heads he bound on with twisted strips of wet gut taken from the animal in the snare. Other strips, tightly twisted, became the bowstring, and sewed the seams of the quiver he made from the salted hide. As the thong dried, it bound tightly whatever it encircled; such was Casey's skill in the wild.

That night I fell asleep in his arms, confident, as the light died, that I was safe with a protector far better armed than any enemy who stalked us.

Later on we met the enemy, there in the dark hollowness of the cavern. I was thrown suddenly aside, awakened by a scream never uttered by a human throat. I crawled away from thrashing feet and grabbed a torch from my pack, then flashed its light around the cave.

Casey struggled with a gangling giant who reached

nearly to the top of the cavern. In one of the creature's hands was a stone axe: in the other, Casey's throat.

Casey held the axe arm back with one hand. With the other he lashed out. His enemy was mighty and determined, and was pushing Casey back toward the wall, though Casey's muscles strained and knotted in resistance. His feet left furrows in the cave's sandy floor as he was forced to give way.

I jumped to my feet, side-stepping them, and they struggled past me. I flashed the light around the cave, fearing other enemies might be about to enter and trying to think of something I could do to help. Casey was no weakling, but he had not yet recovered his full strength.

There in the corner of the cave stood the bow and quiver, which I lacked the skill to use. But there also, stuck in the sand, was the javelin. I ran to it and pulled it free just as a strange sound struck my ears. I flashed the light at the wall. Casey's opponent had kicked his feet out from under him and the sound had come from his head hitting the wall.

The light momentarily distracted the creature. It turned to look at me. For an instant I froze in my tracks as that face inspired pure terror in me, but when it turned its attention back on Casey I knew what I had to do. I brought up the javelin and thrust its head deep into the creature's back.

There was another blood-curdling scream, but it lasted only an instant. Before my eyes and in the torchlight the being literally wilted. A torrent of orange-pink fluid poured from its wound onto the cave floor. It seemed to collapse in sections, like a beach toy deflating. The axe clattered to the ground.

Casey scrambled to his feet. He seized the torch from me and held it on the alien, now curiously flattened and growing even flatter with each passing moment. My nerve broke. I sank to my knees and broke into tears. Casey moved to console me. I struggled for a time to speak, and found words difficult to come by. When they did come they were in broken gasps. "Casey—uh—what is that thing?"

"It is the being who raided our snares, I would guess. It had been tracking us, presumably with this." He pointed to its long snout. "Such noses are found on all earthly creatures with acute sense of smell. I wish you had not killed it."

I was suddenly hurt; defensive. "But you were losing, Casey. I had to do something."

"Its anatomy was strange to me. I needed time to find its vulnerabilities, so I retreated to the wall to explore it. Despite its size it is far weaker than a man. You will perceive it has no bones."

"No bones," I screamed in disbelief.

"It lacks a rigid skeleton on which to anchor muscles, therefore it has great resilience but little strength. That is the reason it died so swiftly once punctured with a deep wound. The fluids expelled were under considerable pressure to hold it rigid, but once released, its form collapsed. Probably it suffocated. I will know in the morning when light permits dissection. That should be fascinating."

I was horrified. "Dissection! I can't stand to look at it now. How can you be so morbid?"

He placed his hand on my shoulder and helped me to my feet. "I have been many things in my long past, Kim, including on many occasions a physician. I was at Waterloo, for instance, and at Gettysburg and Iwo Jima. I was there because while I could not confer my own invulnerability, I could ease pain. I learned from those experiences as I will from this. Perhaps I may even learn to avoid killing any more of these creatures, should we be attacked again."

"I don't want to meet any more of them." I shuddered at the thought.

Casey's answer was firm and resolute. "Nor do I," he said. "But if we do, I do not intend to take another life. My own may be safe, but that of others is so transitory it is much more sacred to me."

I slept no more that night, but huddled in my blanket waiting for dawn. When it came, I avoided Casey. This was illogical, and I knew it. What he said had been true and his grisly work was necessary, but I waited outside the cave while he did it.

When he finally joined me he was grim and seemed puzzled, though not disposed to say why. I packed, while he buried the creature's body in the woods beneath a pile of stones and marked the spot with the stone axe.

We started out, walking silently along the base of the escarpment, searching for a path to the top. Presently we came upon a promising ravine, through which trickled the waters of a small stream. We climbed its slippery rocks as far as the cataract which fell from its summit. There we rested, and drank. I bathed my aching feet in the cool waters of the cataract's pool while Casey kept his bow ready and his eyes on the rim.

Finally I could endure silence no longer. "What disturbs you, Casey? What did you find?"

"I found many things, Kim. All of them strange, most unfathomable. The alien's limbs bore marks on what would be its wrists and ankles were it human. I have seen such marks before, on the bodies of slaves. Manacles and leg irons make them. These were fresh."

I pondered this remark. Casey seemed so sure. "Slavery," I said, "is not new to human culture. It existed on Earth into the last century. I am shocked to find such evidence here on Campbell, where higher life is not supposed to exist at all, but what bothers me more is the possibility that Solar Minerals . . ."

"No." Casey had never interrupted me before. "Solar Minerals has no slaves. They may know of these creatures' existence and suppressed that knowledge, but nothing more. That I know for sure.

"The alien you killed was not a native form. It did not evolve here. There are no anatomical parallels with Campbell's other life. It is grossly unrelated to them. It is, like us, an alien."

He paused a moment to let that sink in, then continued. "There is more. That creature, at least, has been here very briefly. I examined its dentation. In the past it has had caries, repaired with skill few human dentists could match. I found a stainless steel bridge, which implies a very high order of technology, yet the creature was armed with a stone axe *Homo erectus* would have been ashamed to carry. Why?"

I did not know, but the implication sent shivers through me. Suddenly I felt cold and pulled my feet from the water. But the chill was not in the water: it was in my mind. It felt uncomfortable here. "Can we go, Casey?"

He was willing, and we started out. At the top of the escarpment we found flat land, thickly forested. The proto-grasses grew profusely between the clumps of trees, but the bushes were sparse, which made easy travel. The grass was high enough to almost conceal herds of the little grazers, and from time to time we would flush them by stumbling into their hiding places. Toward the end of the day Casey shot two of them: more than we really needed for food, but as he pointed out, I was rapidly tearing my clothing to tatters, struggling through the bush. And while not deerskin, and though it promised to be malodorous for want of adequate curing, it was all we had.

I was reassured, watching this demonstration of his skill with the bow: sure, swift shots that never missed. Less reassuring was the fact that now he kept it always at the ready, while I fell heir to the less complicated javelin, and held it ever tighter.

We stopped well before sundown that night, so that we could have a fire and cook the meat before darkness fell.

Casey picked a thorny thicket and plugged its entrances with branches. "If we have visitors tonight," he said, "they will have to pass slowly through this. I only hope the wood is too green for them to burn us out. The spoor I have seen nearby is old, but it is best to use care."

Spoor, I thought. So, there was more alien activity in the area. He knew it but hadn't told me. Again I spent an uncomfortable night, awakening to a dawn that promised even more danger.

Again we set out in the direction of the rising sun. Long shadows shrank like the dew as the sun cleared the treetops and brought yet another enigma.

Casey noticed it first, of course. His first impulse was to give it wide berth and hope I missed it. I didn't. "What is it, Casey?"

Caught at deception, he owned up. "A building, I think. I am reasonably certain men did not put it there. That leaves the aliens, whose signs abound." Then, as if to forestall alarm in me, he added, "Old signs, though. None have passed this way in recent days."

It lay across our course, and we approached it carefully, stopping about 500 yards away. At this distance its surface was clearly visible. It gleamed in off-white brilliance, standing about three times man-height, with a base of about the same diameter. Concentric stone discs about a foot thick made up its layers, the largest at the bottom. A man would have been hard-pressed to stand on the tiny disc at the apex. We could not tell if these were molded or stacked, the seams were undetectable.

We went nearer and circled it. Casey studied the ground, found nothing recent enough to bother him, then motioned me to come closer.

"It's just a stack of stone steps, Casey. Out here in the middle of nowhere. Why?"

"I cannot even make a conjecture. I can tell you more aliens exist: perhaps more than one kind. I can detect impressions of three distinct shapes and sizes of feet. One fits our dead alien, one is hooflike, and the third is human. All are old and faint."

"Human! Then Solar does know there is a connection."

"They know of the structure." He bent down and walked around it, surveying its base, then picked something up. "Paper fragments, charred and faded. Very old." He stopped again.

This time the retrieved object was larger. He held it to his nose and sniffed.

"What have you found, Casey?"

"Men have been here. One of them smoked cigars. This is tobacco leaf. The paper fragments come from the wrapping of half-pound blocks of nitrostarch, such as we use for blasting. They have tested the strength of this edifice, or perhaps tried to obtain a sample of it. The blast discolored it, nothing more, but the grass and the ground yielded though the stone did not." He pointed.

"Newer growth, though still weeks old, perhaps a couple of months old. They knew long before you came. I think this merits further exploration."

He turned and started off, eyes on the ground, stepping carefully. I walked behind him and waited for him to tell me what I saw. None of it meant anything to me, but I knew he was following tracks of some sort. They led out of one grove and into another. Casey's pace quickened.

Once within it he again bent down; began picking up bones, dried and bleached, which looked to me to be the same as those from the animals we ate. Farther in there was a firepit, edged with stones and littered with more bones.

"The remains of feasts, Kim. Some old, some relatively recent. Some of the parties were large. The last consisted of ten or twelve individuals."

"Men or aliens?" I asked.

"Aliens. I can find no useful tracks among these leaves, but men would leave distinctive signs. And men have metal implements. What ate here had not even flint knives, but only axes, crudely made of stone. Observe the fragments in the fire: seasoned wood was broken and only green wood was cut, because stone blades can handle that. Bones were smashed at the joints, then twisted loose, a somewhat messy, inefficient process compared to cutting.

"And I have noticed something else about this place. I did not climb the structure, therefore I missed it before. Look at this."

He led me to a large, flat, oblong stone set in the ground, obscured by grass. Behind it, in a line leading to the structure, were others. "A marked path, visible from the top of the structure but barely noticeable from the ground. Note the stones are not dressed but natural, though carefully selected. The builders of the structure did not lay them; the diners did. Neither work has been here very long."

"How do you know?"

"The bushes tell me. Outside of a fifty-or-so-foot circle many large ones grow, but few grow inside and they are small. And the grasses within are thinner. They grow in soil recently disturbed to a considerable depth, and therefore poor in nutrients. But come, let us continue."

I followed him around, while he searched for obscure things I would not have dreamed bore information. The

signs led him to another stone. Again it was flat and
very large, sunk deep into the ground and partially
covered with leaves. On its face, crudely scratched in
the soft limestone, were several lines of symbols, each
rubbed with some kind of clay to give it contrast with
the rest of the rock.

"Writing," Casey said. "Several different languages,
too, I'd say. And far from primitive."

"You can read it?" I asked incredulously.

"Of course not. Even so, there is much it tells me. I
am familiar with most human script. Writing begins
with pictograms. Stylized symbols follow, then true alphabets. Alphabets are refined. Their use demands extreme abstraction of thought. Being so fundamental,
their symbols are repetitious: economical. Alphabets do
not occur in non-technical civilizations. Certainly, no
human writing system predates the use of metals."

"Which means?" I wondered if he himself really knew.

"The primitive tools are an expedient to the people
who carved this stone, used because better ones demand technology they don't have. They cannot even
shape flint decently."

"Perhaps they did not come here purposely, Casey,
but were shipwrecked. Perhaps the structure is for
signalling."

He did not agree. "I think not, but I have no better
explanation. However, the writing clearly conveys a
message. The intention of the writers is also clear: it is
to be seen by someone on top of the structure. The
writer intends that the reader first ascend. What intrigues me is why."

"Perhaps the structure is a monument."

"If so, it is poorly placed, hidden in the grove."

For the rest of the morning we explored the area
around the structure. Casey found much more to indicate heavy past traffic through the woods, but nothing
that would tell him why. But from the signs he saw he
concluded the beings came and went from some location to the east. There was a fairly well worn path in
that direction.

We, too, set off to the east, but kept to a nearby ridge
which ran parallel, not wishing chance encounters. The

difficult ground and the need for stealth made the traveling slower, so we had gotten only about a quarter of a mile when Casey suddenly stopped.

His reason was not apparent to me. "What is it?" I asked.

"A strange sensation. I feel peculiar." He looked down at his arm. His sparse hairs were twitching. Then I saw the hair on his head beneath the band move and stand out. I felt my own hair rise like a wreath around my head.

"Some kind of electrostatic field," Casey said. "Let's get off this ridge."

I looked up at the sky. It was cloudless, so it was not an electrical storm that was producing the effect. Nevertheless I followed Casey to lower ground. A noise began: a hiss, then a crackle. It came from behind us, in the direction of the structure. We could see only the top of this. It was glowing.

Soon it was brighter than the sun. The air around it shimmered and the noise rose in both amplitude and pitch. An object, dark by comparison, appeared atop the structure, at first indistinct but rapidly gathering form. It became a great cross: then, as we watched, the image changed, and became a figure with outstretched arms. Abruptly, the hissing died down, and the figure dropped its arms to its sides. Then it ran down the tiers and disappeared from sight.

Again, the hiss grew: the structure glowed. In the same manner as before a being appeared, then fled the pinnacle. Six times more the episode was repeated. Then the glow died.

I broke our long silence. "Well," I said, "Now we know how they got here. It's some kind of matter transmitter. The next question is why. How can we reconcile this with stone axes?"

"We can't, Kim," he answered gravely. "Not without revising our previous speculation. I have the beginning of an hypothesis, but I want to see what happens next before explaining. Let's get up on the ridge where we can watch the trail. Be very quiet."

I followed him to the crest, where we could see in both directions for nearly five hundred yards.

He took note of the direction of the wind and notched an arrow to his bow. "We are downwind," he said, "and thus may not be noticed."

About ten minutes later forms appeared, heading west. There were four of them, all carrying axes. The two in front were the tall, boneless kind. Those behind, and having difficulty keeping up, were short, thick, heavily muscled creatures with hoofed feet. They passed without noticing us.

Twenty minutes or so later six of each passed in the opposite direction, but the newcomers had no weapons.

Casey waited until they were well ahead of us, then motioned me to follow him along the ridge. "I think I know now where we are," he said.

"Another riddle, Casey? Where are we?"

"This is Devil's Island. It's a penal colony, like the one the French used to have in South America. I believe this is where the aliens send criminals, and I think that is what those creatures are. Whoever sends them doesn't know humans have come here. Probably they never visit. There would be no reason for it."

I didn't understand, and said so.

Casey explained his theory. "It fits the facts we have. Consider: these beings possess nothing not obtainable here: not even clothing, if they wear it. This is not compatible with a colonizing or commercial venture, nor with an invasion force, given the means they have of transporting material things of great size.

"Also, note the condition of arrival. The subjects are restrained on crosses. Released, they run and disappear. This may, of course, be necessary to transmission, but I find another possibility more likely: they are restrained because they would otherwise resist. They are freed only when safely trapped here. And they are not slaves as I once supposed, since slaves are useful only when they can be worked.

"But the best support of the convict theory was found on the dead one. He got adequate but cheap dental care: stainless steel instead of gold, porcelain, or silver alloy. It smacks of institutional dentistry: the sort, perhaps, that he'd get from another inmate who had lots of time on his hands, and who employed great skill and patience in the job, but who couldn't get his hands on really first-class materials. The convict dentist's talent shows in the humbler medium, just as the skills of early American goldsmiths showed in the pewter they sometimes substituted when gold was too scarce or too dear.

"Then there are the old signs of turmoil I found at the structure. The first arrivals probably battled one another, then gradually saw that this was foolish and began cooperating. Later they probably organized into some loose form of government and made the guide marker and stone plaque. I think the feasts took place at an earlier time, when they stayed near the structure. Then, as their numbers increased, they hunted the area bare and had to leave. They probably made the plaque then."

"It sounds reasonable, Casey," I said. "But then, so does everything else you say. I am amazed you learn so much from a few simple signs that I don't even notice. Tell me, what have you thought it means for us?"

Casey looked at me and smiled. He was obviously proud of his powers of observation and deduction. "Some look," he said. "Others see. If asked to speculate—and I have been—I would conclude, as I have said, that the makers do not suspect the presence of men here. Perhaps long ago they sent a ship here to build this station, and possibly others elsewhere on this planet, though I think this unlikely. Perhaps they send only a few convicts here, and it may therefore have been a long time since they built the structure.

"In the interim humans came, and the convicts have not molested them, though I believe they know of us. Perhaps promiscuous attack is discouraged by our relatively great numbers and their knowledge that we possess better arms and explosives.

"In any event, I have heard no rumors among the men concerning the aliens. It may therefore be that management knows of the structure, but they think it is sessile."

The impact of that settled on me. It meant that we would now be hunted by both groups.

But Casey reassured me. "I think the alien you killed was a scout, who did not get back to report. Perhaps he saw the forest fire and surmised a skimmer crash. The fire would have been visible for great distances, particularly from atop the escarpment, and the wreck would have represented a valuable source of metal for making tools and weapons.

"He arrived, perhaps, the day we left the site, but dared not attack us then. Instead he followed us to the cave, assuming we would be taken more easily while asleep. He was, therefore, alone at the time, though others may have followed. That too is unlikely, since we had much of value to him and he took nothing. If he were a part of a group he would have selected choice objects for himself. Since he did not, he counted on retrieving them later. Therefore, he was alone."

"That," I said, "is bad enough, even with only half the planetary population against me. I have a real talent for finding trouble, don't I? What am I going to do?"

"The situation would seem to call for skillful diplomacy, Kim. I was about to ask you that question."

"Well, this is obviously going to change Campbell's whole history. I'll have to report the situation as soon as I can, whether Solar Minerals likes it or not, and let the U.N. handle it."

"That is plainly the proper course. The method, however, is critical. This is not a situation of indigenous life having a primary claim; it is a question of who has a better discovery claim. Solar will adopt that position if discovered. I know something of the law, having been a lawyer at various times during my existence.

"However, I have been a human being even longer— and, I hope, a sensible one. It does not seem sensible to me for you to mention any of this to Solar's local management. Remember, we are 114 light years from Earth. The *Wilmington* is our only contact, and it is under their charter. You have a four-month wait until the ship returns, and fifty-two days in space."

"I don't think I can keep the secret that long, Casey."

"You must. Meyers condoned, if he did not order, one attempt to kill you. When they discover their failure there will be another try, unless in the meantime you prove yourself innocuous."

"Why can't we just hide out in the woods until the ship comes?"

"You would starve. I can exist on native foods: you can't. You need Earthly nourishment, and what we brought will not last you."

"So I have to cook up a story, leaving the part about the beasties out of it?"

"It is the only way. You may not succeed in convincing Meyers you are not a danger to him, but it is less likely he will try to harm you at the station with so many others around. And he will have no way of knowing for sure that you have knowledge of the aliens."

I deliberated.

Casey went on. "You have certainly seen enough to make a judgment and complete your survey: you will not have to go out again."

That was true enough, I thought. But I said, "What about you, Casey? You're in it, too. And you can't run like I will."

"Do not worry," he told me. "I'm just a dumb Indian, with more luck than brains. They know I'm too slow-witted to be trouble. Besides, you have seen what my body can do. I cannot count the times I have been killed in the past. As long as a single cell lives, so does He-Who-Waits: though it may take as long as a century to regenerate, my body will rebuild."

That, I told myself, is something else I have to figure out how to handle.

In twenty-seven days we reached the sea. I had gained muscle but lost weight, and was feeling very fit despite the lack of certain nutrients in my diet. But for my red hair and light eyes, I might have been Casey's tribesman, tanned as I was and sporting a set of leather clothing he'd made from the skins of our food animals. They smelled a little ripe, but wore better than what I'd started out in.

There we rested for a day, playing in the surf and sand of the nearly tideless seashore. I felt a certain sorrow fill me. To leave this life and make the transition back to civilized being would not be easy. True, life in the wilderness was not easy, but it was strangely fulfilling. It satisfied my psychological need to find out what was really in me. I was satisfied with what I found. I had the stuff of pioneers. In bygone days I might have been one, seeking fate and fortune in the wild American West or in the harsh beauty of Herschel.

In part, that had been my reason for joining the Ecological Service: to see how much of that I could take, without risking all. Now the work seemed tame. The U.N. was a stodgy bureaucracy, an extension of the old U.S.A., which now dominated planetary government on Earth.

The Earth, though poor now in resources and horribly overpopulated, was still manhome. And Earth assumed that the space around her was hers to control, particularly as man had met no challengers as yet. Mudron didn't count. It was a fluke, an old system which experts felt was not really a part of local stellar evolution: its inhabitants were backward, and would never present any threat to human supremacy.

The beings who'd built that matter transmitter did. That scared me. They were far and away our technological superiors. They might greet our discovery with resentment, perhaps extermination: who knew?

Casey said they could do something worse: ignore us, as the Europeans had his people; pen us up on reservations, leaving us to starve and stagnate. And Casey knew what that was all about.

I felt myself feeling a little fear of him, too. Not of the man, but the idea behind the man. As we traveled it had seemed natural for me to be with him, but what of the end of the journey? What would happen then?

To Casey, all other men were as children. He, who had already lived throughout ages eternal, would still be alive and vital when I was dust. He treated me as an equal, knowing that I wasn't, any more than all the others. He trusted me with his secret, speaking freely of his past, concealing nothing. Perhaps this was the greatest wisdom of all. I understood, yet the secret was still safe. Who would I tell? Who would believe a story so fantastic? He could deny everything without saying a word. Silence would suffice, and the rest of the world would assume I was deranged.

I hoped he would never do that to me: that somehow I would find a way to join him in his destiny, here among the stars, if only for a little while. A dream taunted me. In it, we were together. I knew that he had done such things before with other partners, now long gone, and come away each time a lonely man, without a purpose or the solace of a kindred soul to share his misery. Of all the creatures in the universe, only he was unique, lacking both siblings and descendants.

"My creator gave me wondrous powers," he told me once, "and many gifts are mine. But that which made me truly a man, he took from me."

It didn't matter. I decided, on that last night on the beach, that the rest of the dream was worth it.

We started south in the morning, this time following a trail of a different sort: the *Wilmington*'s. It was as clear as any path could be, even to me. Until the cradle of the landing web was finished she came down on her spacedrive: a process enormously destructive to the off-shore island which served as a landing site. The drive-fields were tame in space, where matter was scarce, but in an atmosphere their inertial force churned the sky and raised cubic miles of seawater into the air. Each takeoff or landing resembled a small hurricane. And as the vessel settled, these forces went to work on soil and crustal rock, fracturing it into powder, which fell to the ground in concentric rings according to its density.

We followed these, taking into account the island lay beyond the great promontory, which itself extended fifty miles to sea. Near its seaward end, on a bay, lay the settlement.

When the net was finished, an array of twenty banks of continously firing lasers dumping power into the system would lower ships slowly into the cradle Solar's crews were building.

One more night we spent out under the stars, there on the sandy lowland. I tried to get back to reality, sifting mental notes of what I had seen so that I could complete a report. I had no written notes or photographs, of course, but I was satisfied I knew what was here: that except for the aliens, I could have passed this world for colonization. I intended to do so.

"I still do." Suddenly I found myself bursting from reminiscence into reality, and shouting at the boss.

Carmody looked at me critically. He had listened politely while I rambled on. He had not interrupted. He did now, though somehow his manner was softened. "I am here to make that choice, Miss Ryan, though I'll take your recommendation into consideration. Actually it's become more political than technical now, in view of your discovery of the aliens. Would it surprise you to hear that we'll probably follow it?"

I was surprised, and showed it.

Carmody smiled. "This may be just the break the human race needs: a chance to get a free lunch, to learn from willing teachers. The government'll probably give you a medal, and Casey too, if they can find him."

"Casey's not likely to be very impressed," I answered. "Now if they made that a necklace of prime serpent's teeth . . ."

"I want to hear the rest of it, Miss Ryan, including all you can tell me about him. Maybe it'll help us find him."

"Okay. Let's see, where was I? Well, needless to say, there was quite a ruckus at camp when we turned up. We walked out of the bush looking like Tarzan and Jane: scared the pants off two guys who were goofing off behind a piling at the construction site. We went back to the settlement in their truck, riding in the back because we smelled bad. Meyers himself met us when we got in . . ."

"We thought you were dead," he told us, probably wondering where he'd failed. "I sent search parties out when you didn't return. We found a burned skimmer and we just naturally assumed you'd been in it."

I did the talking. Casey went back to being the dumb Indian. "Well, as you can see, we're all right. All I need is a bath and some real food. We've been eating what Casey shot with his bow."

Meyers had been watching Casey with a new respect. "Oh, so that's what it's for." He examined one of the arrows. "Certainly looks deadly." He turned to Casey. "I guess you'd better get back to your regular work."

No, you don't. I wasn't about to let myself out of Casey's sight and protection. "Uh—if you don't mind, Mr. Meyers, I'd like to keep him for a while, if you can spare him. I need him to help me with my report."

"Him? What can he do?"

"I want to pick his brains. I lost all my samples and photographs, and I couldn't take notes on the trail, so my report will have to be composed from memory—his and mine. And as you can see, he's a woodsman. He must have noticed thousands of things I didn't."

There was no credible way Meyers could refuse, though I doubt he bought my explanation, so Casey stayed, and we went back to our old quarters together.

"You shouldn't have done that, Kim."

"Why not? I do need the benefit of your observations. And I need your protection. Did you see the way he looked at your bow?"

"I noticed. But a man like Meyers wouldn't be afraid of a savage, and it's difficult to play Dumb Indian when you make me party to scientific studies. I'd have been more effective in the field, where I could keep an eye on things."

"Quit worrying, Casey. Human nature will take care of that problem. We can trust Meyers's prurient mind if nothing else. He'll figure I want to hang onto my stud."

Casey didn't say another word about it. In spite of his vast experience, I guess he still didn't understand women. He settled in with me, and we went to work on a report.

We still needed some information we didn't have, mostly about marine life on Campbell. This provided an excuse for short local field trips, and gave us a chance to reminisce. We spent many days on Campbell's broad beaches or out in a motorboat.

I loved Campbell's mild climate and its friendly sun. "I think," I told Casey, "that I could live here forever. I really like this."

"Have you forgotten the night in the cave," he replied, "or what we saw in the interior?"

"No, Casey, but I can dream, can't I? It will end soon

enough, when my report hits. Then the government will tell us we can't have Campbell."

He was compassionate, and he let me keep the dream a little longer—but there came a day when it died. He came back from a sojourn: they had flooded him with innuendos about "his squaw," but he had learned useful things.

"It has begun, Kim. Great care must be taken now."

Casey always had a penchant to talk in riddles. It irritated me more than anything else he did. I guess it showed.

"What has started?" I demanded.

"Men have begun to vanish. They disappear into the bush around the cradle site."

I was appalled. "If the aliens now exist in sufficient numbers, this might be the beginning of an attack."

"None have been seen," Casey said glumly. "Management has an official explanation. They say that with the web near completion, the missing men have simply taken off, to get the jump on the colonists who will come later. But Meyers knows the real reason."

"How do you know that?"

"The machine shop is making weapons. Lathes turn gun barrels. The smith is making pike heads and short swords. There are armed skimmers patrolling the periphery."

"War, with the aliens?" I saw myself trapped here, perhaps imprisoned or killed, to keep word from getting back to Earth.

"Perhaps. Perhaps not." Casey pondered each phrase. "Meyers may believe he can quietly exterminate the aliens or drive them deep into the bush where they will not be rediscovered. He may bring mercenaries here to hunt them. Certainly he will station marksmen at the transmitter to pick off new arrivals."

"What are we going to do, Casey?"

"For the meantime, nothing. Everything depends on getting you out when the *Wilmington* returns. I now believe the government must be told, even if we lose Campbell. This is better than interstellar war, which man would surely lose."

We waited, and hoped.

I learned later that Meyers and Bigelow *had* tried extermination: had placed a garrison at the alien transmitter. They succeeded for a while in preventing the formation of large concentrations of aliens, but this did not last. Men still disappeared; amusingly enough, some ran off voluntarily, believing Meyers's explanation for the disappearance of others and determined to get in on a good thing.

Not so amusing were the discussions they'd had about Casey and me, which Bigelow admitted to later. To his credit, he balked at murder, but Meyers thought they could blame it on the aliens if they ever got caught.

I was getting packed to leave while this was going on and didn't suspect a thing, not even when landing day arrived. How Meyers talked Corsetti into doing what he did, I'll never know. Casey and I discussed it later and agreed that even a moron should have known it wouldn't work. But some things are just destined to happen, and I guess it was one of them.

We were on the back porch looking at the sky, watching for the great hulk of the ship to descend. On the first down-orbit pass she was just a gleaming point of light which moved rapidly over the station. The second pass would bring her down, and we waited for her to reappear in the western sky. She did not.

"Something's wrong, Kim," Casey told me. He pointed westward.

The air shimmered, and an enormous dust cloud had risen from the ground to race to the top of the atmosphere and flatten out. Then the earth itself started to shake, and there came a series of sonic shocks followed by a great wind. In the dust cloud appeared blazing halos.

Both of us had seen these things before. It was the awful tumult which accompanies a ship's descent on Aschenbrenner drive—but it belonged on the island, not in the bush to the west.

Casey's eyes blazed. He grabbed my arm and shoved me to the door. "Get inside quickly," he warned. "Those fools have turned *Wilmington*'s drive on the alien transmitter."

I found myself on the rough floor with Casey on top of

me, and started to protest his rough treatment. I stopped when I saw the flash, brilliant like a thousand suns. The fireball singed the settlement as it rose, despite the vast distance; then it dimmed. Through the top of the window I could see it rise toward space.

More shock waves followed; more howling wind. The building shook and rattled but it held together.

One, maybe both of them, went: either the ship's engines went critical or the transmitter did. There might be nothing left of either. Casey let me up.

"What now, Casey? What do we do now?"

This time he didn't have an answer.

Outside men could be seen shouting, screaming; vehicles roared wildly through the streets, racing engines and squealing tires. We knew that there must have been casualties.

A few minutes later Meyers came and brought two men, both armed. "Your time has come, Miss Busybody," he said to me.

They herded us off to the brig. The cell looked adequate even to hold Casey.

I sat there on the edge of my bunk, crying. Casey paced.

"I have experience with prisons, too," he said. "There is a way out of all of them."

I was pessimistic. Our cell was essentially a steel box, with walls perforated for ventilation. Its seams were welded, and it was barred and locked from outside, with no openings large enough even to pass a hand. It was also guarded by one of Meyers's gunmen, who sat in a chair outside the door.

After a while Casey came over and sat beside me. "Kim," he said. "I want you to stop that and get control of yourself. That is what I am going to do: understand?"

I hiccupped and nodded my head. I didn't, really.

"Good," he whispered. "I will need three or four hours, and the result may be quite frightening. Do not allow it to upset you."

"Okay," I whispered.

"In the meantime keep me covered, but try not to distract me. If anyone comes you must warn me. Is that clear?"

"Clear."

"I am just going to rearrange a few things."

Then he left me and climbed into the other bunk, covering himself with a blanket.

A new guard relieved the first one. He came to the door to talk to me, but I told him to let Casey sleep. Soon he settled into the chair by the door.

About sundown Casey stirred. I watched an arm snake out from under the blanket and rise to grasp its edge. The arm was pink and covered with a light brown fuzz. It rolled the blanket down, revealing a face I knew and hated. A hand rose to its lips, and Fritz Meyers stood up.

"Rankin." Even the voice was the same. "Get over here."

"Mr. Meyers? How? . . ."

"Never mind: get this door open."

"Yes, sir, only . . . what are you doing in there?"

"None of your business, Rankin: the lady and I made a deal. Get the door open."

The lock clicked and the bar slid back. Casey hit the door like a battering ram, driving it into Rankin's face, smashing flesh and bone alike. He crumpled to the floor.

"Come on out, Kim."

I left the cell, still not completely convinced I was looking at Casey.

He shoved Rankin inside, flipping him onto my bunk, and covered him up. Then he reached over into his own and withdrew a clump of black substance.

"My own hair," he said. "I can't reconstitute dead tissue. I had to get rid of it and start over. We'll hide this somewhere outside."

"Where are we going?"

"Back to our quarters first, to get our equipment and some food for you. Then into the bush. We'll hide there until contact with Earth is re-established. Meyers has to try to kill us now if we stay, and in your case, death's permanent."

We started out into the compound. It was strangely empty. Then I heard a faint popping, and in the south there was a glow in the sky. It looked like a fire, and I thought I smelled smoke, too. For an instant I was afraid it was our quarters that were burning, but the fire seemed to be farther away. We hurried off in that direction.

Others appeared in the street, scurrying about, some moving equipment in the direction of the fire. Casey called to one of them. The man stopped running and came over.

"What's happening out there, Barker?"

"Mr. Meyers. How—I just talked to you on the phone. How did you get way over here?"

"Never mind. Fill me in."

"Well, okay—you mean the fire? Them things set it, we think. I ain't seen none myself, but they're supposed to be all over. There's gonna be a fight, I think."

"What are we doing about it?"

Barker looked at him as if to say *don't you know?*, but he said only, "We got the guys with guns on rooftops, and some in a skimmer. The rest of the men got axes and machetes. We ain't gonna beat fire, though. If they decide to burn us out, we can't stop them."

"You're doing the right thing, Barker. Get back to work."

Barker took off.

"General foreman," Casey explained. "One of the dumber ones. We'd better hurry before the battle really gets started. Barker's right: they can't stop a fire, though I doubt the aliens want to burn up what they hope to get from this raid. Most likely the fire is just a diversion."

We reached our rooms, got what we needed, and left again. I noticed the Meyers form was fading, and commented.

"It takes too much concentration to hold a new pattern until I get really used to it. On occasion I've held them for years—the Compte de Rochambeau, for instance. Now there was a role where I had everybody guessing."

I had not seen the mischievous side of Casey before, but this proved he had one.

We made our way out of the settlement, heading west in the direction of the cradle site. Once or twice we stopped and Casey listened for sounds of others moving in the bush, but we encountered neither man nor alien. Casey led us across the lowlands and into higher country, and by morning we were high on the spine of the promontory about twenty miles west of the station. He selected a campsite where there was both water and cover, and we rested. That is, I rested. Casey climbed a tree and examined the surrounding countryside with field glasses.

I awoke and ate, while Casey explained our situation. "I see little groups of aliens converging on the station. All are poorly armed. As of now there are probably not enough of them to overcome the men, but more arrive hourly. Soon they can start a siege, if they can find the food to maintain one. Still, if the men narrow their perimeter and defend it, they may yet prevail. I think last night's raid was simply a test of human strength."

"Maybe they don't know how many men there are."

"A good point. But neither do the men know the aliens' strength. If the transmitter has ceased to function, their numbers will not grow, but I regard that as a particularly disastrous possibility."

"Why? I should think that would be better for us."

"In the short run, perhaps. But for the race, devastating. If the aliens can detect its malfunction, they may return and find us. Discovery, I think, is something best postponed as long as possible. In the interim perhaps we will be rescued and obliterate our traces from Campbell."

"Do you think we will have to go that far?"

"I cannot see the future, Kim."

"We could have a long wait, Casey. It'll be almost two months before the *Wilmington* is overdue. More time will be wasted deciding what to do, and still more will pass before another ship can get here. What happens in the meantime?"

"Nothing, I hope. We will survive it and do what we can to find solutions. There was a time when I thought we might simply get you back to Earth and let the government handle things. Now that won't work. We're out of time. But I wish we had a better insight into this."

I had thought he did, but something apparently still bothered him. I asked him what it was.

"The aliens are inept. That's not typical criminal behavior, at least not for the human criminals I've known. They're not nearly aggressive enough. Even allowing for cultural differences they ought to show more resourcefulness, particularly in weaponry. We ought to be seeing some spears along with the clubs, and some concerted effort to get hold of human material for weapons. The one thing they do seem to rely on is fire: otherwise, they behave like amateurs."

We moved again, farther into the interior, to find a place which, as Casey said, "You and I can defend by ourselves for long enough to bring this business to an end."

He didn't tell me what he meant by that, but he found our redoubt: a cavern halfway up a cliff face overlooking a broad stream. We had brought much food, and the shrubs from the narrow pathway would provide fuel. Inside the cavern was a pool containing more water than we could drink in years. But farther down the valley was a ford, where aliens sometimes crossed, headed for the settlement.

Casey got me settled in, then told me to rest. "Tonight," he said, "you will not close your eyes at all, but you will be safe here until I return. Even you alone could hold this place against an army, with nothing more than a few rocks and a knife."

When darkness fell he sallied forth armed only with a staff. I waited in darkness all alone for his return, and all alone fought off the savage creatures my imagination conjured up. Once or twice I felt the bow and wondered, if the need arose, whether I could summon the strength to draw it or the skill to find the mark.

With the first light of dawn I heard a noise on the trail below me, and felt a fright. Casey would move more silently than that. And Casey did. But the lanky prisoner he led, tightly bound and stumbling, had no wish to cooperate.

I stood, watching from the cave's mouth, as Casey dragged it in. It seemed to me to be in life even uglier and more menacing than the dead one at the other cave, though it was much smaller.

"I chose it for its size," Casey said. "In time you will understand why. Now I must get to work and learn yet another tongue, so I may speak with it."

And in the days that followed he struggled to master the grunts, hisses and squeals that made up the alien's speech. I despaired of matching his resolve and left the two alone, preferring to speculate on what was happening to the settlement.

Later, when it was over, I learned that these had been desperate times for Meyers, and had finally driven him to self-destruction. By that time most of the outer buildings had been leveled to provide a clear field of fire for what was left, huddled behind barriers of barbed wire. In two months he had lost four hundred men—not killed, but *taken*, dragged away by the aliens.

The cairn had not been destroyed, and the *Wilmington* was sacrificed in vain. Aliens still came through to be cut down by human sharp-shooters mounted in skimmers. Then the aliens ended that; they fire-bombed the motor pool. Immobilized, Meyers sat within his reduced perimeter, along with fifty men who remained, and waited for the end. Casey had been ready.

Again the secretary broke into my narrative.

"That's the part I understand the least," Carmody said. By this time he seemed far more mellow; almost human. His haughtiness was gone. "Perhaps if we could find Kah-Sih-Omah . . ."

"Casey doesn't want to be found, Mr. Carmody. And if he doesn't, he won't be. Until he does turn up this is only a story, a myth, both to us and the aliens." *But he was more than that to me*, I thought. And the thought was painful.

"I want to hear the rest of it, Miss Ryan. Especially the ending."

"I suppose that's the part that really matters most of all," I replied. "I wasn't in on much of it. All I really know was pieced together later, from people I talked to. A lot of my information comes from Bigelow, and has to be considered less than reliable. And I'm sure the aliens don't suspect a thing.

"It all started one morning when I woke to find the message scratched in the sand at the cave mouth. Casey and the alien were gone. By that time, of course, Casey was fluent in the alien speech and . . ."

"What was the message?" Carmody interrupted.

"It didn't make sense, Mr. Carmody. It was only three words. I couldn't really make it out," I lied. "Anyway, Casey was gone, and after that things started happening at the settlement.

"Meyers had succeeded in holding on as long as the aliens simply besieged him, and he was able to fight off their night raids with superior tactics and weapons. The aliens couldn't mount a direct assault.

"Then, suddenly, the aliens brought up trebuchet and used them to reduce the buildings. Meyers shot himself and Bigelow took over. He had guts; I'll give him that, going out to parley with the aliens. You pretty well know the rest."

Carmody did, though he wasn't quite sure how to handle it from there. I wasn't either, and said so.

"I'm leaving you in charge, Miss Ryan, while I go back to report all this. Somehow I can't see the government abandoning Campbell over this; not with all this knowledge available for exploitation. I think we'll get the landing web finished in record time now. There'll be all kinds of people coming in. In the meantime you'll have to keep things stable here. I hope you get along all right with the alien leader."

"Yes," I said. "We understand one another. His English seems to be pretty good."

"Fine, then I won't worry about a thing." He rose from the chair and motioned for me to follow him down to the dock. "This'll mean a promotion for you, you know. Maybe even to an advance scout team. Would you like that?" He had my written report in his hand, and patted it lovingly.

"Yes, if I could get the right partner; yes, I think I would."

He climbed into the launch and I watched it leave,

until at last the image became too small, and disappeared over the horizon.

He hadn't had time to read the report, that I knew. When he did, he would find no reference in it to the extraordinary powers Casey had displayed. So far as that part of the story was concerned, it would remain a myth.

The alien entered the room and sat down in the chair beside me, its legs bent awkwardly, arms resting in its lap. I looked no more than necessary at its face, which appealed to me not at all, though I knew what lay behind it. Instead, I looked away and said, "When, Casey? How much longer?"

"Shh. Not so loud." He raised an arm, but I retreated. I would not allow it to touch me.

"There are," he said, "grave disadvantages to my present form, but until the job is done it is necessary. I grow used to it and it becomes easier to hold. Tell me, Kim, how did your interview go?"

"Better than expected, I think. Carmody appears to be a very prudent man. He will have my report and read it as he travels back to Earth. He believes the aliens can be exploited."

"So do I, and I believe that they will permit this willingly, in the hope that we can someday aid their fellows."

"For all we know they may really be criminals."

"No. Not in the sense you mean. And we do know, in general, where they originate: from farther in on the spiral arm. Their home systems are in foment. They are what they claim to be; political refugees. They are politicians, philosophers, scientists, writers, artists and the like; anything but criminals, and certainly not soldiers. That is why I had to lead them and teach them to make war. They could not even bring themselves to kill, but simply captured humans and dragged them off, often with heavy casualties to their own.

"And they don't want Campbell; at least, not in the sense we do. Their government simply dumped them here with nothing, to fend for themselves on what was thought to be a vacant world. These people embarrassed them.

"To us, they can be partners. We can trade them sustenance for knowledge. The matter transmitter alone is worth that. Spaceships will always be needed for exploration, but commerce needs something better to be really worthwhile. It will make colonization really practical too, and you know what that means."

"We will need many more new worlds."

This time I did not avoid his touch. I knew also what the message meant, that still I pictured scratched in the sand. He-Who-Waits had found a companion, "For A Time."

The Shaman

Kim had been close to the house when the faint slap of skimmer fans attracted her attention. She knew that Casey must have heard them too, and that he would now be heading home, but it would take him longer to get to the house. He was on the far side of the lake.

Without hesitation she called to her children, who were out in the brambles picking berries. They came, Kevin first, followed by his sister, Angela. Neither of them had seen the skimmer, though they had also heard its sound.

Kim could not imagine who the visitor might be. They lived far out in the hinterland, away from any close neighbors, on a world where men were still scarce and skimmers even rarer.

She herded the children together and told them to stay in the woods while she approached the house. They did not understand; they had been raised here on Ithaca and never met a stranger.

But Kim knew this was not one of their neighbors. None of the neighbors had a skimmer. When one called, which was rarely, he came on horseback or in a wagon pulled by an electric tractor. This visitor must be from the city, seven hundred kilometers away. Kim did not find that thought comforting.

Leaving the children at the edge of the glade, she

circled around to the back of the cabin, hoping to be able to enter through the back door and find a robe before confronting whoever it was. Ithaca's warm climate, and their isolation, did not demand a great deal of clothing, and she, like the children, wore the minimum.

Too late, she realized that her visitor had grown impatient and wandered away from his skimmer. He was approaching the back door from the opposite direction. And Kim knew him. At the sight of him, she broke out in a cold sweat.

"Kim! I must say, you're looking good. Colonial life seems to agree with you."

Abashed at her near nudity in the presence of this imposing man, Kim stopped, folded her arms across her chest and stared. "Mr. Carmody! W-what are you doing here?"

"I came to see Casey, Kim."

"What made you think Casey'd be here? I haven't seen him in years."

Carmody sidestepped the question. "Aren't you going to invite me in?"

Kim did not answer immediately, so great was her shock at seeing him, here on their world. It was like meeting a ghost out of the past. Her mind raced. Undoubtably, Carmody had penetrated the maze of false trails Casey had laid, and probably he had tracked her own as well. She had been the weak link. It would not have taken any great ingeniuty for someone with Carmody's resources to deduce that the "Kevin C. O'Meara" she had married on Wolfingham was, in fact, Kah-Sih-Omah.

Proving it, however, was another matter entirely, thanks to Casey's many years of steadfastly holding the O'Meara persona. Physically it was completely unlike his former one, even to fingerprints, retinal patterns and voice print. Kim decided to continue the bluff.

"Of course, Mr. Carmody. You must have had a long, tiring trip. Follow me."

She led him into the cabin's one large ground-floor room, seating him in one of the rough-hewn chairs that surrounded the kitchen table. From a pot on the stove, she poured a cup of steaming liquid. "It's not quite coffee, but it's good. There's something like caffeine in it. We call it 'mescof.' " She did not think it either wise or necessary to tell him it was also mildly hallucinogenic. If he drank only one cup he would barely notice.

"Where *is* 'Mr. O'Meara,' Kim?"

"Somewhere on the lake, Mr. Carmody. He went fishing. It may be quite a while before he gets back. Excuse me; my kids are outside. I have to find them."

Carmody did not show any curiosity about that, and Kim ducked out the back door and into the wood, where Angela was busy stuffing her mouth with berries and at the same time fighting off her brother, who wanted some too. "Stop that fighting, and listen to me. Find your father and tell him Mr. Carmody's here, got that? Ivan Carmody. Then stay with him."

Neither child understood what was happening, but they could assess the tone in their mother's voice. The urgency was a signal to them that something unusual, possibly terrible, was happening.

Kim picked up what was left of the basket of berries and re-entered the house through the front door, stopping briefly to snatch a robe from a peg on the wall. Returning to the kitchen, she poured herself half a cup of the brew and sat down at the table across from Carmody.

"Well, Mr. Carmody. What's happening in the rest of the universe?"

Carmody took a sip, made a face, and pushed his glasses back up on the bridge of his great hooked nose. The piercing blue eyes had lost none of their power to intimidate Kim. "The universe of man may be in danger, Kim. Why else would I travel eighty-eight parsecs to ask for Casey's help?"

Noting the look of confusion on her face, he explained.

"I'm not in the Ecological Service anymore; I'm Commissioner of Alien Affairs now. Quite an important office these days, if I do say so myself. Sort of a promotion. You *must* have been out of contact for a while."

"Fourteen years. And I'm afraid I haven't paid much attention to the news lately. We rarely hear any. Half the time I don't even bother to listen to the local stuff."

"You wouldn't have heard about this on a broadcast,

Kim. None of it's been made public; we're handling it on a 'need to know' basis. And, actually, there may be nothing to worry about. But the human race *could* be headed toward real trouble."

"Because of what happened on Campbell?"

Carmody nodded.

There was a slight creaking sound, very faint, and audible only to someone who was listening for it. Kim was; Carmody wasn't. And the timing was perfect.

"It's a long story, Kim. Things have happened since you left there. By the way, I never repeated what you told me." He looked at her as though he expected to find her grateful. "So you see, my decision to come here was really a very personal one."

"I don't understand what you mean."

"It's my way of demonstrating to you, and to Casey, that I can be trusted, that I won't compromise his secret. Kim, do you remember what you told me about him—how he was altered by extraterrestrial visitors back in prehistory, and how he's lived ever since, wondering what his destiny might be?"

"It sounds melodramatic, the way you put it, but of course I remember."

"This may be it, Kim. Things haven't worked out quite as we expected. When this thing broke, the government was convinced the alien prisoners in that concentration camp on Campbell could help us make a quantum jump up to their level of technology. And that theory was partly Casey's, if you recall."

"Yes, he did open communication with them."

"Uh-huh. And then he disappeared. I guess he figured the job was done."

"As far as he was concerned, it was. Look, Mr. Carmody, Casey's lived a thousand normal lifetimes. Surely his wisdom's vastly superior to anyone else's."

"Perhaps; if he's kept informed. But when he disappeared he left the task to mortal men, and *we* can't handle it. The problem is that almost all the prisoners who come out of that mattercaster on Campbell were political dissidents. They knew a great deal about their own social systems, but very little about anything else.

So they can't do for us what Casey thought they could. At least, that bunch can't."

" 'That bunch'?"

"Yes. What you saw on Campbell was only part of the penal system. There's more to it.

"You see, the two races—we call them the Satyrs and the Skinnies—are part of an actual interstellar empire. Yes, I know that we always considered such things impossible: an empire dependent on space ships for transport could never hold itself together. But that was before we knew about matter transmission.

"This empire came about largely by accident. Each race discovered the transmitter principles independently, and each had a fairly extensive network of stations by the time they met.

"When that happened, the Satyrs apparently got caught with their pants down. They've been the junior partner in this empire ever since. The Skinnies dominate them almost completely—and together, they dominate half a dozen lesser races who are inferior to them in technological achievements. If we aren't careful, humanity could find itself in that category."

"But they don't know we exist."

"True. But we know they're expanding in every direction, including ours. They went to the trouble to put that station on Campbell."

"That's something that's always puzzled me," said Kim.

"They had political reasons. Doing it that way saves them the stigma of executing dissidents and from making martyrs of them. What they'd done, in effect, is to tell the dissidents, 'Here's an empty planet you can have, together with all its resources. Make something of it.' A shrewd move, I'd say.

"But they are capable of getting tough on other kinds of dissidents, and some of their more stubborn scientists. These are the people who interest us."

"Where are they?"

"On their own prison planet. It's organized a little differently from Campbell, but physically not very far away. That, by the way, is illustrative of the problem."

Kim did not comment.

"The idea is to keep the scientists productive, though under firm control. We learned a great deal about it from the prisoners who've turned up on Campbell. We even know its location with a fair degree of certainty. Now, we have to get somebody in there, and we have to get those people out. What's more, we have to do it in such a way that their captors never find out they had outside help."

"And naturally you want Casey to be that somebody?"

"He's the only one who could possibly do it."

"I'm sorry you came so far, Mr. Carmody, but I haven't laid eyes on Kah-Sih-Omah for over fourteen years."

"You don't lie very well, Kim. I can understand your feelings. It would be dangerous, even for him. And the reason why nobody else could do it is that a normal person, either a human being or one of the prisoners, would have the same vulnerability to that peculiar planet as the scientists do.

"You see, something about the prison planet is poisonous to the people who are imprisoned there."

"I don't understand. How can that be, when you just said they keep the scientists productive?"

"The way it was explained to me is that the poison is relatively slow-acting, and there's an antidote. If the antidote's available the damage can be reversed. The poison's called a—" he dug into a shirt pocket and pulled out a notebook, flipped through it and read—"a 'competitive inhibitor.' Does that make any sense to you?"

"Some. Do you know what happens to the person when he's exposed?"

"They become too weak to move. Later, they can't breathe, and then they die. Escape is impossible, because anyone who tried would leave behind the antidote. The supply is well guarded."

"O.K. Then I assume that whatever this is interferes with the utilization of muscle glycogen—or whatever these creatures use to power their muscles."

Carmody consulted his notebook again. "Yes, that's what I have here. In that respect both the Satyrs and the Skinnies are pretty much like us."

"It follows. When we were on Campbell they ate the

same things we did, and survived. But how is it that you know all this?"

"There were some escapes a long time ago, when the place was being set up. But things have changed; nobody's gotten away lately. The dissidents have made a couple of attempts to raid the place, so far without success. The planetary system is heavily patrolled."

"Then how could you expect Casey to do any better?"

"I don't know that he can, but he's the only one who has a chance at all. The dissidents think they know how to get him in. Of course, there's still the problem of getting him *out*, together with all those scientists, and ..."

"It sounds suicidal, Mr. Carmody."

"So's the alternative. Look, Kim. These people *know* something about that technology we need. Some of them are on the cutting edge of it. They're imprisoned because they're balky and because they're in sympathy with the dissidents, which means they might be grateful enough of our help to get us into the club. If we *don't* help them we'll just have to sit here basking in our ignorance until we're discovered and gobbled up. And as I said, we may not have much time."

Kim looked over at him and did not know how to reply. He knew Casey was here, on Ithaca. She was fairly positive Carmody was telling the truth, both about his own silence and the gravity of the emergency. She also knew that, concealed in the room out of Carmody's sight, Casey had listened to every word. And Casey had maintained his silence; he was not ready to make a judgment.

She took this to mean he wanted more information, and there was only one way he could get it: from Carmody, through Kim.

"O.K., Mr. Carmody; suppose Casey were willing. What would the plan be?"

Carmody glanced around, almost as though he sensed he was being tested. Apparently he saw nothing obvious. "We don't know what the antidote is. If we did it might be worthwhile to try shooting it out with the prison defense people. But the prisoners are scattered around all over the planet, and it's doubtful we could hold the aliens off long enough to get everybody out. That's one reason for not trying a direct attack. The other is that then they'd know about us—and if we couldn't shut them off from reinforcements they'd destroy us.

"So what we have to do is get Casey down there. If what you've told me about him is accurate, he could not only assume the physical form of either a Skinny or a Satyr, but neutralize the poison his body took in. We know they have to have a supply of the antidote available."

"That's all he has to do? Go in, get the antidote, collect the prisoners, and get all of them out again?"

"Well, that's an oversimplification," Carmody admitted, eyes turned down. "Actually, there's something I haven't mentioned yet. The guards have a distribution system already."

"I see. Well then, why don't the scientists just take over the place themselves?"

"It's a very ingenious system. It works this way. Each prisoner—or in some cases, two or three prisoners—never more than that—is isolated in some region where he couldn't possibly walk to the main transmitter. That's even assuming he knew how to get there. Each 'cell' has its own one-way mattercaster terminal. The terminal supplies food, water—and antidote. But there's a diabolical catch to it. To get any of this a prisoner has to work. Each transmitter has a crank on it. Every day the prisoner has to turn the crank until his supplies come out. He gets just enough antidote to keep him going one day, until the next cranking period.

"Naturally, all this exertion increases his vulnerability to the poison. In the case of a scientist, they apparently allow a substitution of scientific for physical work, but even there the prisoner gets only what's necessary to sustain normal muscle activity. He can't stockpile any so that he can go see his neighbors.

"What we hope Casey might be able to do is get into the main control area, find some way to organize the prisoners in a revolt, and give them enough resources to carry it out."

"He's *not* a superman, Mr. Carmody."

"Oh, yes he is. Compared to you or I, or any other being I'm familiar with, he is just that. And a superman has obligations, Kim, because of his stature. That's his purpose in *being* what he is."

"No. Casey didn't ask to be anything special; just to be a man. That's all he ever wanted out of life."

For a moment, there was silence. Then a third voice rang out, "He's right, Kim." From out of the shadows a figure emerged; stepped forward into the light.

Carmody had turned. He studied the features of the man. "Casey?"

And then he realized abruptly that he had never seen the man before, only his photograph. This man did not resemble that photograph in the slightest.

"I am here, Mr. Carmody. I have heard your words. I agree."

"Casey! No!"

"The man is right, Kim. It was wrong of me to ignore the problem on Campbell and walk away. I should not have done it."

"But it's not just your problem, Casey. It's everybody's, and it's not fair that you should be . . ."

"No one else can, Kim. You must remember what I did on Campbell. I became one of *them*, and with that physical metamorphosis came some understanding of their culture. They are different from us in many ways, but the basic drive that any race of survivors must have is in them, just as it is in us. We are dangerous to one another."

"And at the moment," Carmody pointed out, "the contest is lopsided. They have the transmatter devices and we don't. Don't you see, Kim? If the contact were made today, human culture would simply be overwhelmed. Do you want that to happen? Think of your children if you don't care about yourself."

Kim was not convinced. Perhaps she would never be convinced. But in the end, she was resigned.

Casey joined Carmody at the table, where they talked at length in quiet tones Kim preferred not to hear. She left, rounded up the children, and went back to berry-picking.

When she returned, an hour later, they were still

talking. She began preparing dinner, assuming Carmody would stay the night.

That he did, though as far as she could tell neither he nor Casey slept. Morning found the two of them still at a table now covered with dozens of thick, plastic-bound reports: statements of prisoners interviewed by the Department of Alien Affairs, and of human experts who had interpreted these.

When Kim appeared she was aloof. She knew what Casey was going to say and didn't want to hear it. But she also knew that any efforts to dissuade him would be useless.

After breakfast Carmody went on a sightseeing trip with the children, undoubtedly at Casey's suggestion, in order to give the two of them a chance to talk. It was largely a one-sided conversation. Casey talked, and Kim sulked.

"It is even worse than he said, Kim. We are surrounded by alien colonies. It is only because of extreme good fortune and the vastness of space that contact has been delayed this long. It cannot last; it could happen at any moment."

"And if they catch you, Casey? What will that do? Make it better or make it worse?"

"They will not catch a human being, Kim. They will never know this is what I am. Besides, as you will recall, catching me is one thing; holding onto me is quite another."

He was right about that. His ability to alter his form rapidly, to assume the features and appearance of any individual he chose, had saved her life during the ordeal on Campbell and given them fourteen years of peaceful anonymity.

"What about me—and the kids? How will we manage in the meantime?"

"I will not be away that long. Mr. Carmody has agreed to care for you while I am absent. He will arrange for people to watch over you until I return. Of course, you could always go into the city . . ."

"No, Casey. Here we are, and here, we stay. We will wait for you—here."

*   *   *

In his time Casey had said many goodbyes to many people, among them many other wives and many children. None of the children had been his biological own, of course. That had not ever mattered before and it did not matter now. Goodbyes were always painful. He would come back; he always had. But he could not be certain that when he did those he had left behind would not be dust. That had happened on occasion, when he had been delayed. A being such as he, who existed outside the bounds of time, must exercise great care in his relationships with those who didn't.

The ship was a cosmetic copy of a Satyr scout. Humanity had been hard-pressed to cobble it together from the fragmented descriptions supplied by the prisoners, few of whom had ever seen one of the interstellar vehicles.

But there had been a few, and from those few they had gained enough detailed information to make the vessel superficially like the real thing. They had not been able to avoid the use of Aschenbrenner engines, and that use had caused delays because of the need to train the aliens in their use.

The six-member crew, chosen entirely from prisoners unaware of human existence, did not know who Kah-Sih-Omah really was. He professed to have come from a remote Satyr colony, and they were satisfied that this was the explanation for his faint accent and somewhat different behavior.

Neither did they know the purpose of their mission. That information was reserved to the planners, both human and Satyr, who rested easier in the knowledge that what the crew did not know they could not tell.

On the surface of things, the operation really made no sense. They were to travel to a nearby colonial world, make a planetfall in the hinterland, and await further instructions.

But the Satyr personality was such that none of them found this unreasonable. They had, Casey observed, relatively little personal initiative, which perhaps explained why the highly individualistic Skinnies were able to dominate them so completely even though their culture was markedly younger. But the Satyrs excelled at teamwork. They could take an idea and execute it with faultless precision. That was the reason they made up the mass of the military forces of the empire, and why they had been chosen to crew this ship instead of the Skinnies. Satyrs could be depended upon to listen to explanations and to follow instructions without deviating.

The voyage took 210 days. The last day found their ship coasting along on reaction drive just outside the orbit of the fifth planet of a rather anemic-looking sun. Their destination within the system was the fourth planet, an Earth-sized body with slightly more than half its surface under water.

Most of the colonization had taken place on an archipelago, offshore of the largest continent in its southern hemisphere. Movement into the continental interior had not yet gotten much of a start, which was the main reason it was selected as their landing spot. The population was predominantly Skinny, the rest were Satyr, with small numbers of three or four other subject races.

After a period of intense observation the crew was satisfied there were no spacial defenses. They moved in and made a fractional orbit polar injection, which brought them down about fifteen hundred kilometers from the coast.

The land was high desert, containing no large vegetable forms. It was windy and sand-scoured and thoroughly unpleasant. It would be, Casey thought, a bad place to be marooned—yet that *must happen*. Once the rest of them had carried out their instructions to establish a camp a sufficient distance away, he followed his own. He set the destroy sequence timer for fifteen minutes later: time enough to leave the doomed ship far behind.

Then, with his little cache of supplies, Casey headed for the sea. Alone and unencumbered by any followers, he would reach the coastal city in twenty days.

Perched atop a mesa with unclimbable walls, set in the middle of a desert no creature on foot could hope to cross, the Imperial prison on Maygarth was a masterpiece of Skinny planning.

New prisoners came in over the transmatter. The transmatter crew was rotated the same way. Only a few

of them ever went out onto the surface, preferring to
avoid the poisonous agents there and stay inside the
sterile dome.

Those who left were protected by airtight suits, and
went only to convey prisoners to their places of captiv-
ity. This was done in a skimmer-like device whose controls were keyed to its pilot's retinal patterns. Once
delivered, a prisoner never left and was never again
visited by a guard skimmer. Whatever he "earned" was
supplied to him from a remote terminal. If he died his
'cell' was reused.

So the guards were quite well insulated from those in
their charge, and so confident they would never have an
escape attempt that no arms were kept in the dome.
The theory was that if the impossible happened there
would be ample time to secure weapons by means of
the transmitter.

Burnollus was an old Skinny, sick already when he
arrived on Maygarth, suffering from degenerating hearts
and leaking valves. Yet he strained as hard as he could.
The accursed crank he labored to turn had moved only
a fraction of a revolution, and the counter to which it
was attached had not clicked off the credit.

The old creature did not know where he would find
the strength to try again. Already his breathing was
labored, not only from the effects of the poison which
was progressively inhibiting his muscular efficiency, but
from the inability to maintain rigidity. Lacking bones,
his form was maintained by hydraulic pressure, which
even before his imprisonment had been low.

If he could not turn the crank the required number of
revolutions and get the antidote, death was certain. He
knew, as every creature does, that this end was inevitable—yet, in spite of his circumstances and his utter
lack of hope, he could not simply give up.

Burnollus was a scholar, an academician of the Imperial University. He was not a quitter. Had he been, he
would still be there, living in comfort and enjoying the
prestige of his station. But he would also be pandering
to the base motives of the Imperium, and building weap-

ons the Imperium could use to enslave or destroy still more cultures than they already had.

Perhaps, had he possessed more political acumen, or more tact, he would not have placed himself in a position of confrontation with the government, but at the time it had seemed unavoidable. He had been working quietly and steadily on a project that he had assumed had no military application. That had been wrong. A chance discovery opened the door—and before Burnollus himself had recognized the possibilities, some underling had.

He had been approached by Imperial agents and ordered to continue his research, but to change the course of that research toward their goal. He had refused, not realizing at the time that, as he did so, he talked his life away. Yet even now, with death so near, he refused to give them what they wanted. Instead he turned the crank, grinding out each day only enough to keep himself alive. He knew that his captors had calculated his needs with extreme accuracy, and that they had also been remarkably shrewd in assessing his physical abilities.

But this time, he thought, *they have over-estimated me. This time, I will not be able to turn my quota.* He wondered briefly if, in hopes of getting what they believed he alone could provide, they watched over him; if, at the last possible moment, they would snatch him from the jaws of death.

He strained again to grasp the crank. It was at the bottom of its stroke, the most difficult position of all. If he could just push it up to the top ...

He couldn't. The effort drained him. He knew his laboring hearts were incapable of maintaining his skeletal pressure. Their muscles were becoming impotent too, even though his body was undoubtedly marshalling all its resources to keep vital organs going. It would not be enough.

He let go the crank. He sank slowly to the ground, then, his pressure dropping rapidly, breath shallow.

Now, without the need for his body to fight the pull of gravity, his failing muscles could keep him alive a little while longer. He could still see fuzzily, though he could no longer move his head.

How long he lay there in his paralysis he could not judge. Because he could not turn his head he did not see where the stranger had come from. But there the stranger stood, looking down at him and fishing around in a pouch he carried.

So, Burnollus thought, *I was right. They don't intend to let me die.* For a brief moment he felt triumphant. He had compelled them to deviate, to notice him. He had interfered with their carefully laid plans.

And then he realized he had really accomplished very little. He had caused them to pause, that was all. He had not permanently deprived them of anything. They would be as stubborn as he was. They would rescue him, time after time, until one day he would grow tired of the pain and the misery. They were merely waiting for that to happen.

Stark reality hit him. He had not considered self-destruction before. He had been confident the planet itself would take care of that. Now he knew it could not be avoided. Since he could not stop them from reviving him, he must take the strength they would give him and use it to end his existence.

He felt a small pain, nestled amongst a multitude of greater pains. He knew the other had injected something into his bloodstream. No doubt it was a dose of the antidote. He would know in seconds, if his strength began to return.

Gradually the labored breathing became more regular. His hearts pumped with more force, and drove away the fuzzy halos that had begun to crowd into his visual field. As the moments passed he felt a newness to his body, more vitality than he had known since the day he arrived. He had forgotten what it was like not to hurt, not to feel tired.

He raised his head, testing the strength of his muscles. His hearts beat strongly now, and his body was rigid. Experimentally, he extended an arm, using it to push against the ground. He was almost instantly in a sitting position, though he did not dare try to rise to his feet.

He turned his head from side to side, expecting to see a skimmer and a guard. He did not.

"Here," a voice behind him called.

Burnollus struggled to get his other arm behind him, and then to scoot himself around. What he saw then amazed him. There was the stranger, standing stark still, within easy reach and unarmed. He wore no clothing other than the belt from which his pouch hung. He did not even have shoes. There was no sign of any vehicle. It did not seem to Burnollus that this could be a guard.

The stranger spoke again. "How do you feel?"

"Stronger. You're not one of *them*, are you?"

"No. I am a friend. It appeared to me that you needed a friend just now."

"How did you get here?"

"I walked."

"Across that?" He pointed out toward the horizon, where nothing which did not grow here had ever been.

"Yes. I will explain later. Now, you must rest. I will turn your crank."

Burnollus allowed the stranger to help him into his little shelter. It was little more than a lean-to, designed to give minimum protection from sun and wind, and from the rare rainstorms.

He could not imagine why the stranger had come, or *how* he had come. But undeniably he was here—and a sensible individual, too. He knew that the crank would have to be turned or suspicious monitors on the other end would wonder what kept him alive.

After a time the stranger returned. In his hand was an ampule filled with antitoxin. The stranger placed it on the shelter's lone shelf. "For later," the stranger said. Then, he slid slowly down the wall and sat on the lean-to's floor. "Now," he said, "I must rest."

Burnollus watched—but the stranger's idea of rest was more enigmatic even than his tale. At first Burnollus believed his eyes were playing tricks on him. Subtle changes occurred in the stranger's form.

First to go was its pigmentation, which in Burnollus' race varied from nearly black to light gray. The stranger became a weak and sickly reddish brown.

While this was going on the shape of his head changed. His face altered. Pressure vessels which held the cranial shape seemed to melt away, yet his head did not collapse, as it might be expected to do.

Burnollus watched spellbound as the same thing happened to the limbs and torso. In place of the pressure vessels, with their interlacing bundles of muscles, an endoskeleton appeared to hold the stranger's body rigid.

These were the norm with every race but Burnollus' own, so the fact that this "creature" had one did not surprise him. But he was not aware of any life form which could alter its appearance the way this one was doing.

It was some time before the creature spoke again. Burnollus could not detect any change in the voice, though he had expected one. Drastic as the change of shape had been, this was peculiar.

"Now," said the stranger, "you see me as I really am."

"What are you?"

"I am a human being. I have shown you what you have just seen so that you will believe what I am going to tell you."

"I have not previously heard of your race."

"This is good. Let us hope that such ignorance continues to prevail."

"Why did you come?"

"To help you escape."

"Escape? To where? You said you walked here. I cannot walk so far. I am too old and too feeble, even if I had enough of the antidote."

"The antidote is available in the necessary quantities. And you will not be alone. Others will come. As many as we can possibly take."

"But how—where would we go? There is no safety anywhere in the Imperium."

"We will go outside the Imperium, to my people, where many of you have already gone and many of those we call Satyrs; you know them as the Kaii."

Burnollus did not respond. He needed to think. This "human" could be what he said he was. But more probably he was an Imperial spy. How else would he get his hands on all that antitoxin? How else would he get around on this god-forsaken world? No doubt, concealed somewhere close by, he had a vehicle. Perhaps companions, too. It could very well be an Imperial scheme to persuade Burnollus to cooperate.

"Tell me more about these people."

Casey did. He started at the very beginning, with the human discovery of the other penal world of Campbell: how the races had met, and how the Imperial government was as yet unaware of human existence. He went on to the subject of the government in exile which had been formed: and explained the human technological weakness.

Burnollus listened, becoming less and less incredulous, until Casey told him how he had gotten to Maygarth. Then he became a little balky. "Are you telling me that you—one creature, all alone—simply went to a colonial planet, assumed the appearance and identity of a local, and transported to the Imperial capital?"

"Essentially, yes. When I arrived, I contacted the underground . . ."

"The what?"

"The dissidents. I entered the prison where they were holding people for transportation to this place, substituting myself for one of them. It was easy to get here."

"For you, perhaps. But even for you it may not be as easy to get out. How do you intend to do it?"

"I am going to rely upon you, and the rest of the scientists here."

"What? That is insane."

"Perhaps. But what alternatives are there? Surely the only practical means of escape is the transmatter system, and there must be many people here who understand it intimately."

"Undoubtedly there are. I am one of them. But we are scattered all over this planet . . ."

"We will do it. We have to."

"It will not work; not with just one of you. Why did you not bring others to help? For that matter, why is it necessary to involve us at all? Why not simply infiltrate the Imperial Government and take control of it?"

"Because there are no more of *us*. I am the only one there is. Now, let us stop this bickering. If we *are* to leave here, you and the others must follow the plan.

You must obey my orders, otherwise we have no chance at all."

"I will not follow you blindly. I do not recognize any authority in you. You cannot give me orders."

Casey turned to him. His own immortality had taught him patience, and this was a virtue he ordinarily culti- vated. But it did not always serve. "I can let you die here, then. I cannot take responsibility for your welfare without taking authority over you also. You will either submit to that authority or I will leave you." Casey knew these words would carry weight. He had learned in his first contact with the aliens that "humanity" was not a matter of body form, nor even a matter of culture. Humanity was a state of mind: a bundle of emotions, including fear and greed and all the rest. Every race had these, needed them, could not exist as a sentient race without them. That was a universal truth.

"But you *need* me. You said your race does not have modern matter transmission."

"True. You could help give us that. Perhaps you could give us even a better system than the Imperials have, but you are not the only one who could do it—and I am the only one who can get you out."

That ended the prisoner's hesitation. "I will agree. Tell me what it is I must do."

Casey did. For the rest of the Maygarth's day he in- structed, while Burnollus made careful notes. When dark- ness approached he walked away, in the direction of the setting sun, toward his next contact.

He would not visit every prisoner in the weeks to come; just the ones his discussion with Burnollus indi- cated would be essential to the escape plan, or who must be given special incentive to stay alive until that plan could be executed. Sometimes he would appear as a Skinny, at others he was a Satyr. Rarely did he use human form; rarer still were there witnesses to the transformation. Always he preached secrecy, persever- ance, and resolve; and always he left with a promise of obedience in return for his help.

Throughout it all, one thing bothered Casey more even than the prospect of failure—that in the interim humanity would be discovered by the Imperials. That fear drove him mercilessly.

The guard, Hagop, was a Satyr. That fact alone complicated Casey's task, since alteration of his bone structure was necessary when he impersonated one of them, whereas with a Skinny it was not. The differences could be camouflaged quite superficially and still be passable.

Hagop was also fat. Satyrs were fat in about the same proportions humans were, and when they were fat they were also inclined to be lazy. Hagop was, but not lazy enough to omit a visual check of the screen when the buzzer rang. The buzzer was his signal to admit someone who had been outside.

Without putting down his magazine, and hardly without taking his eyes off the centerfold he had been examining with such prurience, he flipped the switch on the outside screen pickup.

A Skinny face appeared instantly. He recognized it as the maintenance engineer, Flacco. Flacco was always prowling around the station complaining of something or other, usually the slovenliness of the Satyr guards. Hagop did not like him very well.

Hagop noticed something peculiar, and commented. "Why are you not wearing a suit, Flacco?"

"It is unnecessary to go through the effort for a few moments outside, and it is too cumbersome for delicate work. Open the airlock and let me in."

"How did you get out to begin with?"

"I went through the other lock—just before you came on duty. Now—open up."

"How long did you say you had been out there?"

"I did not say. You are beginning to irritate me, Kaii. Cycle this airlock at once."

Hagop's hand drifted to the control board, where the light was blinking red over the airlock switch. He threw the switch to the first position and the light went out. Flacco's image disappeared from the screen.

Hagop did not know why he continued to watch. It wasn't his custom; certainly he had more entertaining things to do. Nevertheless, he pressed another button and activated a camera in the lock itself.

Flacco stood with his back to it, while swirls of dust blown in from outside curled around him. Had he been wearing a suit, the chamber would simply have been evacuated, then refilled with station air. Since he had not been, the other cycle had to be used, and the air was flushed to the outside, replaced from storage tanks. That cycle was considerably longer.

As Hagop watched, something happened to Flacco, something frightening. His color was fading! Hagop activated an intercom. "Flacco, what is wrong? Are you sick?"

"No," came the answer. "I am fine. Open the inner hatch."

"No! I do not want you in here with me until I know it is safe. How do I know what you might be bringing in with you?"

"I told you, I am all right. Let me in."

Hagop did not reply. He shut off that intercom station and activated another to the station commander, a severe-looking Skinny named Pudlik.

Pudlik answered, a somewhat annoyed tone in his voice. "What is the trouble, Hagop?"

"Flacco is in the airlock. He went outside without a suit. Now he looks peculiar, and I think he is ill. I have refused to admit him until I am certain."

"How does he look peculiar?"

"He is changing color."

"I shall be there momentarily. You have done well, Hagop."

Pudlik did not ordinarily like Satyrs, though he found them to be excellent lackeys. They followed orders to the letter, and properly handled, displayed a servility never found among guards of his own race. Hagop had been quite correct to be alarmed over the color change. A slight paling was a symptom of many diseases to which his people were subject.

Pudlik arrived at the guard station in less than a minute. He found Hagop staring into the video display. He could see Flacco's mouth moving, but since the sound was off he could not hear his words.

"He looks normal enough to me. Turn on the sound, Hagop."

Hagop did as he was told, protesting that Flacco had changed back during the interim.

"Flacco: what were you doing outside without a suit?"

"Adjusting the palagometer fingers."

"The what?"

"It's technical. You wouldn't understand. It is very delicate work, and they are awkwardly located."

Pudlik did not have sufficient acquaintance with the station's hardware to tell if that was true, but Hagop had been right about one thing: Flacco did not seem the same. Pudlik decided he did not like the voice. He devised a further test. "Flacco, who am I?"

"You are the commander."

"Yes—but what is my name?"

"I have always called you 'The Commander.' "

"I see. And who is this?" He motioned to Hagop, who came over and stared into the camera.

"He is the monitor."

"What is his name?"

"Who pays attention to Kaii names?"

Inwardly, Pudlik silently agreed. What disturbed him was Flacco's failure to remember his own name. "Move to the far wall, Flacco."

The image shifted.

"Why are you not wearing shoes, Flacco?"

"They interfere with climbing. I left them inside."

"Where?"

"In my quarters."

Pudlik flipped the switch, turning his microphone off. "Hagop."

"Yes, Commander?"

"Go to Flacco's quarters. Get his shoes."

"Yes, sir." Hagop waddled off.

While he was gone, Pudlik watched the screen. Flacco stood woodenly in one corner, the camera focused on him. Pudlik had to admit he did not look the least bit pale.

"Commander!"

Pudlik turned. Hagop was approaching at a dead run, closely followed by—Flacco!

"Commander, if this is Flacco, who is that outside?"

"I do not know, but I intend to find out."

"I shall send for help, Commander." Hagop picked up his communicator.

"No! We will handle this ourselves. Whoever it is is trapped in the airlock. He cannot escape. I will not have those idiots at headquarters sopping up the credit for his capture."

Hagop put the communicator down. He did not like that idea. It was contrary to standing orders. Under those orders, *anything* out of the ordinary was to be reported before local action was taken. He started to protest, then changed his mind. It was not *his* responsibility, and he would not be blamed if he merely followed orders from the commander.

"Summon the station physician, Hagop."

"Yes, sir." Hagop punched a three-digit number into his communicator, then spoke briefly into its mouthpiece.

Presently another Skinny appeared. This one was aged, and looked harried: an impression cultivated by those in his calling of whatever race. "What is wrong, Commander?"

"Look at the screen, Doctor; then *you* tell *me*."

The doctor did. "Why, it looks like *him*," he said, pointing to Flacco. "A twin?"

"I have no twin," Flacco replied.

"Then who is it?"

"We have no idea, Doctor. He claims to be Flacco, but as you can see, Flacco is here. And he does not know my name. He obviously intended to enter the station and impersonate Flacco."

"Then he must be one of the prisoners."

"We can check that easily enough. We have photographs of all of them. Attend to it, Hagop."

Hagop sat down in front of the control panel and began punching buttons. First he tied the computer into the video camera and extracted a series of still images, which he then commanded the computer to match to the newcomer. It couldn't. "Not a prisoner, Commander," he said.

"Try it against the station personnel records, then."

Fingers flew across the keyboard. The computer hiccupped. "A match, Commander—Flacco."

"Incredible—an impersonation good enough to fool the computer. This *would* have been a dangerous situation. I commend you on your vigilance, Hagop."

Hagop experienced the Satyr equivalent of a blush, but he did not reply. He hoped the commander would remember to make the commendation official and enter it on his records.

But Pudlik, it seemed, was preoccupied with his problem. He turned to the doctor. "What do you have here at the station that will put him out, Doctor?"

"Under the circumstances, I would recommend an anesthetic gas. I would also recommend he not be brought inside. He may carry disease."

"Is that what you think this is? Do you know of any diseases which produce symptoms like that?"

"Well, no. But—"

"Then it is not a medical decision, is it?"

"No, sir."

"Prepare the anesthetic, then. Flacco."

"Yes, Commander."

"The doctor will require your assistance to administer the gas."

"Yes, sir."

Kah-Sih-Omah, He-Who-Waits, waited once again. He was perplexed, but without panic. He knew that his impersonation was suspect, but he did not yet know how he had been detected.

At first, he had considered disabling the camera, but decided not to. It would have the effect of confirming their suspicions, and he could not risk that while there was still a chance he could bluff his way through.

So he waited for them to make a move. He was not uncomfortable in the airlock, merely immobilized. He knew that sooner or later the station people would take some action to examine him closer. Probably they would arrive in sufficient numbers to overcome him. He was ready if that happened. Although unarmed, he had traveled everywhere throughout the centuries he had lived, and studied many things. He was proficient in every form of unarmed combat human beings had developed, and he had the anatomical skill to apply many of these to the Skinny and Satyr bodily forms. He had no doubt that he could at least escape, if it were impossible to defeat the lot of them.

But that would not get him inside the station, and he *must* get in.

Abruptly his train of thought was rudely derailed. Something was happening. There was a faint hissing noise coming from the intake ports, and he felt strangely light-headed. Gas!

In a normal individual terror would have consumed the last few moments of consciousness. Kah-Sih-Omah was beyond that. In his time he had faced such dangers often. He-Who-Waits does not panic. He simply adapts, and waits some more. Thus it had been, on those occasions when he had been buried alive in cave-ins, or choked by poison gases in fires, or trapped in sinking ships.

With the bodily capabilities those mysterious creatures had given him so many millennia ago, he could not be greatly inconvenienced by such prosaic things as anesthetic gases. Almost unconsciously he willed his respiration to cease, so that he would inspire no more of it until he was ready. For long moments his body leached oxygen from non-essential tissues and dumped it into his bloodstream, where it was immediately shunted first to his brain and then to his heart.

In those precious seconds, his mind cleared; his thoughts became sharp and precise. Other commands went out across neural pathways no other creature in all the universe possessed. Some of these went to Casey's liver. There, on molecule-sized samples of the anesthetic, the cells poured out hundreds of hastily fashioned enzymes. When at last one of them fit the molecule better than the molecule fit the hemoglobin in Casey's blood, the liver turned its massive chemical strength entirely on their production.

As soon as this process had begun it dumped them into his circulatory system. Changes had occurred there too. Valves other human beings lacked opened and closed, and soon his heart was pumping the enzyme-laden blood through his pulmonary artery, from whence it seeped into the tiny capillaries of the alveoli.

Only then did Casey's chest resume its regular rise and fall. He was secure in the knowledge that the gas molecules could not attach, and that the vital oxygen still could. The gas would still have some effect, because the volume of space it occupied could not be utilized to accommodate oxygen, but the effect was no more onerous than exercise at a fairly high altitude would be.

He-Who-Waits was ready. In the space of time this had consumed he had carefully feigned the symptoms of unconsciousness. First he wobbled, then he slumped, and finally he collapsed, motionless on the airlock floor.

Suddenly there was a tremendous whooshing sound. High-speed pumps began evacuating the chamber, and through outlets in the walls compressed air began blasting into it.

After about thirty seconds the sound stopped and the inner lock opened. Arms grasped Casey's body and dragged it out of the lock.

He had his eyes closed, of course, but he listened carefully to every word they said. He recognized the voice of the commander.

"How long will this keep him under, Doctor?"

"Not long."

"Hagop?"

"Yes, sir?"

"Fetch rope; tie him up before he regains consciousness."

"Not necessary, Commander," said the doctor. "I have prepared an injection."

Hagop relaxed and remained, waiting for the next order.

"What is in it, Doctor?" Pudlik wanted to know.

"Essentially the same thing he would be getting if he were outside, except in this case it has been refined and will therefore affect him much faster. Uh—it is my own private project. I have been working on it since I came here. I think it might be useful to the military, and I intend to offer it to the government when testing is complete."

"Yes," said Pudlik. "I can appreciate it would be

useful—if it works. Hadn't you better get on with the testing?"

"At once, Commander."

This discourse had been of immense value to Casey, who had, of course, hung on every word. It was a stroke of extreme good fortune that the doctor had picked that particular substance. His body had been neutralizing the toxin since he had arrived, so the mechanism was already extant. It had not, however, had to deal with such a massive dosage as an injection would represent. He would slow the process down.

When the doctor picked up his arm and slid the needle into his vein, Casey promptly ordered his body to close that vessel off at the nearest convenient branch. This maneuver resulted in enough distension of that vessel to alarm the doctor, who terminated the injection without administering the entire dose.

When he withdrew the needle he explained this to the Commander. "Be careful. I couldn't give him all of it without injuring the vessel, but he'll be unable to move for several hours, at least."

"Won't it kill him by then?"

"No. The vehicle I'm using will release it slowly enough so that he still has enough muscle function to stay alive—but not so slowly that his body can eliminate it within that time period."

"When can I start the interrogation?"

"As soon as you like."

"Then," said Pudlik, looking at Hagop, "I will begin now. Take him to the Guard's Lounge. I will use that."

Hagop gulped. Now why didn't he use some other facility? Hagop spent almost all his off-duty time in the lounge, and he would be finished with his watch in twenty minutes.

Nevertheless, good soldier that he was, he slung the comatose Skinny over his shoulders, carried him to the lounge, and laid him out on a cometball table. Several troopers who were playing the billiard-like game protested—until they saw the commander. Pudlik ordered everybody out, closed the door, and ordered Hagop to stand guard—on the outside.

"Now then," he said to the supine figure, as soon as

Casey opened his eyes, "you *will* answer my questions—truthfully. If you do not answer, or if you lie to me, I will have the doctor increase the dosage until you must fight for every breath. Do you understand?"

"Yes." Casey not only understood, but agreed: cooperation was an excellent idea. He had always believed in keeping his plans flexible. Even though the enemy had caught him, or thought they had, he was busy integrating this development into his strategy.

"Good. Who are you?"

"I am Kah-Sih-Omah."

"That is your name?"

"Yes."

"How did you get here?"

"I came through the transmatter, like all the other prisoners, from the Imperial City."

"You lie. The computer could not match your image."

"It had a different image."

"Where did you come from?"

"From Earth."

"Where is Earth? I have not heard of it."

"I do not know how to get there from here."

"But you know how to get from 'Earth' to the Imperial city?"

"Yes."

"I see." Wheels were turning rapidly in Pudlik's mind. He had indeed stumbled upon something sinister; something that obviously posed a grave danger to the Imperium. He saw an advantage in that for himself: a way to realize an ambition; a way to climb out of a dead-end job and get back into the mainstream of the service. Rank and fortune came easily to persons whom the Imperium thought resourceful. Pudlik would demonstrate how resourceful he could be.

"Why did you come here?"

"To free the prisoners."

"All of them?"

"Yes."

"Why?"

"So that they might join the government in exile."

"There is no such thing."

"Very well. I will accommodate you. I will agree; there is no such thing."

Pudlik did not like that reply. He had prepared himself to interrogate a stubborn captive—a deceitful captive—a silent captive. He was not quite certain how to handle one who seemed quite willing to tell him anything he wanted to know. That would require cunning, and though Pudlik did not doubt he possessed that faculty, he resolved to go slow. "Where is this government in exile located?"

"On the planet Campbell."

"And I suppose you do not know where Campbell is either?"

"That is correct."

"But you went from Campbell to Imperial City?"

"No. I went from Ithaca, to Wolfingham, to Gringar, to Imperial City."

"Those names are strange to me—except Gringar. Gringar is an Imperial colony, is it not?"

"Yes."

"It is, is fact, a probationary colony?"

"If you say so."

That fact bothered Pudlik a great deal. Probationary colonists were permitted only limited travel, especially to the Imperial planet. They were a dumping ground for all kinds of misfits, including people who displayed the milder forms of political dissent. Security at the transmatter stations was almost as tight as here on Maygarth. If this person had transported from Gringar to Imperial City he must have done so with the help of station personnel. And that meant there had to be a vast and powerful conspiracy against the empire.

Pudlik decided it could not hurt to ask the prisoner, so he did. "What does this government in exile expect to do with the prisoners you are trying to free?"

"It intends to overthrow the Imperium."

"I see. Is that not a formidable task?"

"Yes. It is very formidable."

"Yet they have undertaken it?"

"Yes."

"Do you know how big the Imperium is?"

"No. How big is it?"

"It occupies 316 planetary systems, populated be fourteen separate races, of which we are the most important. Altogether there are approximately 1.7 trillion individuals. That is many, is it not?"

"Yes."

"How many planetary systems do the exiles have?"

"I do not know."

"How many races, how many individuals?"

"I do not know."

"Are there as many as in the Imperium?"

"I do not know."

"Are we the dominant race among the exiles?"

"We?"

"Yes, our kind. Surely we are."

"No."

"Who is?"

"Human beings are. They are called 'the People.' "

"What is a human being?"

"I am a human being."

"Then we *are* dominant."

"No. I said, *I* am a human being. You are not. I am a shaman of the People. In the shamen reposes the power of the People."

Pudlik did not understand the significance of that answer until it was too late.

With incredible speed—speed so blinding that Pudlik's eyes caught only a blur of it—a long tentacle which had been concealed beneath the prisoner's body lashed out. It whipped around Pudlik, binding his arms firmly to his sides. The end was flattened, like a living ribbon, and it was this tip that suddenly covered his mouth. The scream which had been welling up in Pudlik's throat died, smothered.

The captive rose to a seated position on the table. He reached out with his left arm and drew Pudlik near. "Do not struggle," he said. "It is useless."

Casey extended his right arm. The arm had changed subtly. One of its fingers had grown a horny point. Behind the point it was curiously swollen. He laid the point on Pudlik's arm, then pushed. The point broke through the commander's skin and entered a vein. The swelling behind the point rapidly subsided.

"I trust that the doctor was careful with the dosage, Commander. As you will soon see, I saved the drug for you. To it I have added a little embellishment of my own. In a little while you will become too weak to move. You will still be able to speak, though I caution you to do so softly. If you try to give alarm you will go to sleep, and you will never wake again. The doctor could never identify the substance I added in time to save your life." That last threat was not true, but it was necessary that Pudlik think it was. Casey's carefully contrived answers to the commander's questions had all been designed to reinforce his credibility.

Casey felt Pudlik go limp, and relaxed his grip somewhat.

Pudlik slithered to the floor, sprawling out like a limp rag.

Casey picked him up and placed him on the table, after which he removed Pudlik's shoes from his feet and the harness affair that all the guards wore around the upper torso. He began to don the articles.

"I am about to take your place, Commander," he told Pudlik. "When I have finished, I will be *you*, complete to the pattern of blood vessels on your retinas and the configuration of your vocal cords. I will look like you and I will sound like you. To your people, here at the station and at Imperial headquarters, I will *be* you."

Pudlik glared up at Casey, but he did not respond. Instead he watched in horror as a spike grew out of Casey's forehead.

The spike resembled a horn but as it grew it became thinner and thinner. On its tip another horny scale was forming. Gradually, over the course of several minutes, it reached a length of over two feet and dangled down across Casey's chest.

Then, grasping Pudlik in both arms, Casey rolled him over. He took the new appendage in one hand and jammed its tip deep into the back of Pudlik's neck, while with his other hand, he covered the commander's mouth. "I am about to tap into your central nervous system, Commander. Through the tap I will learn enough about your body to duplicate all the necessary systems. When I am finished there will be nothing about its structure that I will not know, and my impersonation will become indetectable."

That last statement was also not quite true. It would not be completely indetectable. No impersonation ever was. There still remained in Casey's body the basic human structures he was born with, but the cosmetic changes would be complete. These changes would conform his body to Pudlik's pattern in every way his comrades would be likely to check.

The procedure was not a lengthy one, and Casey was, of course, quite skilled at it. He had had millennia to practice, and in this interval he had not confined his experiments to his own species. When it was over he withdrew the probe. It began to recede, reabsorbed into his body as the long tentacle with which he had bound Pudlik had already been. He rolled the commander back over, even as he began making the necessary alterations.

"There, you see how easy it is for the shamen. Watch my features change and become your features. See me become you, as I might become any person in the Imperium."

Pudlik did watch, with horror. Only when the change was complete did he find the courage to speak. "W—what now?"

"Now? Now, Commander, you will go to sleep, and I will call Hagop. Hagop will rush in here and see two of us. I will tell him that I watched your form change with my own eyes, and he will believe me, because he watched the doctor inject the poison into my arm with *his* own eyes. He will examine my arm and find no puncture. Then he will examine your arm, which, as you know, contains one. Is there anything else you would like to know before you go to sleep?"

Pudlik hesitated. His thoughts were a mass of confusion. He could plainly see that this creature had completely destroyed him. Whether he lived through this or not, Pudlik would become an outcast as soon as his superiors learned what had happened. Still, he was curious about this strange 'shaman.' This creature of such sure and effortless power—this superbeing before whom all defenses seemed as flimsy as soap bubbles—what did it want? What would it do to the Imperium?

"What will *we* do, Commander? We will destroy it, utterly. We will obliterate its very memory."

"Why?"

"Because the Imperium is an evil thing. Because it is dominated by venal creatures such as yourself. Because it is oppressive and corrupt. Because, worst of all, it is inept. It cannot prevail over even one shaman. Therefore it is far too weak to protect its citizens from the really powerful forces in this galaxy: forces greater even than the shamen."

Pudlik did a very human thing; he gulped.

"There are," he told Pudlik, "beings as superior to me as I am to you. These beings created me; gave me the powers you have seen me use and many more besides. If I tell you that I have already lived many times as long as the recorded history of my race you must believe that, because it is true. Now sleep."

He placed his hand on Pudlik's arm, just above the puncture. There he had implanted, protected by a crystalline coating, a tiny quantity of one of the Skinny endorphins which his own body had synthesized. The pressure broke the fragile coating and it poured into the commander's bloodstream. A few seconds later, the lights went out for Pudlik.

"Kevin C. O'Meara" was coming home. The skimmer which brought him was piloted by the Commissioner of Alien Affairs himself, no small honor when one took Carmody's personality into consideration.

Carmody was not a very talkative person, and Casey seemed disinclined. He napped throughout the two-hour journey, or appeared to; Carmody couldn't tell. Certainly, if any man deserved a rest, it was Casey. He'd done a yeoman's job.

Still, Carmody was not entirely pleased with the way things had come out. He did not entirely agree that human destiny should depend on anything so fragile as a legend; yet that was the position into which Casey's actions had plunged man.

It did not look very workable. After all, some of the persons who must necessarily believe in it were hard-headed scientists, scientists of a technological level far beyond anything that humanity was likely to reach within Carmody's lifetime, even with help.

The O'Meara homestead had appeared on the western horizon, looking so peaceful and solitary that Carmody could not make himself believe its owner was the man who had probably determined humanity's course for the next thousand years.

He began to cut the power, and the skimmer lost lift, gliding smoothly to a landing in the front yard. Kim and the two children, this time conventionally dressed, emerged from the house and ran to greet Casey.

Casey, by this time quite alert, sprang out like a gazelle and hugged them all, in turn.

Carmody waited a decent interval, then motioned to Kim. She approached the driver's window, looking bright-eyed and relieved.

"You see," he told her, "I brought him back, good as new, just as I said I would. And he got the job done for us just as he said he would."

"I guess it was a little selfish of me to try to keep him from going," she replied. "But I'm sure you understand how much the time we have together means to both of us."

Carmody nodded. The subtlety of the remark was not lost on him, and when he received the obligatory invitation to stay for dinner he shook his head. "No thank you, Kim. I have urgent government business I must return to. I must go now."

They waved goodbye to him as the skimmer rose, and watched it drift off out of sight. When it was an insignificant speck, and after the children had run off to diversions of their own, Kim took Casey into the house and poured two cups of mescaf.

For a while they sat at the kitchen table sipping quietly, each lost in his own thoughts.

To Kim, Casey seemed strangely troubled, moodier than she could remember him ever to have been. It was reminiscent of their first days together.

Finally, just as she had done then, she broke the silence by asking point-blank, "What's wrong, Casey?"

Casey put his cup down, sighed, and looked into her eyes. "Maybe nothing, Kim. But, it occurs to me that I am missing one power my creators might easily have given me. One which would have made life incomparably simpler."

"What power is that, Casey?"

"Prescience. If I could look ahead as I do into the past, I would know whether I had done the right thing. But as it is I can only judge the future by what has gone before. And nothing quite like this has ever happened before—at least, not on the scale I have just attempted."

"I haven't pried, Casey. I know that when you are ready you will explain what you have done; at least, as much of it as I can understand."

"There is no mystery in my actions, Kim. I have once again become a shaman, and I have done what medicine men have always done. It is a calling far older than I, perhaps as old as man himself."

"I guess you'll have to explain it after all, Casey. I don't understand."

And so he did. He told her all: how he had visited the captive aliens, walking up on them out of the desert like a spector and overwhelming their reason with displays of powers which, even to astute scientists, could only be described as magic. He told her how he had labored to build up the mystique of a super-being, immune from the natural laws of the universe in which each and every one of them had previously believed. He had accomplished, consistently and without apparent effort, things which they *knew* to be impossible.

And then had come the threat. Somewhere on the outer marches of the known universe were other creatures to whom this same super-being was a microbe. Beings of awesome power: even the power to create super-beings such as he.

When he had finished this narrative the sun had set and the children hovered near the darkened doorway, hesitant to interrupt what to them was serious and incomprehensible adult talk.

"So you see, Kim, I have told a great lie, and because of that lie man must now become a keeper for his neighbors of the worlds nearby. And the danger in that is that we have, in our midst, many aliens who know the truth about us, together with others who do not know and who are simply unfortunate victims of the times.

"They are now true exiles. None of them must ever be allowed contact with their homeworlds again. Their later generations, yes; but not these. Even now Carmody's people are carting them off to a colony world far down the spiral arm, where they will endure great hardships and where many of them will die. Their maintenance will cost our people most of its surplus wealth for the next two or three generations, but it must be done, and all to support a lie."

"We have the transmatter now, don't we, Casey? That should help."

"Yes. We have that, but even that was obtained by deceit. We told these alien scientists they could go home, and they told us how the system worked. Then we reneged; we sent them on to the colony with all the rest, after smashing any transmatter station they might have used to escape. It is not a deed I am proud to have helped accomplish."

"Don't blame yourself, Casey. It was necessary. I understand that. So does everyone else who knows. Casey, you mentioned prescience a while ago. You said you wished you had it. But maybe prescience fits in here someplace after all."

"What do you mean?"

"I mean, this may all have been foreseen. Not by you, but by your creators. You always said you felt you had a reason to be, that without a purpose in mind they would never have made you what you are. Can you be certain that you have not just fulfilled that purpose in doing what you did?"

Casey did not answer her. But he took the point well; found comfort in it. He could easily envision such a thing: the beings who made him, to him omniscient, looking forward into time and seeing the menace the Imperium would become to the sapient races with which it shared its space.

And it was not unimaginable that even then in the dimness of his remote past that they would choose to alter the course. He found nothing incomprehensible about that, nothing that prevented it from becoming his firm belief.

He wondered would they do it. How would they manipulate races of beings which to them were so primitive as to be incapable of the exercise of true reason?

He found the answer to that question in himself; in what he was and always had been. On the cosmic scale he could detect no difference in what he was doing at the instance of his makers and what he had done for most of his enormous lifespan. He had chanted, and he had rattled bones. He had donned hideous masks and invoked divine powers. He had at once promised mercy and uttered veiled threats. He had used obscure words and innuendos and sleight of hand. He had worked magic which was not magic, but merely the manipulation of natural things by natural laws.

The effect was the same as it always was wherever the ignorant are confronted by the unfathomable, wherever rumor rules instead of fact and logic is driven from the mind to give way to panic.

Every shaman knows what happens next. There is recoil from the unknown; retreat into the familiar and the safer. Within the Imperium there would be bewilderment, while frantic beings pondered what had occurred on the fringes of their empire; wondered what had sealed them off from itself, both physically and within their own minds. The Imperium had been large. It had cloaked itself with the aura of invincibility. It had expanded inexorably, feeding on suns. It had seemed too large, too momentous to ever stop. Now it had—and like a sun gone nova, squandering the energy of its collapse, it would soon find itself a small and insignificant thing.

When a star dies, when an empire dies, darkness comes to both. Casey had seen it many times before. In a few short generations these Imperials would be barbarians again, warring, marching, pillaging and burning. There would be those among them who saw farther and learned more; who would use their wisdom wisely and dole it out sparingly in riddles and mysticism to the beat of the tom-tom and the rattle of bones. He-Who-Waits was *not* alone.

Kismet Station

Two men had served as Commissioner of the Department of Extraterrestrial Affairs during its century of existence: Ivan Carmody, who organized the department, and its present head, Ivan O'Meara, Carmody's namesake and grandson of Kevin and Kimberly O'Meara.

Ivan looked 50, the number of years he had held office since assuming it at age 36. His long tenure testified to his intelligence and his ability to cope with crisis. But a crisis had arisen, too tough even for him, and he had done the intelligent thing—sent for Grandfather.

Grandfather came without a moment's hesitation, though at considerable inconvenience to himself, having been in meditation in the lands of his ancestors, far from modern means of communication or transportation.

He sat now before Ivan's desk, rolling an object in his copper-hued hand, noting its heft, its deformed dull surface and the jagged edges from which fragments of its substance had been torn. Finally he passed it back across the desktop. "Some kind of bullet?"

"A dart, according to the police ballistics experts. They said it was fired through a barrel without lans."

A stranger, watching, would not have understood. Grandfather appeared less than thirty years of age and bore no resemblance whatsoever to his "grandson." Tall and lean, with skin cast in copper, long black braids

trailing past beardless cheeks to fall on buckskins decorated with beadwork, he was as obviously Indian as
Ivan was Caucasian.

There were explanations, of course. The commissioner
owed *his* relatively youthful physique to modern geriatric techniques—vitamins, preservatives that broke down
the destructive free radicals in membranes, DNA and
other vital body components—and to antioxidants and
proper diet.

"Grandfather" owed *his* to a fortuitous encounter,
some 200 centuries past, with creatures who first maimed
him, then rebuilt him. He was Kah-Sih-Omah, He Who
Waits, the oldest man alive.

The relationship was social, not biological, Kah-Sih-
Omah having married Ivan's grandmother and raised
Ivan's father as his own son. Biologically, Kevin O'Meara
had been the son of Ivan's grandmother and a male
donor, since the beings who had endowed Kah-Sih-
Omah with his great powers evidently intended him to
be unique, and he was sterile.

Ivan continued, with mounting concern, "Two days
ago this struck and killed a man named Arthur Anderson as he transported to Earth from the planet Kismet.
We believe an alien fired it as he dematerialized."

Kah-Sih-Omah's calm expression changed and his voice
cracked: "The Imperials?"

"We don't know yet, Grandfather. The evidence is
scant—this object, a few garbled words, and the fact
that Anderson's body was the last object received from
Kismet Station."

"No contact for two days? But haven't you—?"

"Checked? Certainly. We got a test pattern. A test
object made it through—to somewhere—but acknowl-
edgement from the other end never came. We didn't
dare repeat the test—I'll explain why later. Meanwhile,
I haven't told you about the dart.

"Anderson was alive—barely. He uttered something
that sounded like 'aliens, all over,' and died. The Transport Authority notified the police, who gave the matter
priority treatment. And they made the test I mentioned.

"The pathologist recovered this. Its odd caliber"—he
paused and read from the envelope in which the slug

had been kept—".41272 inches, baffled the ballistics people. They said it was fired at extremely high velocity, judging from the amount of tissue destruction, and that the shock killed him, not the poison."

"A poison bullet? What kind of poison is it?"

"There's a whole menagerie of trace elements in it, including arsenic, selenium, gallium sulfide, a couple of the cyanide compounds, and some organics we can't identify. The medical people say none of them were very efficient poisons; they work too slowly to be useful in weapons. Without the high-velocity shock Anderson could have gone on fighting indefinitely. The police couldn't match this slug with any known specimen, by the way.

"But the reason they passed the case to my department was the material their forensic people found under Anderson's nails. It suggested he had struggled with a non-human. They ruled out human tissue first, then when specimens from Imperial forms failed to match they went on to animals, in case Anderson's killer had a dog or something helping him. But this tissue doesn't match that of any animal known to be on the planet."

"Are you sure Anderson came here from Kismet?"

"Reasonably so. That was his assignment. There's no log record he went anywhere else."

"You said 'animals known to be on Kismet'—don't you mean animals we've discovered so far?"

"I can see you don't know anything about Kismet Station, Grandfather. This is one place we're certain there weren't any."

"I don't even know where Kismet is."

"I'll show you." The commissioner leaned forward to pull a keyboard across the top of his desk. For an instant his fingers danced across it. A hologram screen descended from the ceiling.

Kah-Sih-Omah turned to look at it.

Fingers danced again and the display lit. Ivan used a light pointer to trace the route. "Here," he said, "is Earth. Over here, Herschel; then Wolfingham, Brahe, and Mudron off to your right. Here's Campbell. All are settled planets with transmatter installations, all part of our standard exploration route around Imperial space.

"Past Campbell most relay stations are on airless bodies or artificial satellites. Some are continuously manned; most are not. Farther on, the route begins to turn inward again, and there are better facilities."

He moved the pointer along, leaving a long line of red light behind it as far as the last relay. "This," he continued, "is the last station which has been activated."

Kah-Sih-Omah watched the red line trace a loop about a third of the way around the area designated Imperial space. He anticipated that Ivan would move toward that space to indicate the location of Kismet.

He didn't. Instead, he backtracked the pointer to the extreme outer edge of the bulge, far up off the galactic plane, tracing a line which, on the device's logarithmic scale, measured about 150 lightyears. "This," Ivan said, drawing a circle of light, "is Kismet. As you can see, well off the beaten path. Kismet is intended as a vacation planet as well as a relay point."

"A vacation planet?"

"The government plans a sort of park in a decade or so—no permanent population and no colonization. Most facilities are still under construction. Everybody, except a few scientists and V.I.P. tourists—some 13,000 in all—are construction people." He looked over at his grandfather, noted a look of puzzlement, and explained.

"It worked out that way by accident. Kismet was discovered about the time I was born. Ivan Carmody was Commissioner. He named Kismet, salvaged it . . . it was his pet project. You'd have been on Ithaca during that period, I guess."

"Yes," Kah-Sih-Omah agreed. Those had been quiet days—good days. Ithaca was also a secluded world, also well off the beaten path. Outside news had not penetrated easily, and his lifestyle had not promoted involvement in off-world affairs. "What do you mean, 'salvaged'?"

Ivan continued. "Kismet started as a scientific curiosity. And what a curiosity—out in the middle of nowhere, orbiting a first-generation sun that shouldn't have had any planets, much less one entirely Earthlike in size and chemical composition, and ideally located within the primary's life zone.

"It was an enigma. We avoid Imperial space by avoiding the core of the arm. On the periphery most stars are first-generation. Few have sizable planets. Chemical composition of the star and the planet were so mismatched that Kismet was clearly a capture; it couldn't have evolved naturally with that primary." He paused here, anticipating a question.

None came. He went on. "Kismet began evolving life while it orbited some other sun. Whatever force tore it away from there interrupted this process, but it had resumed and was continuing when men found it.

"Kismet was like primeval Earth—reducing atmosphere, no free oxygen, dry land forms, or photosynthesizing organisms even in its oceans. What life it had was extremely simple and totally anaerobic.

"That's why the first relay station was on one of the largest satellite stations we ever built.

"The intention was to permit scientific observation but avoid contamination. In practice, discipline got lax. People began sneaking down, and it was only a matter of time until somebody got himself killed. Eventually there was a casualty whose body couldn't be recovered.

"Kismet's career as a scientific curiosity ended. When natural forces breached the dead man's suit the microorganisms in his body found themselves in virgin environment. They overwhelmed the native life and changed Kismet's evolution.

"The scientists realized they couldn't reverse the process so they accelerated the inversion instead, seeding Kismet with terrestrial life forms, genetically altered and selected for rapid propagation. These spread through Kismet's oceans like wildfire. Within decades the reducing ecology was completely inverted.

"The metamorphosis continues today, of course, but even in that short span Kismet has become an incredibly fecund planet, a paradise completely unspoiled—a paradise that Ivan Carmody believed should stay that way. You'd probably like it there, Grandfather."

Kah-Sih-Omah's memory was as long as his life had

been. He recalled the unspoiled Earth of bygone days. He could not dwell on such thoughts for long without tears, so he changed the subject.

"You said there was an orbital station?"

"Yes—*was*; unused since the surface unit was built. That was the first thing we thought of. In theory, the satellite should still function, but we can't activate it. Whether something disabled or destroyed it . . ."

". . . which brings up the original question—who, or what, shot Anderson?"

"Yes, Grandfather. But for our experiences with the Imperium I'd have gambled and sent someone through to Kismet Station."

"Perhaps it was a human with an alien weapon. Alien artifacts have turned up before, and it's always possible somebody got their hands on one. The police wouldn't have any way of telling."

"Maybe; but aliens seem the only explanation for the tissue."

"I agree," Kah-Sih-Omah grunted. He stiffened. His face was grim. To him, man's first modern encounter with aliens was a recent memory, though it had taken place more than a century ago, on Campbell, where he had met Ivan's grandmother.

Campbell was then a penal planet of the Imperium, a far-flung and evil empire dominated by the Kaii—and at the same time a colony of man. Neither knew of the other, but it was from the exiled scientists rescued first from Campbell and then, almost a generation later, from Maygarth, that humans learned the secrets of the transmatter. With their help a way to lock the Imperium into the volume of space it then occupied had been devised, so that it could not storm out to engulf humanity as it had so many other races.

Ivan Carmody feared that was inadequate. He urged preparation of defense in depth, and humans had embarked on an imperialistic venture of their own, seizing worlds surrounding the Imperial sphere of space.

It was slow going. Matter transmission was instantaneous, across any distance, but required receivers carried in ships, a cumbersome system. In all the time since it came into use, man had traversed a bare 2900 lightyears.

But such cautious detouring had also avoided encounters with new races. Hospitable stellar populations were concentrated in the central spoke, near the galactic plane, and the periphery of the arm contained mostly stars without suitable planets.

When no further hostile encounters occurred, man concentrated his defensive forces around the Imperial sphere, with almost none on the leading edge of his own outward movement.

Perhaps this had been a fatal mistake.

Still, Kismet struck Kah-Sih-Omah as a target both odd and awkward. Kismet was an awfully long way from anywhere. "All right, Ivan," he said. "Let's analyze this. Assuming aliens have attacked, where did they come from and how did they get there? It would seem to me that the transmatter would be the only practical way?"

"The experts don't rule that out but think it unlikely, because we don't seem to be locked out. Instead, they think it was shipborne. If it was we're at a severe disadvantage, with the transmatter in their hands."

"We don't—?" Kah-Sih-Omah's tone was incredulous.

". . . have any military ships out there? Unfortunately not, Grandfather. There wasn't supposed to be any danger in that direction, so the money went elsewhere." Almost apologetically, he added, "Forces are being dispatched from Brahe. They'll be a couple of years getting there."

"A couple of years! Why?"

"Brahe is the nearest big station. Past there ships have to be dismantled, transported, and re-assembled in space at the relay station closest to Kismet, still 140 lightyears away."

Kah-Sih-Omah released an uncharacteristic sigh of despair. "That's far too long, Ivan. Too many human lives are at risk for us to wait. Not just on Kismet—but in all of our space. Someone has to go through and find out what's happened."

"The reason we haven't tried that yet, Grandfather, is that if the invaders used ships it's possible they don't

have the transmatter themselves and won't realize right
away that the main station has off-planet capability.
They won't know where Anderson's body went or where
our test objects came from. We hope they'll assume Kismet Main is just part of the planetary net. With 269
local stations, it would take them a long time to locate,
occupy, and check them all, even with a large force.
We'll get a breather, but we can't afford to be reckless."

Kah-Sih-Omah was dubious. He changed his mind
about Kismet's unsuitability. If it was the Imperials,
hitting humanity on an unprotected flank, then utilizing Kismet Main to make a big breakout could make
sense. He raised the point at once.

"We think it's a brand-new bunch," Ivan replied.
"Granted, we've bottled up only the Imperial transmatter
net, not all space—but the distance, Grandfather! Conventional Imperial ships couldn't make it this soon. And
if they had either superfast ships or transmatter capabilities we don't know about, an attack here would be
pointless. There are better places for it. No, the odds are
much against it.

"So we must avoid giving away any secrets. We need
intelligence; we have only conjecture now. If Kismet
has been occupied, whoever's there will soon discover
we have no fighting ships nearby. If they learn the
transmatter is our sole means of access to the planet,
they're certain to destroy Kismet Main before we can
mount a counterattack.

"The military wants to attack through the station
immediately. I've resisted. An enemy armed and waiting could slaughter them as they materialized. A handful of aliens could hold them off for as long as their
ammunition lasted—and then destroy the transmatter."

"So what *is* the government's plan, Ivan?"

Ivan gave his grandfather a sheepish glance and then
cast his eyes downward. "Right now, *you* are."

He paused again. "You see how indispensible you've
become? Somebody has to go through, and whoever
that is must be able—"

"—to survive long enough to report." To Kah-Sih-
Omah, his grandson's remarks were not callous. This
was, in fact, an eminently rational stance, with which

he quite agreed. He was essentially immortal, and though not invulnerable, certainly closer than any other creature.

So long as a single cell lived, his body could regenerate itself. It had done so many times before and would do many times again before final extinction occurred. Kah-Sih-Omah did not fear that either. He believed his existence had some special purpose to his makers, essential to that of the universe, and that every travail was a part of fulfillment. "I am ready, Ivan," he said without hesitation, "but before I go I want to find out all I can about what happened on Kismet Station. I know you've told me everything you know."

"I'll arrange for you to interview all my people, Grandfather. You can get their views first-hand."

"I'll begin with Anderson."

"Anderson?"

"Yes."

For a time, Ivan tarried in the doorway he had just entered—of a room empty save for three grim men who hadn't even noticed his arrival.

The first and nearest was his Chief Medical Officer, the other two the orderlies who had brought the gurneys they all now watched with such intense concentration.

These three had augmented the brief top-secret biography Ivan had given them, which consisted largely of gross details about Kah-Sih-Omah, with the wildest of the rumors which had drifted back from Campbell years ago. They dwelt on the latter, and not having been told exactly what to expect, quite naturally expected to see miracles.

Ivan watched as intently as they, unable to decide which of the two draped bodies was living and which was dead.

Finally tiring of ignorance, he stepped forward to whisper to the C.M.O., as though this were a funeral.

Holding a hand across his mouth, the C.M.O. whispered back, "I'm not sure just what is happening, Commissioner, but Mr. Omah is the one on the right, and he said he would be going into Anderson's memory."

Fate chose that moment to interrupt. The right-hand

sheet moved, and a small bulge erupted from the forehead of the man lying there.

It rapidly developed into a serpentine form which crept ever so slowly across to the other gurney.

For a relatively brief but highly charged interval all was still. Then, suddenly, both bodies burst into convulsions that threatened to shake them off the gurneys. Orderlies hastened to the sides to bolster the low restraints, but by then the convulsions were over.

For half an hour nothing else happened. Four bored men continued the eerie vigil in silence until, without any warning, one of the figures rose like a cobra from beneath the draping sheet.

Boredom fled before terror. Four full-grown, well-educated, responsible men allowed primitive emotions to overpower reason.

The sheet dropped from a face contorted into a broad grin. Kah-Sih-Omah's seldom-displayed sense of humor surfaced when only he could appreciate it. He gazed at the terrified assembly and said, "One must test one's magical powers occasionally to confirm their potency. We shamen eat from them. Obviously I may continue to feast." He rose and leapt off the gurney, exposing the body on the next as he did so.

It lay face down. Colorless fluid seeped from an incision at the base of the skull.

The C.M.O. examined it.

"Embalming fluid, Doctor," Kah-Sih-Omah advised. "I had a time with it. Quite destructive of tissue and quite disagreeable. Some of the neural pathways were ruined and had to be reconstructed. This is why it took so long. But the electrochemical integrity of the cortex was intact. I was able to bridge across and discharge it. That is what produced the convulsions." He stood at the doorway and stretched. "We are finished in here. Shall we go?"

He did not wait for an answer, but led the way to a terminal in the adjoining room. When the hologlobe descended from its hidden recess it already showed a projection of Kismet Station.

"I have learned a little," Kah-Sih-Omah began. "I know what the invaders look like—or rather, how they looked to Anderson; all such images are highly subjective. His impressions changed from time to time, and either there are several types of aliens or his imagination distorted them. The invaders do not look very much like us, whatever their origin. If they are Imperials it is a species I have never before seen."

Ivan plopped in a chair in front of the desk and stared at the hologram. On it, a red blob pulsed in the center of an arid-looking island continent.

Kah-Sih-Omah began his report. "Anderson was a climatologist. His team was on this island installing recording instruments. When the aliens came down his team was out in the bush in a skimmer. There was a meteorologist named Tim Nix and a xenobotanist who doubled as pilot—Shelley something-or-other; Anderson didn't know her last name, but there must be a record of it. Anyway, there are now three human beings whom we can identify who were killed by the aliens. You'll want to notify their survivors."

"Yes." Ivan cleared his throat.

"An aircraft attacked their skimmer as it was about to take off. Nix and the pilot were in it waiting for Anderson, who was outside and some distance away, making final adjustments to his instruments. Anderson remembered a shrieking sound, and looked up just in time to see an aircraft beginning a bombing run. His strongest recollection is of two fire-filled circles and two trails of smoke—jet engines, I assume, retreating from him. When he looked back at the skimmer it was burning. The aircraft had dropped a huge stone on it. He managed to get the girl out but she was already dead. He could not rescue Nix.

"A stone, you say?"

"Yes; odd, isn't it? But remember, we are dealing with impressions formed by a frightened man, who may very well have been mistaken about what he saw. Anyway, after that Anderson headed back to the transmatter station. He walked for two days. On the way he saw other aircraft, from which he hid. He found the station occupied by aliens and the humans imprisoned, locked in a shed the station crew used as a barn. The animals had been driven outside and the aliens paid no attention at all to them, allowing them to wander wherever they would.

"Anderson watched the barn all day, trying to find a way to contact the people inside. He planned to sneak up after dark and try to overpower the alien sentry, but just before sunset the aliens set fire to the barn and killed any human beings who tried to run away. Then they left in a big helicopter—one of ours, which they apparently commandeered.

"Anderson waited a while to make certain all were gone, then went in the station. He found more bodies, some of which had been mutilated, as though the aliens had tortured them.

"The transmatter controls, scientific equipment, and the station water plant had been systematically smashed. The two remaining skimmers were gone. He believed the aliens took them, but he hoped at least a few of the crew got away. He couldn't tell if any had because so many bodies had been burnt beyond recognition.

"Anderson caught a horse and started overland to the island's other station, up in the mountains. On the way he was spotted by some humans in a skimmer sent out to scout by the mountain station. He told the skimmer crew what he had seen and warned them about the aircraft, which they had not yet encountered. They hid the skimmer and waited for darkness before returning to the station.

"That particular station is in a natural cavern. The country is heavily overgrown. As far as Anderson knew, the aliens never discovered there were two stations on the island, though aircraft swarmed around for days trying to track the source of the radio signals the station had been sending since he told his story. Normally the radios were line-of-sight limited, depending on a satellite relay. The satellite had quit working, so somehow they modified what they had and tried to contact men across the sea.

"They raised no one. They did not know whether the rest of the stations were occupied or if those still in human hands were keeping silent to avoid discovery."

"Were there any?" Ivan asked.

Kah-Sih-Omah paused before he answered. "It takes

a while to search things out, Ivan. Incidentally, sometimes questions help, so keep them coming. Having acquired the memories the way I did it takes the same conscious effort for me to recollect them that it would have Anderson. Yes—he thought so, but he never found out for sure. Anderson thought isolation in an unattractive part of the planet saved the mountain station. He and his companions were reluctant to risk discovery by using the transmatter. So they sent skimmers. These never reported; either the aliens got them or the ocean was just too big for them to cross. Perhaps one, maybe even both, got across but were captured or destroyed. We won't know until I get there."

"Then you think there's a chance—?"

"I have to try, Ivan. If I don't, there may not be anybody alive by the time our ships arrive. Not only that, but by that time the aliens will be entrenched—and they appear to be a belligerent, cold-blooded bunch."

"Can you tell us what is happening at Kismet Station, Grandfather?"

"No. I know only what Anderson observed while he was there. That is not reliable. Anderson was in an extremely excited state when he was killed. Much of what he saw was distorted by his own terror. That is all I can relate."

Kah-Sih-Omah's face was washed with a strangely disturbed look—a look explained in part by what he said next. "The station crew concluded they could not end their isolation unless somebody transmatted. They couldn't know for sure, of course, but they suspected whoever went would be attacked. They had no orthodox weapons but they were resourceful enough to make some from what materials they had on hand. That was a wise decision.

"Anderson volunteered. They put him in a steel box to protect him from alien fire and from his own defensive systems—nail bombs fashioned from seismic explosive charges. The box wore four of these to be triggered by higher air pressure at the receiver station, which was at sea-level.

"These worked as expected. Anderson emerged to find the receiver littered with dead aliens. Unfortunately, there were also dead humans: receiver crews the aliens had held captive while they waited for something to happen.

"Anderson seized a weapon from a dead alien. Curiously enough, this was a human weapon—a pump shotgun. Anderson was not particularly experienced with guns and he learned to operate it barely soon enough to shoot the aliens who rushed in to investigate the explosion. Anderson remembers something about that part of it which he seemed to regard as significant, although under the circumstances I cannot be certain his observation was accurate. His recollection was that alien reflexes appeared to be much slower than man's. He was astonished to find that despite his unfamiliarity with guns he still managed to kill a number of his pursuers and get outside where he could escape in the darkness.

"Anderson then made his way to Kismet Station itself, which was occupied and heavily guarded. For a time he despaired of getting in, but then he remembered the seagates—long tubes that extend offshore and house the transmatter cooling system. He was a good enough swimmer to make it, and by then a good enough assassin to eliminate the one alien sentinel he found stationed there.

"Anderson walked through the maintenance tunnels to the receiver, where he surprised and wiped out the alien force inside. He acquired allies. The human crew was being held at the receiver. Anderson's entrance permitted them time to organize a defense, though most had only clubs. However, they used these with substantial effectiveness.

"Apparently, the transmatter was then inoperable. I cannot determine precisely why; either the aliens had tinkered with it or the humans had deliberately disabled it. Anderson's recollection is unclear because of his highly excited state. Whatever the reason, it delayed transmission for a time, during which the aliens were reinforced."

Kah-Sih-Omah's tone became grim, descending in timbre. "Anderson's last memories were of the doors being blown away with explosives, and of dead bodies, human and alien. Human resistance was gradually overwhelmed. Fighting was hand to hand. Having exhausted his ammunition, Anderson himself killed three aliens this way.

"Somebody got the transmatter into the charging cycle, but Anderson alone reached the transmission cage. His final memory is a sensation of intense pain, followed briefly by absolute astonishment, as though he did not believe he could be harmed while dematerializing."

Ivan was content for a time to join Kah-Sih-Omah in silence, as though some magical event might somehow make further decision unnecessary. When it became apparent nothing of that nature would occur, he made his peace with reality. "I was wrong, Grandfather. I thought you had a chance. You don't—not now. The aliens obviously have a great interest in the system, even if they don't understand how it works. I can't let you go in alone. I'll have to let the military try."

Ivan argued that he had no choice but to let the generals and admirals burst in on whatever it was that controlled Kismet Station—and, for however long it took, spend human lives and human treasure to gain it back, even in the face of almost certain death for a great many of them and almost certain destruction of the off-planet system.

Not very long ago he had hoped otherwise; had sat in his office talking calmly, rationally, and hopefully about finding some other way.

It took Kah-Sih-Omah hours to dissuade him, and even then it might not have happened but for the mention, by a sharp-eyed clerk, of a particularly significant name on the personnel list—Jack Langenfelder. Langenfelder was on Earth, not Kismet, as supposed. He had transported in for some minor but emergency medical treatment and had not been able to get back.

Langenfelder was humanity's leading transmatter expert. He had designed and supervised installation of the Kismet system, which differed from that of most human outposts because it wasn't tied into the off-planet net. The government had wanted to maintain strict entry control. Had it been, any station could have received Earth-Kismet transmissions, limited only by the size of its chamber.

The necessary switching gear fit easily into a knapsack. If Kah-Sih-Omah could get him there in one piece, Langenfelder would be capable, given proper assistance, of tying the local network into the off-planet system and making any station, in effect, the off-planet system. Once that happened, if it did, there would be no way short of destroying the planet itself that man could be dislodged. There would then be too many holes for the aliens to cover.

The central transmatter bank for the entire human network lay on Guam, where the whole Pacific Ocean cooled its mechanism. Each day, waste heat vaporized cubic miles of water and affected the rainfall patterns of the entire planet. Earth Central was huge—bigger than anything else in the net and capable of transmitting a fully-equipped relay ship to any other station large enough to receive it. Unfortunately, the existing line of such stations ended at Brahe.

The useful range of a transmatter relay station was about 250 lightyears, though its theoretical range was infinite. Beyond 250 lightyears there were problems with focus, so relays were needed.

Construction of each relay was laborious and tedious. First the exploration ship had to decelerate. Then a properly stable body had to be found or built in space—one whose co-ordinates could be fixed with extreme precision and whose motions were within the predictive capability of the controlling computers. Finally, the components of the relay station had to be passed through the relatively tiny transmitter aboard the exploration ship.

It was theoretically possible to add propulsion to a relay station, though enormously costly because the stations were at once massive and fragile, requiring vast radiating surfaces to dissipate the heat each transmission produced.

Recovering Kismet Main was the key to defense. Kismet Main could take knocked-down fighting ships in much larger bites than space stations could—and because human ships refueled by transmatter, they should outperform those of any enemy they might encounter.

But everything depended on regaining and holding Kismet Station long enough to get sufficient fighters through. And that could not even be attempted until the primary mission had been successfully completed.

Again grandfather and grandson met in an anteroom of the main transmission chamber, this time looking even less alike than before. Ivan hadn't changed, but Kah-Sih-Omah was different. No longer adorned with feathers and braids, he did not wear buckskins, and his features were no longer Indian. He was a blond, blue-eyed Caucasian. And he was bigger—a full foot taller and a hundred pounds heavier.

But the major changes were inside. Most were invisible, but all required room, thus the increase in size. Kah-Sih-Omah's body now had three hearts—one in the usual site and one on each hip, each protected by a skull-like shield of bone. Armor covered his major blood vessels and motor nerves. Kah-Sih-Omah had stacked his bodily systems, as engineers stacked electronic systems, to increase survivability through redundancy. Switching would go through several new and armored ganglia scattered around Kah-Sih-Omah's body, each doubling in brass as a component of an auxiliary brain, insurance against the possibility his reinforced skull might be breached.

Nestled in pods throughout this augmented system were buds of spare organs—eyes, livers, adrenals, spleens, and pancreases, together with reservoirs of hormones, enzymes, minerals, vitamins and other substances that Kah-Sih-Omah might need in a hurry. He was, in effect, a perambulating spare-parts warehouse—and a fighting machine capable, he hoped, of soaking up whatever the enemy threw at him and still carrying on an offensive.

When he transmatted, he would find out if that was enough. He would arrive at Kismet Station absolutely dependent on the resources he carried.

Ivan had dreaded the moment of Grandfather's departure, not only because he might be sending the race's oldest member to his death but because he might find himself without justification. He did not want to send Grandfather off without apologies for what might well be the vain sacrifice of the race's most precious asset.

Words did come, not from him but from Kah-Sih-Omah, whose vast experience had made him highly sensitive to the emotions of others.

"Before the mammoths died," he said, "I was. For 200 centuries I have been. Until my destiny has been fulfilled, I will be. That is the will of my creators. Trust them, Ivan, even as I do. I believe the road ahead, though hard, is longer yet than all that has gone before. Greater still is my unshakable belief that I will see the end of it." He stepped forward to embrace his grandson, then turned and entered the transmission chamber.

Ivan followed as far as the monitors, and as he watched the hatch close he wondered if he would ever see Grandfather again.

Ordinary transmission chambers were not enclosed, but this time Earth Central was using a special one. It was essentially a pressure vessel. Its usual job was to transmit gases with which protective domes and satellite stations were charged. Before Kah-Sih-Omah entered, it had been flooded with carbon dioxide, which had then been transmatted into Kismet Station.

That station, like most, was largely underground, its air kept fresh by mechanical ventilating systems. The volume of gas transmatted was sufficient both to flood it and to overload the ventilators. The heavy gas would pool—and because it was a gas, the humans hoped its arrival would not be noticed until too late for the invaders to escape.

Kah-Sih-Omah would have preferred to use a less lethal and more reliable agent, but lacking knowledge of the alien physiology he was compelled to choose this method.

A few minutes after the gas went through, Kah-Sih-Omah followed. He intended to rescue any beings, human or otherwise, that he could, as soon as he arrived. He was armed, of course, but Kah-Sih-Omah did not wish to kill if he could help it.

Materialization was anticlimactic, and once it was clear there would be no fighting he relaxed and rose from his crouched position. A quick glance around the room revealed that the gas had worked. Five suffocated aliens lay in the cage and control area and two more near the main doors, which the aliens had repaired. There were no human bodies in the transmatter room.

Kah-Sih-Omah punched the sequence for the Kismet Station test pattern, to tell Earth Central the transmatter was operative, that he had arrived safely, and that they should transmit Langenfelder.

The next three minutes seemed an eternity. Unfortunately, that was the transmatter's cycle, and nothing could shorten it. In those three minutes each relay along the route was reset and reoriented. Fast as they were, the computers at each station needed time to compute locations in proper sequence. If they didn't, Langenfelder would wind up someplace else—if he made it through at all. If they did the transmission would be the equivalent of putting a train on one end of a track and giving it a tremendous shove to the other end.

Kah-Sih-Omah did not waste the time. He observed, though only from just outside the door of the cage. He searched back through the memories from Anderson's last moments and compared them with reality. And he made some astounding discoveries.

First, the aliens conformed fairly well to what seemed to be a universal format for sapient life, in that they were of human size and fairly close in functional configuration. But there were some radical differences between individuals of the species.

He could not investigate minutely, but his cursory study suggested these dead aliens consisted of several races or sub-species, or at least different sexes. The desire to get a better look and satisfy his curiosity became an ache of almost physical proportions.

Behind him the slight sizzling had started—would last about five seconds. He turned slightly so that he could watch the materialization and still see the rest of the room.

Langenfelder arrived in a powered spacesuit complete with oxygen tank and rebreather, as a protection from both the gas and the aliens' projectile weapons.

Kah-Sih-Omah had been managing on internal oxygen reserves which he was fast depleting. He was anxious to get out of the chamber, but had to wait for

Langenfelder to punch a new access code into the station computer.

Langenfelder, hands encased in clumsy gloves of the suit, took an eternity, but in the meantime Kah-Sih-Omah uncovered the ventilator leading to the seagates.

They did no talking, but used gestures, and there was no conversation between them until they had gone far enough to reach breathable air.

Kah-Sih-Omah then moved ahead, weapons handy, instructing Langenfelder in whispers. Through other grills they passed, and from intersecting pipes came sounds of furious activity, but nothing remotely like speech. To Kah-Sih-Omah, the absence of an outcry under these circumstances was enormously disturbing.

They reached the tunnels leading to the seagates and climbed out of the pipe, Kah-Sih-Omah first.

Langenfelder had opened his faceplate and was breathing heavily. The powered suit was not really much help in crawling. "So far," he said, "so good. But won't they be guarding the tunnels?"

"I should think so, since that is how Anderson got in. Follow me as quietly as possible. Perhaps we can surprise and overpower any guards before they can give alarm."

The suit was no better at stealth than crawling, though its boots did have foam rubber caps. The hydraulic system hissed loudly with each step, and Kah-Sih-Omah's ears, tuned to the peak of perceptibility, heard each exhalation as a veritable thunderclap.

But the aliens did not; at least, the sentry at the seagate didn't. At the time, Kah-Sih-Omah assumed their movement was masked by the waves.

The creature stood about a hundred feet distant, fairly well concealed behind the maze of maintenance ladders and piping but discernible because it cast a silhouette against the lights that burned along the water. Kah-Sih-Omah watched it for a long time before deciding it was alone.

He turned to Langenfelder and whispered, "From here on I go alone. Remain until I have overcome him, if I do."

"What do you mean, 'if you do'?"

"There is always a chance, Mr. Langenfelder. If it comes to that, you have weapons. Kill it and get into the water. Throw my body in as well, if you can, then use the suit to get away."

"Uh—well, be careful, will you?"

The concern in Langenfelder's voice was gratifying. It insured he would obey; guaranteed he would not act rashly. In actuality Kah-Sih-Omah was not greatly concerned that his approach would be detected. He had already concluded the alien senses were less acute than humans'.

He advanced, cautiously and silently, adjusting his eye structure to enhance his central vision. Though he lost some on the periphery, he now watched the alien through the eyes of a bird of prey.

Again, an incongruity—the sentinel had a human weapon, like some of those in Anderson's memories. Why? It did not make sense for an invading force to depend on captured weapons. A determined invader would have his own. And, except those of its small police force, all human arms on Kismet were sporting weapons. Surely there could not have been many of these.

He had now approached to within fifty feet of the alien. Its back was to him, and it watched the sea. Briefly, Kah-Sih-Omah considered an attempt to overpower the creature without killing it. The impulse to try this was strong. He was extremely reluctant to take life. But he resisted it fiercely. He dare not endanger Langenfelder, or Langenfelder's mission. He must use violence.

Resolved, he raised the heavy pistol, silencer already firmly fitted on its muzzle, and aimed for the creature's head, the one part of its body where he was certain to hit and destroy something vital. At this range he knew he could not miss.

But had he? True, the creature lurched briefly, giving every indication that it had absorbed the hundreds of foot-pounds of force the bullet carried. But it did not fall. Instead, it began a langorous turn to the right which, in bare seconds, would bring it face to face with Kah-Sih-Omah.

Kah-Sih-Omah hesitated no more. He fired, again and again, until the gun was empty, pumping bullets into every area he thought might reasonably contain a heart, lungs, or brain. As the fusillade ended the sentry slumped to the ground.

A quick motion brought Langenfelder bounding forward. He landed next to Kah-Sih-Omah, who bent over the body and was staring out to sea.

"Into the water, Mr. Langenfelder. I see a boat offshore, and it looks like it's moving closer. There may be aliens in it who could see us if they're looking."

Langenfelder slammed his faceplate shut and sat down on the edge of the concrete step, his feet already in the water.

Kah-Sih-Omah grasped the alien by one limb and dragged it overboard, then he too slipped into the water.

They swam silently out of the little bay into open ocean, where a current carried them toward planetary north. When he was certain they were out of possible earshot, Langenfelder opened his faceplate and spoke. "Why are you dragging that body along?"

"For study. We would have had to conceal it in any case. Perhaps the aliens will think it fell in and was drowned."

"And bled all over the place first?"

"A good point, Mr. Langenfelder. So—they will not be deceived. Still, there is something decidedly peculiar about these creatures. I want a better look."

That 'better look' became a full-fledged post-mortem when they gained the beach a few miles north. Kah-Sih-Omah, with little more than a trenchknife for instrumentation, carefully dissected the body while Langenfelder discarded the powered suit and repacked the equipment stored in its backpack. By the time he had this arranged in a lighter fabric pack, Kah-Sih-Omah was finished.

"Well, what did you find?"

"Riddles, Mr. Langenfelder. Had I better facilities I might have learned something useful, but that will have to wait. In the meantime, I suggest we bury my victim and the evidence of our presence and find some cover while it is still dark."

Langenfelder got the message. Whatever Kah-Sih-Omah had found, he wanted to think about it before he discussed it. He helped Kah-Sih-Omah dig a great hole in the sand. They pushed the suit and the body in and covered them, then retired to an area of brush and low trees behind the dune line.

Risking a small light, they studied the map. Drawn by computers, using satellite data, the map was remarkably complete as to topographical features. But human presence on the planet was so slight there were great distances between their possible points of destination.

"What now, Casey?"

"We find you a station."

"I can alter any one of them, provided the controls and power at Kismet Main are O.K. I wish there was some way we could check that out."

"Going back would be too dangerous, Mr. Langenfelder. Without you, we really would lose Kismet. It'll have to be someplace else. How about this one? It looks well off the beaten path."

Langenfelder huddled to look. "It is. I remember it. It's up in the mountains. There's nothing there except the station and a couple of hotels, quarters for the construction crews. There shouldn't be anybody there."

"That's the one we want, then. There's less chance the aliens would go there if there are no people. Shall we get started?"

"I don't know, Casey. It seems to me we ought to try to find somebody who knows what's going on here before we go off on our own."

"Perhaps we'll meet somebody on the way." He knew, of course, how unlikely that was, given Kismet's small population.

But it seemed to satisfy Langenfelder. They started off for the station, about 80 miles away. Before long, Kah-Sih-Omah found himself wishing they had transportation. He didn't need it for himself, but Langenfelder was looking bedraggled. Being unable to modify his body the way Kah-Sih-Omah could and being biologically older, he was having a rough time with the thick brush. Besides slowing them down, the frequent rest stops provided opportunity for conversation Kah-Sih-Omah would have preferred to avoid until he had things better sorted out.

They came to the fall line, where a ridge of limestone had risen nearly forty feet above the plain they had been crossing. They stopped so Langenfelder could rest before tackling it. Kah-Sih-Omah's extended legs, looking odd on his normal torso, bent poorly, so he stood. Langenfelder flopped to the ground at his feet.

"Where do you think they came from, Casey?"

"You want speculation? We have nothing else at this point."

"Well, you've been inside the Imperium . . ."

"These are not Imperials, Langenfelder. I met many different races and heard of many more. I would have heard of these, I'm sure. Not even the Imperium is large enough to hide this."

"Hide? What are you talking about?"

"That was no sapient we buried, Mr. Langenfelder. It had no business doing what it was doing."

"I don't understand."

"Neither do I. That is why speculation at this point is useless. We need more data. Now, get up. We must go before the sun rises higher and it grows even hotter." He loped off, trusting that Langenfelder would follow.

Langenfelder did, though from that moment he was morose and silent, a mood that suited Kah-Sih-Omah well.

He was immensely disturbed by what he had seen. Though his post-mortem had been a very crude one, certain things were obvious—and these both shattered his pre-conceptions and contradicted his experience. Despite superficial differences, all intelligent creatures of his acquaintance had some features in common, dictated by natural laws. Except these.

Though he told himself this was only one of many types, he doubted that any of the others would conform either. He couldn't reconcile the facts with orthodox theory. It was bad enough the creature he had killed had no ears, and only rudimentary eyes. But neither was its central nervous system centralized. It had one fairly large brainlike organ in its torso and another chicken-sized one in its head. To use Langenfelder's metaphor, it was wired all wrong, and very inefficiently.

Yet he recalled the events at the dock—the boat, off-shore, which raced straight for them as soon as the creature was hit, though whatever was in it could not possibly have seen or heard them from that distance. He hadn't seen a radio, or anything that looked like one, and he'd kept the creature too busy to signal.

Kah-Sih-Omah longed for another specimen to examine, to search thoroughly for implants. There had to be sound physical reasons why these creatures, provided they were all like that one, weren't stumbling around over their own feet. Yet the ones he'd seen through Anderson's eyes were hardly stumbling. They seemed efficient killers of men.

"What's wrong, Langenfelder?" Kah-Sih-Omah leaned over the 'older man's' shoulder, watching fingers fly across the console's keyboard.

"I don't know. I can't access Kismet Main." He punched in more and more number combinations, glancing at the screen between each sequence and muttering aloud. "Power's O.K., and I've got the transmission links cleared; there's no orientation problem between fixed stations—everything works that should work, but I can't get in."

"Damage at Kismet Main, perhaps?"

"Possibly, but none shows on the board. No, I think it's on this end. I'll have to check."

Langenfelder toiled for hours prying off panels and checking circuitry. They couldn't get any other stations either, though it was a long time before he knew why.

"Here it is, Casey." He held up a circuit board. "Somebody rewired the transmission circuits into a closed loop. The computer reads it as a completed signal, though it's really only an echo. The computer is tricked into thinking the system is operational when it isn't even connected."

"Hook it up, then."

"Can't. Parts are missing. Whoever did it knew his stuff. There won't be any in inventory either."

"Aliens?"

"Uh-uh; men. You see, this station can still receive,

which means somebody could pop in, make repairs, and have it operational in a few minutes. It's really quite ingenious."

"Why not aliens?"

"Because of the complexity of the physical system. Even if they understood the theory they'd have to know where all the circuits go and what all the components do. No, Casey, not without the diagrams—it has to be one of the station crews, trying to keep the system out of alien hands. They must be hitting every station. It's a resistance movement. After all, these are men, and men fight back. We should be trying to get in touch with them."

The innuendo was not lost. Kah-Sih-Omah had steadfastly refused to expose them to discovery by any of the skimmers they had seen flying overhead. He believed there were aliens inside, an impression reinforced by the lack of human traffic on the radio. Langenfelder, on the other hand, refused to believe it. He was getting ugly.

"We'll try another station, Mr. Langenfelder. I understand how you feel, but right now you're too important to risk."

They headed south and planetary west, keeping to the central valley that followed the coastline. Again, Kah-Sih-Omah avoided exposure to aircraft, while Langenfelder fumed that they had seen no signs of alien presence.

When they reached the next station, which was also inoperative, Kah-Sih-Omah showed him proof—tracks of alien feet, outlined in cement on the concrete forms they had used to build a ramp alongside a stairway leading to the station. "They came in a skimmer, Mr. Langenfelder. It landed here." He pointed at impressions on the ground. "They carried these forms, used them for planks to build the ramp. Underneath, where the rain could not reach them, I found footprints better preserved. Apparently the alien leg cannot take quite as much riser as human legs can. That would follow. The specimen I examined did not have the offset ball-and-socket hip that men do. Its pelvis was more like that of a reptile."

"So, they've been here. So were men."

"Yes, but the aliens are now getting interested. I found broken wires, bent back and forth until the metal crystallized and snapped, with their insulation cut by pincers."

"Pincers?"

"Pincers like crab claws, and of a like material. Tiny barbs broke off on contact with the metal, which was harder. But then the wires were spliced, apparently after the aliens learned to disconnect the power in the conventional manner. The important thing is that I found no evidence of the use of tools. Perhaps they have none."

"That's absurd, Casey, and you know it."

"Is it? I am beginning to question our original conception of the aliens. Consider: they rely heavily on human weapons and transport. They have not used tools. They are evolutionarily immature, yet they have taken this planet. How?"

"Because there are lots of them."

"I wonder. Where are their ships?"

"In orbit—where else? We haven't seen any on the ground."

"Then where is the shuttle traffic? Why haven't we seen their ships in orbit? They'd be big enough, if the force is of any size."

"Maybe they're 'way out?"

"Possible, but unlikely. They would know we have no ships. Low orbits would be preferred for easier communication and fuel economy."

"So?"

"Perhaps we see none of this because it does not exist. Perhaps there were only a few ships and they have landed. Perhaps there is only one. Kismet was designed around the net, so the very nature of the system works against us. Without the net, we, not the aliens, are effectively immobilized."

"That's a pretty iffy theory, Casey, but if you're right it's even more reason to connect with the underground."

"I doubt any exists, Mr. Langenfelder, for the reasons I just gave. There only could be isolated local pockets, with no way to mobilize. We will continue with my plan, as modified."

"Modified?"

"Yes. The answer undoubtedly lies with the aliens themselves. There are aliens at Kismet Main. We will return. On the way we will watch for men, though I doubt we will find any."

They didn't. There was a ranch, one of many set up to feed the population Kismet was expected to support someday, along the course of a river some fifty miles upstream of Kismet Main. The aliens had been there too.

Casey was examining the exterior of the house when Langenfelder came out.

"Uh—what's that you have?"

"Spent brass, Mr. Langenfelder. Someone shot a rifle from here, probably at the large aircraft, or shuttle, or whatever it was. I saw tracks from landing jacks farther out. Aliens shot back. That hole in the stucco was probably made by one of those strange darts. What did you see in the house?"

"Looks like the rancher took off. All the clothes are gone, and the skimmer and radio. The gun cabinet's been cleaned out."

Kah-Sih-Omah went in for a look. He disagreed. "The humans were either killed or captured, Mr. Langenfelder. Do you see all this food?"

"Yes." Langenfelder was standing before the open door of a pantry, filled with cans and freeze-dried packages.

"If the humans went for the bush they would have taken food as well as clothing and weapons."

"What would the aliens want with clothes, Casey? I can understand the other stuff, but clothes?"

"I have no idea why, either."

It was obvious Langenfelder wasn't buying it. No amount of evidence could convince him that the woods were not full of guerillas, just waiting for them so they could go off together and fight aliens. Langenfelder's glands had taken over. He insisted that they find these people before trying Kismet Main, even though Kah-Sih-Omah made a convincing case for learning more about the aliens.

"You forget why we came here, Casey. We came to

take Kismet back, and it's beginning to look to me like that'll take more guts than you've got. I say get a skimmer and hit the boonies. That's where the men will be."

"And I say 'no' to that, Langenfelder. I am still in charge. We go to Kismet Main."

This time they had transportation—a canoe made from a culvert pipe, its ends battered shut and smeared with roof cement to make them watertight. Langenfelder grudgingly helped construct it, working silently while Kah-Sih-Omah whittled paddles. But it was clear that he wasn't resigned.

At dusk they embarked downriver, taking advantage of the gathering darkness. By traveling continuously, taking turns paddling and sleeping, they expected to reach the sea in less than two days.

For hours Kah-Sih-Omah paddled while Langenfelder snored. He held the clumsy canoe in midstream where the current did most of the work, alert for sandbars, the only hazard he expected. There were no rivers like this on Earth anymore; hadn't been for centuries. The water was clear and pure, and the absence of very old trees eliminated the worst hazard of night travel—sunken logs.

Soon it would all change. In a couple of generations Kismet would be crowded. Already the plant and animal population was exploding. Fish, hatched on Earth and transported to Kismet's virgin waters, leapt from the water to gulp hapless insects, ignorant that the presence of both was the design of man. How long, he asked himself, can such luck hold? How long before some error of judgment or accident brings a pest to Kismet? Perhaps, he thought, that has already happened, since man himself is here.

Langenfelder awoke. For a while they held a banal, meaningless conversation; then, though Kah-Sih-Omah was not really very sleepy, he yielded the watch and willed his body into slumber. There was little reason not to; there were no signs of aliens, and running aground on a sandbar would be no great tragedy. Wet feet for one of them would be the only penalty.

He thought that this was what had happened when

the dawn sun broke through and glared into his eyes, and that Langenfelder had gone overboard to free them. So, for an instant after waking, Kah-Sih-Omah kept his eyes closed, to spare Langenfelder embarrassment over his ineptitude. His ears, however, were alert. Suddenly, they told him the truth. Langenfelder was not in the water struggling to free the canoe—Langenfelder was gone.

Kah-Sih-Omah's eyes opened, flashed across the panorama of dawnlit landscape. He saw verdant growth, a sign this was no sandbar but the bank. He moved experimentally. The canoe did not rock, meaning it was grounded firmly. Ahead, the surface of the river was clear of any signs of trouble.

Only then did Kah-Sih-Omah move. His hand first went to his holster, feeling for the butt of the heavy-caliber pistol, and slowly drew it out, his thumb simultaneously depressing its hammer. That low click was the loudest sound to be heard.

He rose slowly, carefully examining the scene around him, noting that the silence did not extend to the birds the sun's arrival had also stirred into activity—a good sign in part, because it told him danger did not lurk here; a bad one, because it meant Langenfelder was not nearby on shore.

Gun now back in the holster, he checked the other signs. More bad news—his automatic rifle was gone, as was Langenfelder's pack, the compass, and the map. Langenfelder had not simply wandered off on some local excursion. He meant to leave for good.

Kah-Sih-Omah had as yet no inkling why. He speculated there could have been alien activity onshore during the night. But reason told him that if there had been Langenfelder would have wakened him.

But was he really that certain of the man? Langenfelder's hot-headed character had surfaced only hours before. Suppose he had seen aliens and plotted vengeance? The thought was chilling. He could imagine Langenfelder, armed as he now was, out in the woods, waiting in ambush, perhaps at any moment to open fire on the aliens.

All Kah-Sih-Omah could do was search. He dragged

the canoe far up the bank, covered it with branches hacked from nearby trees, and obliterated the worst of Langenfelder's tracks, which stood out prominently in the soft soil of the bank.

These led inland, toward the top of a ridge paralleling the river perhaps a thousand yards from the water, then melted into a bluff half a mile upstream. Kah-Sih-Omah saw the base of the bluff had been quarried. Great mounds of gravel lay around it where the conveyor belt from the rock crusher had piled them, and behind the crusher was a large tractor with a scraper blade.

Kah-Sih-Omah studied the scene from the heights. He could not imagine why Langenfelder would suddenly bolt and run here. He knew there had to be a reason, but it was not apparent. In the rubble of crushed rock that littered the quarry area there were no useful tracks, but a careful look around revealed what might be signs of an alien visit.

Back near the woods, partially concealed by brush, were the ruins of a burned cabin. He circled around until he was close enough to tell if there had been any recent activity. He found nothing, and started to circle behind it through the woods, hoping to pick up Langenfelder's trail again.

When the angle changed, so did his perspective, and he saw the excavation. He had almost missed it. It was hard to see, concealed as it was from the river and no doubt from the air, hidden by trees and partially under an overhang. It must have been Langenfelder's destination—but how had he known about it? Kah-Sih-Omah began a cautious approach.

At length he reached a point where he could see past the mass of wilted foliage evidently meant to camouflage the entrance. This was partially thrown aside. Using all the cover he could find Kah-Sih-Omah crept forward, then stopped abruptly when he saw a figure stagger from the shadowy depths of the cave.

The features were still obscure at this distance, even to Kah-Sih-Omah's augmented vision, but he knew it was a human being. It looked like an elderly man, wounded—an impression confirmed a moment later when he stumbled and fell.

Kah-Sih-Omah watched a few moments longer to see if anything followed him from the cave, and when nothing did he threw caution to the winds and broke his cover.

The man was probably near ninety, though like most people these days he benefitted from modern geriatric techniques. Except for a large cut on the back his head, he appeared healthy.

Kah-Sih-Omah examined him superficially, then carried him back inside the cavern. At various times during his long lifetime he had been a medical man, and he recognized the symptoms of concussion readily enough.

Slowly he brought the man around to where, though still disoriented, he could speak.

"What happened to you?" he asked.

"A guy hit me. He came last night. I don't know where from. Wanted to know if I was in the resistance."

"Was he big? Gray hair, bald on the top?"

"Yeah. He had guns—and a pack; said he'd just come from Earth."

"Langenfelder."

"Yeah, I think that was his name. He told me when he first came up. I didn't see him until he was inside the cave."

"How did he know you were here?"

"Probably saw me setting trout lines. He got here right after I finished. Fish's all there is to eat now. The food burned up with the cabin."

Kah-Sih-Omah eased the old man back to the rear of the cave, where there was a makeshift bunk, a lantern and a fire pit. "Do you live in here?"

"Yep. I do since *they* came. 'Course, I was gone when all this happened. Good thing—that's why I'm alive now. Uh—who are you, anyway? Where'd you come from? You from Earth, too?" Apprehension crept into his voice.

"Yes. My name is K. C. Oma. Langenfelder and I were together—until last night. He sneaked off while I was asleep."

The old man relaxed a little, then suddenly stiffened. "Hey, you're him! You were the one—from Campbell."

"You know me?"

"Sure—and you know me. I was there—when that other bunch came—I'm Rankin. The last time I saw you was when you broke my nose—but you looked like Fritz Meyers then."

"I suppose I should apologize, Rankin, but you did have me locked up in a cell."

"Naw, I didn't mean anything by that—I had it coming, I guess. Uh—but what they say about you—it's all true, ain't it? I gotta admit, even with what I saw I didn't really believe it."

"It's me, Rankin, and it's true."

"Then, everything's okay?"

"Not exactly. Tell me, Rankin—what were you doing here?"

"Running the quarry, Casey. Pretty soft touch—until *they* came. 'Course, like I said, I wasn't here when that happened; I was up river, and I seen that thing come down."

"What thing?"

"A shuttle—or something. I knew it wasn't ours. We didn't have anything like that; didn't need it—we got the net."

"And as you say, you were on Campbell."

"Right. Anyway, the thing was loud, and up pretty high. I was in my skimmer—he took it by the way—and when . . ."

"Langenfelder took it?"

"Yeah—hit me when I tried to stop him. All he's gonna do is get himself caught. There's no 'resistance' so far as I know."

"He thinks there is, Rankin. But go on; tell me about this shuttle."

"Well, like I said, it was big, and noisy, and it was going down the river—like whatever was in it was watching for something on the ground. I dropped down under the trees and watched it—I was maybe ten, twelve miles from here then. It dropped straight in, and for a minute I thought it was gonna crash. But it didn't—it landed, right out there on the riverbank where the boats tie up—we don't have a transmatter here, so barges took the gravel to Kismet Station.

"I watched quite a while. I didn't know what to do. I

listened on the radio but there wasn't anything on about it. Maybe nobody else saw it—maybe they'd just landed then, or something. There's a whole lot of planet and not many people.

"Then it went up again—I heard it first, then saw it. When it was gone I took the skimmer up, and then I saw the smoke. Back here the buildings were burning, and everybody was gone. The aliens took them, I guess. I hid the skimmer in here and laid low ever since. I figured the army'd get here sooner or later and take care of it. You with the army now, Casey?"

"No. No, Rankin, I'm afraid not. Things are a little more complicated than that. I guess you deserve to know. I'll tell you all about it."

That took a while, and when he was finished Rankin's mood was glum. "I wish I could help, Casey, but the fact is I don't know much. There was some talk on the radio for a couple of days after these things came but that was mostly people like me, hiding out, and they didn't seem to know any more than me."

"What kind of talk, Rankin?"

"Well, the aliens were in Kismet Main, and out hunting men. They were ramming skimmers with that big shuttle. I listened to a couple of guys get it that way—that's why I stayed down. That's about all I know. Like I say, I figured the army'd be here pretty soon, and that they'd get that ship, and . . ."

"Wait a minute, Rankin—what ship?"

"I only heard about it once, Casey. And that was from one of the guys who got rammed."

"Did he say where it was?"

"No. They were chasing him."

It was Kah-Sih-Omah's turn to be glum.

Rankin caught this immediately, and tried to help. "It sounded like he was a long way off, if that helps. 'Course, it coulda been his radio; I just don't know."

"The ship was down?"

"Yeah; I guess so. The guy talked about flying over it."

"You only heard it mentioned once?"

"That's all."

There were long moments of silence, which Rankin finally broke. "What are we gonna do, Casey?"

"I don't know. I wish I knew where Langenfelder went."

"He headed southwest."

"Is there anything in that direction that might have interested him?"

"Carmody Station's about 90 miles, as the crow flies."

"What's in Carmody Station?"

"Well, it's about the closest thing we had to a town besides Kismet Main. There's a couple of mines where they get rare earths, a big warehouse, couple of labs for the eggheads, machine shops; they got an industrial-size terminal there. Gonna be a big city someday. You say the stations have all been sabotaged? That's probably why he went there—it'd be the best bet for spare parts."

"And occupied by aliens?"

"Oh yeah, sure. They couldn't miss it. They'd hit it before this place. This is peanuts compared to Carmody. If he goes there there's no question they'll get him."

"Then it's up to me, Rankin, and I don't know the new access code."

"What do you mean?"

"Langenfelder's a transmatter engineer. He was afraid that the aliens might find out how to operate the station, so he changed the code. He wrote it down on the map, but he took that with him."

"Oh! So if anything happens to him . . ."

"Right. I know that there are people on Kismet who could crack it in time, but we might not *have* time. It's one more obstacle."

"I can't help you there, Casey."

"There might be something you can do, Rankin. You know the territory pretty well, don't you?"

"Sure. I had lots of time to goof off, Casey; I go around."

"I'll bet you know everybody on Kismet."

"Most of them—and I'll be more'n happy to go along. I'm sick of this cave; sick of eatin' fish."

"Not so fast; you're safer here. I only want part o you."

"Part of me? What do you mean?"

"Your memories."

"I don't understand."

"Then I'll explain."

He did. Rankin listened wide-eyed. When Kah-Sih-Omah finished, Rankin looked up at him and gulped.

"You say it ain't gonna hurt?"

"You won't feel a thing, Rankin, and I'm not taking anything—it'd be like making a copy—and only as far back as when you came here; I won't pry into you past. Okay?"

"You'd have to go way back to find anything exciting, Casey. Okay."

Kah-Sih-Omah left with a far better understanding of the situation than he'd arrived with. He now had memories of the area's physical features and inhabitants. He had Rankins's impressions of the aliens. He knew what the shuttle looked like, and how it behaved. He could recall the radio transmissions Rankin had overheard.

It gave him a new impression of the aliens, a composite of his observations and those of his mentor. The resulting portrait was of clumsiness. There was no other word that fit as well. It added to his conviction that somehow everything had been misinterpreted—that it was all wrong. Of course, there might very well be a substantial invasion force; perhaps in a very large ship. But it all sounded so inefficient he could not help but equate the alien appearance with accident.

He found himself wondering what would have happened had they come down on a human planet with a sizable population, and the answer he got was reassuring. They would have been wiped out in no time, unless they had overwhelming firepower off planet. He was already betting himself that there was no such firepower—and hindsight was making the original plan seem foolish now. That was the reason for the original choice of objectives when he left Rankin.

Kismet Station loomed ahead, a small settlement by normal standards, but still the largest, most important on Kismet. It had perhaps a hundred and fifty buildings of assorted sizes, mostly shops, warehouses, and industrial facilities, scattered along several dozen broad streets. Between the main settlement and the transmatter was a broad, clear area, intended someday to be a park. Currently it was a storage yard for lumber, pipe, and building materials, and a parking lot for vehicles that hauled cargo from the loading dock at the terminal's side.

The terminal was a huge concrete building housing the transmatter equipment and the nuclear powerplant which drove it, located atop the seawall on the edge of the bay across which Kah-Sih-Omah and Langenfelder had escaped.

Kah-Sih-Omah lay on the small knoll just to the south, along the spit of land through which the river poured into the ocean. Alone, he had abandoned the clumsy canoe and adapted his body to swim swiftly and unseen beneath the surface, periodically rising to search the sky for signs of activity and scan the shores for humans or aliens. He had seen only animals, mostly cattle, who grazed contentedly along the riverbank, oblivious to the foreign masters now ruling their adopted world.

Even here they wandered about pretty much at will. This gave him an idea, sparked by what Anderson had observed—that the aliens ignored animals. He decided the risk was slight, considering what he knew of alien senses, and he made the change.

For almost an hour a nervous cow was shadowed by a strange calf that looked extremely odd and incomplete. It had substantially the right bulk and shape, but it appeared so—so unfinished.

As indeed it was. Kah-Sih-Omah avoided specialization. He wanted to retain most of his human abilities, and changed appearance just enough to fool observers with bad eyesight and from long range.

Beyond assuming a four-footed stance and reproportioning his torso, he kept the differences cosmetic, raising a ruff of hair to give his head a roughly bovine shape and using still more luxuriant growth to fill out his body and conceal his pistol belt. Beneath the reproportioned legs were fingers and toes, as fit as ever for manipulation and grasping.

Herding the nervous cow closer and closer to the

center of the station, he watchd his surroundings as warily as she did hers.

He saw few aliens, and concluded most were inside buildings. Those he did see went in and out of the various outbuildings. He decided to enter one of these and see why. Choosing for his first target a warehouse well away from the terminal building but still in sight of it, he entered less than gracefully through an open window, landing on the wooden floor with a rather loud thud.

For an instant afterward he listened for signs of discovery. Continued silence reassured him. He made the necessary changes, then carefully set about to explore the interior.

For the most part it was stuffed with mundane things—shingles, sacked cement, bundles of reinforcing rod and wire, milled lumber, and assorted tools. The office section, partitioned off by panels of frosted glass, held a grisly surprise.

Kah-Sih-Omah opened the door cautiously. He was startled when the lights went on, relieved when he realized they had responded to a sonic switch, and appalled when he saw what it was the darkness had concealed.

Bodies, rows and rows of them, male and female, all nude, covered three quarters of the exposed floorspace. At first he thought they were all dead, but closer examination revealed that each chest rose and fell about once a minute.

He reached down and touched the nearest, a young man whose body bore fresh-looking scars on his temporal lobes. The body was cold, confirming what he already believed—that, somehow, life processes had been slowed down to almost nothing; too low for the body to maintain its normal temperature.

He was, of course, exhaustively familiar with that technique. He had been in this state himself many times over the past 200 centuries, but he would not have believed it possible for the unaltered human body.

It could only be the work of the aliens, but try as he might he could not make himself believe they had either the knowledge or the skill, particularly considering their own pathetic physiques.

He checked each body for life signs, briefly considered a cortical tap on one of them to determine the exact state of health, but abandoned the idea when he heard a noise outside.

He searched for a place to hide. Whoever approached moved rapidly toward the room he was in. Through the opaque glass he saw shadows of figures, the size of men and moving somewhat like men, but he could not see enough detail to be certain.

Seconds remained before certain discovery if he did nothing, so he did the only thing he could—ripped off the pistol belt, threw it under a nearby desk, and flopped down on the floor beside the other bodies. Fortunately, having been in transformation at the time, he wore no clothes.

They were altered aliens. They looked a little like human beings but weren't. He could glimpse them only through a tiny crack under his eyelids, but it was obvious all they had done was superficially mimic two of the humans in this room. The disguise was close enough to enable him to pick the two models out, but details were so sloppily copied they would have fooled no one. They had not even altered the skeleton—arms and legs still bent in the wrong places. It did not approach his standards.

They carried a man, dormant like the rest of the people in the room. His eyes were closed and it took a very close look to determine that he was still breathing. They dropped him on the floor near the door and left.

Kah-Sih-Omah's curiosity mounted. Now more than ever he would have liked an opportunity to probe one of the sleeping people to determine what it was the aliens had done to them. He recognized many of them through Rankin's memories. All of them, so far, had been station operators, computer technicians, communications people, or scientists, all essential to either the operation of the transmatter terminal or to the nuclear reactor that powered it.

He speculated on the aliens' purpose, but he could not come up with a theory which would explain everything.

Perhaps the aliens were trying to neutralize the

transmatter by disabling all essential personnel. That would make little sense, since it should have been obvious that much of the system was automated, that human control was largely supervisory.

True, if they persisted long enough malfunctions, either in the transmatter or the power plant, would cause an automatic shutdown if not repaired. But it didn't strike Kah-Sih-Omah as a very efficient way to commit sabotage, and he didn't believe that could be their objective. More likely the aliens realized the human population of Kismet was small and scattered and were utilizing this means of neutralizing it.

Even that supposition had serious objections. Killing was easier than capture, and the aliens had shown no compunctions about killing men since they had come here. Why were they saving these?

For what remained of daylight Kah-Sih-Omah hid in the warehouse, speculating upon the likely and the unlikely, including the possibility that the aliens intended to use human corpses for food. He decided that to be particularly absurd, since they allowed the animals not only to live but to roam freely. Even could they digest terrestrial proteins, the animals were a far better source than men. No, there had to be a better reason.

By dark, ready to renew explorations, Kah-Sih-Omah had decided that the aliens' ultimate purpose was to gain information; that they must plan to revive a few human beings at a time and question them. Perhaps, unlikely as it now seemed in view of what he knew of them, they *could* communicate, and had some plan of conquest beyond Kismet.

He left, and in his superficial animal form wandered freely around the station complex. Occasionally, through lighted windows, he saw aliens, some in human disguise, most not. He could distinguish many physical types. Some were quite bizarre—figures with jointed exoskeletons and many limbs, some ending with claws; some tall and thin, others short and squat. They came in all colors, sizes, and configurations, but somehow he got the impression that all were the same inside.

He did not know why this should be, but only that it could be, because *he* could be. The existence of his own abilities suggested to him that they might be capable of the same physical transformations as he was, and to Kah-Sih-Omah, whose own origins were an enigma to him, this was fascinating.

Yet there were important distinctions. When he assumed a persona, human or alien, he tried his best for as complete and faithful a reproduction as possible. The aliens, if that was their objective, were abject failures. They could not seem to get things right.

He moved as close to the terminal building as he dared. Such aliens as were about ignored him, until he entered a paved area where there was no grass, and then they began casting occasional glances in his direction. Luckily, he noticed before straying too far from the normal habitat of a cow, and ducked behind a clump of bushes for another change of form.

This time he reappeared in the form of the creature he had killed at the seagates, and unlike the sloppy aliens this was faithful in every way to the external appearance of that being, even the misjointed appearance of the knees and elbows. Thus transformed, he brazenly walked toward the entrance to the terminal building.

A human military force, in the same circumstances, would have guarded the entrance. The aliens did not. Kah-Sih-Omah walked through the unlocked portal as if he were one of them, astonished that it was so easy. There were not even many aliens about.

Rankin had been exhaustively familiar with the layout of the station, and Kah-Sih-Omah drew from these copied memories to find his way around. He walked swiftly through the maze of corridors from the front of the complex, past the administrative offices and the many laboratories and shops, finally into the traffic control section, located at ground level but in effect a mezzanine that ran around the transmatter chamber dome and overlooked a part of it through windows.

Some windows had been broken, perhaps during the battle below when Anderson had been killed. Kah-Sih-Omah went to one of them and looked down, expecting to see the transmatter chamber as it had been when he and Langenfelder had arrived.

He drew back, shocked at what he did see—smashed controls and debris strewn all over the floor, piles of charred furniture and ashes in the center of the cage, evidence that a fire had been built there in an effort to destroy the focusing ring itself.

That would have worked, he knew. The ring was formed of an osmium alloy, very hard and very dense, but it contained delicate circuitry in its core. Those devices would not have survived the intense heat of a big fire. Kismet Main was out of business.

And it was his fault—his fault for resisting a military effort, for insisting that he and Langenfelder could do the job alone. As a result, before warships could arrive, the aliens would have time to subjugate the planet—to round up all the human beings on it and reduce them to zombies like those in the warehouse.

He looked away from that scene of destruction, glanced around the room he was in now. It was filled with banks of instrument consoles apparently untouched by the mindless vandalism as those below had been—banks controlling the routing on the 269 stations of the local net.

Then he knew that the aliens's destruction had not been mindless at all, but a very sound military stroke. They had been threatened, and they had eliminated the threat. Somehow they must have puzzled it out—discovered what the device could do. How?

And then he remembered the young man in the warehouse—the one with the scars on his temples; the torture victim. That had to be it. But he wouldn't have known the new code. Maybe that was why they'd destroyed the ring instead. And maybe he was wrong about why the aliens captured and imprisoned all of those other people. Maybe it wasn't to get them out of circulation—maybe it was to preserve them in an untroublesome state until the aliens had time to pry their secrets loose.

Kah-Sih-Omah's impression of the aliens underwent a change then. Previously he'd regarded them as clumsy and inept, but he could see now that wasn't true. They were clever enough in their own way, and very different from any others he had previously met.

No, they were not fools. Because they were not fools they had one of man's planets, with assurance that they could not be molested for a long time. And by the time men were able to menace them they would know how to use the hostages they held: 13,000 men and women who by then would no doubt lie asleep in alien strongholds all over Kismet—strongholds which humans must attack to take their planet back.

And it was all his fault. He had been blind to all of it; too blind even to listen to Langenfelder and do what human beings naturally did when that which is theirs is threatened—fight.

Langenfelder! Where was Langenfelder? What was he doing now? What would Langenfelder do if he were here now, in this control room, the central mechanism of the domestic transmatter system? Was there still a way to tie it into the off-planet net? Langenfelder would know; Kah-Sih-Omah did not. He left the room cursing his ignorance—the ignorance of he who was the most experienced of all men, because he had lived the longest of all men. He felt small, against the might of the universe.

Once out of the corridor he found there had been change. The plaza in front of the terminal building had been dark and empty. It was now brightly lighted and filled with more scurrying aliens than he had seen since coming to Kismet. They were very busy.

A big cargo skimmer had landed, and the aliens were loading it. Kah-Sih-Omah gasped when he saw the cargo: the sleeping people from the warehouse.

He went as close to the skimmer as he dared, and looked inside. A rack of sorts had been built. Shelves of roughly sawn lumber, nailed haphazardly together as though by children, formed containers for the bodies, stacked like so many bottles of wine in a cellar.

He could not be indecisive now; he had to act, and do what he could to save those he could from whatever fate awaited them. Not even the disciplined mind of 200 centuries' experience could resist the impulse to act.

He sprinted for the skimmer's cab, yet twenty yards away, where there sat an alien whose limbs rested immobile on the controls.

Kah-Sih-Omah's presence had been ignored before, because he looked and behaved like them. Now his behavior attracted immediate attention. He had supposed it would, but never had he envisioned the scenario that was about to play.

All alien motion stopped. Those carrying bodies froze in mid-stride and remained rigid. Some, off balance at the time, fell over, but their limbs remained in the pose they had held when the command—there was no other word for it—came through.

In the cab the alien driver's limbs immediately animated. With sure, steady motions and single-minded determination it activated the skimmer's controls and tried to lift it.

But the fans had not yet reached lifting speed, and Kah-Sih-Omah was able to leap aboard and begin a long, laborious crawl up to it. He was attacked from behind, and struck a glancing blow with one of the high-velocity alien missiles.

By the time he could turn, the skimmer was airborne and banking, the purpose of the maneuver obvious; to bring him under fire of three giant creatures who had rushed up when the episode began.

Kih-Sih-Omah had not seen any like these before, though he knew it must have been they who removed the lock and cut the wires at the second transmatter station he and Langenfelder had visited. They had the claws for it, and were exoskeletal.

It was then also that he learned the guns that fired the darts were biological—pipes of chitin that folded out on hinges from the front of the creatures' carapaces.

Hanging there in midair, making such observations, though fascinating, was enormously dangerous. Kah-Sih-Omah ducked down behind the nearest shelf, sheltering himself with the body of a sleeping human. He did not want the man to be hit, of course, but by now he had his priorities straight—he was the active agent. He could do something and the slumbering man could not. Therefore, his own welfare was paramount.

The chitinous creatures fired in unison, by expanding the tissue between the front and back sections of their carapaces until they looked like giant bellows. When in a split second the muscles contracted, darts blew through the pipes at bone-shattering speed. Two missed. One struck the sleeping man and killed him.

Kah-Sih-Omah could allow no more of this. Before they could reload he leapt upon the driver, seizing it and dragging it off the seat. The skimmer lurched as tenaciously stubborn alien hands froze to the lift lever, depressing it as Kah-Sih-Omah pulled on them.

And that was all right—altitude was fine for the moment. But lateral movement would be far better, if he could manage it. He could and did. He broke both the creature's arms, pried its three-fingered hands off the controls, and hurled in to the floor.

But even as Kah-Sih-Omah himself sprang into the driver's seat and began to fly the skimmer away the alien persisted, flailing at him with its dangling hands and with its feet.

Finding this useless, the alien next butted Kah-Sih-Omah again and again with its head. While this did no real damage, it made a bumpy ride, so he dropped the skimmer to the ground and threw the creature overboard.

Even as the skimmer flew away the alien stood staring upward, as though it would continue the fight if its enemy were still reachable.

Kah-Sih-Omah pondered where to take his grisly load. Clearly the best choice would be where there were other human beings, preferably with medical skills and medical facilities. But so far as he knew, none of these things existed on Kismet anymore.

The next best place was a secure shelter where he could himself investigate. He headed for Rankin's cavern.

Rankin received him with a blast of buckshot, breaking the skimmer's windshield before Kah-Sih-Omah's desperate yell convinced him he was human.

He landed outside the cave entrance, and as soon as he was certain Rankin would fire no more he got out and started clearing away the brush.

Rankin guessed his plan and didn't like it. "Casey, are you nuts? You can't take that thing inside—they'll be all over this place by morning. Hide it out in the woods where it'll take some work to find it."

"I will, once we get the people out."

"People?"

"Look inside, Rankin."

Rankin did. He gave a low whistle and muttered a curse. "Stiffs!"

"These people are alive, Rankin. I'm hopeful we can revive them. Whatever the aliens did, it drops the metabolic level to almost nothing. Here, let's get this skimmer inside." He climbed back into the driver's seat.

Kah-Sih-Omah selected as his first subject—the young man with the temporal scar, because he wanted to try to find out how much the aliens had learned from him. The exercise was not just frustrating, it was terrifying.

He had injected a probe and attempted a cortical tap, using the horny tip to penetrate the muscles at the back of the man's neck. Following this, an enzyme dissolved a passage through the first cervical intervertebral disc. Then a different, less destructive enzyme pierced the outer sheath of the spinal cord, and selective filaments from the probe attached to sensory nerves leading through the foramen magnum into the brainstem, Kah-Sih-Omah's immediate objective.

So busy was he inserting the probe that he did not take the usual precaution of testing feedback. Saving time seemed more important than confirming that even in its dormant state the host's brain was receiving the same sensory input his was.

Thus, until he had linked with his host's cerebral cortex, Kah-Sih-Omah did not know this was completely inactive—that no sensory data penetrated beyond the limbic, where it simply looped endlessly and never reached the biological processors within the hippocampus and the amygdala which would have edited and preserved parts of it as updated memory.

So it was, that with a shock as great as any he had ever felt, that Kah-Sih-Omah realized this man's mind was essentially empty. His fact memory, long and short term, was completely blank.

When this shock passed, as it did in time, he searched for confirmation in the cells, analyzing one after another. He found them small and stunted, and of the wrong configuration, as in a newborn baby—not only reformatted, but reformed.

All the while Rankin watched him work with growing concern, somehow sensing something was wrong. "What's the matter, Casey?"

"This man's mind is—well, it seems to have been erased."

"Erased?" Rankin's facial expression remained unchanged. He didn't understand.

Kah-Sih-Omah tried to explain. "With a cortical tap, Rankin, what I do is go through the same nerves the host would to recall a memory. I have to hit all these centers, because they're sensory-oriented. And I only get declarative memories—memories that have been acquired by seeing, hearing, feeling, and so forth. These are stored near areas of the brain which use them. When a memory is stored, it changes the cell it's stored in, both in shape and in electrical charge. That's how I know this man's memories are gone."

"But I've still got mine."

"I—I know. That's why I don't understand. I don't know of any way this could be done." He gave a low sigh. Actually, that wasn't quite true. He did know how it could have happened, though he couldn't duplicate it—the same way it had happened to him when he had been changed. The implications were at once terrifying and tantalizing. He couldn't believe the creatures he had seen possessed any such skill. There had to be another intelligence at work.

"What are we gonna do if they're all like this, Casey?"

"What?"

"I mean, maybe that's why they're all sleepin'—maybe they just don't have enough sense left to stay awake. Maybe they're all like babies. How are you and me gonna take care of a bunch of big babies all by ourselves?"

Practical! Leave it to a man like Rankin to pick out the practical things. He was right, of course. If further probes did reveal more empty minds, they would be foolish to awaken any of them.

Still, Kah-Sih-Omah wanted to know if he *could* awaken them, whatever the risk of inconvenience. Accordingly, though Rankin was against it, he removed the probe from the scar-faced man and chose another subject, this time a middle-aged woman. And this time when the probe connected, Kah-Sih-Omah's face lit up. "She's all right—she seems to know you."

"And I know her; that's Belva Nichols. If you're doin' what I think you're doin', you already know how we met. Belva's in the entertainment business."

"I try not to pry, Rankin. Find her something to wear, while I see if she can be aroused."

Rankin shot Kah-Sih-Omah a facetious glance at that remark, smirked, and went off to find something.

He need not have bothered. Though Kah-Sih-Omah knew what had been done to Belva and the others, and could reach their memories, he could devise no fast way to purge their systems of the alien drug.

The woman's memory of capture was typical. Aliens had entered her establishment unannounced, pointed guns at those inside, then injected them with massive doses of this substance. It went into the liver, which stored it as it would glycogen and dispersed minute amounts into the blood. The trouble was that the liver's metabolism was slowed to the same rate as that of the rest of the body. Revival was possible, but would require far better facilities than Kismet had.

"So I'm stuck with all these bodies, Casey?"

"We'll take that rack out of the skimmer and stack them up again, Rankin. You could use the company, and I have better use for that skimmer."

"So do I," boomed a voice from behind.

Kah-Sih-Omah recognized the voice before he turned. "Langenfelder."

"Hello, Casey." He pushed aside the curtain the two of them had hung across the doorway to keep the light in. He was carrying Kah-Sih-Omah's rifle, and he was not alone.

"I brought some of the underground people that don't exist, Casey. For an invisible outfit, there's quite a few of us. We don't intend to wind up like that." He poked a thumb at the rack of bodies. Then, suddenly, he gasped— "No, God, no!"—jerked the rifle barrel up and emptied the clip into the scar-faced man's body. There was nothing left of the man's head when the echo died.

Kah-Sih-Omah had gathered his muscles, ready to spring and seize the rifle from Langenfelder's grip. But the scar-faced man was already dead. There was no point in provoking further shooting.

Langenfelder shouted, "That was a changed one, Casey. We all have to get out of here."

"What are you talking about?"

"They'll know you're here—through that—that thing. Casey, that's not a man anymore. It's like them."

"He's right, mister," one of the other men chimed in. "We learned the hard way. Come on. Get in that skimmer and get it moving, before they come down on us." His gun was pointed at Kah-Sih-Omah, and it looked like he meant to use it.

"Casey." Rankin's eyes were pleading. "I don't want to go like that. If they're comin', let's get out of here."

Kah-Sih-Omah didn't know whether to believe them or not. He hadn't found any implants in the dead man's body, and he didn't see how its presence could alert the aliens. Besides, there had already been hours for such a thing to work, and no aliens had appeared. He explained that to Langenfelder.

Langenfelder's jaw dropped open momentarily. When he spoke, his voice was crackling. "T–then, they've been watching you—they know?"

"Know what?"

"What you are. Casey, we've got to leave, now, before they jump us. They must be hiding all around here— they probably watched us come in."

"All right," Kah-Sih-Omah answered. "Into the skimmer—how'd you get here?"

"We've got our own—uh, Rankin's skimmer outside . . ."

Suddenly, shots echoed into the cavern. A tiny voice squeaked out from under the jacket of Langenfelder's companion.

He reached down and jerked out a hand radio set. "Where? How many?"

Static crackled through the air. "Ten, maybe twelve— they're all around here—them big ones, mostly. We need your firepower."

"You'll get it," the man replied. "Get ready to leave. We're coming out in a cargo skimmer."

Kah-Sih-Omah was already in the driver's seat, revving up the fans. He couldn't lift right away because of overhanging tree branches, and he hoped none of the aliens were near enough to shoot into the cave entrance.

They weren't. One or two had been, but marksmen outside had gotten them. Aliens ran through the woods, trying to hit the other skimmer with shotguns. It was still in range of them, and a charge into its fans would make a real mess.

"Get us up, Casey. Get us away from the shotguns but stay in rifle range; I want all of them."

He got a few. So did riflemen in the other skimmer, but then the roaring sound that signalled the approach the alien shuttle drummed across the night. They couldn't match its speed or shoot it down. They'd have to hide.

Kah-Sih-Omah followed the other driver, using his augmented night vision to good advantage. The other driver followed the course of the river, which he apparently knew well. He led them, at breakneck speed, up a tributary creek where overhanging willow trees effectively concealed the water from above.

Here, both skimmers stopped, close enough together so they did not need radio communication. The men aboard held their breath and listened.

"Chances are we ditched them, Casey," Langenfelder whispered. "That thing's a shuttle, not an atmospheric fighter. We don't think they have much instrumentation on it. If they lost sight of us, then we're probably safe, at least for now.

"Uh, Casey—about the guy I shot—"

"You proved your point, Langenfelder. I wish I knew how they did it. I'm certain there wasn't anything in that man's body."

"So am I, Casey."

"You are?"

"They're all like that, Casey. All the aliens."

"What do you mean?"

"Have you been close to any?"

"Once or twice."

"Ever hear any of them say anything?"

"No. But that could be coincidence."

"Believe me, it isn't," Langenfelder said earnestly. "I've been with these men a few days. They started fighting aliens as soon as they knew they were around. They kill them now; they don't take prisoners, because every time they tried it led the aliens right to them. The aliens don't talk, Casey. What's more, they don't signal. Like it or not, we have to consider the possibility they're telepathic."

"What?"

"They do communicate. If they don't use sound, how do they do it?"

"Maybe they use radio. Maybe a biological radio system is possible. We have electric rays, and eels, and catfish; we've got fireflies . . ."

"Casey, you dissected one. Did you find anything like that?"

"No, but I could have missed it. It's an unfamiliar lifeform, and working conditions were bad. Now, if I'd done a tap . . ."

"You did a tap on the altered human. You didn't find anything."

"All right. I'll accept it as an hypothesis—until the real explanation comes along. But I don't buy it until I can identify the mechanism."

"Fair enough. Hey, I don't hear that thing anymore. I think we can get out of here now."

"Where do you plan to go?"

"There's a couple of safe stations. One of them's in a cave up on that big desert island. That's mostly where I've been since I left."

"I know the place. You went through the net?"

"I got lucky. When I left Rankin's place I picked up the chatter from a raiding party—part of the bunch that has been disabling stations—and joined them instead of going to Carmody. As I said, the underground is only looping the transmitters, not the receivers. And it seems there aren't enough aliens to garrison them all, so what they've been doing is stationing a couple of these big lobster things at each one. We zap them with gas, then come through with masks and take the station."

"Wait a minute—assuming, as you said, these things

were telepathic, don't their buddies know as soon as you get there?"

"Sure. But by the time reinforcements arrive we're already gone—and when we want to go back we just take another station. Neat, huh?"

"Maybe for a while. What happens when they catch on and start smashing the net?"

"So far, they haven't done that. It's plain they want it intact, to use themselves when they find out how it works."

"Langenfelder, they smashed Kismet Main."

"What?"

"Didn't you know?"

"No, I didn't. The underground had plans to try to take it, but we didn't have the muscle yet—not enough weapons, not enough skimmers. I gather you got back in there?"

Casey nodded. "It's bad. They used a fire to warp the focusing ring."

Langenfelder's features became grim. "The ring's not essential; we could detour around that. But the power is—the local stations haven't got the oof—and it's all routed through the terminal's control system. That's been down since just before I met these guys. I'd have to take a look. . . ."

"You should have gone with me. That was your mission; not to play soldier."

"Wait a minute. I thought the idea was to tie in the local net. If we'd joined the resistance, like I wanted to, and gone before the link with Kismet Main was cut, it might have worked out. I had the components. But they'd already cut it by the time you got there. I couldn't have helped if I had been there."

"I'll concede that point. But the fact is that we're marooned now, with no choice but to wait for the fleet."

Langenfelder thought a minute. "No, Casey, you're wrong. There's still the orbital station."

"But it isn't operative—and the aliens may be there too. And how do you get there?"

"Maybe we can take that shuttle away from them."

"And maybe you can't. And if you do, they still have a ship."

"Their ship's down—we think. But don't worry, we'll find it and take that too."

Kah-Sih-Omah gave up in disgust. His optimism was gone. It was quite apparent that things had been handled all wrong from the very beginning and that, in the main, it was his fault. He had discouraged military intervention. He had chosen to go out and check the net first. He was the one who'd thought the aliens would leave Kismet Main alone, and the one who believed the aliens would be a long time in learning to subvert humans.

True, what had happened was against all his experience with extraterrestrials. Who would have believed a race could function without vocal communication? This had been what had convinced him they had a little time.

Well, time had run out. There wasn't enough left to do things in the safe leisurely manner he preferred. It was time to take some risks and get some answers. There were times when a tiny bit of audacity equalled tons of reasoning. He, the most experienced of all men, should never have forgotten that.

Kah-Sih-Omah stood alone beside the concealed skimmer, watching aliens swarm through the station the resistance had just left.

Langenfelder had taken the sleeping humans back to his sanctuary, where such medical people as were still at large would try to revive them. Langenfelder—now a relatively useless part of the original plan, who now talked of taking the aliens' shuttle away from them to reach the dormant satellite, though he knew the aliens might have disabled that too. Humanity on Kismet was reduced to clutching at straws.

Kah-Sih-Omah felt remorse more strongly than ever. He had gotten used to the adulation of mortal humans, to their supreme confidence in him and their undying and unshakable belief that he, their superman, could never be defeated. Worse, he had himself begun to believe it. Now, when it appeared the impossible had happened—that he had failed—he was stricken with a devastating panic.

He had made mistakes in the past. Twenty thousand years of life left lots of room for miscalculation, and it had occurred with tedious regularity in the early millennia. But as he grew experienced he stumbled less and less frequently, until compared to ordinary human beings he seemed not only invincible, but infallible. The temptation to believe this himself overpowered him, and he had fallen—fallen inordinately hard—at the worst possible time, when what he did next might affect the future of the entire race.

He had underestimated an opponent. He had been deceived, by that opponent's apparent ineptitude and clumsiness, into thinking it weak. Now he knew better. It was not weak. It was simply different, with different strengths than men had.

He resolved to learn more about it, find its weaknesses, take the step he should have taken many days ago.

And so he did. He left the skimmer in the bush and started out on foot toward the station. He would take an alien, a live one, and perform the tap he should have made on the first day—invade its mind and seize its memories so he could understand it, if that was possible.

That was the rub; he might not be able to do it. The aliens were totally different from anything he had ever encountered before, with their brains dispersed throughout their bodies, as these seemed to be. He was a competent, skilled pathologist, but he hadn't understood what he saw.

Nor, it occurred to him, might it be possible to decipher what was stored in its mind, because the common format for recording sensory impressions seemed absent. That was why cortical taps on animals failed. Animals lacked speech. There was no common denominator. It might well be the same with these creatures.

Kah-Sih-Omah didn't know, but would soon. He skulked through the heavy brush which surrounded the station, alert for a solitary alien. He saw several, but they were exoskeletal types and he did not want them. They would be difficult to disable quickly, and he did not know any details of their anatomy. Avoiding a protracted battle with his victim required a patient wait for the kind he had killed at the seagate.

It was a long time before one came along, and even then it appeared in the open, within sight of other aliens, beside the skimmer in which they had arrived.

Kah-Sih-Omah stalked it nevertheless, with a new plan—to abandon the skimmer he had hidden out in the woods and steal the one over which this alien stood guard.

He watched it from concealment, noting that same strange behavior he had observed back at the warehouse. It was as though it was only "on" part of the time—most curious. Of all the characteristics these creatures had this struck him most starkly.

He surveyed the clearing. Other more active aliens could be seen moving around the terminal. He wondered what they'd found to do here, and hoped they were not demolishing this station as they had Kismet Main. That would be disastrous.

He was ready. He crept from the bushes behind the creature, walking swiftly, though in a crouch, until he was upon it—then struck it a blow in the abdomen, at a point where he had seen the massive bundle of nerve tissue in the dissected specimen. The punch would have been more than sufficient to disable a man.

But nothing happened. The creature lurched from the force of the blow, but did not fall. Its limbs remained rigidly beneath it. It merely toppled toward the skimmer.

Flabbergasted, he glanced again toward the building, horrified to discover that though his victim was motionless, its companions weren't. Fully a dozen of them, including some of the exoskeletal types, raced toward him.

They would arrive in a few seconds, and long before that they would be shooting at him.

He threw the alien's poker-stiff body into the skimmer's back seat and jumped into the driver's chair, punching at the "start" command. He raced the fans up to lifting speed.

As he rose, he saw flashes of gunfire from the ground and heard the clatter of buckshot striking the skimmer's underside. If one of them had a rifle . . .

But none apparently did. No high-velocity slug tore through the fanblades and unbalanced them, to throw the skimmer back toward the earth. But something was wrong. Acrid fumes began to pour from the stern, suggesting that one or more pellets had pentrated the tough plastic hull and that the electroylyte in the skimmer's molded plastic batteries was leaking. He had to get down again, fast, but where?

The other skimmer—parked concealed in the brush. It was somewhere below.

He turned, and dropped to minimum altitude. If he fell now it would be from a height where he and his passenger might still survive—unless they burned first. Added to the fumes was the first odor of smoke, and the umistakable smell of overheated insulation. Kah-Sih-Omah knew that if fire did start it would engulf the entire hull in no time; and that there might not even be time for him to get out before the thing became a fireball.

So, taking a bearing on the place where he recalled the other skimmer to be, he dropped the burning one to the turf below, grabbed his prisoner, and jumped out with him, running as fast as he could.

The fireball came, and the skimmer's hull split, spraying superheated chemicals on the dry vegetation, setting it afire.

Kah-Sih-Omah took note of wind direction; was relieved to see it would take the fire away from him, and redoubled his efforts to reach the other skimmer. The way was not easy and the burden of the alien slowed him down, but within a few minutes he had it in sight. In a few more the alien, hastily bound with tape from the skimmer's tool locker, lay draped across the back seat and Kah-Sih-Omah was airborne.

This time, fairly sure none from the station area would see him if he kept low, he threaded the skimmer between the stunted trees that shared this arid valley with brush and grasses. He hoped the aliens would believe he and his prisoner had been in the skimmer and consumed by the flames.

For more than twenty miles he hugged a dry creekbed overhung with trees, and only when he could not see the smoke any more did he rise to a hundred feet or so and divert the major portion of the skimmer's thrust astern. All the same, he kept a wary eye out for pursuit.

He headed straight to the ranch where he and Langenfelder had stopped on the way to Kismet Main, because he knew that he could raid its supplies and because it was somewhat familiar to him.

He landed next to a large barn, and taxied the skimmer in through its open door. The alien, still bound and rigid, he lifted from the back seat and draped over his shoulder. He carried it into the house and laid it face down across the kitchen table, ready for the tap.

Forming the probe took time, even though he had long since modified the frontal bone of his skull with a removable plug. He used the time to study the alien and to try to decide where to enter its body.

Eventually he chose the abdominal "brain," reasoning that the one in the cranium was far too small to be the seat of sentience. No theory he could formulate explained why this was, though Kah-Sih-Omah was certain there was a sound evolutionary reason for it.

It would have to be a good one, he told to himself, to justify using such extremely long neural pathways as ran between this being's eyes and the sight center in its brain. Such extended cells would be grossly inefficient, and seemed sufficient reason in themselves for the slow reaction times the aliens displayed.

But not always. Sometimes they moved very swiftly, like the one who'd driven the skimmerful of human bodies. It had put up a pretty good fight.

The probe was finished. Kah-Sih-Omah inserted it into the alien's body, taking care not to provoke extensive bleeding.

He found and followed a motor nerve into the mass of neural tissue located where a human liver would have been, then extended filaments into the surrounding area. The procedure was gross, hit or miss, but there was no other way to do it. Tragically, it was mostly miss, and when he did happen on a sensory area it proved extremely disappointing.

He now explored the visual. He was able to perceive a faint, fuzzy view of the linoleum on the floor, where the creature's gaze was focused; but it was so poor an image he could not believe it was how the creature normally saw.

This experiment had a purpose: to provide the feedback he needed to determine if his tap was working. The fact that it had been the visual into which he had intruded was extremely fortunate. The visual was the one sensory area he was certain man shared with this species.

He went on, inserting thousands of tiny neural filaments into the creature's peculiar brain. He tapped into an olfactory channel, found it strangely acute, and spent a long time mapping the nerves that carried the data from the muzzle. Again, he struggled to reconcile this keen sense of smell with the wastefulness of these extended nerve channels. It made no evolutionary sense for a creature to have such fine sensory apparatus yet waste time with processing, as this system did.

Then a thought struck him. Suppose the neural transmission speeds were faster than those human beings enjoyed? It seemed unlikely, considering his observations, but he put it to the test anyhow, by segregating a small nerve down which he sent a signal speeding. The result confirmed his observations. If anything, the creature's transmission speed was slightly slower.

With yet another enigma to haunt him he turned his attention back to the primary task and began a careful layer-by-layer examination of what in a human being's brain would be its sensory cortex. The visual and the olfactory were now fairly clearly defined. With persistence and some measure of luck he would find connections to banked masses of cells whose function would be to process and store the data these two systems accumulated.

Kah-Sih-Omah worked at it for a long time, but his efforts failed utterly. At first he put this down to simple bad luck—chance, such as had impelled him to choose all the unproductive alternatives first. But gradually he concluded it was more than that, and when he reached a large cable-like bundle of cross-connecting neural filaments and could not breach it, he was certain.

This was most peculiar. Following the sensory trunks he had identified he could go so far and no farther, yet it was apparent that the data continued onward nonetheless.

Mystified, somewhat irked by this blockage, Kah-Sih-Omah bridged it with filaments from his probe, which consumed considerable time in the growing. When he was finished, the problem was edema. The creature's system was filling the surrounding tissues with fluid, almost as though it were fighting the completion of Kah-Sih-Omah's bridge.

Kah-Sih-Omah would not allow this. He pushed his probe forward and eventually was in position to tap on the other side of the bundle. From its location and configuration he believed this was the connecting cord to the rudimentary chicken-sized ganglion he had observed in the cranium of the specimen he had dissected.

When the tap was secure, he changed the configuration of its cells, polarizing them in the direction of current flow, or what he thought would be the current flow. He received no data. He reversed, and tried again. Still nothing.

That was unthinkable! Even if it was totally indecipherable, there should have been a discharge. But the neural tissue seemed totally inert.

Dismayed, he backed his probe out, hopeful that the edema would subside, but fearful that the creature would suffer an immune reaction and become ill. He did not want that.

He set to work laying out a network of thousands of tiny exploratory filaments whose task would be to measure the impulses that coursed through the alien's brain. He intended to proceed layer by layer, from the core outward. It would be a long, time-consuming process, but he hoped that this would give him an image of its electrical structure.

After this process had been active for a while Kah-Sih-Omah saw that it would not provide a solution to the puzzle. He found that he could understand the organization; that in general the cells closely approximated the behavior of earthly neural tissue, a development hardly surprising because physical laws bound all lifeforms in equal degree.

However, he could not tell what the alien brain was

doing with the data it collected. It seemed to have no capacity to process or store data, even though most nerves transmitted charges readily enough.

Baffled, he abandoned this course to reassess the situation. He knew he did not understand its organization as well as he thought. He had believed that once he had identified and invaded the sensory areas he could follow them to the creature's seat of reason. Now, he was not so certain he had correctly identified these. He resolved to explore the motor areas.

His own senses could aid in that effort. Feedback was instantaneous. When he moved an alien muscle his eyes could see that it moved. He tried many samples, observing each in turn, and concluded the motor system was as straightforward in its function as his own—except in one respect. Again he came across connectors to the great impenetrable bundle which led into the cranial adjunct.

Frustration mounted. Never before had he encountered anything like this. Never before had he suffered such an unmitigated defeat.

And defeat it was. He was ready to admit that. He began making preparations to withdraw the probe and try more conventional methods of communication with this creature.

When the probe was completely extracted and the creature's wound closed as best he could manage, Kah-Sih-Omah sat there silently, without moving, while his body reabsorbed the probe's mass. Throughout his long life Kah-Sih-Omah had observed that every experience, even failure, teaches something. This was certainly a failure of the most dramatic kind—but where was the lesson in it?

Suddenly, he knew where to find the answer. The answer was in the cranial adjunct—it had to be. That was the only place where the data could have gone. Or rather, it was the conduit through which it traveled—to someplace else outside the creature's body.

The proof of that was all around him—but it was now too late. A movement outside caught Kah-Sih-Omah's eye. There was proof indeed: in the form of several hundred divers aliens who now surrounded the house—and were advancing upon it.

Kah-Sih-Omah shuddered. *They had known. Impossible as it appeared to be, the telepathic theory now stood as proven.*

Kah-Sih-Omah rose to his feet, grasped the alien and flipped him over on his back.

The eyes were open and were looking into his; worse, they seemed lit with a glint of intelligence Kah-Sih-Omah knew could not really be there, because the creature simply did not have the biological equipment.

Therefore, he reasoned, what he was seeing was not this individual's spark of intellect, but that of whatever it was with whom it was communicating. *But what are its plans for me?*

He raced to the window and looked out, to see a ring of aliens tightening around the house. None of them were armed, but certainly that was not a disadvantage, considering their numbers. And he had been taken unawares. There was no time to alter his body, to use the physiological edge which had always saved him in the past. He would have to take them on in present form—if he took them on at all.

Perhaps, he decided, making a fight of it would not be wise. They could not know he was not the same as other human beings. There was no reason for them to treat him differently. And it was clear that they did not kill indiscriminately anymore, but chose instead to drug their captives into the dormant state—a state that he could easily feign, and from which he could recover at will.

While he pondered his course he began to hear noises: doors opening, footfalls on wooden floors. He knew they were in the house, and that there might be only seconds left to deliberate. In the next instant he committed himself to surrender.

The alien ship was huge. Perched on three immense landing jacks its globular form rose almost 200 meters into the night sky. Kah-Sih-Omah studied these and gained another fact: it was ancient, so ancient that the joints of the jacks were frozen into immobility.

seems to lack any conception of the passage of time, which explains what I meant when I said maybe 'somewhen.' This may be the explanation for what I saw on Kismet."

"But you haven't told me what that was, Grandfather."

"So I haven't—sorry. I guess I'm too excited." He smiled at Ivan.

Ivan smiled back, but said nothing. He had never seen his grandfather in such a flustered state.

Kah-Sih-Omah must have realized this. He paused for a long moment, struggling to control his exuberance, before he spoke again, this time in a calmer tone. "It was that ship, Ivan, one maybe as old as the universe itself. Its fuel had completely decayed into lead, yet the creature had somehow used it to transport its probes to Kismet; probes it had collected from other expeditions throughout the universe. It was these probes that men were fighting, Ivan."

"You mean, they weren't alive?"

"Oh, yes, they were very definitely alive. But they weren't sentient, except in the sense that the controlling organism was. I dissected one when Langenfelder and I first arrived on Kismet. Later I tried a cortical probe—which, by the way, was what finally got this creature's attention.

"What baffled me at the time was that I couldn't imagine where the sensory data were going. There was nothing in the probe's body to process data."

"I don't understand, Grandfather."

Kah-Sih-Omah embarked on a long and detailed explanation of his findings during the post-mortem and the tap. When he was finished he thought Ivan understood, until his next question.

"I don't see how that could be."

"Neither did I, Ivan. I hope that someday I can find out. But I do know the sequence from the tap onward, now. You see—and this is what makes me think a difference in time may be involved—these probes were all so amateurish. I can deduce what must have happened if we follow the theory a ways.

"Picture this: a being whose intellectual powers transcend time and space, whose own existence may have been more or less accidental or incidental to the creation of the universe, but who largely lacks tools to explore the physical.

"Add to this that lesser lifeforms also developed in time—lifeforms which eventually came to the attention of this being, who copied them with less than absolute fidelity and used them as its bridge to the physical universe, transporting them in a derelict ship it found somewhere. Perhaps at the time of its initial experiment these creatures were the best that the universe had to offer—I think that is a good possibility in view of the creature's apparent awe of me . . ."

"Awe of you?"

"That is what I said, Ivan—and I think you commit a common error, by assuming that the possession of great intellectual powers necessarily equates with great intelligence. What I see in this creature suggests that either this is not the case or that it is immature. In fact, in many ways its behavior seems infantile."

"Oh?"

"It professed to admire my organization, Ivan."

"It did?"

"It did indeed. It discovered this during the tap. While I was exploring its probe it was exploring me, without my knowledge. You see, the cranial adjunct served only one purpose: to transmit sensory data to the creature, wherever it was, and to receive commands. All the rest of the neurological system was devoted to motor and maintenance functions. They had no need of memory, so they didn't have any.

"It had already experimented with a human subject. It found the human organization fascinating but unusable in the form it was in—until it got to me, that is.

"Other humans had fixed-format nervous systems, cluttered with memory and with too much sensory data for the creature to assimilate without disorientation. It found direct contact unpleasant. As a result, during its early experiments it killed the humans in the captured transmatter station. It was afraid they would interfere with the functions of its probes, as in fact they eventually did.

"Later it tried again, found that it could erase the

human cortex, and reasoned it might be able to make the necessary modification. Then it set about collecting specimens for conversion and use on Kismet. To the creature, men appeared far better adapted to the local conditions than what it had been using."

"Why does it want Kismet, Grandfather?"

"I have been unable to determine that precisely, Ivan. Its discovery of men's presence on Kismet was evidently serendipitous. It noted what on its time-scale was an instantaneous transformation of the planet's ecology, and sent sensing organisms to investigate the reason. Now, the closest I can come to a theory is that it eventually intends to come here—because of me. Somehow, it deduced my nature."

"It likes you?"

"Not the way you mean, Ivan. No, it would be more proper to say that it finds me interesting. I am unique in its experience. I am an entity with both a memory of my own and the capacity to link with its own systems. I do not confuse it because my mind is orderly and under control. My mind can adjust and accommodate itself to the creature in a way no other ever has. It has created a probe through which this can be done. This probe is an exact duplicate of me."

"A clone?"

"More than that, Ivan; less, too. The physical part of it is on Kismet. The intellectual part has become a compartment of the creature's consciousness and lies wherever it does. But the combination of these two enables us to join our minds, to share data and experiences. Its own are, of course, vast compared to mine, and will take an eternity to sort and process."

"Process?"

"The creature does not really know what most of its data means. That is why I said that it was childlike. It does not know what to do with the data it has because its perception and contacts with the physical are too obscure. It is, in my opinion, like a computer, full of data, but with no program running to organize and analyze the data.

"It has one now; it has me. I will be that program, and where before it merely groped it will soon set forth to explore all of creation: all of space, and perhaps all of time. It is time that I find to be the most intriguing area of study, considering that my roots are buried in it."

"Grandfather, it's beginning to sound like you intend to control the creature."

"That is exactly what I propose to do. Someone must. I shall change it; bring discipline, provide order. You will perceive its present lack."

Those words! Where did they come from? Why did I say them? They—they popped into my mind. Kah-Sih-Omah began to sweat. Suddenly, he knew where he had heard—perceived—those words before. He fell silent.

"I can't do it, Grandfather."

"What?"

"Evacuate Kismet; I can't take a planet away from man and give it to some alien creature. The people would never stand for it."

"It's not for the creature, Ivan; it's for me. The creature doesn't need it—I do."

"You do?"

"Yes. I'll be joining the creature in the probes, as well as sorting its data for it. I have related to the creature such facts as I know of my transformation. The creature is intrigued, and wishes to help me find the beings who did this. And it may well be that within the stupendous mass of raw data it has already collected, or in that more disciplined exploration, that we will make together there is the key to my own nature, and perhaps my own end.

"I know that the creature's understanding of my explanation was imperfect, and so I will be experimenting as well—sometimes with forces that may prove very dangerous. It may be necessary for my own body to grow quite large."

Ivan's mouth was hanging open, and he was attempting to sputter out the words he was thinking. He could not seem to make it.

Kah-Sih-Omah took the opportunity to clinch the argument. "Ivan, consider this: with mental power alone this creature hurled that devastated ship across space and time and set it on a planet that would have killed its probes just decades earlier. Don't you see what that amounts to?"

"Maybe something too big for man to handle, Grandfather."

"There are no such things. Look at this realistically. This is mattercasting without the net, without the need for slow ships to creep across space to the next destination in order to set up stations.

"You and I have worried and fretted over the Imperium. We were afraid the Imperials would find us, and overcome us while we were still weak. But we found this, *we*. The threat is ended now, Ivan—over—for good—as are all other threats that might ever menace the race. We are free of them; we are free to go out there and see what there is to see—and I want to go.

"That is my reason to be."

"I still can't do it, Grandfather. I'm sorry."

"So am I, Ivan. I'll miss you."

"Wait—where are you going?"

"Back to Kismet, to begin the evacuation."

Ivan reached for the phone, punched a button, and spoke: "No further traffic to Kismet unless I give the order in person." He put the phone down. "There. Well, I suppose you *could* manage my impersonation rather easily. . . ."

"Not necessary, Ivan. I said man doesn't need the net. That's not quite true. Other men still do—but I don't. The next step will be planned evolution, Ivan, when I find the way to connect the rest of the race to the link—like this."

Kah-Sih-Omah vanished, leaving Ivan sitting speechless, frozen into inaction. It wasn't until the phone rang that he moved again, and then it was only to raise the receiver to his ear. He didn't even speak; he listened.

The voice at the other end said, "Commissioner, this is Harry Bainbridge, at Earth Central Traffic Control. We've got a malfunction. I know you gave orders, but . . ."

". . . but people are coming through. I know I'll take care of it."

But he wouldn't. Grandfather was doing that.

A giant space station orbiting the Earth can be a scientific boon ... or a terrible sword of Damocles hanging over our heads. In Martin Caidin's *Killer Station*, one brief moment of sabotage transforms Station *Pleiades* into an instrument of death and destruction for millions of people. The massive space station is heading relentlessly toward Earth, and its point of impact is New York City, where it will strike with the impact of the Hiroshima Bomb. Station Commander Rush Cantrell must battle impossible odds to save his station and his crew, and put his life on the line that millions may live.

This high-tech tale of the near future is written in the tradition of Caidin's *Marooned* (which inspired the Soviet-American Apollo/Soyuz Project and became a film classic) and *Cyborg* (the basis for the hit TV series "The Six Million Dollar Man"). Barely fictional, *Killer Station* is an intensely *real* moment of the future, packed with excitement, human drama, and adventure.

Caidin's record for forecasting (and inspiring) developments in space is well-known. *Killer Station* provides another glimpse of what *may* happen with and to all of us in the next few years.

Available December 1985 from Baen Books
55996-6 • 384 pp. • $3.50

**For
Fiction with Real Science In It,
and Fantasy That Touches
The Heart of The Human Soul . . .**

Baen Books bring you Poul Anderson, Marion Zimmer Bradley, C.J. Cherryh, Gordon R. Dickson, David Drake, Robert L. Forward, Janet Morris, Jerry Pournelle, Fred Saberhagen, Michael Reaves, Jack Vance . . . all top names in science fiction and fantasy, plus new writers destined to reach the top of their fields. For a free catalog of all Baen Books, send three 22-cent stamps, plus your name and address, to

*Baen Books
260 Fifth Avenue, Suite 3S
New York, N.Y. 10001*

HAVE YOU FOUND YOURSELF ENJOYING A LOT OF BAEN BOOKS LATELY?

We at Baen Books like science fiction with real science in it and fantasy that reaches to the heart of the human soul—and we think a lot of you do, too. Why not let us know? We'll award $25 and a dozen Baen paperbacks of your choice to the reader who best tells us what he or she likes about Baen Books. We reserve the right to quote any or all of you...and we'll feature the best quote in an advertisement in <u>American Bookseller</u> and other magazines! Contest closes March 15, 1986. All letters should be addressed to Baen Books, 260 Fifth Avenue, New York, N.Y. 10001.

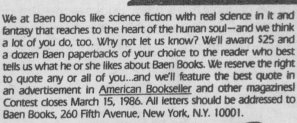